Praise for Th[...]

The Bri[...]

"The slowly simmering sensuality a[...]g bonds of family hold readers' interest and hearts.[...]

—*RT Books Reviews*, 4 Stars

"Historical details enrich Burrowes's intimate and erotic story, but the real stars are her vibrant characters and her masterful ear for dialogue."

—*Publishers Weekly* Starred Review

"A rich, emotion-filled tale to be enjoyed more than once."

—*Long and Short Reviews*

"This delightful Scottish Victorian romance will engage readers with emotion and sensuality. Burrowes has a talent for filling traditional romance situations with depth and the unexpected."

—*Booklist*

"Grace Burrowes has become an auto-read author for me... With an honor-bound Scottish groom, illicit romances, and hidden secrets, *The Bridegroom Wore Plaid* is a book historical romance fans will not want to miss."

—*Book Savvy Babe*

"Deliciously sensual, intricately plotted, and filled with a cast of appealing characters...pure pleasure."

—*Library Journal*

Once Upon a Tartan

"Writing this lush and lively deserves to be savored."

—*Library Journal* Starred Review

"Burrowes creates a powerful story replete with heartfelt emotion and rich characterization. An instant keeper."

—*RT Book Reviews* Top Pick of the Month, 4.5 Stars

"Grace Burrowes weaves her magic with words…a memorable love story—excellent and exquisite."

—*Long and Short Reviews* Best Book

"Warmth, sensuality, and humor infuse Burrowes's writing, and fans of Suzanne Enoch and Sarah MacLean should enjoy this series."

—*Booklist*

"Charming… Expert prose, likable characters, realistic relationships, and believable complications create a pleasant and satisfying keeper."

—*Publishers Weekly*

"As in all Grace Burrowes novels, this one has beautiful scenery, a well-knitted family, a hint of mystery, and a love story that will wind itself around your heart. This author has a way of luring you away for a few hours of utter bliss."

—*BookLoons*

The MacGregor's Lady

"A powerful and moving romance... A deeply engrossing, well-written, not-to-be-missed novel!"

—*RT Book Reviews* Top Pick, 4.5 Stars

"Both Asher and Hannah are well rounded, and I found them to be some of the most likable characters I've read about in a historical romance."

—*Fresh Fiction*

"Torture. Torment. Delicious despair. Those words pretty much sum up *The MacGregor's Lady*. Reading this book is ultimately a rewarding, if cathartic, experience."

—*Heroes & Heartbreakers*

"Burrowes has done an outstanding job of taking the plot to a thrilling end. It will not only amuse readers, but might make a movie producer request a script."

—*Historical Novel Review*

"Burrowes has a knack for giving fresh twists to genre tropes and developing them in unexpected and delightful directions. This novel is a perfect example of her consistently excellent writing."

—*Publishers Weekly*

"Grace Burrowes has a remarkable ability to bring the environment to life. However, her special talent for developing strong, memorable characters is the very best part of her novels."

—*Long and Short Reviews*

Also by Grace Burrowes

The Windhams

The Heir
The Soldier
The Virtuoso
Lady Sophie's Christmas
Wish
Lady Maggie's Secret
Scandal
Lady Louisa's Christmas
Knight
Lady Eve's Indiscretion
Lady Jenny's Christmas
Portrait
The Courtship (novella)
The Duke and His Duchess
(novella)
Morgan and Archer
(novella)

The Lonely Lords

Darius
Nicholas
Ethan
Beckman
Gabriel
Gareth
Andrew
Douglas
David

Captive Hearts

The Captive
The Traitor
The Laird

The MacGregors

The Bridegroom Wore Plaid
Once Upon a Tartan
The MacGregor's Lady
Mary Fran and Matthew
(novella)

WHAT A Lady NEEDS for Christmas

GRACE BURROWES

sourcebooks
casablanca

For those of us to whom the holidays present a challenge, which is to say, ALL of us, at some point.

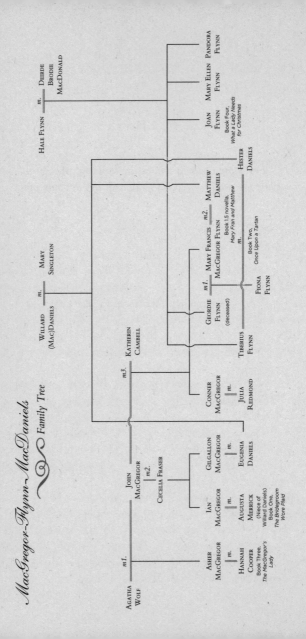

MacGregor~Flynn~MacDaniels ~ *Family Tree*

One

"BUT, PAPA, WE SHOULD HELP THE LADY!"

The childish soprano carried over the hum and bustle of a crowded train station, jabbing at Lady Joan Flynn's composure like a stray pin making itself known in her bodice as she swept into the first turn of a waltz.

Joan nonetheless beamed an unfaltering smile at the ticket master.

"Surely you can find *one* seat on the westbound train? I have little luggage and need passage only as far as Ballater."

Her luggage consisted of a carpetbag clutched in her right fist. That she'd fled Edinburgh without even packing a single trunk of clothing spoke of Joan's first experience with true desperation.

"Papa, *we're* going to Ballater. We should help her." The girl's voice, if anything, had grown louder.

"Like I said. Nary a single seat left, ma'am. Ye'll have to step aside now." The old gnome made his pronouncement with the malevolent glee of a clerk exercising his petty—but absolute—power.

Joan most assuredly did not step aside.

"Christmas is coming. We're supposed to be nice, Papa."

The child's intentions were good, though Joan wanted to turn around and wrap her scarf around the little dear's face. A soft, rumbling Gaelic burr replied to the girl, while Joan let her smile wobble as she fished a handkerchief from her reticule—the white silk with the holly-and-ivy trim around the edges.

"I'll ride with the livestock," Joan said, touching the handkerchief to the corner of her left eye, where tears would, in fact, soon gather. "I must rejoin my family, and they'll be so worried, and—"

White eyebrows climbed aloft on the ticket master's pink forehead, then crashed down as inspiration struck.

"Ye canna ride with the beasts. 'Tis against regulations." He flourished the *r* of *regulations*, then swooped on the *g*, an officious Scot relishing the delivery of bad tidings—rrrreg'ulations. "Ye can buy a ticket for Monday's train."

No, she could not. "But I have nowhere to stay until Monday. I have the fare if—"

"Her ladyship will ride with us," said that same rumbling baritone from directly behind Joan.

"Because we're going to Ballater," the child added helpfully.

Joan turned without giving up her place at the counter. "Sir, that's most kind of you, but if we have not been introduced—"

Except, thank all the angels, Joan *had* been introduced to the man, not three weeks past.

"Lady Joan." Mr. Dante Hartwell bowed, as much

as a man can bow when he has a small child perched on his hip. "You are welcome to travel with us. Charlie reminds me that we're going as far as Ballater ourselves, and we have plenty of room."

Charlie was of the female persuasion, though she had her father's sable hair and a lighter version of his green eyes. He whispered something in the girl's ear, then pressed a quick kiss to her cheek, which had Charlie grinning at Joan.

Mr. Hartwell's expression was not nearly so genial.

In Joan's experience, Mr. Hartwell and geniality were not well acquainted, though if Joan had spoken out of turn at Charlie's age, her lordly father would not have whispered his scold or followed it up with a kiss.

"Your offer is generous, Mr. Hartwell, but I cannot travel with you unchaperoned." Or could she?

"You were willing to travel with the beasts," he shot back. "I smell a bit better than they and can offer you more than straw and a cold loose box for the duration of the journey."

"Papa smells good," Charlie supplied, "but not as good as Aunt Margs. She took Phillip 'round back."

"Madam," the ticket master interrupted. "Ye're holding up the line, and ye either travel with the gentleman and his family or ye bide here until Monday's train. Next!"

Joan had danced with Dante Hartwell and found him lacking many of the attributes she associated with a proper gentleman. He neither gossiped nor flattered nor took surreptitious liberties in triple meter.

In short, despite his many detractors—some called

him Hard-Hearted Hartwell—she'd liked him. Little
Charlie was also right: her papa smelled good, of
wool and heather, unlike the fellows wearing their
cloying Paris fragrances in ballrooms already redolent
of manly exertion. Mr. Hartwell savored of simple
tastes, fresh air, and Scotland. Then too, his hair stuck
up to one side, as if Charlie had made free with her
papa's coiffure.

"Your sister is traveling with you, Mr. Hartwell?"

"Aye. Is this your only bag?" He appropriated the
carpetbag from Joan's grasp.

"Aunt Margs has lots of bags," Charlie said. "I think
our Christmas presents might be in them, but Aunt
says it's all her dresses."

The ticket master had apparently had enough.
"Madam, I really must insist that ye—"

"Stow it, MacDeever," Mr. Hartwell said. "*Lady Joan*
travels with us, and ye'll no' be spoutin' off about yer
pernicious regulations if ye want my continued custom."

The eyebrows climbed halfway to the North Pole,
but MacDeever remained silent.

"Thank you, Mr. Hartwell, and thank you, Charlie,"
Joan said, for it appeared she was to share a compartment with Mr. Hartwell and his family. How she'd
travel from Ballater to Balfour House, she did not
know, but surely hacks, drays, and other conveyances
could be had for a few coins at a busy train station.

Because a few coins was all she had.

"Aunt Margs!" Charlie bellowed, waving madly as
they tromped out onto the platform. "We're being
good. Papa says Lady Joan is to travel with us because
we're going to Ballater and she only has one bag."

The girl had shouted directly in her father's ear, and yet, Mr. Hartwell simply stood in the freezing wind, his bare knees exposed by his kilt. As rescuers went, he was an unlikely specimen. Pine swags draped over the station's entry luffed above him; he had Joan's purple brocade traveling bag in his big hand, a child affixed to his hip, and a grouchy expression on his face.

A petite woman approached, leading a small, dark-haired boy by the hand. Her cloak was a nondescript green with an unevenly stitched hem, though the wool was passable quality.

"Dante, has someone joined our party?" She spoke with the soft, broad vowels of the native Scot, and while her brother was tall, dark, and lean, Margaret Hartwell was short, fair, and comfortably rounded.

And smiling. Margaret had the sort of open, friendly smile that would put any guest at ease and warm any heart.

"Lady Joan Flynn, may I make known to you my dear sister, Margaret," Mr. Hartwell said, his tone as close to warm as Joan had heard from him. "The rascal by her side is my boy, Phillip. Phillip, make your bow."

"Pleased to meet you, ma'am," the child piped, flopping over at the waist.

"Miss Hartwell, Master Phillip, the pleasure is mine." Particularly when it was Margaret's presence that allowed Joan to accept Mr. Hartwell's kind—if begrudging—offer.

As for the "boy"—a gentleman of more refined breeding would have referred to the child as his son—he looked entirely too angelic. Dark hair in need of a trim framed green eyes too serious for such a small child, but then, what did Joan know of small children?

Much less than she needed to.

As Joan cast around for small talk, Mr. Hartwell strode off toward the back of the train.

"We'd best hurry," Margaret said. "Dante likes to oversee the loading of the luggage, and he'll forget that Charlie shouldn't be out in this weather any longer than necessary. Normally Dante would make this journey in a single day, but with the children..."

She bustled off after her brother, though why Mr. Hartwell had to oversee the porters, Joan could not fathom. Her brother, Tiberius, would have, because Tye was the most responsible fellow ever to stand in line for a marquessate, but Mr. Hartwell's prospects were nowhere as daunting.

Mr. Hartwell was *in trade*, a fact Joan had heard whispered behind fans, mentioned at card tables, and casually brought up in the course of numerous dances. The longer Mr. Hartwell had gone without stumbling on the dance floor, insulting the hostesses, or showing up for a Society ball in riding attire, the more frequently Joan had heard of his plebeian antecedents and unfortunate preoccupation with commerce.

A whistle blast signaled those milling on the platform to board their respective compartments, and at the end of the train, Mr. Hartwell, the child on his back now, oversaw no less than three porters stowing bags in the last car.

"Should we find our compartment?" Joan asked as she caught up with Margaret and Phillip.

"We're in here," Margaret said, gesturing vaguely

toward the passenger cars. "Dante, that child should be out of this weather. You will put her down this instant."

"I'm helping," Charlie said, clearly enjoying her perch on her papa's back.

The girl might have weighed less than a sparrow for all the notice her father took of her.

"The fools put the small trunks in first," Mr. Hartwell groused, "which means the largest trunks have nowhere to go but atop the heap, and that isn't the most stable—"

He broke off and leveled a look at Joan.

"Take Charlie." He peeled the girl off his back in a smooth display of one-armed muscle and more or less threw her in Joan's direction. "Charlene, mind Lady Joan while I—"

A spate of cursing in Gaelic followed as Mr. Hartwell disappeared into the baggage compartment, and three porters vacated it, rather like rats scurrying for safety upon the arrival of a particularly large, ferocious terrier.

"Dante likes things just so," Margaret observed in what had to be a diplomatic sororal understatement. "Let's get these children out of the weather, shall we?" She led Phillip to the steps and allowed him to scamper onto the train ahead of her.

"You can put me down," Charlie said. "Papa only carries me when I can't keep up. His legs are longer than mine."

"His legs are longer than most people's," Joan said, taking the child by the hand, though she'd rather liked Charlene's solid weight against her hip. "Shall we find our seats?"

Charlie peered up at her, her expression perplexed. "We don't have seats. We have the last two cars of the train."

❧

"She's hiding from you," Dante said, wondering how much his guest's cloak had cost. Contrasted with Lady Joan's red hair, the velvet was so purple, it shimmered in waterfalls and waves of light that had no visible source. A dark, luminous purple that shouted—quietly, mind—of warmth, pampering, and class, even as it made a man's palms itch to stroke it.

"Miss Hartwell is hiding?"

Miss Hartwell. Not "m' dear wee sister, Margs," or whatever Dante had said when he'd introduced Margs to her ladyship. A powerful thirst came upon him, the same thirst he experienced whenever he was forced to prowl around the parlors and ballrooms of his betters.

And what a waste of time and fussy tailoring that had been.

"Aye. Margs is shy. May I offer you something to drink, Lady Joan?" Margs was scheming and determined too, which accounted for her pressing need to "see the children settled" in the other car.

"Have you any tea, Mr. Hartwell? I left Edinburgh in something of a hurry."

Her very diction carried light and elegance, and yet bore a certain warmth, as did she. Dante owed this woman—and he always paid his debts—but he also liked her.

"Tea, we have, and we'd best drink it before it

cools." The train had yet to pull out of the station, so pouring would be little challenge—but for whom?

Lady Joan sat at the small mahogany table secured beneath the curtained window, while Dante prowled around the parlor car like a bear in a tinker's wagon.

Did he sit across from her?

Ask permission to sit?

Serve her while standing, as if he were a bloody footman? Sit and then serve her?

Ask her to pour?

Would Father Christmas please bestow on one hardworking Scotsman some command of the manners and mannerisms necessary to move among those with titles and wealth?

"Do have a seat, Mr. Hartwell, and I'd be happy to pour out."

Dante retrieved the tea service from the sideboard, set it down before her with a small "clank," and wedged himself into the seat across from her.

Train cars were built to the scale of fairies, though for all her height, Lady Joan looked comfortable enough.

"So what were you about, stranded at some widening in the cow path halfway to the Highlands?"

He should probably have stashed a "my lady" or two somewhere in that question. She belonged in the ballrooms, the elegant parlors, the best shops, while he did not.

"I was all but going to pieces," she said, her smile wry. "I cannot thank you enough, Mr. Hartwell, for your kindness and generosity. How do you take your tea?"

Dante Hartwell was known for neither kindness nor generosity.

"If that's your idea of going to pieces, then I'm not sure what you'd call some of Charlie's worse behaviors. The girl can be—"

Just like her father, but Dante didn't say that. He was too absorbed watching a lady execute the gracious and baffling ballet of the tea service. Lady Joan had lace at her wrists, the white a brilliant contrast to her deep purple sleeve. The dress wasn't as dark a hue as the cloak, but complemented the cloak and was every bit as shimmery. Against the purple velvet, the dab of lace looked like snow on violets or hyacinths or some damned posy.

"Your daughter is charming," Lady Joan said. "Shall I add cream and sugar?"

"Nay." He accepted the tea and downed it in a swallow. It was hot, and—

Not by word, deed, lifted eyebrow, or firming of her rather full lips did Lady Joan call Dante on his misstep. He rather wished she had.

"I bungled that," he said, setting the silly little cup back on the tray. The service was sized for one of Charlie's endless tea parties, not for use by thirsty adults. "I was supposed to wait for you to serve yourself."

His entire foray to Edinburgh had been one long exercise in bungling, and he was weary to his soul of it. When he'd been on the point of retreating to Glasgow, tail between his figurative knees, Lady Joan had given him a waltz and shown every pretense of enjoying his company. That single dance had silenced the worst of the gossips and prompted invitations from all manner of titled hostesses.

"You were supposed to enjoy your tea," Lady Joan

said, pouring him another cup. "You should hear my brother prosing on about tea, and how the empire would fall apart if we were denied our tea for a week straight. He's full of opinions, is Spathfoy."

This time, Dante let the cup sit on the tray until the lady had poured for herself. "The empire's finances would certainly falter if tea consumption stopped."

Another bungle, referring to commerce that way. He was in fine form today.

She took her tea with cream and sugar, and in her hands, the little porcelain cup with the gilded rim looked perfect—also a tad shaky.

"My nerves would falter as well. This is very good."

"Bit of Darjeeling in it, because Margs prefers it. You've avoided my question, Lady Joan. One doesn't find daughters of English marquesses milling about wee, cold, smelly Scottish train stations every day." Not alone, not without their luggage, not desperate for a seat on any westbound train.

She cradled her tea in her hands, giving Dante a moment to study her. The Lady Joan he'd come across socially had never had a hair out of place, never so much as a crumb on her bodice or a less-than–pleasant expression on her lovely face.

This Lady Joan's green eyes were shadowed with fatigue, her red hair was coiled in a simple chignon any serving maid might use for Sunday services, and her fine brows were slightly pinched, as if a worry had taken up residence behind them.

"One *shouldn't* find daughters of English marquesses in such condition," Lady Joan said, trying for humor and failing.

While Dante was trying for manners and not exactly succeeding.

He pushed the plate of scones at her then nudged the butter to her side of the tray, because he wanted to give her something to ease her distress. His bare knee bumped the same portion of her velvet-clad anatomy under the table, because she was no more built to fairy proportions than he was.

"You're trying to concoct a falsehood, my lady." Perhaps that was what creased her brow so she resembled Charlie on the verge of a bouncer. "You needn't bother. Have something to eat."

While she remained perched on the edge of the seat, teacup in her hands, Dante split a scone, slapped some butter on both halves, set it on a plate, and passed it to her.

"Many have nothing to put in their bellies this winter. You aren't among them today. Eat and be grateful."

He'd sounded like his papa—he sounded like his papa more often the older the children grew, and this was not a happy realization.

And yet, Papa hadn't been entirely wrong, either. The parlor car boasted a small Christmas tree on the table in the corner, complete with tiny paper snowflakes and a pinchbeck star. The cost of the tree and its trimmings would likely have bought some child a pair of boots.

"This scone is very good," Lady Joan said, tearing off a bite, studying it, and putting it in her mouth. "Your hospitality is much appreciated, Mr. Hartwell. Your discretion would be appreciated even more."

The silver service rattled as the train lurched

forward then eased into a smooth acceleration away from the station.

While Lady Joan made deft references to Dante's *discretion*.

"You're not trying to insult me." Dante didn't feel insulted, exactly, more like excluded—again. Excluded from the ranks of gentlemen, whose faultless discretion would be evident somehow in their very tailoring and diction.

"I mean no insult," Lady Joan replied, munching another bite of scone and looking...bewildered. "I'm trying to trust you."

"Try harder. I don't gossip, and I don't take advantage of women who find themselves in precarious circumstances. I've a daughter, and a sister, and I employ—"

She peered at him, as if perhaps he might have sprouted an extra head or two in the past minute.

"The rumors in Edinburgh were that you were looking for a wife, Mr. Hartwell. Nobody mentioned that you had children, though."

He recalled something then, about their passing interactions among the Edinburgh elite: he'd seen her dancing most often with Edward Valmonte, a mincing, smiling, nasty bugger of a baron—or possibly a viscount.

Pretty fellow, though, all blond grace and heavy scents. Lord Valmonte had done a lot to queer Dante's chances of finding a wife among the titled and moneyed set Valmonte called his family and friends.

"Keep your secrets then," Dante said, buttering another scone for her. "You're safe here, Lady Joan

Flynn, and while I cannot call myself a gentleman, I can
be discreet." He rose, though in the presence of a lady,
some damned protocol probably applied to that too. "I'll
send Margs to you. The sofa there is a decent place to
nap, and we'll not make Aberdeen for two hours at least."

He headed for the door that would lead him across
the platform to the other car.

"My maid fell ill," Lady Joan informed the bite
of scone she'd accepted. "She had to turn back for
Edinburgh, but I wanted to push on. My family
is gathering in anticipation of the holidays, and I
wanted—I have to be with them."

She wasn't lying; she also wasn't allowing him to
aid her any more than was necessary.

"To be with family for the holidays is a fine
thing," was all he could think to say. "Margs will be
along directly."

But not immediately, because as Dante well knew,
sometimes the only kindness a person in difficulties
could accept was solitude in which to contemplate
their troubles.

~∾~

"We're going visiting," Charlie informed Joan, scram-
bling into the banquette flanking the table. "We have
to be on our *best* manners, or Father Christmas will
only give us lumps of coal."

"Coal costs money," Phillip added from across the
parlor car. He sat on the sofa, his booted feet dangling
above the floor, a storybook open in his lap.

"Papa has lots of money," Charlie assured Joan
earnestly. "Does your papa have lots of money?"

"I'm sure I wouldn't know." Papa and Tye were both quite well set up.

"Our papa does." The child buttered herself a scone and inspected both Joan's teacup and the one Mr. Hartwell had used. "Papa owns tex-tile mills. Tex-tiles are like my dress."

"Textiles are fabrics," Phillip added. "Everybody needs textiles."

"Or"—Charlie's eyes danced as the door to the platform opened—"we'd be *naked*!"

"Charlene Beatrice Hartwell," Margaret said, advancing into the car. "Mind your tongue."

Charlie scrambled down, her scone in her hand. "Well, we would be. That's what Papa says, and *you* say we must mind Papa."

Papa, who had disappeared into the next car just as Joan had been about to ask him what, exactly, he'd heard about her in all the smoking rooms and gentlemen's retiring rooms of Edinburgh's best houses.

Mr. Hartwell would have told her, too, honestly and without judging her for what the gossip implied. How she knew this had something to do with his magnificent nose and with the manner in which his kilt flapped about his knees. His steadfast demeanor was also evident in the way he cursed in Gaelic and tossed full-sized trunks around as if they were so many hatboxes.

Even as he handled his daughter with much gentler strength.

"Charlie, perhaps you'd like to finish that scone sitting here next to me," Joan suggested. "If the train should lurch while you're larking about, you could choke."

Though he'd fled to the other car, any distress to Charlie would likely distress her papa greatly too.

When Charlie shot a curious look at Phillip and his storybook, Joan stroked the velvet cushion next to her seat.

"I thought I might pour you a spot of tea, and you too, Miss Hartwell. The tea will soon grow cold, and Mr. Hartwell said we're a good two hours from Aberdeen."

"I like tea!" Charlie skipped over to the table, leaving a few crumbs on the carpet. "Phillip doesn't, not unless it has heaps and heaps of sugar."

Phillip did not deign to reply, his little nose being quite glued to his book.

"I prefer some sugar in my tea as well," Joan said.

Now, Phillip raised his face from his stories long enough to stick his tongue out at his sister, but only that long. Charlie returned fire, grinning, then resumed her seat across from Joan.

"You two," Miss Hartwell muttered, sliding in next to Charlie. "They aren't bad children, exactly. Dante says they're high-spirited."

"Papa says we're right terrors," Charlie supplied, taking another bite of scone. "I like being a terror."

While Miss Hartwell looked as if she'd expire of mortification.

"Even a terror must know how to serve tea," Joan said, passing the girl a plate. "And even a terror knows that somebody must clean up all the crumbs strewn about, and cleaning up isn't much fun, is it?"

Charlie looked at her last bite of scone as if she'd no idea how the food had arrived into her hand. Her shoulders sank as she studied the carpet. "I made a mess. I should clean it up, or Papa will be *disappointed in me.*"

"Only a few crumbs' worth of disappointment," Joan said, because she knew well the weight a papa's disappointment might add to a daughter's heart, and would soon know it even better. "We'll tidy up when you've had some tea."

How to serve tea was a lesson a lady absorbed in the nursery, her nanny guiding, her dolls in attendance. Joan's own mama had joined in those earliest tea parties and turned the entire undertaking into a game, eventually adding real tea and—Mama had a genius for raising little girls—real tea cakes.

"What's the most important thing about serving tea?" Charlie asked, and the ring of the question suggested Papa, in addition to the other pearls of wisdom he showered upon his adoring daughter, tended to prose on about Most Important Things.

"The most important thing," Joan said, "is to make your guests feel welcome, otherwise, they won't enjoy their tea, or even their tea cakes."

"It's not to avoid spills?" Miss Hartwell asked.

Interesting question, and Miss Hartwell offered it hesitantly.

"Spills are inevitable." Spills on the tea tray, and in life too, apparently. "That's why we have trays and saucers and extra serviettes. If the hostess spills a drop or two, then a guest who makes a similar slip won't feel so ill at ease."

Joan poured out for Miss Hartwell, though to do so was presumptuous when Miss Hartwell's brother owned the parlor car—and everything in it.

As a younger man, Dante had ended up in bed with any number of strangers. The cheaper inns were like that—a man might share a room, even a mattress, with some fellow he'd never met, share a table with a family he'd never see again. The locomotive had conferred that same quality upon the traveling compartment, where impromptu picnics, shared reading, and gossip turned the cheaper cars of each train into a series of temporary traveling neighborhoods.

Dante hadn't expected that his private car would fall prey to such informality, but there Lady Joan lay, cast away with exhaustion on the settee bolted to the wall.

She did not fit on her makeshift bed.

Her ladyship was tall for a female. Had she been male, Dante would have called her "lanky," but because she was *not* male, the applicable term was probably "willowy." The luminous dark purple cloak swaddled her to the chin, but one half boot dangled free of her frothy lavender hems, an escapee from warmth and decorum both.

The question that dogged his very existence of late loomed once again: *What would a gentleman do?* He'd probably retreat to the other car, where Charlie was busy making enough noise for three little girls, a pair of small boys, and a barking hound.

If the gentleman were very pressed for time, would he ignore his guest, sit at the fussy little tea table, and plow through Hector's stack of figures? Would he close his eyes for a moment and snatch a badly needed nap when nobody was looking?

That way lay two wasted hours, and yet, Hector's reports were a daunting prospect.

Lady Joan looked daunted. Her eyes were shadowed with fatigue, and on this rocking, noisy, stinking train car, she was fast asleep.

In addition to her half boot and frilly hems, a slender, pale hand now emerged from under the purple velvet. A row of small nacre buttons started at the wrist of that hand—more subtle luster—marching right up the underside of her forearm to disappear under her cloak.

The poor woman would take forever to get dressed. Or *undressed*.

Trying not to make a sound, Dante sorted through the half-inch-thick packet of documents he'd taken from the top of his traveling valise when he'd fled the other car.

Five minutes later, he was studying the rise and fall of Lady Joan's chest beneath her velvet swags. Her stays did not confine her much, was his guess, and maybe that accounted for the freedom she exuded in her movement and in her smiles.

"You've caught me," she said, opening her eyes. She started to stretch, her boot hit the end of the settee, and she subsided beneath her cloak. "Not well done of me, falling asleep where any might chance upon me."

"I meant only to retrieve my reports. I'll go back to the other car," Dante said, shuffling the reports into a stack but making no move to rise.

"No need," her ladyship said, pushing halfway to sitting and then stopping, awkwardly, half reclining, half sitting. "Gracious. I seem to have become entangled."

She could not lift her hand to peer at the difficulty,

because her lacy cuff was caught on one of the buttons fastening the upholstery to the settee's frame.

"Hold still." Dante extracted his folding knife from his coat pocket. He was across the parlor car in two short strides and on his knees before the settee. "I'll have you free in a moment."

Dante still wore his reading glasses, so he could see that three of those tiny, fetching buttons—that would inspire a man to stare at her slender wrists by the hour—were now twisted up in the lacy cuff. He flipped open his knife, prepared to deal summarily with troublesome fashions, when Lady Joan's free hand landed on his shoulder.

"Please, do not."

"You're trapped, my lady. A quick slice, and you'll be free. You can stitch up the lace by the time we're halfway to Aberdeen."

Her contretemps put them in close proximity, Dante kneeling before the settee, the lady's cloak and skirts brushing his knees. What he felt crouched beside her semi-recumbent form was not a temptation to sniff at her spicy fragrance, not a desire to unbind all that fiery hair, but rather, an itch to divest her of the velvet covering her from neck to toes.

"But that's a *knife*, Mr. Hartwell."

"Aye, and I keep my blades honed."

"One doesn't…velvet and lace should not be…a knife is…oh, bother. Give me a moment."

He knelt before her, feeling helpless and stupid, while she tried to use her free hand to worry the buttons from the lace. She was doomed to fail—one hand wouldn't serve for this task—and Dante had every intention of allowing her to struggle while he returned to the boring safety of Hector's reports.

Except, when she bent forward to work at the trap she'd fallen into, Lady Joan shifted so her décolletage was a foot from Dante's face. The spicy scent of her concentrated, nutmeg emerging from undertones of cedar, clove, and even black pepper.

The lace of her fichu was a cross between pink and purple—she could doubtless tell him the name for that shade in French and English both—and the cleft between her breasts was a shadowy promise between two modest, female curves.

"I can't get it," she muttered. "Drat this day. I can't even properly sneak a nap or occupy a settee."

She occupied a settee quite nicely, but one didn't argue with a lady. Dante knew that much.

"Let me have a try." He scooted two inches closer and covered her hand with his own. "You're at the wrong angle."

She slid her hand out from under his. "Please do. At some point I must leave this train, and dragging furniture behind me will make that a difficult undertaking."

"You could always take the dress off," Dante said, studying the problem. Because of the way she'd twisted things up, the trick would be to free the buttons in sequence, top, middle, bottom. He carefully spread the lace around the top button, making an opening for the button to slip through.

The quality of her ladyship's silence distracted him from the buttons.

What had he said? Something about taking the dress—

She stared at him, her brows drawn down, her

mouth a flat, considering line. Then, the corners up her lips turned up, hesitantly. "Taking off the dress would extricate me from the settee's clutches, though it might be a bit chilly, too."

She was not chilly. When Dante considered the picture she'd make, all lace, silk, and pale garters— probably embroidered with lavender flowers—he wasn't chilly either.

"I'll have you out in a moment," he said, focusing on the two remaining buttons.

The third button was not, in fact, the charm. Number two obeyed Dante's fingers as he created another temporary buttonhole for it, but the last button was tightly caught, and Dante's efforts to rearrange the lace resulted in a small tearing sound.

"Oh, no," Lady Joan moaned, trying to still Dante's fingers by covering his hand with hers. Her palm was cold, her grip stronger than he would have thought.

"Ach, now, my knife—"

"*No*. No knives, not on my cuffs, not on my sleeves, not on my buttons." Her tone was pleading rather than imperious, but she'd covered the junction of button and lace with her hand so Dante could not have freed her if he'd wanted to.

The moment turned awkward, with the lady trapping his hand against her wrist, as if she'd protect a bit of cloth from the infidel's knife.

A single hot tear splashed onto the back of Dante's hand, and the moment became more awkward still.

Two

JOAN DID NOT HAVE A FAVORITE FABRIC, A FAVORITE
color, a favorite style of dress. She loved them all—
right down to the smallest lacy cuff—with a dangerous, undisciplined passion.

Her passion for fabric would soon cost her everything she held dear.

"I'm sorry," she said, trying to straighten, but even
this small attempt at dignity was thwarted by the
perishing sofa. "I'm fatigued, and the day has been
t-trying, and no matter what I—"

"There we go," Mr. Hartwell said, lifting Joan's
wrist from the arm of the sofa. "You're free." He dug
in his sporran for a handkerchief, which Joan accepted.
Her white silk handkerchief was for show, and these
tears were all too real.

"My thanks, Mr. Hartwell. I do apologize. I'm not
normally so easily—"

A large, blunt finger touched her lips. "You're
about to spew a falsehood, *another* falsehood. In case it
has escaped your notice, we are alone in this train car,
and nobody's on hand to whom you need lie."

Lie was a blunt word, and Mr. Hartwell's touch was far from soft, but the kindness in his eyes was real. Rather than fall into that kindness, Joan smoothed her fingertips over the corner of the plain cotton handkerchief.

"Who embroidered this?"

"Margs."

"She does lovely work." The small square was monogrammed in green with exquisite precision. "She must have excellent eyesight."

Mr. Hartwell took the place beside Joan on the sofa, draping her cloak over the arm. "She's determined, is Margs. Why were you crying?"

A gentleman wouldn't ask, but a friend—if Joan had had a friend—wouldn't have let the matter drop.

"Allowing me to share your parlor car doesn't mean I can inflict all my petty difficulties on you, Mr. Hartwell."

Though her present difficulties would be the ruin of her, if not of her sisters too.

"I was married," her companion said. "Sufficiently married to have two wee bairns, and that means I have a nodding acquaintance with women, if not with ladies."

Soon, Joan wouldn't be worthy of such a distinction. The notion prompted more tears, not because she would be a discredit to her title, but because her family would be so *disappointed* in her.

She was disappointed in herself, come to that.

Mr. Hartwell wrapped a heavy arm around Joan's shoulders, and she gave in to the comfort he offered. For long moments, she simply curled into the solid bulk of him and cried, all dignity, all self-control gone, while the train rumbled and swayed ever northward.

When her upset had eased to sniffles, his arm was still around her shoulders, and she could not have moved off the sofa to save what remained of her reputation.

"The wool of your coat contains a quantity of merino," she said, rubbing her cheek against his sleeve. "The blend is lovely, if unusual. Why aren't you horrified when I cry?"

"I'm Charlie's da. You think a few tears will put me off?"

Joan's father would not have sat with her like this, a quiet, tolerant presence offering handkerchiefs and a calm that had something in common with loyal hounds and plow horses.

"Tears put *me* off," she said, dabbing at her cheeks and trying to sit up. "I must look a fright."

His big hand settled on the side of her neck, his callused palm an interesting contrast to her velvet and lace.

"You look frightened, Lady Joan, and tired, and much in need of a friend. You have nowhere to run for the next two hours. The children have gone down for naps, Margs is reading some improving tract, and you have no one else to talk to. I am not—"

Joan waited while Mr. Hartwell chose his words, because she liked the sound of his voice, and she had a soft spot for merino blends.

"I'm not refined," he went on, "not *of your set*, but I have a few resources. I'll help if I can."

He was rumored to be wallowing in filthy lucre.

"You are helping. You are helping me flee Edinburgh, where I am sure scandal is about to erupt all over my good name. I was foolish."

"Edinburgh must breed foolishness, then, because I certainly did not acquit myself well there either." His admission was grudging, self-mocking, and endearing.

His thumb rested right below her ear, and abruptly, Joan was assailed by a memory of Edward's nose mashed against her neck. He'd been on top of her, breathing absinthe all over her and wrinkling her gown terribly. If she could forget a man nearly crushing her, what else had she forgotten about last night?

"I cannot imagine you being foolish, Mr. Hartwell. You strike me as the soul of probity." He was certainly the soul of sober colors, at least when he took to the ballrooms. No extravagant jewels, stickpins, or even formal Highland dress, which was common enough in Scotland.

Joan knew with a certainty that Mr. Hartwell wouldn't slobber on a woman's neck while he yanked at her bodice.

"I am the soul of low birth," he said. "I should know better than to impose myself on my betters, but Margs needs a husband, and someday, Charlie and Phillip will need prospects their papa's money cannot buy. I sought to start securing those prospects, and found the task utterly beyond me."

Joan set aside her troubles for a moment—they weren't going anywhere, heaven knew.

"You're giving up on Polite Society after a few weeks of waltzing and swilling punch? This isn't even the social Season, Mr. Hartwell. The prettiest debutante knows she must campaign for more than a few weeks."

"And I am not the prettiest debutante, am I?"

He was in trade. Even if he had been the prettiest and best dowered debutante, or the handsomest, most charming bachelor, being in trade would follow him everywhere.

"You sought a wellborn wife, I take it? One who could open doors for your daughter and your sister?"

He tugged off his glasses and slipped them into a breast pocket. "I certainly haven't any need to polish my waltzing skills."

"You waltz beautifully. You don't haul a woman about, as if it's her privilege to smile and simper at your every word while you step on her toes and leer at her attributes."

She should not have been that honest. She should have asked him which clan plaid was draped over his knees. The pattern was mostly blue and black, with thin intersecting stripes of red and yellow. A hunting tartan, possibly.

"Was one of these leering, stomping idiots involved in your foolishness, Lady Joan?"

The train whistle sounded, and beyond the velvet curtains caught back at the parlor car's windows, snow had started. The landscape was bleak, and Joan's mood more bleak yet.

She said nothing.

"I'll tell you a story, then. Charlie vows I've a gift for telling a tale," Mr. Hartwell said, easing back a fraction against the cushions, as if getting comfortable. "Once upon a time there was a lovely, graceful young woman whose papa was a marquess—an *English* marquess, the very best sort of marquess to be. She was friendly and kind, also every inch a lady—and there were many inches, for she was tall. Along came a young man, probably handsome, full of charm. He'd be blond, for the handsomest young men usually are—also English somewhere not too far back in his pedigree. Does the tale sound familiar?"

Had he already heard the gossip? Not twenty-four hours after the debacle, and even Mr. Hartwell, who could not belong to the best clubs or have the ear of the worst gossips, seemed to know the particulars.

"Go on."

"The handsome young swain exerted his charm, he made promises—he served the young lady strong drink and stronger compliments, and he made more promises. He took liberties, and the young lady was perhaps flattered, to think she'd inspired a handsome, charming man's passions to that extent."

Joan's head came up. "I wasn't flattered. I was muddled." Also horrified.

"You have made a wreck of my handkerchief," Mr. Hartwell observed, gently prying the balled-up cotton from her grasp.

"I've made a wreck of my life."

⁓

Nothing good came from a fellow involving himself with damsels in distress. Dante knew this, the way a lad raised up in the mills knows to keep his head down and his hands to himself, lest some piece of clattering machinery part him from same.

Rowena had been a damsel in distress, and look how that had turned out.

And yet, Charlie hadn't allowed him to ignore

Lady Joan, and some vestige of chivalry known to even clerks, porters, and wherry men hadn't allowed it either. Now that Dante had rescued his damp handkerchief from her grasp, she traced the lines of the Brodie hunting plaid draped across his thigh.

Joan Flynn was a toucher, a fine quality in a woman, regardless of her station. Charlie was a toucher. She had to get her hands on things to understand them, the same way Dante had to take things apart to see how they fit together.

"You have not made a wreck of your life, my lady. The worthless bounder who stole a few kisses will keep his mouth shut about it, and not because he's a gentleman."

Gentlemen tattled on themselves at length over their whiskey and port, and called it bragging. Worse than the waltzing and bowing, listening to their manly drivel had affronted Dante's sensibilities.

"Why should he keep his mouth shut?"

"Because it reflects badly on him that he'd take those liberties. Your papa could ruin the man socially, to say nothing of what your mama might do. Pretty English boys who take advantage of innocent women need their social consequence if they're to pursue their games."

Her brows drew down in thought, which was an improvement over tears, and her fingers stroked closer to his knee.

"You are certain of your logic, Mr. Hartwell."

"I am certain of young, charming Englishmen." He was also certain that Lady Joan ought not to be cuddled up with him this way, now that her tears had ceased.

And yet, he stayed right where he was.

She wrinkled her splendid nose. "He's engaged, that Englishman."

"Which he neglected to tell you as he was leering at your bodice." Her attributes. She'd used the more delicate word. The woman beside him wasn't over-endowed. Even in her feminine attributes, Lady Joan had a tidy, elegant quality. "That little omission on his part had to hurt."

She left off patting his knee—a relief, that—and worried a nail. "The announcement was in this morn-ing's papers. I was an idiot and I panicked."

Whoever the English Lothario was, he'd upset a good woman, and done it dishonorably. Many a man had stolen a kiss, but not when promised to another, and not by using cold calculation to muddle the lady.

"You were an innocent, and I suspect you still are. Nobody can tell, you know."

His blunt speech had her sitting up.

"I beg your pardon?" Her tone was curious rather than indignant, and Dante was glad he didn't know which mincing fop had taken liberties with her.

"Nobody can tell which favors you've bestowed on whom. Maybe you kissed him witless; maybe he put his hands where only your husband's hands ought to go. Maybe he saw treasures no other fellow has seen. If it was only you and he on that darkened balcony or in that unheated parlor, then it's your word against his regarding what transpired. If he threatens gossip, you threaten some of your own."

She fingered her lacy cuff, which wasn't torn exactly,

but the drape of the lace was disturbed by the mishap with the snagged buttons. "A lady doesn't gossip."

He was in the presence not only of goodness, but innocence. May his daughter grow up to be just like Lady Joan.

"Many ladies seem to do little else but gossip," he said, "and the gentlemen can be just as bad, because they apply spirits to their wagging tongues."

He retrieved his arm from around her shoulders, though that did nothing to take her delicate, feminine scent from his nose, or the warmth of her along his side from his awareness.

"What sort of gossip would a lady bent on revenge start?"

He liked that for all her soft, velvety elegance, she'd ask such a thing, and he liked more that she'd ask *him*.

"His charming young lordship can't kiss worth a damn. He gambles indiscriminately. His hands are clammy, his breath stinks." Because the damned fool fellow had it coming, Dante added, "He makes odd noises."

Auburn brows flew up. "How ever did you guess? He makes whiny little moans, and it's distracting, and not very manly, the same sounds his lapdog makes when in urgent need of the garden. I'd forgotten his moaning."

Oh, Dante liked this woman. He liked her very well.

"If he has a lapdog, you're well rid of him." The blighter probably had a tiny pizzle, too. If Dante told the lady to bruit that about, she'd likely leap from the train.

Though Dante would catch her.

"Perhaps I am well rid of him." The first hint of a glimmer of a smile tugged at the corners of her mouth. Not a pleasant, social smile, such as she'd bestow on shop clerks and churchyard acquaintances, but a true, warm, merry smile, such as she'd share with a friend. "Perhaps I am well rid of him at that."

Dante loved that he'd made her smile, loved that she wasn't as upset as she'd been, and all because he'd spent a few minutes talking with her—and letting her pet his knee.

So he smiled right back.

⁓

Mr. Hartwell was honest, friendly, and kind, which to Joan was a significant improvement over handsome and charming. He also smelled good—of heather and cedar—and he wore the most marvelous merino blends.

Over thighs that put Joan in mind of the mahogany table under the window. Smooth, warm, hard.

Gracious heavens.

"What has you traveling into the mountains at this time of year, Mr. Hartwell?"

His smiled faded but didn't leave his eyes, suggesting he was permitting Joan to change the subject.

"The same thing that has me getting up most mornings and ruining my eyes with a lot of reports most nights: business."

"You're in textiles." The polite version of the ballroom *on dits*.

"I'm in *trade*," he said, rising. "I'm not ashamed of working for my bread, Lady Joan. I'm responsible for three mills, and they turn out fine products. They do, however, require both management and capital on a regular basis. Capital being money."

Tiberius was always going on about capital.

"My mother has ensured that I have a thorough grasp of economics, Mr. Hartwell. Your mills also require land and labor, among other things." Without his bulk beside her, the train car was not quite so cozy, though it was a good deal more proper.

Mr. Hartwell wedged himself into the bench at the small table, looking momentarily puzzled. "Your mama educated you thus?"

Mama was notorious for her financial skills, at least in Polite Society. Mr. Hartwell couldn't know that.

"She educated all five of her children regarding money, and Papa thoroughly—if quietly—approved."

To the extent Papa approved of anything.

Mr. Hartwell retrieved his spectacles from his pocket and picked up a sheaf of papers from a stack on the table.

"Do you mind if I read, Lady Joan? When I reach my destination, I will have little time to acquaint myself with these reports, and a successful negotiation always starts with a thorough grasp of the pertinent facts."

"You're not traveling for pleasure, then."

She had withheld specific permission to read, and Mr. Hartwell must have grasped that subtlety. That's how desperate Joan was to avoid what memories she had of the previous night.

He put the papers down and stared into the middle distance. "Had I any other choice, I'd not make this journey. I'm invited to spend the holidays with acquaintances too wellborn to dirty their hands in trade where anybody might notice, and because they cannot abide the notion I might raise such a topic where polite ears could overhear, I'm enduring the fiction that I'm a guest at a house party."

House parties could be delightful—though they were usually tedious in the extreme and at least a week longer than necessary to make that point.

"If you're not a guest, then what are you in truth?"

Bleak humor crossed his features. He took out a second plain handkerchief and rubbed at the lenses of his glasses.

"I'm an opportunity."

A shaft of cold tricked into Joan's belly. Edward had said something similar about Joan, though the exact words refused to show themselves from the undergrowth of her memories.

"That doesn't sound very pleasant."

"It's business." He held his spectacles up to the window, as if inspecting for smudges. "I understand that, and they are an opportunity for me. The land can no longer support the aristocracy in the manner they prefer, and trade is a means of diversifying revenue—of making money in more ways than one. I don't suppose a lady enjoys talk of the shop, though."

Gracious heavens, Mama would have Mr. Hartwell's suppositions for dessert. "Diversification requires a greater management effort, though it ideally spreads risk."

Drat and a half, she ought not to have said that.

Pronouncements along those lines—which Joan had heard at the family dinner table since she'd put up her hair—made gentlemen smile as if their baby sister had just recited a piece of the royal succession—without a single error!

Or the fellows would wince and see somebody else they had to speak with on the other side of the ballroom.

Immediately.

Mr. Hartwell unwedged himself from the banquette and knelt before the parlor stove. "Diversification ideally spreads risk. Explain yourself."

"Risk has to do with the probabilities and eventualities," Joan said. "With how likely it is that matters could go awry, or succeed wildly. If you have invested in one solid venture, then your profits are likely to be more reliable than if you invest in two risky ventures. Over time, however, one of the risky ventures might do quite well."

Risky ventures could also, however, see a lady precipitously ruined.

He added coal to the fire, closed the stove door, and dusted his hands, but remained kneeling, as if he could watch the flames dance through the cast iron.

"I do not believe I have ever heard another female use the word *probability* regarding anything other than a marriage proposal."

The greatest risk of all. Joan tucked her feet up under her and came to two conclusions.

Mr. Hartwell had noticed that she might be cold, and rather than ring for the porter to tend to the stove, he'd seen to it himself. Trains were messy and smelly, even as far from the engines as this car was, and yet,

Mr. Hartwell had dirtied his hands without a second thought. This suggested he was heedless of strict decorum, but not of the consideration due a guest.

The second conclusion was that Joan's lapse into territory through which Mama gamboled with heedless abandon had not put Mr. Hartwell off, but rather, had *interested* him.

"You have the right of it," he said, rising lithely and bracing himself on the narrow mantel over the stove. Somebody had draped pine swags from the mantel in another nod to the approaching holidays—or possibly in an effort to cut the stench of coal smoke permeating any locomotive. "Diversification can mean greater management effort, so when my betters seek to diversify, they expect me to provide the management, while they reap the profits."

As if he were a shop clerk, and not owner of the very mill. "You would manage anything in your keeping responsibly."

He rolled up the pine rope, unhooked it from whatever held it up, and pitched the entire fragrant bundle out the door at the far end of the parlor car.

"How can you assess the management ability of a man you met only weeks ago, Lady Joan? I was born in a dirt-floor croft. I married for money, and I'm known to pinch a penny until it screams for mercy, hence the frequent references to me as Hard-Hearted Hartwell."

Mr. Hartwell propounded these notions as if they were facts, while Joan suspected they were mostly myths—though a dirt floor was hard to argue with.

"I have witnessed you with your children, Mr.

Hartwell. I've watched you stack your sister's trunks. I've seen you eyeing those reports as if they were sirens calling you ever closer when I know you need a nap."

She had also danced with him. Any matter put into his care had his undivided attention.

"I'll not argue about the nap, but soon the children will be underfoot again, and they tend to frown on Hector's reports."

Joan wasn't too fond of Hector's reports, and she'd never met this Hector fellow. "Have your nap," she said, rising. "I had mine, and if you're headed for a house party, you will need your rest."

When she might have put her hand on the door-knob, he stopped her by reaching it first. "While you do what?"

He really had no notion of polite discourse. Joan's chin came up, rather than admit she might have liked a peek at those reports.

"I will explain diversification to your children."

"How?"

Yes, how? "The holidays are approaching, Mr. Hartwell. I can put it in terms of holiday gifts. Would they rather have one large gift or four smaller ones, any one of which might hold their heart's desire?"

"Charlie's heart's desire is a pet."

"And Phillip's?"

Mr. Hartwell studied Joan, which was a lovely opportunity to study him. He was a man in his prime, not a boy. The architecture of his jaw put her in mind of Arthur's Seat, a geological formation overlooking Edinburgh. The cast of his face wasn't stubborn so much as ageless. Enduring. His looks wouldn't change appreciably for decades, and already, his children bore the stamp of his features.

"Phillip wants a baby brother to boss around. The boy is a born manager."

"A baby—?" He was teasing her, the wretch. Joan patted his cheek, which was rather like patting the surface of the stove—warm and unyielding. "There's always next Christmas, Mr. Hartwell, particularly for those who are well behaved."

As Joan had not been.

Somebody ought to have been blushing and stammering—Joan suspected it was she—but instead, two people were smiling. Two adults.

Joan slipped through the door, her smile fading as the cold, smoky air assailed her on the noisy platform.

She had no business teasing Mr. Hartwell like that, no business touching him, no business even sharing a private car with him. For while she might, indeed, discuss diversification with his darling children, most of Joan's mental efforts should be bent toward trying to recall what, exactly, had transpired in Edward's parlor the previous evening.

❧

Dante rooted through the stack of papers until he came up with the report Margs had put together for him. The document read like a book of the Old Testament, one begat after another, followed by was-brother-to, and wed-the-daughter-of.

Aristocrats tended to inbreed, and even line breed, particularly on the Continent. Prince Albert's father, on the occasion of his second marriage, had chosen his niece for his bride, a common undertaking among the pumpernickel princes, for it kept land and wealth in the family.

The English weren't quite that medieval, but memorizing the intermarriages of the aristocracy was sufficiently narcotic that by the time Dante's daughter came barreling into the parlor car, his chin was on his chest, and his eyes were closed in…thought.

Marriage was a sort of diversification, or it could be. The titled and wealthy families understood that, as had the clan chiefs of old. The parallel hadn't occurred to Dante previously, and he didn't like it.

"Papa!"

"No need to yell, Charlene." And no need to be fully awake to catch the child up in his arms as she scrambled onto his lap.

"Lady Joan is showing Aunt some fancy stitches. It's boring."

Sewing on board a swaying train could not be easy. "Is she stitching up her cuff, then?" The cuff Dante had torn.

"She did that first." Charlie made herself comfortable on her father's lap, a conquest simplified by the fact that Dante had folded the table down and propped his feet on the opposite bench. "Why did you take the decorations down, Papa? Christmas is coming!"

Christmas had been coming since Michaelmas, according to Charlie. Shortly after the Yuletide holidays had passed, Easter would approach, and May Day, too.

"I took them down because anybody who would drape pine swags directly over a burning parlor stove is an idiot."

"The decorations could catch fire?"

The girl was tempted to suck her thumb, Dante could feel it in her, though she'd never sucked her thumb until her mother had died.

"Almost anything can catch fire." He took her right hand in his and kissed little knuckles that tasted sweet—also a bit sticky. "If you could choose between four small Christmas presents and one big one, which one would you choose?"

He asked, because a discussion of fire was not conducive to a small child's peaceful dreams, and because he enjoyed the way his children's minds were unburdened by adult preconceptions.

"How small?"

"Smaller than a kitten, larger than a ring." Charlie cared nothing for rings, yet.

"How big is the big one?"

"You're gathering your facts, which is smart. The big one is smaller than a pony."

"Not smaller than a dog?"

Neatly done. "Not smaller than a dog, no."

"I'd want both. I've been very good, though not as good as Phillip. He and Lady Joan were talking about bad things happening or good things happening."

"They were talking about risk." Why had Dante never thought to broach such a topic with his small son? The boy would take to the subject with relish—to the extent Phillip did anything with relish.

Dante rose, Charlene affixed to him like a particularly large neckcloth. "Let's join their discussion, shall we?"

"Aunt said I was to fetch you."

Well, of course. Because Lady Joan was pretty and single, and Margs was determined to see Dante remarried—Margs was also oblivious to the ironclad rules of Polite Society.

"Then you've completed your assignment," Dante said, making his way from one car to another. The countryside was blanketed in white now, the pines on either side of the tracks bowing branch by branch with a burden of snow. "Pretty out here."

"Pretty, but cold, Papa."

A good description of most of the women Dante had met in those fancy ballrooms, though not of Lady Joan. He left the bracing air of the platform for the other parlor car, coming upon a scene of such domestic tranquillity, it might have been some cozy sitting room in Edinburgh.

"Ladies." Dante put Charlie down and bowed slightly, which folly made Margs's eyes dance. "Charlene said I'd been summoned."

"Charlene misheard," Margs replied, all innocence as she bent over her embroidery hoop. "I said it was a shame you had to bury yourself in your reports when we see so little of you."

Charlie had excellent hearing, also a soft heart.

"Reading on the train is difficult in the best circumstances." Dante took a place beside his sister on a silly undersized blue sofa bolted to the wall. Clearly, train cars had gender, and the paneled, dark, *decantered* car he'd left was for the fellows, while this space was for the ladies.

For the back of the sofa curved exactly in the shape of a heart, or of a woman's breasts at the top of her décolletage.

Phillip, as ever, watched the exchange from across the room without saying a word. The boy had made gathering facts into a life's work.

"Would you like a chocolate, Mr. Hartwell?" Lady Joan held out a box of sweets, more silliness, but Dante suspected the polite thing to do was to take one.

"Thank you." Except the blasted confections were nestled among colored paper, so Dante had to dig to extract one—any one at random—and he nearly ended up causing Lady Joan to drop the lot.

"Perhaps I might suggest one?" Lady Joan asked.

Was that how polite people went about such an undertaking? In none of the etiquette books Dante had trudged through had he seen a discourse on the proper method of selecting a chocolate.

He did not want a damned chocolate. He wanted to stand out on the platform until his temper and his cheeks cooled, and then stand out there until his awareness of Lady Joan cooled as well.

Which could well see him frozen before they reached Aberdeen.

"Any one will do." Because he did not favor sweets, and had said so to more than one titled hostess. He did not say so to Lady Joan.

"No, not just any treat," she said, peering into the box. "For you, this one, I think."

In her hand was a treat for which the French probably had a name. Dante took it from her fingers and popped it into his mouth, aware that every other occupant of the car was watching him for a reaction.

"Quite good...quite..." He'd had chocolate before, which came in varying blends of bitter and sweet, much like life. He didn't care for it, but this was ambrosial. "What is it?"

The flavor was interesting, substantial, appealing, and neither too sweet nor too bitter, and the pungent chocolate balanced whatever the filling was.

"Marzipan," Lady Joan said. "Mostly ground almonds, some sugar, eggs, a dash of vanilla, that sort of thing. I'm partial to it myself, particularly as the holidays approach. This box was a gift from a family friend."

She'd treated him to her favorite sweet. Any thought of returning to his reports evaporated, as did a pressing need to make a solitary visit to the frigid platform.

"Shall you join our discussion of risk, Mr. Hartwell? Phillip raised an interesting point, about risk varying with the person taking it."

"Did he now?" Phillip was a man of few words, and fewer smiles, and yet, as Lady Joan spoke, the boy beamed at her.

Beamed. When was the last time wee Phillip had beamed?

And why hadn't his father noticed?

"I have a few opinions on risk," Dante said as the last of the marzipan melted from his palate.

"We thought you might," Margs murmured. "About avoiding risk whenever possible."

His sister was twenty-five years old. She had never, as far as Dante knew, been kissed, and she was lecturing *him* about avoiding risk.

"I'll take a prudent risk," Dante said. "Witness our holiday destination, Sister."

She might have stuck her tongue out at him, but for Lady Joan's presence.

"Phillip and I were discussing the risks inherent in a business that depends on women's fashions," Joan said, searching with an index finger through the box of chocolates. "Purely as an example of a difficult undertaking."

"Because women are fickle," Phillip volunteered, his expression wary.

"Fashion is fickle," Dante said, though the boy was quoting his own papa. "The textile market is fickle, and competition is fierce. Ladies' fashions are not a business I'd advise anybody with any sense to go into."

Lady Joan put the lid back on the box of chocolates and scooted closer to Margs. "Perhaps you're right, Mr. Hartwell."

Her tone—and her unwillingness to offer him another treat—said clearly, "And perhaps you're dead wrong."

He wished she'd argue with him, and he wished she'd offer him another one of those almond treats—or get her cuff caught, or something.

Stupid wishes. He should have brought his reports along with him from the other car. Instead of studying the slight furrow between Lady Joan's eyebrows, he might instead have tried—again—to get straight all the interlocking dynastic connections of the prigs and buffoons with whom he'd be spending his holidays.

Three

TIBERIUS FLYNN, EARL OF SPATHFOY, LOVED HIS countess and his family, though both could try the patience of a damned saint.

"You have that 'I wish I could use foul language' look on your face," his countess said, bussing his cheek.

They were on a train headed for Ballater, and thus Tye's store of retaliatory kisses was limited.

"How is the boy to learn manly discourse if I never let loose around him?" Tye groused. "Some things a fellow needs to learn by example."

"Perhaps I should refuse your overtures on occasion, then, hmm?" Lady Spathfoy tucked the blankets up around the baby more snugly, though the child seemed to take to train travel easily enough. "Then you might have had an example for how to refuse Balfour's invitation to this house party?"

"I could not refuse him. Give me that baby." Tye plucked the child from his mother's grasp. "He's growing too heavy for you to be carting about all the while, and it isn't as if we're lacking for nursemaids."

Both of which had been given leave to stretch

their legs, because the train was an hour from Ballater at least.

The other men in the family had warned Spathfoy: once the child started toddling, a papa's role was sorely limited. The ladies closed ranks about the youngster, as if realizing that once a lad was in breeches, the menfolk would have the raising of him forevermore.

Spathfoy's firstborn son and heir smacked his papa on the chin. "He'll have a bruising right cross and fierce uppercut."

Lady Spathfoy—Hester, by name—treated her husband to the gentlest of you-are-ridiculous looks. "I wouldn't dream of arguing with you, Tiberius. Do you suppose we'll be the first to arrive?"

She was small, blond, and argued with him brilliantly and often. Her uppercuts were delivered by virtue of embroidered peignoirs, and her bruising right cross was a function of kisses, caresses, and soft asides that rendered a man witless.

Though happily witless.

"I hope we are not the first on the scene. Ian and Augusta promised they'd meet us there, and I cannot imagine my parents lingering in Northumbria when Mama might be matchmaking for my sisters."

May God help them. Joan was racketing about between Paris, London, and Edinburgh, intent on designing fashionable dresses for the women of the aristocracy. The eccentricity of this objective bothered Tye, not because his sister lacked the talent to succeed at such an endeavor, but because Society dealt poorly with eccentricities in an unmarried female. For a man, any hobby, interest, or peculiar start was considered a charming sign of intellect and passion.

While all a lady needed were pretty manners and a fat dowry.

"Balfour House will be damned cold." Bloody, goddamned cold, though Tye restrained his vocabulary in light of present company.

Her ladyship peered at the baby meaningfully. "Cold sometimes inspires you to great feats of cuddling, Tiberius. Is that baby wet?"

"Very likely." Train travel inspired infant digestion—another salient fact to which the men of the family had drawn Spathfoy's attention. "I'll change him."

Her ladyship dug more purposefully into the traveling bag, likely to hide her merriment. Tiberius was determined that he should be able to look after the boy in every needful fashion, which even his Scottish relations regarded as a queer start, indeed.

Determination, however, was a familial trait the Flynns prided themselves on, and thus—while the results were often lumpy, off-center, or droopy— Tiberius honed this aspect of his nursery maid's skills on the rare opportunities to do so that came his way.

He laid the child on the bench of their first-class compartment, while his wife studied the frigid scenery of Deeside as it swayed past outside the window.

"Do you know who will join us for this holiday house party, Tiberius?"

Tye let the question wait—a wiggling child, a wet nappy, and a dry replacement required concentration. "Family, mostly."

"You're getting better at that," his wife observed.

"Quicker." Though the results exhibited a damnable lack of symmetry. Tye tucked the child's dress down and folded the plush, cream-colored blanket about him. The hem was a riot of leaping, rolling, bounding rabbits—Joan's work, no doubt—while the blanket itself was the softest wool Tye could recall touching.

"Dora and Mary Ellen will come with your parents, won't they?"

Tye picked the child up and held him at arm's length, blankets and all. "Kicking and screaming, but even my sisters wouldn't abandon Joan to the heathen Scots in the dead of winter." Much less to Mama's tender machinations.

Next he hoisted the baby over his head, which provoked the boy to smiling hugely and waving his fists.

"Gahg!"

Both parents stared for a moment at the prodigy who'd uttered this pronouncement.

"Gahg-gaa!"

So of course, the next five minutes were spent waving the child about the train car, until Tye's arms honestly grew a bit tired. "He'll sleep now."

"He'll remain wide awake," Lady Spathfoy countered. "Do you ever worry about Joan, Tiberius?"

And thus, they came to the real reason her ladyship had shooed the nursemaids off to the parlor car.

"Incessantly. I had envisioned her finding a genteel companion and establishing herself as a fashionable adornment to Paris society, but that hasn't happened."

"Gahg-gaa-gaa!"

The viscount—for the baby was the grandson of a marquess, and in the direct line to inherit the title— struck out at his father's nose this time.

"Enough," Tye said. "If God meant for little men to fly about train compartments, he would have given papas greater arm strength."

Her ladyship waited patiently because it suited her, though she could be marvelously impatient under certain circumstances when private with her husband.

"Joan is my sensible sister. I hadn't foreseen that she'd cause anxiety," Tye said, putting the baby to his shoulder and rubbing the child's small back. "She is doomed to fail with her little fashion venture, and it distracts her from finding a husband, another venture at which she does not seem destined for success."

"Joan's dresses are striking," Hester countered loyally. "You're putting the child to sleep."

Tiberius slowed his caresses to the boy's back. "Joan's dresses are striking *on her*. That's not entirely a good thing when men seek agreeable, biddable, retiring qualities in their spouses."

"They seek broad hips and empty heads," Hester sniffed. "Most titled men are dense beyond belief when it comes to seeking a marriage partner. Joan is not in the common mode and deserves a man who can appreciate it. Perhaps she'll find a prospect at this house party."

No, she would not; not if Tye had anything to say to it.

"Balfour has invited mostly family, but also a few Scots with interests in trade. He's of a mind to mix business with pleasure, and shift some of the earldom's investments from shipping to local ventures."

The child let out a sigh so great as to shake his entire body.

"That's it, then," Hester said. "He's down for the nonce. The maids won't thank you."

Tye would not admit it, even to his wife, but the pleasure of holding the sleeping child was worth all the dark looks and long-suffering mutterings of the nursery crew.

"Joan should have found somebody by now in London, Paris, or Edinburgh," Tye said, leaning back so he could wrap an arm around his petite countess. "If she can't snag some prancing dukeling or German prince, then I'll not have her yoked to a cit with more money than manners."

Hester nestled against her husband in a most agreeable fashion. "I am the daughter of a mere baron, Tiberius. I would caution you against such rigid expressions of fraternal concern."

"I do not want to see my sister hurt," Tye said against his wife's hair. She was blond, a surprising contrast to her big dark husband, and she always felt just right in his arms. "If one of Balfour's upstart business prospects thinks to entice Joan to the altar in a weak moment, I'll soon have him thinking otherwise."

The countess rubbed her cheek against her husband's shoulder and closed her eyes.

❧

A foul, foul stench pervaded Edward Valmonte's awareness, more foul than usual the morning after his lordship had overindulged.

"Go away," Edward muttered at the source of the odor.

Fergus yipped, which happy sound ricocheted around in Edward's head like so many stray bullets. Waking up to hot, smelly terrier breath ought to number among the biblical plagues.

"I said"—Edward rolled over to bury his face in clean linen—"get the hell away from me."

Another yip, which bore a warning quality.

"I don't care how deep the snow is. If you tee-tee on Mama's carpets again, she will have you made into a fricassee."

After she'd done worse to her firstborn son. The woman had no sense of her proper place in the scheme of things. Fergus was mostly a very good fellow, much like Edward.

"Yip! Yip!" The dratted pestilence followed up with enthusiastic licking about Edward's ear, which made Edward smile and rather put him in mind of Lady Joan's breathy—

"Shite." The worst curse Edward could manage under his mother's roof, and still inadequate for the combination of woe and queasiness that welled up from within. "Shite and dog breath and tee-tee in the front hall." He sat up, cradling the dog to his chest. "I am in such trouble. Fricassee will be too good for me."

The outer door to the adjacent sitting room banged open loudly enough to make Edward wince. One instant too late, Edward understood that Fergus had been trying to alert him to Mama's approach.

"One hopes you are awake, though Kyle says he has not attended you." The Viscountess Valmonte's heels drilled into Edward's meager store of composure as they clattered against parquet floors. "And"—her ladyship barreled right into Edward's bedroom—"you had best be up and about, for we're expected to take tea with Lady Dorcas and her family in light of the day's developments."

Mama was no respecter of Edward's privacy, as if he were still a boy in dresses.

"I'm not decent, your ladyship. You will please allow a fellow a few moments with his valet of a morning." Against Edward's chest, Fergus was a warm, reassuring little ball of canine loyalty. He gave a short bark, doubtless agreeing with his master.

"It's past noon, young man." Mama's scolds were all the more effective for being delivered with a hint of a French accent. "And I am sorry to inform you, your lady wife will not take kindly to allowing animals of any description into her bed."

She clapped her hands, the ultimate insult to Edward's throbbing head and roiling belly. "Kyle! His lordship has need of you!"

What Edward needed was to apologize to Lady Joan Flynn before the woman's brother sent his seconds to call.

"Mama, please leave. I must have peace and quiet, a pot or two of black tea, and somebody to take Fergus for a stroll in the mews."

"I'm here, your ladyship." Kyle bowed to the viscountess, Edward's shaving kit in the man's pudgy hand, a towel over his arm as if he were some damned waiter. "We can be ready in less than an hour."

We? As if Kyle were Edward's nanny, getting him ready for an outing to the park.

"Excellent. When you are finished with Edward,

you can see to the dog. Lady Dorcas deserves her day to preen and gloat, and of course, his lordship must show himself as her devoted swain."

Lady Dorcas Bellingham—Lady Dorcas-Rhymes-with-Orcas, according to a zoological wit at Edward's club—was not a bad sort, though she was prodigiously fond of sweets, and rather an armload to wrestle about on the dance floor. She had an agreeable dimness to her mental faculties, and a nice smile.

"I am not her devoted swain." Edward fumbled about beneath his pillows for his nightshirt. "Kyle, procure a fellow a pot of tea, if you don't mind."

Edward set Fergus down, got a nightshirt more or less on, and mentally prepared himself for the ordeal of standing upright. The bed was elevated two steps for warmth, though what good did warm covers do a man when he broke his neck tumbling from bed in the morning?

"You look positively bilious, Eddie. Were you up late sketching? I must say, those drawings in the sitting rooms are quite the cleverest efforts I've seen from you to date." Mama seemed to look at him for the first time, while Fergus bounded off the bed and turned an encouraging pair of bright black eyes on Edward.

"I was up quite late." Joan had been sketching—at first—beautiful, flowing, ingenious sketches that provoked Edward to equal parts envy and admiration. And curiously enough, the sketches were apparently still here. "Mama, you really ought not to be in my bedroom."

"Nonsense. You've nothing to display I haven't seen before. We'll be stopping by the salon on our way to Lady Dorcas's, and I cannot afford to indulge your penchant for dawdling. Lady Dorcas could cry off, despite the announcement."

Edward was focused on navigating the steps, but it didn't do to ignore Mama's nattering entirely. "What announcement?"

"Coyness doesn't become you, Eddie. The announcement of your engagement to Lady Dorcas. Brilliant match, if I do say so myself."

Edward's ears began to roar, and his stomach rebelled against his mother's words, even as his head-ache escalated to a point past agony.

"I never proposed to Lady Dorcas Bellingham. She and I cannot be engaged." Though a dim recollection of Mama chattering about productive discussions, and Uncle nodding approvingly suggested Edward's objection was too little and too late.

Mama regarded him with her head cocked to the side, making her look like a small, puzzled French bird—a bird of prey.

"Don't be tedious. Bended knee and dramatic declarations are hardly necessary among the better families. The girl has pots of money, and she has the look of an easy breeder. Get dressed, lest we be late for a call on your intended. The announcements went out this very morning, and if we're quick about it, we can have you married before the New Year."

Oh, God.

Oh, Joan.

"I'm going to be sick."

As his mother fled the room in another tattoo of heels, Edward was indeed sick, barely missing her ladyship's prized Axminster carpets, while Fergus looked on with sympathetic eyes.

❧

How soon after conceiving could a woman turn up queasy?

Joan knew of no treatise she could read on the subject, and she had no doting auntie to whom she might discreetly put the question. Tiberius's wife, Hester, was a good sort—witness, she'd taken on the care and handling of *Tiberius*—but Joan could not test her sister-in-law's loyalties with such an inquiry.

"He works all the time," Miss Hartwell muttered, biting off a length of green thread. "Dante, that is. For Christmas, I wish my brother would be given the gift of the occasional afternoon or morning spent at leisure."

"What about you?" Joan asked, wondering if another chocolate might settle her digestion. "Do you spend the occasional afternoon or morning at leisure? Sometimes example is the best teacher."

Miss Hartwell regarded her hoop, which sported a pair of doves amid a riot of green-and-gold leaves. "As if Dante would be guided by my example in anything. Charlie can occasionally make him laugh."

The train was slowing, perhaps in deference to the thickening snow.

"Maybe your brother won't be *guided* by your example, but he might be *tempted* by it." Just as Joan might tempt Mr. Hartwell with the lone piece of marzipan remaining in the box of chocolates.

He'd sampled that marzipan with the same focus

he'd brought to reading his reports or to stacking luggage. Joan could not imagine what such a man would *do* with a morning's leisure, much less how he could need one.

While Joan needed for her belly to settle, and for Edward Valmonte to magically acquire unfailing discretion.

"We're coming to Aberdeen," Margaret said, putting down her embroidery and going to a window. "The children will want to leave the train, lark about for five minutes, catch a chill, and generally get in the way."

Something was afflicting Miss Hartwell's spirits, for she struck Joan as a sanguine lady, and yet her litany was nearly a complaint.

"Fresh air sounds lovely. Shall we bundle the children up and get off for a few minutes too?" Gray, bleak granite structures flashed by the windows, a few draped in pine roping, some sporting wreathes on doors. In the occasional window, lone candles tried to shed light amid a thickening gloom.

"Darkness will soon fall," Miss Hartwell said. "So yes, let's get off the train, stretch our legs, and chase the children about."

They retrieved the children from the part of the car partitioned off for sleeping cots. Charlie had been lecturing a doll about reading reports, and Phillip had countered that dolls didn't read reports.

"You can have that argument outside," Miss Hartwell said, "provided you're bundled up to your noses. The day has done nothing but grow colder and darker."

True enough. Joan assisted with dressing the children—Phillip stood still, while Charlie's mouth and all fourteen of her limbs were in constant motion—then wrapped herself in her velvet cloak.

By the time the children and both women were appropriately attired, the train had come to a halt at the back of yet another gray stone building, this one larger than many of the others. Miss Hartwell gave the children a final stern admonition about running off—running *anywhere*—and turned to open the door.

A man stood directly outside in his kilt, the fellow tall enough to be higher than eye level with Miss Hartwell, even when she had the advantage of the train's height. His age was hard to determine, but likely fell between thirty and thirty-five.

A gust of frigid air accompanied the moment of silence while Miss Hartwell and the fellow stared at each other, then Charlie tore a hand free from Joan's grasp.

"Hullo, Hector!" She launched herself at the man, who caught her easily.

"Hullo, ma bonnie wee lass! Did ye save me a kiss?"

The next instant was full of the sort of impressions designed to make Joan feel like an interloper: fellows named Hector should be short, skinny, wear too much pomade in their hair, and eschew kilts.

This Hector had the sort of cliffs-meeting-the-sea features that were the embodiment of sternness in repose. A sloping brow, deep-set eyes, and a prominent nose came together with a determined jaw to form a countenance that would have looked well on an opinionated conservative bishop or a Highland chieftain. Dark hair—no pomade—did nothing to lighten Joan's impression of the man.

And yet, his waistcoat was bright, even loud plaid, along the lines of the Royal Stewart tartan.

Charlie's greeting effected a transformation, bringing merriment to blue eyes, and a broad smile to Hector's face. His affection for the child and hers for him was unabashed and charming.

"We saved you chocolates, too," Charlie said. "Or Lady Joan did. You mustn't eat too many sweets, or you'll get a bellyache. Did you miss me?"

"Fair t'broke ma heart for missing ye," he said, setting Charlie down but keeping her hand in his.

He was difficult to understand, having a thick Scottish burr—not heart, but hairt. Untangling his speech didn't spare Joan from noticing the way Hector glanced at Miss Hartwell as he flattered the child.

Fair to broke my heart for missing ye.

Oh. Dear.

Mr. Hartwell's man of business—or whatever Hector was—had directed his sentiment at least in part at Mr. Hartwell's sister. Miss Hartwell was busy rewrapping Phillip's scarf about his face and likely missed the innuendo entirely.

Or was polite enough to pretend she had.

"Shall we step out for a few minutes?" Joan suggested.

Hector's smile faded as he treated Joan to a visual inspection. "Hector MacMillan, ma'am. I haven't had the pleasure…"

"Well, move aside, Hector," Miss Hartwell scolded. "We're letting all the heat out of the parlor, and the children aren't getting any fresh air."

His expression, if anything, grew more shuttered. "My apologies."

Miss Hartwell got the introductions wrong, presenting Joan to Mr. MacMillan first, which was three kinds of a blunder. Joan offered her gloved hand, which Mr. MacMillan took in his bare fingers without bowing.

"I don't recall that a guest was to join the party."

"I'm not a guest," Joan said as Margaret bustled off after the children, and two young ladies with the harried countenances of nursery maids hopped down from cars farther along the platform. "I'm a charity case. Mr. Hartwell and I became acquainted over the past few weeks in Edinburgh. When I needed to journey north on short notice, he offered the hospitality of traveling with his family."

"Don't insult my guest, Hector," Mr. Hartwell said, climbing down from the second car. "Lady Joan helped Margs with the children, and for that we must all be grateful."

Mr. Hartwell shook hands with Mr. MacMillan, then slapped the fellow on the back and offered him a dented silver flask. Not only did the temperature drop and the light fade as one journeyed north, but apparently manners also grew less formal.

"A wee nip, Lady Joan?" Mr. Hartwell asked when Mr. MacMillan had declined the proffered libation.

Joan had an older brother, and she and her sisters had been duty bound to sneak a nip from his flask. The memory was not happy, for Mary Ellen had snorted the contents of the flask into her nose, and accused Joan of trying to poison her loudly enough for Mama to hear.

Mama had made them finish the flask, though she'd diluted the contents with water.

Why had Joan not taken that lesson in the evils of strong spirits to heart?

"No, thank you. A pleasure to meet you, Mr. MacMillan. I'll see how Miss Hartwell is getting on with the children." Those children had run down the platform, trying to catch snowflakes on their tongues and narrowly missing collisions with other travelers.

The men moved away, back toward the second train car as the wind snatched at terms like "profitability" and "rate of return" and "damned Sassenach."

Joan qualified as a Sassenach—a rather cold, miserable Sassenach. She was no longer on the swaying train, and the brisk wind blew the coal smoke away from the platform, and yet, even standing still in the frigid air, Joan's stomach was still unsettled.

Perhaps she was a damned Sassenach after all.

❧

"Charity cases don't wear velvet cloaks that cost more than my grandda's entire harvest of wool would have brought in a good year."

Hector was a master of the casual observation.

I see you haven't made notes on these reports yet.

How interesting, that you're now in correspondence with the very English earl who damned near tried to shoot you on your own grouse moor.

Margaret appears a wee bit wroth with you.

"And yet, Lady Joan had no way to travel home to see her family, dirty weather was closing in, and Margs seemed in need of some company," Dante *observed* with equal casualness. "They're getting on well enough."

Hector paused before climbing into the second parlor car—the one with the decanters, but lamentably lacking in that marzi–whatever confection.

"I don't believe I've ever seen Margaret try to catch a snowflake on her tongue."

Another observation. Down the platform, Lady Joan, Margaret, and the children were holding hands in a circle, everybody's face turned skyward, while some sort of silly game got under way and a queer sensation tugged at Dante's chest.

"Into the train with you," he said. "I have questions about Balfour's holdings, and if we're quick, we can snatch the box of chocolates and nobody will notice."

"Nobody will notice for about five minutes," Hector said, climbing aboard, "and Balfour's situation was hard to gather information about. Until a year or so ago, the present earl was presumed dead, and a younger brother was styled as the earl. An older relation had the keeping of the earldom's trusts, and the family has been wrangling ever since."

"They're Scottish. Of course they'll wrangle," Dante said, while outside, the sound of laughter cut through even the bustle on the platform. "The present earl owns ships, I know that much. Bloody fast ships, if the captains at the Edinburgh docks can be believed. Where there are ships, there can be capital."

Dante hung his coat on a peg while Hector lingered at the window.

"Margaret isn't wearing a bonnet."

Neither had Lady Joan been wearing a bonnet.

Perhaps Hector's habit of observation was conta-
gious. "A good wool scarf is better protection from
the elements."

They fell silent while porters appeared with another
bucket of coal, more tea, and scones—in this modern
age, could Her Majesty's rail services boast no fare
more imaginative than tea and scones?—and a few
disapproving looks aimed at the swag-less mantel.

"I'd kill for a pair of hot bridies," Dante said. "The
spicy kind my grannie used to make for my nooning."

"Shall I have meat pasties delivered on your
next trip?"

Hector was quintessentially Scottish—in his diction, his substantial build, his stubbornness—and yet
he made the occasional swipe at English vocabulary.
Dante had no idea why.

"Not meat pasties, a batch of damned bridies.
Somebody's mama likely sells them out front of the
station, fresh and piping hot." Dante grew hungry
even thinking about them. "Stay here and prepare to
explain to me about Balfour's personal assets when I
get back."

Hector raised one dark eyebrow high enough to
let Dante know that attempts to deliver orders were
humored rather than tolerated—Hector was plenty
Scottish when he wanted to be.

When Dante returned with the box of chocolates,
minus the last piece of that almond sweet, Hector had
wedged himself in at the table and was making notes
in pencil on a sheet of foolscap.

A conductor's whistle sounded a single blast.

"I didn't quite manage to memorize the guest

list for this holiday farce," Dante said, "much less untangle all the begats and wed-the-daughter-of's. Tell me about Balfour's money. Why would an earl who owns a shipping enterprise want to involve himself with my mills?"

And how much could Dante charge him for that privilege?

"You could sell the mills," Hector said, running his pencil down the side of the page as if a few scribbled notes held the key to untold riches. "They're profitable."

In two words, Hector managed to put a strong whiff of disapproval in the air. The mills could be *more* profitable, of course. Significantly more profitable.

"If the mills aren't to become more dangerous than they are at present, improvements are necessary. If I sell them to some greedy Englishman, nobody will make those improvements, an entirely avoidable accident will transpire, and then somebody—maybe a hundred somebodies—will have a gravestone, and my profits will be buried with them."

If that accident took the form of fire or broken machinery, there'd be no wages for the hundred women employed at each facility, some of whom had held their positions for more than ten years. This signal fact kept Dante from selling one mill to finance improvements on the other two.

Which one would he sell?

How would his suppliers and buyers—many of whom were English—react to the news that he was liquidating a major asset?

How would the women fare when the new

owner realized how much more profitable the mill could be if hours were extended, wages cut, younger children employed?

"I can't imagine Margaret brought a box of chocolates along on a journey that involved the children," Hector said, helping himself to a pair of sweets.

Dante sprawled lengthwise on the couch, pleased to think he might be napping in the same place Lady Joan had.

"Can't you simply ask, Hector? Where did the chocolates come from? Maybe I bought them. Christmas is coming, you know. A few holiday treats might be in order."

A silence from across the car was punctuated by a double whistle blast. The sound of laughter and thumping feet came from the adjacent car, and another queer pang assailed Dante.

Had that been Phillip laughing along with Charlie?

"You are attending this house party to find investors to capitalize updating your mills," Hector said, folding the table down and crossing his feet on the opposite bench. "Your efforts to catch a wealthy titled bride having failed, I'd think you'd want to focus on business, and not on cadging treats provided by charity cases wearing ermine cloaks."

"Lady Joan wears a velvet cloak." Also a velvet dress, lots of lace, and a lovely scent.

"Your efforts to find a bride did fail, then?"

Finally, a direct question.

"Spectacularly. English mamas aren't stupid. They aren't about to marry off their darling titled daughters to a climbing Scottish cit when so many of the English variety ooze about the ballrooms with better manners and their knees decently covered at all times."

"What do knees have to do with it?"

Another question, nearly drowned out by the third whistle blast.

"I should have left my kilts in Glasgow. Balfour has a wealthy brother, doesn't he?"

"Several, in fact. Connor MacGregor is married to a wealthy Northumbrian widow. Ian MacGregor married an English baroness with significant assets, and Balfour—Asher MacGregor—is doing very well for himself. A third brother, Gilgallon MacGregor, also married money—pretty, English money. The MacGregors are Scotsmen. If you can't scare up interest among them, then you really ought to consider selling one of the mills."

"Tell MacDermott to start stocking that almond sweet in this car."

"It's expensive, if you're talking about marzipan."

"Not as expensive as my trip to Edinburgh. Everybody in town knows I tried to find a well-connected bride and failed. That will make attracting investors for the mills that much harder."

"Then you'd better give it your very best effort, hadn't you?"

In the next car, Charlie was laughing uproariously, and a lady in a velvet cloak was probably wondering where her box of chocolates had got off to. In *this* train car, Dante was trying not to become annoyed with Hector, who had a sniffy little answer for everything.

Dante closed his eyes and crossed his arms over his chest.

"You were telling me about Balfour's assets." One of the man's assets was family. Three brothers, all doing well, plenty of family wealth to help out any sibling whose fortunes suffered a reverse, a nice big country house to gather everybody together for the holidays...

While Dante had a few dependents, and Hector's reports.

"Are you even listening, Dante?"

Dante rose and crossed the car, which was lurching and swaying away from the train station.

"I always listen, but be patient with me. Margs sprang the nursery maids before we'd even reached Edinburgh. My nerves are delicate right now."

His patience was delicate, for Hector's very competence grated. Dante opened the parlor stove and used the wrought iron poker to redistribute the fresh coal.

"It's only a house party," Hector said, helping himself to another chocolate. "You eat and drink, flirt a bit, dance and sing, play cards, and casually mention that the mills are doing well enough to support a few more investors."

Dante closed the stove, the poker still in his hand.

"Do you ever think maybe those old fellows with their claymores and targes had an easier time of it? No mincing and flirting involved—you wielded your sword against any who opposed you, plain and simple. No investment opportunities, just life and death with a wee dram now and then." He made a few passes at thin air with the poker, then felt silly at Hector's pitying expression.

Dante would feel equally silly dancing and flirting

away the coming weeks, much less playing cards night after night with men he'd likely never see again.

"Edinburgh was worth a try," Hector allowed charitably. "I don't suppose Miss Margaret met anybody there?"

"She met plenty of fools sniffing around for her dowry, and an equal number of well-bred ladies I wouldn't turn my back on. Maybe MacGregor will have a spare relation who might catch her eye."

Though the children would miss Margs terribly if she married and moved away.

"Maybe MacGregor will have a relation who might catch *your* eye."

"That would at least quiet the gossips I left snickering behind my back in Edinburgh. If she were a well-dowered relation, then she might spare me all that mincing and toasting and caroling too."

Also warm his bed, which notion a tired, single, and possibly lonely fellow shouldn't be blamed for contemplating wistfully on a cold, snowy afternoon.

Hector's pencil paused in its journey down the right side of a page of notes.

"Maybe marriage and money ought not to be on the same ledger page. The English aristocracy has bound up matrimony and wealth for generations, and look how they're turning out."

Lady Joan was an English aristocrat—a rather pretty one—though the woman had a peaked, pinchy look to her Dante couldn't approve of.

"I hate it when you make a good point. Move over and pass me the chocolates."

Four

WHEN SILENCE DESCENDED NOT FIFTEEN MINUTES OUT of Aberdeen, Joan missed the chatter of the children and Miss Hartwell's gentle clucking and scolding. One of the nursemaids was coming down with a sniffle, so both had been banished from the parlor cars for the duration of the journey, lest the children take ill too.

A lady did not pace.

A lady did not worry the lace at her cuffs, much as a child might compulsively stroke a corner of a favorite blanket or doll's dress.

A lady did not allow herself to become inebriated by strong drink, then overcome by a man's illicit passions.

The sheer shame of Joan's folly with Edward Valmonte threatened to choke her and had her heading for the platform between the train cars. As she opened the door to one car, Mr. Hartwell opened the door to the other. He had in his hand the box of chocolates Joan had stashed in her bag before making a hasty departure from Edinburgh.

"My lady, where is your cloak?"

Cloak. She'd come outside in the dead of winter

on a speeding train without her cloak. A lady probably didn't do that either.

"I forgot it."

Something shifted in his regard, though his stance on the swaying platform was utterly solid. Feet spread, chocolates in hand, he looked to Joan as fixed as the enormous trees dotting the white landscape whizzing by.

"Were you going to jump, my lady?" he asked gently.

"No." Her reply lacked conviction, though Joan had no more intended to jump from the speeding train than she'd intended to become inebriated in Edward Valmonte's company.

Mr. Hartwell reached past Joan to open the parlor door behind her. In the limited space of the platform, that brought him near enough that Joan could catch a whiff of his heathery, piney scent.

"Let's get you back inside. You'll catch your death taking the air out here."

Her teeth had begun to chatter. Mr. Hartwell took her by the arm and steered her back into the cozy light of the parlor car. He sat Joan down at the small settee, then came down beside her and passed her the chocolates.

"I ate all the almond ones. I think you had better tell me what's amiss."

No, she had better not.

"I wanted air. My insides are unsettled."

He set the sweets aside on one of the fussy, scaled-down tables beside the settee. "Charlie lies better than you do, though falsehoods don't sit well with her, either. Whatever is bothering you, it's not worth jumping from a train."

Margaret and the children were napping behind a closed door not twelve feet away, and yet, outside, darkness had all but fallen, suggesting they'd remain asleep as long as the train kept moving.

"I had no intention of jumping."

"How about if you have no intention of trusting me, but you give it a try anyway? Nothing is so desperate it can't be shared with a friend."

The wind had disordered his hair, again. Joan searched for a way to remind him that he and she were not friends.

"I need a spouse," came out of her mouth. "Rather desperately. Before the holidays would do nicely, but I'm off to join family, where the prospects will be lamentably l-limited."

How could she become so chilled in a few short moments out of doors?

"Damnedest thing, needing a spouse," Mr. Hartwell said. "They get thrust at you when you've no notion one might come in handy, and then when you need one…not a blushing bride to be found."

Surprise cut through Joan's misery, accompanied with a frisson of amusement.

"Everybody said you were hunting a wife in Edinburgh. I couldn't credit why they'd believe such a thing, but I suppose your children need a mother."

He smoothed the fabric of his kilt over a large male knee.

"True enough. I was also hoping Margs might see a fellow she could tolerate, but we made no headway on that score either. Spouse hunting is a dismal business, probably invented by the English."

Joan's situation remained unchanged. She was still horribly compromised, and quite possibly in anticipation of a troubling event, and yet, Mr. Hartwell's commiseration comforted.

"I was so stupid."

He produced his dented silver flask, then offered it to Joan, who shook her head.

"I know of nobody else who's ever been stupid, my lady. I myself have been a paragon of common sense and prudence, as any will tell you. This sojourn into the mountains to cavort for weeks among strangers only *looks* like sheer, bleeding folly."

His foul language relieved Joan of an urge to air similar vocabulary. *Sheer, bleeding folly*, indeed.

"You'll manage, Mr. Hartwell. The holidays are a merry time."

He put his flask away and patted her hand. "Tell me his name. I'll pass along my compliments."

The hand covering Joan's knuckles would close into a delightfully formidable fist.

"That won't help anything, and it might try the gentleman's meager store of discretion. I was *exceedingly* stupid." Though Edward was vain as a peacock with four hens, and a few ugly bruises were the least he deserved.

"*Exceedingly* stupid. You have an English way of making that sound dire indeed. I suppose the bastard kissed you?"

Bastard was such a hard word. Joan's free hand went to her belly, which had calmed a bit, while her other hand remained in Mr. Hartwell's warm grasp.

"I do recall kissing." Enthusiastic, naughty kissing,

at first, for Joan had been curious and surprised by Edward's overtures.

Then there had been struggling. She had struggled, and now recalled this for the first time.

"Doesn't sound like he got the kissing bit right. You poor wee thing."

Joan was skinny. She would never be wee. "Poor wee, exceedingly stupid thing."

"Did you mind the kissing so awfully?"

What had that to do with anything? "Not awfully."

"A spouse will probably expect some kissing, you know." He gave her fingers a squeeze.

He had been married, and he was a father twice over. He was also not a fussy, proper fellow who'd blush beet red at matters pragmatic and biological. Joan pushed out a question before the tattered remains of her dignity could stuff themselves into her mouth and silence her.

"How soon might a lady experience digestive upset upon conceiving a child?"

He reached into his coat for his flask, his hand stilling short of its goal.

"Some presuming twit needs killing. You must have menfolk who can see to the matter. You said this embarrassment to the male gender was engaged, too, which tells me his death ought to be slow and painful."

Mr. Hartwell did not sound as if he were teasing.

"As heartening as the notion of justice for my partner in folly might be, that would not solve my problem." Joan tossed her dignity out a figurative window and seized her courage with both hands. "Such measures would not solve a child's predicament either."

The train swayed along through the cold darkness for a few moments, while Joan marveled that she'd confided in a man more stranger than friend.

"I like you," Mr. Hartwell said, his pronouncement the sort of gruff, unpolished sentiment Joan suspected hadn't aided his cause in the ballrooms. "You are honest, and you don't put on airs. Do you suppose you might stand to kiss me?"

Then he went and said things like that. Joan withdrew her hand.

"I am not wanton, Mr. Hartwell. If I've said anything to make you think my favors might be available in the general case, then you're sadly, severely mistaken. I made an egregious, imbecilic error—one misstep—which I sorely regret and have no intention—"

He put his hand over her mouth, gently. "I meant no insult, ye ken?"

Joan managed a nod, but he'd leaned closer and whispered his question, and abruptly, his company no longer comforted. Mr. Hartwell grew larger with increased proximity, also stronger and more…more masculine.

"My family is on the other side of that partition, my lady. I'll no' ravish you in a damned parlor car. If you can't abide my company, then all you have to do is say so. Before I offer you marriage, we'd best establish that we can tolerate a shared kiss first, aye?"

❧

The nobs considered business a dirty, dull, tedious undertaking, but in truth, commerce was exciting. Something close to sexual anticipation attended the rattle and hum of competition, cooperation, and the myriad challenges attendant to keeping three mills profitable.

Wolves and tigers lurked in the jungles of commerce, and a man needed quick wits and courage to avoid disaster and capitalize on good fortune.

Lady Joan's situation was good fortune; Dante was almost sure of it.

"You would *marry* me, Mr. Hartwell?"

Her incredulity should have been that he'd *presume* to offer her marriage, not that anybody would have her.

"I would," Dante said slowly, because he was acting on a hunch, on an impulse somewhere between cold calculation and hot instinct. "You're in want of a spouse; my children need a mother."

And he needed entrée into the aristocratic strata of investors. What a lovely coincidence. Lady Joan's people had to include at least an earl, or she wouldn't be called lady.

Her ladyship fingered the mended lace of her cuff. "Marriage is a serious business."

"It's a permanent business," Dante said. "I do recall occasionally laughing with my first wife." Not often, and not until they'd rubbed along together for a few awkward years. "She broke me in, I'll have you know. Put some manners on me, though it was uphill going, I'm sure."

She'd put a terrible lot of sexual restraint on him, too, though Dante would hardly burden Lady Joan with that truth.

Her fingers slowed as she stroked the mended cuff. "I like you too."

"Does that surprise you?" For it surprised him—and confirmed his sense that marriage to Lady Joan was a brilliant solution to several problems.

"My husband cannot be titled, because the child might be a boy—if there is a child."

"I'm in no danger of acquiring a title. Are you sure you're carrying then?"

She stopped fussing her lace altogether, her gaze going to the darkness beyond the windows.

"I have not had occasion to familiarize myself firsthand with all of the definitive symptoms... That is to say, I might... Or I might not. I don't know. Yet. I ought not to be discussing this with a gentleman."

A *gentleman* would pretend that babies arrived from celestial realms with little involvement from the mother, and that such arrivals were attended by angelic choruses instead of a lot of fuss, discomfort, and bother.

"My dear, I'm not likely to be mistaken for a gentleman. You will take that into account when considering any proposal of marriage from me. You would be marrying quite beneath you."

He was compelled to point that out to her, not because he was a gentleman, but because fair play alone called for such a reminder. Women got muddled when they were expecting. Men grew muddled when their women were expecting, too.

"A failure to marry on my part would occasion disaster for my good name," she said, "and for my child, while marrying down happens to somebody every day. I suppose we'd best try a kiss."

Fair play poked Dante hard in the arse.

"Before we endure that trial, you need to understand that I'm offering you a real marriage, not some prissy little formality that sees you in Paris and me in Scotland. You will be a mother to my children, my hostess, the lady of my households."

He'd expect her in his bed, in other words, which was probably ungentlemanly of him.

"I like to sew."

"I beg your pardon?" And could they please get to the kissing part, because now that the notion was running loose in Dante's imagination, he was curious to see if they could manage it.

"I wanted... I love fabrics, love the feel of them. Did you know you wear merino blends? Did you know Margaret's clothes are all wrong for her? From the colors, to the fabrics, to the designs?"

She took his hand and ran it over the wool of his kilt, then the wool of his jacket.

"Can you feel how soft those are? How full of warmth? There's lamb's wool in this weave too."

He hoped *she* was soft and full of warmth. "You can sew all you like when we're married, woman. If we marry."

Whatever point she was trying to make, he was missing it. That happened regularly between spouses too, and yet, Lady Joan kept her hand over his.

"I not only sew, I design clothing. I design my own clothes, and sew them myself. I love working with fabric."

While Dante ran three textile mills, which was probably irrelevant to whatever queer start she was on.

"You love fabrics," he said. "You will love your child, too, I think."

That got her attention. "You will treat my baby the same as you do Charlie and Phillip, or we have no bargain. A child born into circumstances such as these will be especially in need of a father's guidance and protection."

She meant, in need of a father's love, but she was too English to use the word. Dante was not. He rose and drew her to her feet.

"I'll love our firstborn as if he or she were my own. That I can promise you."

She'd likely never held a newborn, never experienced the helpless surrender to sentiment such a moment engendered, never known the ferocious sense of protectiveness one wee bairnie could arouse in a man.

The prospect of sharing such a moment with her was strange, exciting, and also uncomfortable. A prudent man *did* look a gift horse in the mouth, for the beast would require food, shelter, and care, regardless of its age.

A gentleman merely murmured his thanks.

Lady's Joan's hand was cool in Dante's. "How do we go about this?"

"It's quite complicated," he replied, leading her over to the wall beside the door. "My lips and yours, smack up against each other. It might take a few tries before we get it right—I'm rusty, you see."

A clumsy attempt at humor, and yet, something he'd said pleased her, for those lips he'd soon be smack up against curved upward.

"I've hardly had any practice myself."

Well, then. They weren't a pair of virgins, which

was a relief, truly, and yet, they could bring something of newness to their first kiss nonetheless. Dante maneuvered her between himself and the wall, and before the surprise fled Lady Joan's green eyes—he hoped it was surprise and not trepidation—he set about kissing her.

❦

Mr. Hartwell hauled Joan around and settled her against the wall, rather like he'd rearranged the trunks in the baggage compartment. She closed her eyes and braced herself for a mashing of lips and teeth, some heavy breathing, and a male body pressed into hers.

Her hands gripped the comforting softness of velvet, for her cloak hung on a peg behind her—the cloak she'd walked right past in her headlong dash for fresh air.

Mr. Hartwell's lips grazed Joan's forehead, a warning shot, perhaps. The next thing she felt were those same lips on her cheek, a gentle buss that put her in mind of a cat nudging its owner to encourage petting.

Cats were soft too.

"I've changed my mind, my lady."

"You've *what*?"

He was braced against the wall with a hand above her shoulder, a relaxed quantity of kilted male who could loom over even a woman of Joan's height. The thoughtful look on his face boded ill for Joan's chances of finding a husband by Christmas.

"I've changed my mind. My plan was to kiss you witless, and while that plan has appeal, I'm thinking you ought to be the one doing the kissing."

"But I don't—" *Know how*, while his kisses came with thought-out plans. And yet, without having a proper sense of how to conduct a kiss, Joan had known enough to get into tremendous trouble with Edward Valmonte—as best she could recall.

"This might take some time, Mr. Hartwell."

He settled close enough to whisper in Joan's ear. "I'm a patient mon, though I will mention, one parent to another, that children have a tendency to wake up at the least convenient moments. In the usual case, they wake up full of questions, too."

One parent to another. The reminder steadied Joan.

"I'm not sure I'll become a parent any time soon, but I am sure that my good name has been compromised."

"Stop dithering, woman. I'm only a man, and it's only a kiss."

He took her by the middle and traded places with her, so he leaned back against the folds of her cloak, legs spread, Joan standing between his thighs.

Only a kiss—that could lead to a marriage.

A married woman, in some regards, was more free to do as she pleased. Mama managed the family's finances, held her salons in Edinburgh, and had separated from his lordship for nearly two years. A married woman could design dresses all she wanted, in fact.

Joan framed Mr. Hartwell's jaw with her hand, the texture beneath her palm a contradiction of warm skin, bristle, uncompromising bone, and interesting angles. For balance, she laid her free hand against the wall and again encountered her velvet cloak.

The feel of the fabric soothed her, as did Mr. Hartwell's unmoving patience.

He closed his eyes, which courtesy emboldened Joan to trace her fingers over his eyebrows. His lashes were dark and thick against his cheek, an incongruous dash of luxury on a countenance otherwise devoid of softness.

And his nose… Joan ran her thumb down the length of that nose, tracing the bump near the bridge. His nose was straight, unbroken, and yet the bump suggested something untoward had occurred somewhere along the way. The arches of his eyebrows were perfect curving sweeps, almost graceful, except his brows were too dark and heavy for grace. As an old man, those brows would grow bushy.

"Will you kiss me with only your fingers?" His whisper had developed a rasp.

"I like to touch. I learn by touching." And he might become her husband, the one man she was at liberty to touch intimately. A weary caution tried to issue from Joan's mind—*why* was he so willing to become her husband when they were complete strangers and the children were managing well in their aunt's care?—but time was of the essence, and a husband by Christmas a necessity.

She took a leaf from his album and pressed an experimental kiss to his cheek.

No heavenly chorus erupted; neither did revulsion stir. Mr. Hartwell smelled good, and his claim to patience was apparently well-founded.

"Again, my dear."

Joan's next attempt landed closer to the corner of his mouth. She wasn't tall enough to kiss his forehead.

"Charm on the third try, my lady." He was teasing

her, and the idea that he could laugh about this kiss allowed Joan to breathe.

"Stop nattering, Mr. Hartwell. I have another use for your mouth."

She kissed that mouth, their lips coming together in a pair of smiles that boded well for their future. Putting responsibility for prosecuting the kiss in her hands had been generous on his part, giving Joan the latitude to linger on new sensations.

Mr. Hartwell was utterly solid, unlike Edward, whose bones were not wrapped in any particular quantity of muscle.

Mr. Hartwell didn't grab at a lady. His hands on Joan's waist were steadying rather than clutching—or wandering. He let her know where his hands were, and left hers free to acquaint themselves with his wool-clad person.

His clothing was a delight—soft, warm, and fitted to him with the precision and quality found in the best tailoring.

"Taste me, Joan. I'm dying for you to taste me."

She left off stroking his chest—his coat, rather—long enough to decipher that whispered suggestion.

Taste him—with her *tongue*. Joan pressed her face to Mr. Hartwell's throat and withstood the recollection—clear, for the first time—of Edward's tongue intruding into her mouth like illness rising from the wrong side. She had been so disoriented with drink and bewilderment, she'd had trouble figuring out how to breathe.

"Like this," Mr. Hartwell said, making a soft, slow pass with his tongue over Joan's bottom lip.

"You taste like chocolate."

"You don't want a husband who tastes like chocolate?"

A husband who tasted like chocolate, and who knew how to invite with his kisses rather than plunder was an agreeable prospect. "I'm partial to chocolate."

She imitated his kiss, which, like a magic word uttered from the exact right location, had the effect of parting his lips.

He drew her closer—right against the solid length of his body—and what followed next defied Joan's ability to keep sensations organized in her mind. Mr. Hartwell's embrace had a sheltering, comfortable quality, the very opposite of the entrapment Joan had felt mashed beneath Edward on his too-short settee.

Joan could breathe in Mr. Hartwell's arms; she could enjoy his height and muscle; she could revel in how delicately such a large, dark fellow could share a kiss with a woman who knew precious little about the entire undertaking.

"Relax, woman. Let yourself have a bit of fun." His kiss grew playful, his tongue dodging and feinting, his mouth retreating then fastening over Joan's again. She had to go up on her toes to recapture his kiss, and finally let go of the velvet cloak to sink a hand into his hair.

The texture of his hair was distracting, much softer than it should have been, softer than Joan's own russet locks.

"I like it when you pull my hair," he growled. In contrast to his voice, his hand on Joan's hair was light. "I like your kisses too, Lady Joan."

Relief coursed through her, for the kiss had been

interesting and not at all unpleasant, but Joan had no frame of reference for what constituted an adequate kiss from a prospective fiancée. She let herself rest against him, yielded to the warmth and relaxed security of his embrace.

"Are we to marry, then?"

He spread his legs a few inches wider, his chin coming to rest against Joan's temple. "Ye daft woman, will ye no allow a fellow to propose? That kiss was your inspection tour of me. I had best warn you I work too much—Margs is forever scolding me about it, and has nearly poisoned Hector's soup in an effort to gain me respite from my business."

Joan rubbed her cheek against soft wool and hard, honest man. "Are you trying to talk me out of marrying you? My options are limited—you or scandal—and that flatters neither of us."

"I'm warning you: work is all I know. I have no... no, what you English would call *address*. I loathe the quadrille. I prefer the freedom of a kilt to the fussiness of ballroom attire. I raise my voice indoors. I forget my glasses, and even forget I'm wearing my glasses. I'm late to meals. I have no head for names and family connections. When I'm tired, I can be testy—"

Joan kissed him to stop his litany of self-revelation.

"I'm the same way about my sewing. I'd sew all the time if allowed. Dancing with men who are eye-level with my bodice has been a trial since my come out." She hadn't meant to say that—hadn't quite admitted it to herself even. "My father raises his voice indoors and even at table, as does my mother. When I'm tired, one of my eyes has a tendency to turn in when I look down."

Her younger sisters had delighted at this discovery, the wretches. As a result, Joan had spent years never allowing her chin to dip after supper.

Mr. Hartwell's chest bounced—a chuckle.

"A terrible shortcoming, that. Perhaps we should loan you a pair of my spectacles. When will you know if you're carrying?"

As Joan stood in the circle of Mr. Hartwell's arms, the tension she'd arisen with so many hours and miles ago eased by a small increment. His kisses tasted of chocolate, he wore beautiful wool blends, and he could go from teasing to blunt, necessary inquiries in a sentence or two.

She had liked him when she'd danced with him. Respect, and something greater than liking took root where all of Joan's upset had been.

"If I am in an interesting condition, I will have definite indications within a week, ten days at most." If she were regular, which she was—sometimes.

His hand passed over her hair, a thoughtful gesture.

"Will you marry me, Joan Flynn?" That same hand landed gently over Joan's mouth. "Don't answer that. A child needs two parents, but you might well not need a husband. If the offending twit who took such advantage of you keeps his mouth shut, and nature is kind, then your prospects are undiminished, and you need not take me on as husband."

But she—

She *wanted* to take him on as husband. Wanted an uncomplicated man for her spouse, a man who wasn't afraid to apply himself to his goals, a man who cared naught for the social whirl and whose kisses were full of humor and patience.

"The offending twit isn't likely to keep his mouth shut. He revealed a tendency to grow bosky, and gentlemen in their cups have no discretion." Tiberius had warned her of that repeatedly. Tiberius was a great one for issuing warnings...

Tye would be much in evidence over the holidays.

"My parents' union was not happy," Mr. Hartwell said. "Marriage is a great challenge, trust me on this. If we marry, then the less we do so in haste, the better. I'll expect to bed you."

That again. He wasn't teasing, and he wasn't asking. He shouldn't have to ask and yet... The pleasant hopeful glow of the kiss faded, and Joan pushed away from her reluctant suitor.

"I may well be thoroughly used goods, Mr. Hartwell, though my recollections are lamentably unclear. Pretending I'm a blushing innocent would hardly serve."

He remained leaning against the wall, Joan's aubergine cloak forming a black backdrop in the limited light of the parlor car. The dark velvet looked like the background for a portrait—and Mr. Hartwell's expression had grown abruptly stern.

"How can a woman not know if she's been ill-used?"

Joan dropped onto the settee. "I was bosky too. Have you ever partaken of absinthe?"

He wrinkled his substantial nose. "Hateful stuff, particularly if you haven't a head for it. The flavor is strong enough that it can be mixed with laudanum and no one's the wiser. Did you lose consciousness?"

"I cannot recall." The words held equal measures of shame and relief. "Pieces of the evening come back to me when something prompts the memory. I was inappropriately intimate with a man who cannot marry me. I know that much. I cannot think I'm still a maid, and I might well be on my way to motherhood."

He pushed away from the wall with his back, and such were his reflexes that when Joan's cloak came free of its hook, Mr. Hartwell caught it easily before it could brush the floor.

"I'm sorry, then." He drew Joan to her feet and wrapped the cloak around her. "A lady's first time should at least be a pleasant memory, contrary to what your mama might have told you."

He was sorry.

Joan was so far beyond sorry. The cloak settled around her, a comfort in dark velvet that eased her sense of regret.

"I'm sorry too, for my family would not understand what drove me to such folly."

"Probably more important that you understand it yourself." His fingers went to the frogs of her cloak, reminding Joan that Mr. Hartwell had children already. This was a good quality, and not simply because it made a man adept at bundling his womenfolk up against the weather. "I will not tolerate infidelity in my spouse, Lady Joan. The typical aristocratic marriage is a disgrace by my plebeian lights. You will endure my company even when I'm less than charming, and I will endure yours."

Gracious saints. "Will you force yourself upon me?"

Dark brows knitted as he tugged the fastenings to her cloak closed. "Are ye daft?"

The memory of Edward's inert, bony weight pushing against Joan's chest suggested she was, indeed, lacking in sense, for the entire debacle with Edward had been her doing.

"*Will you force yourself upon me?*"

"I *canna* force myself on a woman. Neither my spirit nor my flesh would comply with such a heinous venture. Where will you bide over the holidays?"

Joan did not understand his reply—many intimate details of married life were kept from young ladies—but she understood his question.

"I'm joining my family at the home of relatives-by-marriage. My brother has arranged this, and I owe him much. I'll endure Christmas in the wilds of Aberdeenshire at his invitation."

At Tye's insistence, though he meant well. The whole Flynn family hadn't been together at Christmas for years, and acquaintance with one's in-laws was seldom a bad idea.

Though even in the snug train car, the temperature had dropped, suggesting the wilds of Aberdeenshire would not offer cozy holidays.

"We're both to endure house parties, then," Mr. Hartwell said. "Hector will give you my direction. And you will apprise me of the status of our betrothal within the next two weeks. If I don't hear from you, I'll assume other options have become available to you."

His expressions were already becoming readable to her, for the careful diffidence of his words didn't fool

Joan. Mr. Hartwell sounded like he was discussing some option in a business contract when, in fact, he was being gallant.

Allowing the lady to change her mind, though Joan's behavior had been far from ladylike.

"Thank you, Mr. Hartwell. I cannot envision those options arising when I'm limited to the company of family, but I appreciate the gesture."

She wanted *him*. Wanted a man who was certain of his aims in marriage, and held to the old-fashioned requirements of loyalty and fidelity. She wanted honesty from her spouse, not manipulation and over-imbibing. Mostly she wanted her child—if she was to bear a child—to have a father who wasn't preoccupied with matters of succession and social consequence.

If that man also allowed her to sew to her heart's content, and his kisses tasted of chocolate and smiles, then Joan could be not simply content, but happy.

"You're thinking," Mr. Hartwell observed, caution in his tone. "Has one of those options occurred to you?"

"No, it has not." And likely would not. "My digestion has been tentative all day."

"Train travel does that to many people."

"I feel perfectly fine now." For indeed, the upset in Joan's belly had entirely settled, which made no sense.

No sense at all.

Five

WHEN THE CHILDREN CAVORTING UNDERFOOT OR MARGS bustling about might have for once been convenient, when even Hector's nagging might have been helpful, Dante was left more or less alone with a woman he'd had no intention of marrying even an hour past.

"If you'll excuse me, my lady. Hector hasn't finished haranguing me."

She settled on the settee in a rustle of velvet and grace. "Don't let me keep you, Mr. Hartwell. It grows dark quite early, doesn't it?"

He suspected her observation was a Proper Lady's version of announcing a desire to nap.

"This time of year and this far north, we have more darkness than anything else. Makes sense we'd have holidays amid all the gloom."

Small talk had ever eluded his grasp, but this was his potential prospective wife. They need not *make* small talk. They could, God willing, soon make love. Dante strode over to the woman perched on the fussy settee, kissed her on the mouth, shoved the box of chocolates at her, and got the hell out of the parlor car.

He stood for a bewildered moment on the platform, hoping the lethal cold might clear his mind. A woman of refinement and poise had been shamelessly taken advantage of by one of her own kind, and Dante had offered her marriage, friendship, and a solution to her problems.

Damned well-done of him, too.

Joan would know everybody who was anybody—and know who among them had wealth. Joan would help Dante find a husband for Margs. She would take the children in hand, and take her husband's heathen ways in hand as well.

His proposal had been brilliant from every pragmatic angle.

The lust still stirring through his veins was not pragmatic in the least.

Rowena had not been a martyr in the marriage bed—she'd wanted children, after all—but neither had desire for her plagued Dante when he was out of her company. They'd both preferred it that way.

Now he recalled why. Desire could knock a man sideways, destroy his focus, make his parts ache, and render him daft. Desire could send him back to his earliest youth, when sex, getting sex, recalling sex, and enduring times without sex, could order a young man's entire existence.

He was out of practice was the problem. Thirst after a drought was predictable, and while Dante hadn't been celibate since becoming a widower, he *had* made work a priority—the highest priority.

So for Christmas, he might end a sexual drought and be better able to focus on work for doing so.

On that steadying thought, he took his practical—if temporarily randy—self into the back car, where Hector remained at the folding table, scribbling away, despite the swaying of the train.

"I might be giving the children a mother for Christmas this year," Dante said, somewhat to his own surprise.

Hector didn't immediately look up but kept writing for another line or so, then put his pencil down and stared out at the passing darkness.

"I thought you said Edinburgh was a failed attempt."

"I met Lady Joan in Edinburgh, and she and I might suit."

The pencil went behind Hector's ear, a ready writing implement being as necessary to Hector as a handy dirk was to others.

"Marrying her ladyship would be quite a sacrifice," Hector said, tidying his papers. "I thought you liked your women merry and sonsy."

"I barely recall how I like my women." Was Lady Joan eating the remaining chocolates and recalling their kiss? She was the farthest thing from merry and buxom.

"I suppose she'll do," Hector said, scratching at his nose. "She's the daughter of a marquess whose affairs are reported to be quite in order."

Quite in order. "You're sounding English, my friend. Lady Joan's people have money—her very clothing makes that much plain." Though Hector's news was welcome—as easy to esteem a wealthy bride as a poor one, wasn't it? Dante busied himself tidying the decanters rather than admit to Hector that Joan's finances hadn't, in fact, been a consideration.

Which was foolish when a man could take only one bride at a time.

"Her brother Tiberius, Earl of Spathfoy, manages the family's mercantile interests, abetted by her mother, a formidable woman," Hector said.

The parlor car boasted a selection of whiskeys, mostly from the islands, where a liberal hand with the peating ensured richness and subtlety accompanied the burn of good spirits.

Lady Joan had been brought low by a scoundrel wielding spirits, and yet, she was a formidable woman too. Dante braced his back against the sideboard.

"I expect if we wed, we'll wed over the holidays. The lady has yet to give me an answer, though I'm hopeful she'll have me."

"You're courting her?" Hector asked, folding the earpieces of his spectacles.

"A bit of courting wouldn't go amiss." Courting and a few more kisses. And yet, Dante would not relay the details of Joan's folly to another. A husband—even a prospective husband—owed his wife loyalty.

"I'm fairly certain the courting is supposed to come before the engagement."

"Are you scolding me on this too, Hector? Bad enough you inundate me with reports I can barely decipher, quiz me on the royal succession of a bunch of dead Sassenach kings, carp at me for wearing my kilts, and refuse to take any holidays for yourself."

Hector became absorbed with polishing his spectacles, which hadn't sported a smudge since Moses had been found among the bulrushes.

"Shall I leave you to your house party, then? Give you a few weeks respite from my irksome company?"

Irksome was another of Hector's prissy words, and yet, coming from a braw, bonny fellow who never seemed to do anything but write and read reports, irksome had an off quality.

"If you did not join us at this infernal gathering, you'd be down at the mills, pacing the floors like a hungry pantry mouser, flooding the King's mail with more correspondence than I can read in this lifetime, and aggravating the women in my employ."

"A woman's hair must be tidily braided if she's to work in a mill. If it's aggravating to insist on simple safety precautions from your employees—"

The sideboard dug into Dante's back as the train shook its way over some rough patch in the tracks. "Cut line, Hector. We need to find you a wife."

Abruptly, Hector's linen handkerchief ceased circling on the right lens of his spectacles.

"Do you suppose Margs might marry if you take a wife?"

Interesting thought, and exactly what Hector's restless appetite for angles, details, and contingencies might seize upon.

"Joan will likely be an asset when it comes to finding a fellow for Margs. She'll be an asset in many regards—if she'll have me." And increasingly, he hoped she would.

"Can I fix you a wee dram, Hector? Ballater will be colder than hell."

Hector stashed his glasses away and rose. "Marrying a woman because she's a marquess's daughter with money is colder still."

"I thought you, of all people, would approve of an advantageous match, Hector." Though Hector had been notably silent regarding Dante's sortie to Edinburgh.

Hector stalked over to the door, for once leaving his reports lying all about on the table. "I'd like to make the acquaintance of the English lady who'd consider taking you on as a spouse."

Dante did not particularly want to be cooped up in the same car with a man of business who'd grown moody at the mention of an advantageous match.

"Hector, if I don't replace the floors in Faith Mill, we could have an accident. That equipment is deuced heavy and shakes like doomsday hour after hour. Hope Mill needs a new roof, and the looms in Love will need replacing by this time next year."

From Rowena, Dante had inherited a great lot of problems—also ridiculous names for the mills—mostly because she and her father before her had taken a shortsighted view of profit. Five years after Rowena's death, many of those problems remained unsolved.

"Court your lady then," Hector said. "I'm off to see if Charlie and Phillip might be up for a game of marbles."

Even in this comment, Dante felt a hint of the Parthian shot from Hector—for Dante had not been invited to join that game of marbles.

"I'll finish with your reports then."

Dante sat at the folding table and saw that Hector's most recent list had been of Christmas presents Dante might purchase for his family. The possibilities for Margs were damnably few—they always were—while Charlie's list was as long as Margs's and Phillip's put together.

Dante set aside those lists—Christmas was several weeks off—and tried to focus on estimates for the new roof on Hope Mill. A roof could be constructed to allow light into the facility, but such innovation cost money.

Everything cost money.

In her situation, Joan would not want a lavish ceremony, and while Dante was in favor of saving coin wherever possible, he wished that particular economy not be imposed on the woman he might take to wife.

⁂

Joan's dignity lay in tatters all over her satin-lined cloak, which—much to Joan's consternation—had been shanghaied into service as a field of play for the Great Christmas Traveling Marbles Tournament. The children and Hector had delivered a handy defeat to Joan and Miss Hartwell, amid much merriment and forfeiting of chocolate treats. Phillip played with a concentration and skill far above his years, Charlie made a lot of noise, and Margaret and Hector assiduously avoided the near occasion of flirting.

While in the other car, Mr. Hartwell did…*what*?

"The train is slowing down," Charlie announced, springing up and going to the window.

"It's dark," Phillip said, also getting to his feet. "You can't see anything out the window."

"I can see lights. We're coming into Ballater."

"Somebody had best tear Dante away from his ciphering," Miss Hartwell observed as she gathered her skirts. "Children, get your coats."

Hector reached a hand down to Miss Hartwell.

Rather than wait for the same courtesy, Joan rose and poured the marbles into a decorated jar. Her cloak was a bit wrinkled, but otherwise in good repair.

"Will your family meet you?" Hector asked, for Miss Hartwell had taken on the burden of fetching her brother.

"My arrival will be something of a surprise. I'm sure a conveyance is available to take me to them."

"And all you have is that cloak to keep you warm?" *That cloak?*

"I love this cloak, Mr. MacMillan. I stitched every seam and buttonhole of it myself, chose the fabric and created the design." His expression wasn't contemptuous, so much as disbelieving, and Joan had the thought: So what if he doesn't appreciate my cloak? After today I'll likely never see him—

Except, after today, she very well might see Hector regularly for years. A sense of unreality wrapped her more closely. She was alone, in the Highlands, with little money, and—quite possibly—a child on the way. Yesterday at this time, her only dilemma had been which pattern to cut out first.

"As long as the station's open, you should be safe enough," Hector said. "Charlie, come here and let me do those buttons."

The station at Ballater was a low, unprepossessing gingerbread cottage, nothing like the granite edifices Joan was familiar with to the south. The Hartwell party was the only one to debark, and as the train chugged away, Joan appropriated her traveling bag from the heap of luggage on the platform.

The cold and dark here exceeded even what

Joan had grown up with in Northumbria. Breathing through the nose was a curiously invigorating exercise, and more stars blanketed the night sky than the eye could count in a lifetime. Pine roping adorned with red velvet bows decorated the little station, the ribbons whipping in an arctic breeze.

Joan had to wait while Mr. Hartwell groused at the lone porter and tossed trunks about—weren't his knees cold, for pity's sake?—before she could have a word with him.

"Mr. Hartwell?"

His gaze was on Miss Hartwell, who herded the children into the small waiting area while Hector took over the transfer of bags from the platform to the street side of the station.

"Lady Joan?"

"I wanted to thank you."

He peered down at her, as if she'd used a strange word or two. "Thank me? For proposing marriage?"

"*What?* Oh, yes, for that too. For bringing me this far."

His brows drew down, suggesting Joan had misspoken.

"You're welcome. Here." He passed her a folded piece of paper. "My direction for the duration of my holiday sentence. You'd best get into the station. When it's this cold, the horses can't stand for long."

She heeded his suggestion, for her teeth were about to start chattering, also because this exchange with her possible intended had been toweringly awkward.

Though kissing him had not been awkward at all.

"You'll be in touch?" he asked when Joan had moved several yards away.

He stood on the platform, the bitter wind whipping his kilt around his knees and playing havoc with his hair. His expression was unreadable, and Joan abruptly didn't want to leave him.

He was practical, he was kind, he was competent, and he didn't judge her, as her family must should they learn of her folly.

Joan offered him her most brilliant smile. She'd perfected that smile when faced with yet another dancing partner half a foot too short, or overheard yet another comment about the pathetic lot of a Long Meg.

"I'll send a holiday greeting to Miss Hartwell, at the very least."

"Aye, do that." He turned his back on her—a mercy more than a rudeness—and marched off in the direction of the porters wrestling with the luggage trolley.

"Happy Christmas," Joan whispered to his retreating back.

From the chilly confines of the station, she watched as the Hartwell party organized itself into two sleighs—one for the people, one for baggage. Hector and Margaret each took a child on their laps, Margaret and Charlie wedged between the men. Lap robes covered Margaret and the children nearly to their eyes.

How warm the Hartwell womenfolk would be.

"I'll be closing up now, miss. We'll have no more trains through here until Monday, and my missus will have held supper for me."

The only other person in the station was the lone porter, who also apparently served as stationmaster. He was a man of middle years and prodigious salt-and-pepper whiskers. His eyes were tired, and he was already wrapping a red plaid scarf about his neck.

"Can you hail me a cab before you go?"

He paused between donning one glove and next. "A cab? We've no cabs in Ballater village, miss. You can wait in the pub for your people to fetch you, but in this weather, nobody would make a decent beast loiter about in hopes of custom. I can lock up your bags for you, if that would aid matters."

Joan's bag or the oxen and horses were due more consideration than she was herself, and she had her own ignorance and folly to blame for this.

"I can wait in the pub," she said, though she'd never entered such an establishment without a male escort before. "Will I be able to hire a vehicle in the morning?"

"Depends on the weather," the fellow said, blowing out one candle after another. "And depends on where you're going—and how much coin you have."

Joan had no idea whether Tye's house party was two miles from the station or twelve. She left the station with the stationmaster, and for the first time allowed that velvet might be more pretty than warm.

The stationmaster toddled off, nipping from a flask, leaving Joan standing before the dark station. A team approached, harness bells jingling, and her spirits lifted. Somebody was willing to hire their conveyance despite the weather, and she would find her way to her brother's temporary household.

She'd come this far safely, and in this season of Christian fellowship—

The dray trotted past, and because Joan had been in

anticipation of hailing it, she'd approached the street more closely than was wise. Frigid slush splashed up her cloak to the knees, ruining the fabric and dashing Joan's spirits.

"So much for Christmas." Joan clenched her jaw against the possibility her teeth might start to chatter, and took stock of her surroundings. Not a soul walked along the streets; not a beast of burden was in sight.

And she had no clue where the pub might be.

❧

"Are you lost?" Hector asked.

Yes, Dante was lost—or his common sense had gone begging. "Nobody was at the station to meet Lady Joan."

"The train was on time," Hector said from Margs's other side. "Nobody expects the trains to be on time."

"Dante's right," Margs said from the depths of her scarf. "We should not have left her there alone."

Margs's support had the feel of an opportunistic swipe at Hector, and yet, Dante was grateful for it.

"I liked Lady Joan," Charlie volunteered from Margs's lap. "She's nice, and she shares her chocolates."

She shared her favors too, or believed she had. She'd spoken as if she hadn't been forced, but inebriating a lady was the opposite of gaining her consent.

He turned the team back into the oval before the train station, the baggage sleigh following behind, and at first saw nobody.

Well, more fool he. "Her ladyship must have found accommo—"

A figure emerged from under the eaves at the

station's door. Tall, clad in a cloak far too light for the weather. For Dante, genuine relief replaced the feigned variety, despite a niggling unease that rescuing the same damsel twice in one day could not be a positive trend. He passed Hector the reins and leaped down, the cold sending a hard ache up his legs.

"You daft woman, have you nobody to take you in out of the weather?"

She wiped at her cheeks with her fussy purple glove. "Don't scold me. I was about to ask a passerby where the pub was."

Dante whipped off his scarf and wrapped it around her fool neck. "A fine plan, as long you don't mind freezing to death in the next quarter hour." When she might have offered some genteel retort, he wrapped the scarf directly over her mouth.

"You," Dante barked at the coachy driving the baggage sleigh. "Trade with me. Charlie and Phillip, mind your aunt and Hector."

"Or we'll get lumps of coal for Christmas," Charlie yelled.

"Into the damned sleigh," Dante said to the shivering bundle of womanhood beside him. She managed it, despite the folds of her cloak, and Dante soon had hot bricks under her feet and thick wool lap robes layered over them both.

"Budge up," he said, taking up the reins. "We've only a few miles to travel, but a little Highland cold goes a long way."

"Th-thank you."

"Keep your damned manners, and pray God you don't get a lung fever for your holiday treat."

◈

Joan tucked herself under the heavy lap robes and reviewed a day that had been a series of revelations, starting with the awful realization of how precarious a woman's good name truly was. In a few hours, Joan had laid waste to a lifetime of decorous behavior and risked her family's standing too.

Matters had deteriorated from there, for Joan had the lowering suspicion that her maid had suffered from an attack of self-preservation rather than a bilious stomach. If Bertha had pieced together the details of Joan's previous evening, then the maid's search for another post was already under way.

Then had come the lowering news that despite an uncommonly competent grasp of economics for a lady, Joan wasn't very familiar with money.

What did a meal cost?

A train ticket?

A plain wool cloak ready-made?

She knew even less of train schedules, or she would never have debarked halfway to Aberdeen to ensure passage back to Edinburgh for her ailing maid.

Small shocks had followed: How did a lady unlace herself without aid at the end of the day? What food was safe to eat at a train station? Did pickpockets frequent such locations?

After overimbibing, did memory never fully return? How did men endure the frequent occasion of overimbibing?

"Are you falling asleep, my lady?"

"I'm thinking."

"About?"

Brave fellow, or perhaps Mr. Hartwell was simply bored.

"This day had some positive aspects." Joan was tucked up against one of them, and Mr. Hartwell's sheer animal warmth featured prominently among his winning qualities.

"Always a good day when one doesn't die of exposure in the Highlands. If you'd like a wee nip, my flask is in my hip pocket."

He thought she was an idiot, and Joan agreed with him.

"Drinking spirits is part of how I nearly died of exposure in the Highlands." She fished in his pocket nonetheless, a curiously intimate undertaking.

"Firstly, if we share that flask, there's not enough to get either one of us drunk. Secondly, it's too damned cold to tarry by the roadside, even for the pleasure of sampling a lady's charms. Thirdly, if we do not appear at our destination directly behind my family, a searching party will soon come looking for us."

Joan took a very *wee* nip, cautiously, for she was stupid but could learn from her mistakes.

"This tastes of...sherry? I find it odd that the same spirits that authored my social downfall now serve to warm my insides."

And warm them *agreeably*. She did not find it odd that her charms were no temptation to Mr. Hartwell, despite his references to the weather.

"Good whiskey goes down with all manner of subtle glories, and it wasn't the spirits that authored your downfall, if indeed you've fallen."

As the road climbed, the sleigh ahead marked the

path at a greater distance. The baggage sleigh didn't sport harness bells, giving Joan the sense of all gaiety and light receding from her life the farther they traveled from the village.

She burrowed closer to Mr. Hartwell. "I authored my own downfall, and I have the sorry premonition that the consequences are only beginning to manifest."

"Then you've nothing left to lose, have you?"

Mama would kill her, Tiberius would lecture her within an inch of her life, and Papa would shout.

"I have nothing to lose but my good name, my welcome in my own family, my self-respect, and my dreams of designing clothes that make a woman feel pretty without beggaring her pocketbook."

"If your family turns their backs on you now, then they aren't much of a family."

Joan passed him the flask, and after he'd taken a considerable swallow and handed it back, she capped it and tucked it into his pocket. She kept her hand in his pocket too, for warmth.

Or something.

Because Mr. Hartwell's observation about Joan's family turning their backs on her was the most lowering of the entire miserable day.

"Are you crying, my lady?"

She had the oddest conversations with him. "Would you mind I if were?"

"A cold wind can bring tears to the eyes, but mine host would likely take it amiss if I showed up with a blubbering female among my baggage. Charlie will be enough of a trial to the man's hospitality. Hector and Margs's feuding will add a cheery note to the festivities too."

A shaft of insight struck, every bit as warming as the whiskey. Mr. Hartwell was teasing her, or riling her, distracting her. In any case, he was trying to help with a problem so much larger than a mere awful day.

"You are a nice man, Mr. Hartwell. I like you quite well."

"No more whiskey for you, Lady Joan."

His tone was gruff, which Joan suspected meant he might like her a little too.

He turned the horses down a dark tree-lined drive. Up ahead, the outline of a sizable edifice loomed, though ten windows sported a single candle each, in a four-three-two-one pattern. The effect—a rising triangle of illuminated windows—was lovely, rather like a Christmas tree.

Hector and Miss Hartwell had already shooed the children into the house before Mr. Hartwell handed Joan down from the sleigh. She retrieved her bag, which Mr. Hartwell plucked from her grasp, and accepted his escort as a footman held up a lantern, porters tackled the luggage, and a groom dealt with the horses.

"Whose hospitality am I imposing on?" Joan asked, for their arrival was certainly meeting with every courtesy.

"Some earl or other. He's in shipping and looking to diversify. Lots of interests in the New World and doesn't socialize much. Supposedly quite wealthy, though I've likely offended you by saying as much. Why?"

The day was to end with a small mercy, apparently. "I don't know any earls with interests in shipping, and if he's reclusive, then there will be that much less talk about my having to depend on your good offices to see me back to my family."

Or about her possibly ending up married to Mr. Hartwell, another unfathomable element to this most unfathomable day.

They paused on the front stoop of a house built of mellow gray granite. The footman stood patiently with one hand on the doorknob, suggesting nobody in these surrounds let the night air in for an instant longer than necessary.

"You're not looking forward to explaining *me*," Mr. Hartwell said. "Don't suppose I blame you."

The footman opened the door, and a rush of warm, piney air greeted Joan. A small crowd was knotted in the house's entryway, Charlie's voice piping above a hubbub of greetings and introductions.

A tall dark-haired man in a kilt detached himself from the group and extended a hand to Mr. Hartwell.

"Hartwell, welcome. This must be your wife."

Their host was broad-shouldered, and his burr was laced with some subtle accent Joan couldn't fathom. About the eyes and jaw, he looked familiar, and he was much younger than Joan had anticipated, probably about Mr. Hartwell's age.

She noted these details with the part of her mind adept at social gatherings, while the part of her that had endured a long, hard, bewildering day scrambled for a reply to their host's error.

"Lady Joan—" Mr. Hartwell began, only to be interrupted by a cultured, very English baritone from over Joan's shoulder.

"She is most certainly not his wife, for that lady is my own dear sister. Joan, a pleasure to see you—an unexpected pleasure."

Joan had always viewed the ladies who succumbed to a convenient swoon with amusement, and yet... A varied diet of whiskey, chocolate, self-recrimination, and anxiety did not make for steady nerves.

Mr. Hartwell's arm, though, was steady indeed. Joan manufactured a brilliant smile, turned, and faced yet another challenge in this endlessly challenging day.

She also lied—convincingly, she hoped.

"Hello, Tiberius. Delightful to see you too, as always."

Six

VALERIAN FONTAINE HAD NO SENSE OF FASHION, AND
the only figures that turned his graying head were of
the mathematical variety. Edward might have forgiven
his uncle these shortcomings, but the old boy had no
sense of fun, either.

"If you are to take over this business someday, you
will have to learn to *work*," Uncle barked, closing a
ledger book with a decisive snap. "You must leave off
mincing about the ballrooms and leering down ladies'
bodices, and spend more time seeing to business."

Uncle came from the practical French side of the
family, after which Edward did not now and never
would take if he could help it. Times were changing,
true, but having a hand in trade was hardly a rose on
the family escutcheon.

"Don't scold the boy," Mama said as she leafed
through Edward's sketches for next year's ball gowns.
"Where do you think all the latest fashions are to be
seen, hmm? Edward is an English aristocrat and must
be seen comporting himself as such."

"Those ball gowns are to be *seen* night after

night, the same fashions on the same ladies from the same modistes and the same houses of fashion. The boy needn't become a fixture in the ballrooms to know that bustles are smaller this year, or larger, or whatever."

The size of a fashionable bustle was not a *whatever*, and Edward, at twenty-seven years of age, was not a boy.

"Eddie, where are your new drawings?" As always, Mama was composed and lovely. Mama might not be able to design a pretty dress, but she could still wear one to excellent advantage.

"I believe you're looking at my most recent drawings, Mama."

And when would Uncle renovate this shabby, cluttered, dingy office? Customers never saw this part of Salon du Mode, but Edward was spending rather more time here of late than he preferred.

"Not these," Mama said, setting aside hours of Edward's work, "the ones you did at home, the ones with the different bodices and all that flouncy business about the hems."

An image flashed into Edward's mind, out of context, the way recall of a hard night always popped up unexpectedly. Lady Joan had been so eager to show him her sketches, and not very eager at all to show him her other treasures. She'd prattled on and on about seams, flounces, nap, drape, and all manner of subtleties, while Edward had watched her hands moving on the page and become aroused.

"What drawings?" Uncle asked, for even Uncle understood that a clever design yielded profit, of which there had been too little for too long.

"I have them in my case," Edward said, because he had spent hours trying to imitate the innovations Joan had tossed off in a few moments of sketching. "Might we have a tea tray sent up?"

"Show them to your uncle," Mama said, waving her hand languidly. "They're your best work so far. When you apply yourself, you astonish me, Eddie."

The hour was late enough that Edward ought to be dressing for his evening's entertainments— Uncle's misguided notions of *work* meant long hours spent on the business premises. Edward was hungry, bored, and—

The sense of his mother's words registered. "Those sketches you were looking at at home are not mi—"

Between one heartbeat and the next, Edward came smack up against a choice. Lady Joan had left her designs behind in Edward's parlor, only a few of the many brilliant ideas she was unfairly endowed with. He'd wanted her help without having to ask for it—the reason for the entire debacle—but he hadn't strictly planned to appropriate her work.

She wouldn't miss the sketches, and she certainly wouldn't be asking for them back.

Would she?

A man must take charge of his destiny.

"Those sketches are not my best work, though some of them have potential," Edward said, untying his portfolio. He carried the leather case with him so that all and sundry might know that his contribution to the family venture was artistic, and nothing so pedestrian as arithmetic or ledgers.

That would be *ungentlemanly*. Also tedious, and in

Edward's case, doomed to failure. Then too, a port-folio was a good place to stash a spare handkerchief, a comb, some mints, and a sheath or two.

"I'm still refining most of them," Edward said, passing Joan's sketches across the table to his uncle—and pray God the man would not turn them over to see the signatures.

Uncle dressed like a latter-day Puritan, and his grasp of women's fashion likely matched Edward's grasp of ledgers. What mattered was that Mama had liked the drawings.

"Damned lot of fabric involved," Uncle muttered. "Though they're quite fetching. Silk, I suppose?"

Silk was expensive; Edward knew that much. "Well, perhaps we might use—"

"Of course, silk," Mama said, turning the stack to consider a drawing. "Nothing else drapes quite like silk, and it's warm without being heavy. Spring nights are the very devil for being chilly."

How could a woman be chilly when wearing all those confounded layers? Lady Joan had certainly worn layers beneath her skirts—Edward recalled that much—and each one had been soft, delicate, and complicated—also mouthwateringly pretty.

"Matching capes and shawls then," Uncle groused. "More damned silk."

"Matching stockings," Edward said. A silly notion, one that had both of his relations peering at him. Joan had worn purple silk stockings, the sight of which on her slender calves had parted Edward from his next-to-last shred of common sense.

"Brilliant," Mama cried.

"Costly," Uncle countered. "I suppose we can charge exorbitantly for them if they're dyed to match."

Mama nattered on, while Uncle offered a counterpoint in dolorous estimates and dire predictions, and Edward wrestled with what amounted to purloining Lady Joan Flynn's sketches.

The sketches she'd abandoned when she'd stolen from Edward's embrace in the dead of night.

"These aren't final designs," Edward said, though neither Mama nor Uncle appeared to heed him. "I said, these still need some work. I'm not finished with them."

Because with a flounce here and a puffier sleeve there, Edward might obscure the fact that he'd committed larceny in addition to trespassing on a good woman's virtue.

While Mama and Uncle went blithely about another of their many arguments, Edward tied the portfolio ribbons closed. It would not do for anybody to catch sight of what he carried about where pencils, paper, charcoal, pastels, and erasers should be.

⮞⬟⬟

A big dark-haired fellow came sauntering past the crossed ceremonial claymores gracing the first landing, his unsmiling gaze fixed on Lady Joan. He looked ready to launch into lectures Dante was too tired to tolerate.

"Are Dora and Mary Ellen with you?" His tone was more inquisitive than concerned, and beside Dante, Lady Joan stood taller.

"They made separate arrangements."

"Lady Joan traveled out from the station with my family and me. I'm sure her day has been quite taxing."

The confused quality of the other man's scowl reminded Dante that—heaven help him—they had not been *introduced*.

MacGregor remedied the oversight. "Lord Spathfoy, may I make known to you Mr. Dante Hartwell. Mr. Hartwell, Tiberius, Earl of Spathfoy, whom I consider a cousin by marriage."

Without giving up his hold of Joan's arm, Dante bowed to his lordship, wondering what the fellow had done to merit a first name address from Lady Joan. Spathfoy was English, and impeccably turned out, which would matter to Joan.

"Hartwell, my thanks," said his hoity-toity English lordship. "Now you will please turn loose of my sister that I might inflict a proper greeting on her."

Sister. Dante did not turn loose of Joan so much as she eased from his grasp and slipped into her brother's embrace.

"Is Hester here?" Joan asked, drawing back but not leaving the circle of her brother's arms. "I have missed you both terribly, and I'm sure my nephew is ready to ride to hounds."

Spathfoy was fooled by that diversionary tactic—he went into lordly raptures about some baby, and needing rest, and his countess believed this and that about the rearing of a child—but Joan was bluffing.

She was exhausted, anxious as hell, possibly even scared, and her brother wasn't to know any of it. And yet, the entirety of her miserable day had been given into Dante's confidence.

Where it would remain.

"MacGregor, if you'd complete the introductions?" Dante asked. "The children in particular have had a long day."

As had Dante. MacGregor—the earl of Balfour, rather, dammit—said something to his red-haired wife, an American whose name or title or proper form of address Dante would worry about tomorrow, and soon that lady was leading Margs and the children up the curving stairway.

The noise level dropped considerably with Charlie's departure, and in the ringing quiet, fatigue crept up behind Dante and clobbered him stoutly.

"You're probably for bed too," MacGregor—Balfour—said. "Her ladyship will have trays sent up, and the sideboards are stocked in all of the bedrooms. Will you need a valet?"

What Dante needed was to know Joan would be provided the same solitude and comfort MacGregor was offering him.

"I see to myself," Dante said. "A tray would be appreciated."

"Joan!" A small blond woman came barreling into the entryway. "Oh, you've surprised us! It's so good to *see* you!"

Dante liked this woman on sight, for her arrival had saved Joan from further interrogations by Spathfoy, and she was effusive in her greetings. She was so petite, however, that Joan's height looked even greater by contrast.

"It's lovely to be here," Joan said, flashing another smile. Her stamina, when it came to facial dissembling, was prodigious. She reached for Dante and drew him forward by virtue of linking their arms. "Lady Spathfoy, may I make known to you..."

Dante bowed over the lady's hand, while he tried to absorb that this bright, cheery little woman was married to Joan's lordly brother. Perhaps opposites did attract. And while Spathfoy made sheep's eyes at his wee countess, Dante renewed his request to MacGregor.

"Might we prevail upon you to show us to our accommodations, MacGregor? I confess I'm about asleep on my feet."

He could go another twenty-four hours before that was so, and had on occasion, but he was damned if he'd let Joan's brother get a free shot at her before she'd had some rest.

"This way, then," MacGregor said, leading them up the stairs and past the claymores. "Spathfoy, Countess, until breakfast."

They were shown to rooms across the hall from each other, which suited Dante well enough. MacGregor's ancestral pile sported a modern bathing chamber on the same corridor as the guest rooms. The house was well appointed—the mirrors shone brightly, the sconces sported clean chimneys, the scent of the place was fresh and cedary with a homey undertone of peat.

For all its cleanliness and size, the house fell short of pretentious—and thank God for that, because Dante could not have borne to do business with a Scotsman given to fussiness and airs.

"Lady Joan, I'll bid you good night," MacGregor said. "Breakfast is on the sideboard by seven. Any maid or footman can direct you if the scent of bacon isn't guide enough. Mr. Hartwell, good night."

He bustled off, kilt swinging, maybe to find his countess, or perhaps to give two weary travelers privacy to seek their beds.

Joan paused with her hand on the glass doorknob. "He's Balfour, not MacGregor, though Asher is quite the democrat. He didn't seem to care how you addressed him."

Her hand dropped without turning the knob. Dante was across the hall in an instant, scooping her up against his chest and carrying her into his room.

"*I* don't care how I address him," he said, shoving the door closed with his shoulder. The room was warm, a few candles were lit, and a fire burned cheerily in the hearth. "We need to get our stories straight before your brother resumes his interrogation of you."

"You *need* to put me down, Mr. Hartwell."

No, he did not. Lady Joan was no sylph, she was a proper armful of feminine curves—unhappy feminine curves.

Dante sat her gently on the high, fluffy bed, and then he locked the door.

❧

"Your brother will be after you at breakfast," Mr. Hartwell said, stalking about the room. He peered out at the darkness past the window, opened and closed the wardrobe doors, opened and closed the drawers to the night table, and generally inspected his accommodations much as his daughter might have. "And don't be fooled, that wee, cheery wife of his will abet his questioning."

"Would you please sit, Mr. Hartwell?" For his per-egrinations, particularly among the green-and-white plaid decor of the room, were dizzying.

He took a seat next to her on the bed, and his bulk was such that Joan settled against him.

"I wasn't expecting Tye to be here," Joan said. "I wasn't expecting *your* house party to be *my* house party, rather. This complicates matters."

Mostly, she wasn't expecting to be ruined.

Oh, that again.

Mr. Hartwell took her hand, his grip warm and unexpected. "Family members excel at the art of the public ambush, lass. We need to think."

We. Joan's regard for Mr. Hartwell rose with his choice of pronouns, and he was right. Tiberius would note the absence of a maid, the absence of baggage, the absence of explanations for those departures from normal expectations.

"My maid did fall ill. Perhaps I'd already joined your party when that happened?"

"Your maid returned to Edinburgh, and her version of events will be different."

It would. Family excelled at the art of public ambush, as Mr. Hartwell had noted, while Bertha enjoyed excellent and unwavering recall of the truth, also a loyalty to Joan's mama that was occasionally inconvenient.

"Perhaps I knew your sister was traveling north, and agreed to join her party?"

"Your path never crossed Margaret's in public before today, for my sister finds Polite Society tedious."

A point in Miss Hartwell's favor.

"Who knew you were leaving Edinburgh, my lady?"

Joan tried to turn the gears of her recollection, but the going was made difficult by fatigue and anxiety bordering on panic.

"Everybody knew my general plans. My family has not been together for a winter holiday for several years, and my mother crowed about this year's plans to all and sundry."

Edward knew she was coming north for the holidays and had asked her under whose roof those holidays would be spent—as he'd offered her another drink and sat near enough to her to admire her sketches.

And to leer at the meager treasures in her bodice.

Maybe depression was the exhausted form of self-loathing, for when Joan should have crossed the hallway into her own room, she instead turned her face into Mr. Hartwell's wool-clad shoulder. The inevitable scent of coal smoke clung to his clothing, but beneath his attire was solid muscle and common sense.

Also, apparently, a goodly quantity of decency.

"Perhaps you and I are already engaged," Joan said. "Or we have an understanding until you can talk with my family."

By virtue of a hand anchored at her nape, Mr. Hartwell turned Joan's face up, so she had to meet his eyes.

He was tired, he lacked the refined appearance and pretty manners of Joan's peers, and she wanted to kiss him.

"If you bruit it about that we're engaged, Lady Joan, your reputation will suffer if you have to break it off. You might cast aside a fellow of your own set as a queer start, but I'm...I'm not...an expected choice for such as you."

Such as you. Mr. Hartwell forgot his host's title, but he could be delicate when it mattered.

"You own mills," Joan said, smoothing his hair back, because touching soft things soothed her. "I love to design clothing. Maybe you're not so unexpected."

He said nothing rather than remind Joan of his parlous upbringing. She appreciated that consideration too.

"Will you sit by me at breakfast?" she asked.

"I'll not go down without you."

He'd wait above stairs until spring for her if need be. Tiberius was equally stubborn, though in a brother—or a father, mother, and sisters—the quality was not half so attractive.

"I'll think of something," Joan said, "and confer with you before breakfast. I'm too tired to think now."

Not too tired to feel, though.

Mr. Hartwell patted her hand. "You might tell your family the truth, my lady. That brother of yours looks like he could sort out a presuming twit or two without much trouble."

"But Tiberius would *know* then, wouldn't he? He'd know I was ruined, and he'd feel compelled to tell my parents. They'd all smugly conclude that were I not so preoccupied with matters of fashion, I would not have been led astray, and the one thing—the single pursuit I've chosen for my own—would be taken from me."

He kissed her temple, the same way he'd kissed Charlie's temple hours ago in a chilly rural train station.

"Your dresses are more important to you than honesty with your family?"

What had that to do with anything?

"I'm tired," Joan said, rising. "You're tired, and things will look brighter in the morning."

They would not, of course. By tomorrow, Edward might have already let all and sundry know of Joan's fall from grace.

Mr. Hartwell remained sitting on the bed. "Shall I unhook your dress?"

This had been a worry, in that small train station as Joan had put Bertha on the southbound train. How did a fashionably attired lady undress at the end of the day if she was unfashionably stranded without the services of a maid?

She could destroy her clothing or accept assistance.

"Lord Balfour neglected to offer me a maid's services, though I could ring for one." Who would probably take a half hour to appear.

Mr. Hartwell rose, his expression grave.

"If we marry, my lady, we will marry quite soon and consummate the vows immediately. For the child's sake, and for yours."

Understanding bloomed, a blush along with it. "So the child's paternity might be shrouded in ambiguity?"

He did not so much as nod. "Shall I unhook your dress?"

The second time he asked the question, it bore a significance Joan hadn't grasped earlier. Mr. Hartwell had been married, and married couples at his strata assisted each other to dress and undress. He'd unhooked any number of dresses, unlaced endless numbers of stays.

While Joan's experience of unclad men was limited to marble statues without faces.

She'd enjoyed kissing Mr. Hartwell, despite all odds to the contrary. Had he enjoyed kissing her?

Joan turned her back to him and swept her hair off her nape. As deft fingers undid her gown, she marveled that with Mr. Hartwell, she was safe even when he was *undressing* her, though with a man she might have considered her equal, she'd been ruined.

"Thank you," she said a few moments later, more able to breathe than she'd been all day.

He stepped away, his hands behind his back. "Get some rest, and we'll talk further in the morning."

Joan headed for the door but had to pause to unlock it. "In the morning, we might become engaged."

And within the week, they might well be married.

❧

Edward stared at the blank stationery before him, one thought filling his awareness: a gentleman should apologize for abusing a lady's sensibilities, particularly when that lady was connected to a wealthy family, moved much in Society, and possessed prodigious talent when it came to designing pretty dresses.

"You aren't making much progress with your correspondence, Edward. Are you preoccupied with thoughts of our wedding?" Lady Dorcas asked.

What wed—? *Oh, that wedding.*

"Of course, my dear. Have you chosen a recipe for the cake yet?"

Because the cake was the central concern in this blushing bride's list of wedding details. The dress, she'd confided, would be of her fiancé's design—God help him.

"I'm debating between vanilla and orange flavor for the cake. To whom do you write, Edward?"

Like most engaged couples, they were given significant latitude beyond the rules imposed on the unattached. Edward's mother would reappear at some point, though not soon enough, and she'd announce her impending arrival with a song or an overloud proclamation to the footman posted six feet outside the door.

"I'm writing to a friend, trying to word an apology that isn't too obsequious, and asking for the loan of a…particular walking stick left in my care."

Dorcas put down her lorgnette. "Apologize for what? You're a viscount—why should you apologize?"

"My friend and I were a bit naughty—a bit too free with the spirits, you know."

Was he telling her this as a sort of backhanded confession?

"If he's careless with his things, you need hardly apologize for looking after them in his absence. I know somebody else who was naughty. Mama's abigail heard it from her sister, who's a chambermaid in Lady Quinworth's household, and the abigail told my lady's maid."

Dorcas had a certain practical charm, for all she thought more of cakes than dresses, and she had a fiendish memory for gossip.

Edward tossed his pen down and took a place on the love seat beside his intended.

"We're to be married, my dear, and that means we

should be in each other's confidence when it comes to juicy gossip."

For why should he be the only one making the occasional, entirely understandable, hardly-his-fault misstep?

"Lady Joan Flynn's maid went north with her yesterday—very little luggage, no tickets purchased in advance, bad weather closing in—and came back without Lady Joan before midday. The family is sending the maid off to spend the holiday with her sister in the south."

Of all the names that might have come out of Dorcas's rosebud mouth...

"Lady Joan was to spend her holidays at some house party in the hills, I believe." At the Earl of Balfour's house party, a coveted invitation extended to a select few, and those mostly MacGregor family connections.

Wealthy MacGregor family connections.

Dorcas's expression was indulgent. "Edward, Stirring Up Sunday is tomorrow. Nobody starts a Christmas house party this early, particularly not in the frigid and dreary Highlands. The maid came back *alone*, which means Lady Joan apparently met somebody to the north, or traveled on without any accompaniment. One is left to wonder why she fled, or whom she met."

"I thought you liked Lady Joan." Edward liked Joan—when he wasn't trying to cadge kisses and sketches from her.

"How could I like a woman who manages to look wonderfully turned out despite having a long nose, no figure, and far too much height? Badly done of her, if you ask me. She's overdue for a comeuppance. Do you favor vanilla or orange?"

Sweets in general had no appeal for Edward. "I'll favor whatever you choose, my dove. So Lady Joan is courting scandal?"

Dorcas picked up the lorgnette and went back to studying her recipes.

"A woman who values her wardrobe as much as Joan Flynn would never part with her maid when in her right mind. Joan was going to meet a lover is my guess, and the maid figured it out and wanted no part of such debauchery. Skinny women get desperate."

Joan was not skinny, not where it mattered. "Maybe her ladyship was *fleeing* a lover." Or fleeing the announcement of a lover's engagement, which had been all over the morning papers—bad timing, that.

"One doesn't flee a lover," Dorcas said, wrinkling her nose. "Whoever heard of a chocolate wedding cake?"

Joan *had been* fleeing, though, suggesting…

"Chocolate might be a nice change," Edward said, kissing his intended's plump cheek and returning to the escritoire. "Sometimes, one needs to set trends, not follow them."

"Chocolate with orange frosting? Very pale frosting, with maybe a hint of orange and peppermint?"

Edward's stomach churned at the notion. "I must be guided by your judgment in all culinary matters, my dear."

While Dorcas billed and cooed over frosting, icing, and candied flowers of various descriptions, Edward considered his situation. He'd indulged in some illicit affection with a woman not his wife, and she'd left a few sketches in his care. Now that woman was using bad judgment, scampering off as if she were hurt or insulted or...

This was why the apologetic note had been so hard to write, because an apology was not how a man seized his destiny or dealt with women who sought to use their feminine wiles for commercial profit.

For that's what Joan had been about—Edward was nearly sure of it. She had probably wanted him to commission designs from her—a scandalous notion in itself, given her lofty birth.

He picked up his pen and wrote a note that contained not one hint of apology, while Dorcas rhapsodized about how clever her future spouse was, and about peppermint and orange with a hint of lavender.

Seven

LADY JOAN LOOKED BETTER FOR HAVING SLEPT through the night, and yet, she was wearing the same purple dress she'd had on the previous day. Her brother would notice that—or the brother's wife would.

Dante had tapped on her ladyship's door, his empty belly unwilling to tarry above stairs any longer than necessary.

"Mr. Hartwell, good morning." Hovering in the doorway, she was so pretty, and so scared. What would it be like to wake up to this woman across the breakfast table each morning? To sleep beside her each night?

"Might you call me Dante?"

She opened the door a few more inches. "For the fellow who wrote all that verse about hell?"

"He wrote about heaven, too, my lady." Also purgatory.

"Dante is better than had you been named for some misguided Papist lady saint who came to a martyr's end trying to lead a bunch of fool men on the battlefield," she said, opening the door farther. "I need to put on my boots, though."

She did not like her own name?

He was probably supposed to wait outside her door, like a dutiful hound, but what other opportunity would they have to talk privately?

"Is it proper for you to put on your boots in the presence of a gentleman?" he asked, following her into a room less laden with plaid than his, but no less comfortable.

"Certainly not. A glimpse of even *my* ankles will send you into a passion." She took a seat in a chair before the hearth and peeled thick wool socks off to reveal feet covered in purple stockings.

Dante lounged against the bedpost, a good eight feet away from the heat of the fire. "Even *your* ankles?"

She stuck out a narrow, high-arched foot. "Not the stuff of raptures, Mr. Hartwell, though my feet serve me well enough when I'm dancing."

If he married her, he'd make it a point to kiss her ankles, mostly because they were pretty, but also because she apparently needed such attentions. She slipped on a pair of white half boots sporting purple laces, and tied a perfectly symmetrical bow on each one.

"Those can't be very warm," Dante said.

"I had them made with low heels, Mr. Hartwell, and for that—"

The little blond appeared in the doorway, tidily turned out in soft green. "Oh, I see Mr. Hartwell has beat me to your door, Joan. Good morning, Mr. Hartwell. Will you escort us down to breakfast?"

"Good morning, Hester," Lady Joan said, smiling creditably as she rose. "You may lead us to our destination, for I vow I'm famished."

The smaller woman was married to Joan's brother, who was earl of something. Dante bowed and prayed he was guessing right. "Countess, good morning."

"You may call me Hester," the lady said. "I wasn't raised lady anything, you see, and all this formal address, it doesn't seem very friendly or Christmasy, does it?"

This woman was too good for the glowering, imperious Spathfoy, of that Dante was certain.

"Good morning, Hester. You must lead on before I'm reduced to devouring Lady Joan's boots."

The ladies exchanged a look, confirming that idle banter was not one of Dante's strengths. The children, Dante was informed, were settling in nicely, Miss Hartwell was taking a tray in her room, and Mr. MacMillan would appreciate a moment of Mr. Hartwell's time after breakfast.

Dante did not understand the niceties of formal address, he wasn't sure where the honorables stopped and the plain misters began, but his grasp of management principles was solid, and this small, busy woman in green was clearly the hostess's aide-de-camp. He was careful to seat Joan beside her as a result, and took the seat across from the countess for himself.

Spathfoy, of course, came sauntering in before Dante had enjoyed his first cup of coffee, but the Earl of Arrogance did not turn his gun sights on his sister. He kissed his little countess on the cheek then settled in on Joan's left side.

"So, Hartwell, how did you and Balfour meet?"

While his lordship started in on a prodigious quantity of eggs, Dante endured a predictable inquisition.

"We met in a card game down in Newcastle, when an early storm temporarily stranded us both in the same hotel. Butter, Lady Joan?"

"Please."

Spathfoy's fork paused halfway to this mouth. "On the strength of that one encounter, we're blessed to have you join our family Christmas gathering. That must have been some card game."

A brother was entitled to be protective of his sister, but Dante had the sense Spathfoy's questions would have been equally rude regardless of the context.

"Balfour and I traveled on together to Edinburgh, and found we had some interests in common. We kept in touch and have shared a few meals since. Jam or marmalade, Lady Joan?"

Something was amusing the lady, which suited Dante fine.

"Jam, please. Tiberius, would you like some butter and jam?"

"No, thank you. What were these common interests, Hartwell? Perhaps I share them too."

The countess reached over and appropriated a slice of his lordship's toast, then applied both butter and jam.

"We had a rousing argument regarding child labor, your lordship. Balfour believes any child over the age of ten can be given some quantity of useful work, and while that might be true in a domestic setting, I will not hire a child under the age of thirteen for the mills."

"Seems an arbitrary distinction to me. I was certainly expected to endure a day's labor at my studies by age twelve."

Eton was not easy, particularly not for the younger boys. Short rations, bullying, strict discipline, and high academic expectations were the typical reality, or so Dante had heard. And yet, he answered honestly.

"I was permitted to remain at my studies until I was twelve," Dante said. "It seemed only fair I accord other children the same privilege."

"And after age twelve?"

The countess's brows were furrowed, while Joan had become fascinated with her toast.

"I went down to the mines, until I became too big at age sixteen. I was fortunate, though, because my father was a senior foreman and well liked by the mine owner. I was kept from the most dangerous work. Many of the other lads were not so lucky."

Mining was the filthiest work on the planet. After Dante had left the mines, six months had passed before his fingernails had been fit to be seen in Polite Society.

"Fascinating. Does mining still interest you?"

The conversation no longer *interested* him, and Joan had barely eaten a quarter of a slice of toast.

"My wealth comes from the mills, your lordship. I will never own any interest in a coal mine, nor will I burn coal in my private residence. Would anybody like more coffee?"

"You have an aversion to good English coal, Hartwell?"

Spathfoy was tenacious, also more rude than Dante

could tolerate with Joan sitting quiet and miserable at her brother's side.

"My lungs object to coal smoke, Spathfoy, and the same sensitivity has presaged the death of many of the fellows I worked with as a lad, though they, of course, went down the shafts until they were too sick to work. My objection is not to good English coal, it's to a constant reminder of the lives given up to get that coal to your cozy English hearth."

Rather than embarrass Spathfoy, Dante's show of temper seemed to mollify the man. He helped himself to a sip of his wife's tea, and sat back.

"My condolences on your losses. Are you up for a ride when we've finished our meal? Balfour keeps guest mounts, and it looks like we might have some sun today."

As if Dante would spend one avoidable minute in this buffoon's presence? And yet, the buffoon likely had money, so Dante did not have the luxury of putting him in his place.

"My man of business has spoken for my time this morning, and I must look in on my sister too. My thanks for the invitation—perhaps another time."

Food should not be wasted, so Dante finished his eggs, bacon, and toast while three feet away, he could feel Spathfoy mentally loading more questions to fire across the table.

"Are you also off to the nursery?" Lady Joan asked.

Well, of course, though mentioning that to Spathfoy hadn't seemed quite politic.

"I am." A man with better manners might linger at the table until his host or hostess showed up—though Balfour could well have already broken his fast.

"I'll go with you."

"But, Joan," Spathfoy said, "I haven't seen you for weeks. Surely you're not leaving the table without catching us up on all the gossip from Edinburgh and Paris?"

She rose when Dante held her chair for her. "Gossip is ill-bred, Tiberius. I'd rather renew my acquaintance with Mr. Hartwell's children, who have at all times and in all company exhibited delightful manners."

Spathfoy ought to have accepted this chiding with some chagrin, though it was no less than he deserved. Instead, the man saluted with his toast—his wife's toast?—and blew his sister a kiss.

Joan appropriated Dante's arm in a rather snug grasp as they quit the breakfast parlor.

"Do you even know where the nursery is?" Dante asked when they were a safe distance from Spathfoy's personal interrogation chamber.

"Upstairs. Nurseries are always upstairs, so girls might spend their entire childhoods, peering out windows at the wide world unavailable to them while they practice deportment and elocution, and write letters to the brothers who are off at public school, playing cricket and making friends."

She churned along beside him, hems swishing with what Dante fancied was a sartorial testament to indignation. The exchange with her brother had upset her, for which Dante was tempted to haul the man up short.

"You escaped the mines, Lady Joan, and they can never make you go back there. You were smart enough to grow too tall."

She led Dante up a set of stairs he had not seen before.

"Tiberius is not generally rude, though he's protective. I'd apologize for him, but there is no apology to be made for the men in my family. The older he gets, the more Tye becomes like my father, and between the two of them—"

While Dante had been deflecting rude questions from dear Tiberius, Joan's breakfast had likely been ruined by fears of impending scandal. She'd probably taken those same fears to bed and held them close through the night.

The stairs took a turning, up to a landing between floors. Dante paused and pulled the lady into his arms.

"Settle, woman. Your brother was having some sport with the new fellow, is all. It's on the curriculum at all the fancy schools and even for those of us who worked the mines. Balfour suggested Spathfoy might be looking to diversify his investments. Those questions were not aimed at ferreting out your secrets, they were intended to unearth mine."

She took the space of a slow breath to accept his embrace, then her forehead dropped to his shoulder.

"I cannot grasp that I could be with child. I simply cannot—"

What she could not grasp was telling her family she was with child—and without a husband.

"Even were you happily married, conceiving a child would have an element of disbelief, my lady." She nuzzled his shoulder, like a kitten missing its mama. "My late wife explained to me that her condition became real to her only when she could see the changes to her body in the mirror."

Joan pulled back. "She examined herself in the mirror *without benefit of clothing?*"

"Clothing is not always a benefit." He had offered marriage to this woman, a shrewd, bold move that would also…put him in bed with her. Unease joined the bacon, eggs, and toast in his belly.

"Clothing is a benefit to me." She strode up the next flight of stairs, her pace moderated, perhaps by the novel notion that for some people, even some female people, clothing served a function other than social armor.

"Joan?"

She paused at the top of the stairs, while Dante remained several steps below her.

"You should tell your brother what's afoot. He's pompous, arrogant, and completely lacking in subtlety, but he cares for you and would take your situation to heart."

"While you would take my situation to the altar, which outcome will do something to solve the problem, while Tiberius would only make it worse. Are you coming, Mr. Hartwell?"

He climbed the last few steps, so he and Joan stood nearly nose to nose.

"What if your brother opposes our match, Joan? Will you choose the cold comfort of marriage to me over the warm regard of your family?"

He could see the gold flecks in her green eyes, could pick up the fragrance of spices and flowers from her person—and that subtle hint of black pepper.

"I do not anticipate that marriage to you would be entirely cold, Mr. Hartwell. In fact, you have assured me it would not be."

His assurances were moot, if Spathfoy took a notion to spoil Lady Joan's matrimonial schemes.

"Dante," he said. "You agreed to call me Dante."
Like the fellow who knew so much about hell.

❦

Asher MacGregor, Earl of Balfour, had not precisely slept late, though he had tarried in bed overlong. His countess yet slumbered there, exhausted by her husband's marital enthusiasms.

And her own.

"Good morning, all," Balfour said to the breakfast room at large, and then, because Spathfoy's dark brows lowered a telling quarter inch, "And, Countess, you are in particularly good looks today."

"You are to call me Hester," the lady said, pushing the teapot up to the head of the table. "My cousin Augusta is married to your brother Ian, my brother Matthew to your sister Mary Frances. Titles at such close range would be silly. The tea is lovely, by the way."

"A blend with some Darjeeling," Balfour said, crossing to the sideboard. Here were all good, delicious things. The footman, one of at least three Donal MacGregors on Balfour's house staff, held up a dish cover so the earl might enjoy steam rising from fluffy eggs. Crispy bacon was piled next to the eggs, kippers sat farther down the sideboard, along with Spanish oranges, ham, and—Balfour had insisted—a steaming bowl of porridge that had apparently appealed to nobody.

The porridge wasn't to feed Scottish national pride, it was to feed Balfour's countess, for Hannah occasionally suffered delicate digestion in the mornings.

A peat fire added to the cozy scents of breakfast, and later today, the Christmas pudding would be set to soak in its brandy bath—provided the kitchen staff remained sufficiently sober to manage a few English Christmas traditions.

Balfour piled his plate with eggs and ham, then served himself a bowl of porridge too, in the name of marital sympathy.

"Shall you go riding with me this morning, Spathfoy?" Balfour asked as he took his place at the head of the table.

"He will not," Hester said, passing the newspaper up to Balfour. "I am concerned my husband is coming down with an ague, and it's beastly cold out."

"Madam, I am in excellent health," her husband retorted, and something about the way Spathfoy smirked at his wife suggested he, too, had started his day with an exhibition of marital devotion.

"No, Tiberius, you are not in excellent health, for at this very table, I witnessed a display of rudeness from you, which could only have been the result of bilious humors. Mr. Hartwell is a guest of my lord Balfour's, and you treated him as if he were a French spy. I have never seen you behave so poorly. What were you about?"

Hester Flynn, formerly Hester Daniels, was young— not much more than twenty—and diminutive. Balfour had not thought her up to Spathfoy's weight, as countesses went, and then he'd seen the lady in action.

She would scold the earl over breakfast, more or less in public, and Spathfoy would be purring like a very large kitten by the time she'd finished dressing him down. Gave a Scottish earl some hope, to see that even Spathfoy—English to his big, fussy bones and in line for a marquessate—could be brought to heel by the woman he loved.

"Have you read the papers, my lady?" Spathfoy asked his spouse.

"No, I have not, because you appropriated them first thing after you sat down. You didn't even offer them to your sister or Balfour's *guest*."

"For an Englishwoman, your wife takes Highland hospitality seriously, Spathfoy. You should be pleased."

Both husband and wife glowered at Balfour and spoke in unison. "Half-English."

For they were both half-English and half-Scottish, while Balfour was...

"Good morning." Hannah MacGregor, Countess of Balfour, came sailing into the breakfast parlor, smiling directly at her husband.

Balfour's heritage lay partly in the Highlands and partly in the New World, but his heart was entirely in the keeping of his American countess. "Good morning, Wife. Spathfoy ate all the eggs. I'm reduced to foraging for porridge, but you're welcome to share what's on my plate."

"Have our recent arrivals been seen yet?" she asked, serving herself a bowl of porridge and taking the place not at the foot of the table, where a proper countess would seat herself, but at Balfour's right elbow.

"They've already eaten," Hester said. "Tiberius ran them off with his inquisition, though Joan put him in his place easily enough." Her comment bore as much affection as reproof.

"Hand me that paper," Spathfoy said, gesturing at Balfour.

Spathfoy was not a bad sort—Hester approved of him, and her judgment was sound—but he was terribly assured of his own consequence, and single-minded to a fault.

"Say please," Balfour replied while Hannah kissed his cheek. "I'm practicing for the coming paternal ordeal, when my children are in need of correction, and I must stifle the impulse to indulge them as my countess indulges me."

"I am going to be sick," Spathfoy informed the ceiling. His manners would not allow him to reach for the paper when in company at table. "My lord Balfour, mine esteemed host, mine pain in locations unmentionable before the ladies, would you please pass the paper down this way, that I might enlighten my wife as to my motives?"

"Better," Balfour said, surrendering yesterday's copy of the Edinburgh daily. "Though your pleading wants polish, Spathfoy."

Hester patted Spathfoy's big paw.

"Read that," Spathfoy said, tapping a finger at a small article on what looked to be the Society pages. "Joan has suffered a blow."

Balfour had passed Lady Joan in the corridor. She had looked magnificent in deep purple, while Dante Hartwell had trundled along obediently beside her. This blow did not appear to have daunted the lady in the least.

Though Hartwell had looked slightly dazed.

"What sort of blow?" Hannah asked as Balfour poured her a cup of tea.

"Edward, Viscount Valmonte, is engaged to Lady Dorcas Bellingham," Hester murmured, studying the newspaper. "I'd say Lady Dorcas is the one enduring a blow. I've always found her charming, while Valmonte is a prancing ninny with artistic pretensions."

"Joan fancied Valmonte," Spathfoy said in the same smug tones somebody at the British War Office had once read a pigeon dispatch reporting Wellington's defeat of Napoleon. "She was forever turning down the room with him, whispering about hems and gussets and fichus. Mama was hopeful Valmonte might offer for Joan."

Balfour left off watching his wife eat porridge, though nobody ate porridge any more appealingly than his Hannah. "Do you even know what a gusset is, Spathfoy?"

"I know what heartbreak is," Spathfoy retorted, chin jutting. "Joan isn't the typical simpering dimwit, she's getting long in the tooth, and her preoccupation with fashion doesn't help matters. Valmonte might have indulged her little hobby, or even encouraged it through the Valmonte family enterprise. Now she's likely scurried north to avoid all the pitying looks."

Lady Joan would not know the first thing about scurrying.

"So naturally," Balfour said, "you had to offend Mr. Hartwell, whose great crime was to share a ride out from Ballater with your sister. Makes perfect sense to me."

Hannah gave him a chiding look, but Spathfoy's wife had declared open season on her earl, and public thrashings were the English way.

"I can't have Hartwell sniffing about Joan's ankles," Spathfoy said. "She's tenderhearted, is Joan, and has her head in the fabric shops to the exclusion of an appreciation for conniving scoundrels. Besides, Hartwell owns *mills*."

This last was offered with such dark foreboding that even making allowances for fraternal concern, Balfour could not remain silent.

"I'm looking into owning a few *mills*," he said. "As much wool as we raise here in Scotland, it seems to me our mills ought to be in Scottish hands."

"But he married those mills," Spathfoy shot back. "Married the owner's daughter, knowing she'd inherit them. A man like that bears watching around a fellow's brokenhearted sister."

"Now that is odd," Hannah said from Balfour's side. "Husband, would you like more tea?"

"No thank you, my love." And because he was a well-trained husband, Balfour served up the rest of the line. "What strikes you as odd?"

"I'm under the impression all three of your brothers married wealth, and yet, Spathfoy doesn't hesitate to break bread with them. Didn't you suggest to me that Spathfoy himself might take a look at investing in these mills? I must have misheard, based on his lordship's comments this morning. Perhaps your brothers would like to invest in those mills if Spathfoy isn't interested."

Spathfoy's countess set the paper aside and patted her husband's hand, while the English earl busied himself with the remaining portion of the eggs growing cold on his plate.

❧

Anger, like excessive height, did not become the woman exhibiting it, but Joan lacked the cleverness to mask either effectively as she and Mr. Hartwell escaped the breakfast parlor.

"Have you brothers, Mister—Dante?"

"I do, twins. They're in school in Edinburgh. A younger sister, too, twelve going on twenty-nine. She terrifies me, rather like spending my holidays among all these titles terrifies me."

They paused to let a footman go hustling by with a bucket of peat.

"The Earl of Balfour is new to his title, relatively," Joan said, because she owed Mr. Hartwell—Dante—as much information as she could convey to him. "He trained as a physician and turned to the New World to ply his profession. I gather he disappeared into the wilderness for several years and was presumed dead."

"Don't."

She had apparently amused her escort. "I beg your pardon?"

"Don't start concocting schemes that see you and your unborn, possibly *unconceived* child, living on bread crusts and bear meat in the northern woods of Canada."

Drat his perceptiveness. "Italy is said to be cheaper and warmer."

They'd reached the nursery, and while the corridor was chilly, part of Joan wanted to tarry with Mr. Hartwell, choosing a destination where she could serve out the sentence for her disgrace.

He took her hand, courtier-fashion. "Bear meat is

disgusting, and much of Italy is hot. If you flee there, no more wool blends or velvet cloaks for you, *signorina*."

Joan took the space of a silly kiss to her knuckles to comprehend that Mr. Hartwell was teasing her—mostly. "You've never eaten bear meat."

"And you should never have to."

The moment was sweet, and put Tiberius and his infernal meddling at a slight, much-needed distance.

"Did you come to play marbles?" Charlie had opened the door to the nursery suite, and stood peering up at them. Her hair was in one tidy braid, her pinafore clean. At the sight of her, something in Joan's insides turned over.

I might even now be carrying a daughter. Mr. Hartwell's word choice came to mind, for the notion was, indeed, *terrifying*.

"Good morning, beloved child," Mr. Hartwell said in Gaelic, lifting his daughter to his hip. "I smell bacon, toast, and mischief. Have you broken your fast?"

"We did. A footman named Donal brought it, and the nursery maid—her name is Our Daisy—says Donal is cheeky but quick, so the food is still hot when it comes up to us from the kitchen. Did you know we'll have a bunny here in the nursery next week when Fiona comes to see her family? Did you know Lord Balfour's family used to take in paying guests here? Did we have to pay to visit?"

We, us, we.

"A guest in any house is expected to repay his host's hospitality with excellent manners and a future invitation, not money. Laddie, what are you reading?"

Phillip sat at a table positioned to take advantage of

the window's natural light, while a short, plump, red-haired nursery maid sprang to her feet from a reading chair near the hearth. Peat was burned here too—had that been at Mr. Hartwell's request?

"Down to the kitchen with you, miss," Mr. Hartwell said. "Grab yourself a cup of tea."

Our Daisy bobbed a curtsy and slipped away, probably to share that cup of tea with the cheeky, quick footman.

Joan took a chair at the table, envying Daisy the innocence of her assignation.

Mr. Hartwell sat as well, but rather than read to his son, something Joan's father had been known to do with his children long, long ago, he instead asked Phillip about the book. Soon the boy was prattling on about breeds of sheep, and which ones were big, which ones woolly.

"Do you suppose you could draw them, these breeds of sheep?" Mr. Hartwell asked.

"He could," Charlie replied, dipping her finger in a jar of honey on the breakfast tray. "Our Daisy showed us where the paper and pencils were, and even the pastels."

"Charlene Brodie Hartwell." Her papa took her finger and wiped it off on a linen napkin. "You are a *guest* here."

The child's expression was comical, and easily read. Joan could all but taste the pleasurable sweetness of the honey Charlie had anticipated.

"Sorry, Papa. C'mon, Phillip. Let's draw some sheep. I want wings on mine, and a horn, like a unicorn."

As the children scrambled off to assemble supplies

on the floor before the blazing hearth, an argument ensued about what arrangement of horns would best suit flying sheep.

"Did you love their mother?" Joan asked, for Mr. Hartwell surely loved his children.

He lifted a covering quilted in the MacGregor red-and-green plaid from a plain white teapot, and peered into the pot. "Fancy a cup?"

"Please."

He served her a cup of warm, weak, milky tea sweetened with honey, and while Joan appreciated the solicitude and the sustenance, she also understood that Mr. Hartwell was stalling.

"I loved Rowena, and it might relieve your fears to know she loved me, after her fashion."

Nothing would relieve Joan's fears.

"My parents love each other 'after their fashion,' which is often loud, dramatic, and unhappy. In fairness to them, the unhappy part grew much worse after my brother Gordie died."

"I'm sorry you lost a brother."

So was Joan. Gordie had had charm, and not the superficial ballroom variety. He could be a selfish lout too, of course, but he'd also had the ability to make even his awkward, too tall, younger sister feel like the most important person in his world.

For a few minutes at a time.

"Tell me about your wife, Mr. Hartwell."

"My first wife," he said, rummaging about on the breakfast tray. Before the hearth, the children had quieted down as the serious business of drawing winged sheep got under way.

"Ro was a scrapper," Mr. Hartwell said, his tone wistful and affectionate. "It took several years to understand what she was about. I'm not one for noise and rumpus. I like an orderly existence with a certain amount of routine. Ro kept things stirred up, and I realized, eventually, she mostly wanted to know I was paying attention. Charlie takes after her in this regard, or maybe many women do because men leave them little choice."

Was that what Mama's great rows had been about, making sure Papa noticed her?

How could one not notice the Marchioness of Quinworth?

"How did you meet your wife?"

He applied a dollop of butter to a thick slice of toast. "My father was a foreman in her father's mine. I would have been far beneath her notice, of course, but then came a fire."

"You rescued her from a fire? How romantic." And here he was again, offering to rescue Joan.

"I did no such thing. Their big, fancy house burned to the ground, and while Darrell Shatner had insurance for his mines and mills and even his railway cars, he had no insurance on that house or its contents."

The tea was very good, and just the right balance between bland and sweet. "So you rescued your lady from poverty?"

"Hardly." He drizzled honey on the buttered toast, a slow, careful operation punctuated by a squabble from the hearth over who got to use the green pastel. "To appearances, the fire was nothing more than an inconvenience to Shatner. He had another house, in

Edinburgh, and a fellow who owns mines and mills is hardly in straitened circumstances."

Nonetheless, Joan was convinced that in some regard, Mr. Hartwell had rescued somebody. "And yet, this fire saw you married to the man's daughter."

He studied his toast and added a touch more honey. "Not directly. Shatner's wife had long since died, but he'd kept her jewelry for Rowena. He was convinced we could find those jewels in the ruins that had been his house. I'd come up from the mines and was helping my father in the foreman's office. We organized volunteers to search the mess for the master's jewels, sifting through the rubble and ash as if looking for gold."

Cleaning a hearth of a day's ashes was a messy enough undertaking. "I can't image it was enjoyable work."

"And old Shatner knew the men would do it for free, too, up to a point. They wanted his favor, and wanted the chance to slip a stray earbob into a pocket. Eventually, though, they gave up. A man must feed his family before he feeds his ambitions."

"You did not give up."

He passed her the piece of toast.

"We Scots are sentimental, though we're not given to the noisy verbal flights of you English. Had Shatner been unable to pass that jewelry on to his daughter, he would have felt like a failure as a father. I did not stop searching, and eventually, I found the damned jewelry, including a slightly melted version of Mrs. Shatner's wedding ring. I suspect, in hindsight, that single piece was the point of the entire endeavor."

Joan took a bite of toast. The bread was no longer

warm, but the butter and honey were a perfect counterpoint to its crispness. Damn Tiberius for disrupting breakfast, anyway.

"Go on."

"My tenacity recommended me to Shatner, though I was too big to be of use down in the mines. My father suggested I might be helpful in the mills, and by God, I made myself indispensable."

"You became the son Mr. Shatner never had." For powerful men were much taken with their sons.

"Oh, I did better than that," he said ruefully. "I became the son he'd lost to smallpox ten years earlier. Damned old fool didn't hold with vaccination. Phillip is named for the uncle he'll never know."

Without doubt, Charlie and Phillip had been vaccinated, as had Joan.

She took another crunchy, contemplative bite of toast. "And Miss Shatner fell in love with you?"

"She resented the hell out me, for she fully intended to run those mills when her father stepped aside. She might use foremen and stewards and crew chiefs to do it, but Rowena loved those mills."

"You do not love them?"

Joan loved fabric. She loved watching a design emerge from the trial and error of a pencil wandering for hours over a clean page. She loved the way each fabric had its own feel, and specific preferences for dyes and drapes and even seasons of the year.

"I love that my son will never watch his friends cough themselves to death. I love that Charlie can aspire to more than hiring puppets to run her mill upon her papa's death."

What did Dante Hartwell consider *more* than doing a man's job in a man's world, however indirectly?

"And yet, you loved your wife."

"We learned to appreciate each other. Shatner left her the mills in trust, provided she married me, otherwise the mills would have gone to me directly. He saw what Rowena did not. She and I were a good team. I had know-how and the expected gender for running the mills. She had ambition and shrewdness, and the mills benefited."

Joan finished the toast only to find another perfectly buttered, honey-sweet slice passed to her. "This led to love?"

"She wanted children. We were young, and fighting is both exhausting and in some regards exhilarating, for some. I would have said we entertained a proper respect and affection for each other, but then one morning, in the middle of another rousing argument over how much debt the mills ought to carry, I noticed that my wife's face was thinner."

Fashion favored a full figure on a woman, with her waist cinched to make her bosom look more generous, and yet, Mr. Hartwell had noticed his wife's face.

"You will tell me the rest of it," Joan said gently because she had the sense this tale was seldom, if ever, recited.

"I at first attributed the change to maturation, to being run ragged by the children, the business, entertaining…but my wife was unwell. She'd hidden it—we had separate quarters—and then she'd told me it was fatigue, but fatigue does not strip the very flesh from a woman's bones and take the light from her eye.

When I accepted that my wife would not recover, I also realized I would lose somebody I loved."

"I hope she did not suffer." Except Rowena Hartwell would have suffered terribly, to have come to the same realization about her husband, and know that their time together was over all too soon.

"She left the mills to me to manage in every regard, though eventually, I'm to pass one to Charlie and one to Phillip. I took that as an indication that my sentiments were returned. She was Scottish."

And thus sentimental, but not loquacious with it.

Joan finished the tea and toast, much restored by the breakfast she'd been served from the nursery tray, and in some regard, fortified by the tale Mr. Hartwell had served up with it.

When the maid returned, Joan sent Mr. Hartwell off to meet with his man of business, while she repaired to the floor before the hearth, there to learn all she could about sheep who had the claws of a lion, the horn of a unicorn, and the wings of a dragon.

Eight

"TIME FOR A TRIP TO THE KITCHENS," HECTOR announced from the nursery door. A petite white-capped nursery maid, napping in a rocking chair, gave a start. From the floor before the hearth, Lady Joan, Charlie, and Phillip looked up at him with expressions suggesting they'd been expecting somebody else.

"My drawing is almost done," Charlie said. "May I show it to you?"

The girl was on her manners, probably as a function of being in new surroundings, or maybe because Lady Joan was here, sprinkling sweetness and fairy dust on all and sundry.

"Later we'll have an art show," Margaret said, wedging past Hector.

And what a blow that was. Margaret didn't believe in lacing herself tighter than perdition, and preferred the old-fashioned country stays to the modern variety. Her female attributes were thus in soft, abundant evidence as she squeezed through the doorway and into the nursery.

"Good morning, children!" Margs said. "The cook

is making the Christmas pudding today, and that means every member of the household must give the batter a stir, especially you weans."

"Everybody? Does that mean Papa, too?" Phillip asked, replacing pastel chalks in their box, ordered from brightest to darkest.

"Everybody," Lady Joan replied, neatly stacking the drawings. "That's the tradition."

"English tradition," Hector said, extending a hand down to the lady. "In Scotland, we don't emphasize Christmas as much as we try to prepare for the New Year."

Lady Joan put her hand in his, a slim, pale hand sporting not a single freckle. She rose easily, nearly matching him for height, and set the drawings on the mantel, face out.

"How fortunate, then, that we shall have the benefit of both traditions this year." Her smile was pleasant, her tone entirely civil, and Hector nearly hated her for it.

"Come along." Margaret waggled her fingers at the children, while Hector endured the knowledge he was being ignored—again. "Lady Balfour says the servants like to sing when they're mixing up the pudding, and you two both have such strong voices."

"Especially me!" Charlie grabbed her aunt's hand. Phillip was slower, looking around for a place to store the box of pastels. Lady Joan took the box from him before Hector had the chance, and put it on the mantel.

"We can draw more when you're done in the kitchen, Phillip," she said. "You were making great progress on your dragon." Slow progress, no doubt. Phillip was a plodder, and Hector had sympathy for all plodders.

"Shall you come with us, Lady Joan?" Hector asked. She might be English, and a distraction Hector's employer could not afford, but, to Hector's eyes, she could use a few servings of pudding, for all that.

"Let's fetch Mr. Hartwell. His children will enjoy having him take part in the merriment. I'm sure Balfour and even Spathfoy will put in an appearance."

Charlie's happy voice faded as Margaret and the children left for the kitchen. A cool draft from the hallway cut through the nursery's peaty coziness.

"You refer to your own brother by his title, my lady?"

Lady Joan appeared to consider Charlie's drawing, a fanciful amalgamation of wings, fangs, horns, and God knew what in every color of the rainbow.

"Of course—also by his given name and even his nickname. He answers to all of them, unless he's absorbed with some problem on the estate, and then he answers not at all. I think you know the type?"

She sent the merest glance in the direction of the nursery maid, who was studying the fire as if a pot of gold might be contained therein.

That glance was a rebuke to a mere man of business who would pick a fight with a proper lady before the help—a deserved rebuke, at least in part. And yet, Hector presumed to offer the lady his arm, which she took with easy grace.

"I'm protective of him," Hector said when he'd intended to maintain a stony silence through four stories of elegant Highland decor. "If it weren't for Dante Hartwell, my family would still be freezing on the coast, living on mackerel, kelp, and stubbornness."

Lady Joan smelled good, all female spiciness with a hint of something expensive. Margaret, by contrast, smelled like vanilla and common sense.

"Protectiveness can be smothering, Mr. MacMillan, all the more so for being well intended. I'm only a female, what can Mr. Hartwell possibly have to fear from me?"

She wasn't pretending they were making small talk, for which he accorded her a few grudging points.

"He has everything to fear from you. You sport a passel of wealthy, titled English family at your back. They will not understand. They will stand against him, and Dante deserves better than that."

Better than you.

That was her cue to drop his arm, stick her sniffy nose in the air, and beat him down the corridors with lectures on presumption and knowing one's place.

She patted his arm. "Margaret needs to see this protective side of yours, Mr. MacMillan. Making allies of the children is clever, and I can understand that Mr. Hartwell might take some winning over, but when the lady herself doesn't know she's being pursued, it's time to reevaluate your tactics."

"I'm not pursuing her." Hadn't dared.

"The holidays are a fine time to win a woman's notice," Lady Joan went on, as if Hector hadn't spoken. "And while your Scottish heart probably winces at all of our English silliness, you can work it to your advantage."

"Margaret's not English." And when had he lost control of this discussion, which was to have been about how daft marriage between Dante and Lady Joan would be?

"Margaret's not English, but she's a woman much in need of kissing and cosseting, and you're just the fellow to take on that challenge."

Lady Joan did stop then, right where two hallways converged on the balcony leading to the main staircase. She pointed straight up, to some greenery hanging from a crossbeam.

As if pine boughs...

And then she kissed Hector's cheek. "I can be protective too, Mr. MacMillan. This is your only warning."

She sashayed on down the stairs, all purple grace, and while Hector had no idea what she might be warning him about, he did grasp that mistletoe was a fine old English tradition.

❦

Dante had made a sketch of the Balfour family tree, for the MacGregors had managed, repeatedly, to marry English wealth. Balfour himself had married an American heiress less than a year ago, while each of his four siblings had plucked a matrimonial English goose.

Ian MacGregor, the next oldest to Balfour, was married to Augusta, Baroness of Gribbony.

Gilgallon, described by Balfour as the family charmer, had married Augusta's cousin, Eugenia Daniels, another heiress and a beauty.

Connor, the youngest brother, and "whatever the opposite of a charmer is," had married a wealthy

Northumbrian widow, with whom he was hatching up a brood of fat, noisy bairns.

Mary Fran, in addition to being the widow of Spathfoy's late younger brother, had married another of Augusta's cousins, Matthew Daniels, whose substantial assets included nothing less than the personal favor of the Queen and the Prince Consort.

And finally, the youngest of the Daniels cousins, Hester, had the dubious honor of the Earl of Spathfoy for a husband.

The lines on the page crossed and recrossed, forming the sort of genealogical fortress a Highland laird would have been proud to call family— wealthy family.

Lady Joan interrupted Dante's musings, striding into the library—no hesitating on the threshold for her—her purple skirts a-swishing.

"Are you hiding, Mr. Hartwell?"

She was a master at hiding, even in her velvet and snowy lace. Dante ever so casually folded the family tree in half, so the various golden apples dangling from it were not visible to Joan.

"I'm working. Hector gets frantic when we have to be away from the mills for any length of time, and he knows I'll use the Sabbath to catch up."

"It is Sunday," she said, stopping short of the armchair Dante occupied near the hearth and veering off in the direction of the bookshelves. "The trains won't run. You're not supposed to work on Sundays."

He liked the look of her, wandering around Balfour's high-ceilinged library. She was made for lofty spaces, for places that flattered her height.

"You work on Sunday, madam."

Her ladyship left off studying a portrait of some Highlander of old directly over the crackling fire. A fierce old fellow who yet had a twinkle in his eye.

"I don't work, ever. This is a point of contention between my family and me. I'm a lady, and worse than that, a lady blessed with a papa who thinks I'm to be ornamental."

She was very ornamental. "I assume this papa will arrive on one of those trains you're so worried about."

"This painting needs a good cleaning. Peat smoke will ruin it in another generation or two."

"Why don't you clean it?" As soon as he'd made the suggestion, Dante realized that if Joan were busy in the library throughout the day, he'd have to work elsewhere if he wanted to be productive.

"I *could* restore this portrait. I studied in Paris for a few months." She was lost in the painting, which prompted Dante to rise and take a closer look at it himself.

"You could get started today, assuming the supplies were on hand. Restoring the laird here would give you something to occupy yourself."

Because she needed that.

"I don't seek merely to be busy, Mr. Hartwell."

"You're fretting. Being busy can help the fretting times pass more easily." Though it had never particularly helped Dante, not when *busy* meant closeting himself with Hector's blasted reports.

"I'm not fretting. I'm fetching you down to the kitchen, so you can have a turn stirring the plum pudding. The servants are all gathered there, along with the children, my relations, and Balfour's family."

What was she looking for in that mahogany desk?

"Balfour's doing the English this year?"

"He's doing the hospitable. Tiberius likes Balfour, and that's no small endorsement."

Dante was more inclined to think of Spathfoy's blessing as a millstone for a Scottish earl.

"What are you searching for?" Besides a husband.

"This." She held up a silver-handled quizzing glass. "That painting isn't uniformly dirty. It's darker near the bottom, and probably has more cracks near the top, where the temperature has varied more. The project wants study before I approach Balfour about it."

"You'd commend me to the mayhem in the kitchen all on my lonesome?" Not that he'd set foot in a noisy, crowded, tipsy kitchen without her. "Come with me, for Balfour will have punch and sweets to ensure we spoil our digestion."

Then too, it couldn't hurt for dear Tiberius to grow accustomed to the sight of his sister on Dante's arm.

She slipped the quizzing glass into some secret female pocket in her velvet skirts. "Don't talk to me of spirits. I know now why the fussiest ladies never partake of strong spirits."

"They abstain because they've never faced winter in a Scottish croft. Spirits in moderation never hurt anybody."

He'd said the wrong thing, for this time, when she perused the old fellow in his fancy kilt, she blinked furiously.

"Joan, I'm sorry. I did not mean to judge you." Though it was a dicey proposition, Dante put a hand on her shoulder. Tension vibrated through her, or indignation.

Or hurt.

"I *wish* I had a familiarity with strong spirits," she said as the first tear trickled down her cheek. "I wish I had a strong head for them, in fact, because then that dratted man would not have been able to, to—"

Dante pulled her into his arms, where she fit so well, and so reluctantly.

"Sooner or later, everybody drinks too much. I get the sense that much of what we call a university education is an exercise in teaching the sons of the aristocracy to hold their liquor. That strong head you're so envious of takes years to acquire, and some never do."

From the same secret pocket, she produced a square of silk, white with green trim. "When will I remember?"

Women should always wear velvet, for when a man stroked his hands over a woman clad in velvet, he was soothed and aroused in equal measure. "When will you remember what?"

"When will I recall what *happened*. I got so muddled, and when I woke up, he was sprawled on top of me, my skirts in complete disarray, the candles guttering, and nothing made any sense."

Dante kissed her temple, though she wasn't Charlie, that her hurts and indignities could be made better with a kiss.

"Nothing made sense because you were still tipsy. The drink can take a full day to leave your system, and more days before your body entirely rights itself." That assumed she hadn't been drugged as well as inebriated.

"The drink is not in my system now, and I still can't make sense of what happened. I don't recall what I said. I don't recall what I did. Not the half of it, only bits and pieces that are of no help."

He let her go, because her indignation was doing more to dry her tears than his embrace—or his kisses.

"You might never recall more of that night than you do right now," he said, pulling the fireplace screen back and tossing another square of peat onto the flames. Joan held out her little handkerchief to him, for handling peat was an untidy business.

"Your handkerchief will get dirty, my lady."

She lifted one eyebrow, looking much like her lordly brother. "A bit of dirt will wash, Mr. Hartwell. Most fabrics know the difference between a smudge and a permanent stain."

Though Society, of course, did not, and neither did Lady Joan. Dante took the bit of silk, rubbed the dirt from his fingers, and stuffed her handkerchief in his pocket.

"Don't focus on trying to recall what you said or did. Let it come back to you on its own. If you were drinking absinthe, then the scent of it might trigger some memories, a snippet of conversation might, a whiff of his shaving soap. You can't stitch this down and put a perfect hem on it, Joan."

The library door opened, revealing none other than dear Tiberius, but of all things, the man had an infant affixed to his shoulder.

A smiling infant sporting a head of bright red hair.

"There you are. My countess insists that I join the riot in the kitchen, which means you two are subject to the same decree."

Joan was across the library in four swishy strides.

"Give me that baby, Tiberius. You'll feed him sweets until he has a howling bellyache, then feign innocence and mutter darkly about women who are overly indulgent to their children. What was Hester thinking, putting him in your care on such an occasion?"

"While you'll feed him marzipan, and not let me have him back until Whitsun?"

"Too late," Dante said as Joan settled the child on her hip and swept from the room. "Your son has been taken captive, and you might as well surrender with good grace—unless you must be the first to stir the Christmas pudding?"

Joan went on her way, her prize in her arms. His lordship's expression drained of the puzzled wistfulness with which he'd watched Lady Joan make off with the infant and filled with characteristic disapproval.

"You were alone in here with my sister, Hartwell."

The remaining weeks of the house party loomed with the never-ending dimensions of the new boy's first semester at public school.

"Spathfoy, you insult me, your sister, the holidays, and the very books with your innuendo. Balfour has offered the library as a place I might work and meet with my man of business. Lady Joan came to invite me to the merriment in the kitchen, exactly as you did— more or less—and she lingered to inspect that portrait over the hearth."

Spathfoy turned his scowl onto the hapless laird twinkling over the fireplace.

"Lady Joan says the painting is in need of cleaning," Dante went on, "and she might undertake the project herself. If you doubt my facts, ask her to turn out her pockets, and you'll find a quizzing glass among her effects."

Joan would find her temper, did Spathfoy ask her to turn out her pockets like some naughty child, and she'd direct that temper at her infernal brother.

"My apologies, Hartwell, but Joan is not in good spirits, and she might turn to an unlikely source of comfort. If you think my regard for her is overbearing, my father is positively backward when it comes to my sisters."

At least Spathfoy grasped that Joan was in need of comfort, though it had apparently escaped his lordship's comprehension that a man with two motherless children knew plenty about offering solace to those afflicted with heartache.

"Is your backward papa due on the next train?"

Spathfoy was a big fellow of solid dimensions and strong features. Women would call him handsome, with his dark hair and green eyes. Men would say he had plenty of muscle, and Hector attributed significant wealth to him as well.

And yet for a fleeting moment, Spathfoy had looked haunted.

"Quinworth will be here tomorrow, with my other two sisters—*and my mother*. If you know what's good for you, you'll develop pressing business down in Aberdeen, and absent yourself for at least the next week."

His lordship followed Joan from the library, leaving Dante to wonder if that admonition was Spathfoy's idea of a friendly warning—or a threat.

❧

Hale Flynn, Marquess of Quinworth, hated Christmas. He hated the foolishness of eating like a market hog when the weather was too foul to allow a man to regularly ride his acres. He hated the social deception of claiming to be glad to see people whose names he'd happily forgotten. He hated eggnog. He hated endless renditions of Handel, and this latest business of whacking down entire trees to dress them up like debutantes at an engagement ball...

Sheer buffoonery.

But he loved his marchioness, and if Deirdre, Lady Quinworth, wanted to spend the holidays draped in plaid and harassing their children, then Hale was pleased to oblige her.

"Damned trains get smellier every year," he remarked to his son. He handed Lady Quinworth down from the sleigh, and watched bemused as she nearly tackled Spathfoy into the snow.

"Tiberius, you naughty boy! I was expecting to see you at the train station, and instead you send poor Balfour, who should not be away from his lady if it can possibly be helped. Where is my grandson, and, Quinworth, why are you standing about in this dreadful cold? Take me inside and do not think of disappearing into the game room until you've done the pretty for Lady Balfour."

Quinworth winged his arm, the only response

DeeDee needed when she was in one of her flutters. Spathfoy had the slightly dazed look so many fellows wore in DeeDee's presence, and the faint fatigue of a man parenting a small child.

"Hello, sir." Spathfoy said to his father.

"Hah. Warn your sisters that her ladyship and I are on the premises, and pray for an early spring. I don't know whose idea this infernal house party was, but if I find *him*, he'll have much to answer for."

Spathfoy had his mother's sweet, winning smile, though he was more parsimonious about sharing it. "Happy Christmas to you, too, sir. And might I say, you and Mama are in great good looks."

DeeDee preened, and well she might. For a woman of a certain age, she showed to excellent advantage. Tall, red-haired, and formed by a generous and loving God, she was more Christmas gift than any one marquess deserved in a lifetime.

"Save your flattery for your wife, Tiberius," she said. "Your father doesn't tolerate the cold as easily as you young fellows do." She ran a maternal eye over Spathfoy's knees, in evidence because the boy was wearing a kilt—the Flynn tartan, of course.

Inside Balfour house, Quinworth endured more greetings, to the point that a near crowd had gathered in the entrance hall. Most of the fellows were in kilts, and many of the assemblage seemed to know one another. Hester greeted her father-in-law cheerfully—as well she had better—while DeeDee swanned about and kissed cheeks left and right.

"Who's the solemn little fellow?" Hale asked his daughter-in-law, for the petite Lady Spathfoy was a canny sort and a worthy ally. A small boy peered through the banisters of the balcony in the time-honored tradition of eavesdropping children.

"Mr. Hartwell's son, Phillip. A shy lad, likes his books and is completely overshadowed by his younger sister."

"Younger sisters can be the very plague," Quinworth muttered. "Just ask your husband."

"Dora, Joan, and Mary Ellen will all be down in a moment," Hester said—she was also the informal sort, which likely caused Spathfoy no end of consternation. "Dora and Mary Ellen were on the noon train. You made good time out from the station."

They'd made good time because DeeDee loved to feel the wind in her hair—also because the lady needed to dote on her children and grandchildren regularly, and brought a certain urgency to her activities.

"I assume you and Tiberius are managing adequately?" Quinworth asked. Balfour had decorated his home in the English style, with greenery hanging from the rafters, cloved oranges dangling here and there, and wreaths on the doors and in the windows.

All in the tasteful excesses called for by the season, of course.

Hester was not fooled. She waited until Quinworth had visually inspected every corner and cranny of the entrance hall before she deigned to answer.

"I might well be again in anticipation of a blessed event, your lordship. Tiberius wants to wait until after the holidays to share the news with her ladyship."

Tiberius was waiting, no doubt, because DeeDee had buried a son, and her nerves should not be tested unnecessarily with good tidings that could turn out to be no tidings at all.

"The little fellow wants to come down," Quinworth said. "Where is his nurse?"

The longing in the child's eyes was discernible at twenty paces. He'd have imprints on his pale cheeks from the banister railings. As Quinworth and Hester watched, a blond woman no longer in the first blush of youth knelt beside the boy. She wasn't dressed as a nurse, and yet...

"Joan needs to take that young lady's wardrobe in hand," Quinworth muttered. "Though I doubt her ladyship or Dora and Mary Ellen will allow her the time."

"That is Mr. Hartwell's sister Margaret," Hester said. "We're finding her very agreeable company."

Of course. Everybody was agreeable for the first few days of a house party, and then the flirting and overimbibing and overwagering began. Miss Agreeable Company took the boy by the hand, but the child cast a longing glance over his shoulder.

DeeDee had once confided to Quinworth that her secret for managing any gathering was to look about the room and find the person who seemed the most out of place, the most uncomfortable, and attach herself to that person until others had joined their conversation.

Other children were in the entrance hall, darting between the adults, adding to the racket, and nearly tripping the servants taking winter wraps and offering hot cider to the new arrivals.

Quinworth tipped his chin to get the lad's attention. The boy stopped long enough that Quinworth could wink at him and earn a smile for that breach of lordly decorum, before the child was dragged away from the balcony.

DeeDee's smile connected with Quinworth's gaze in the next instant. Not her "The Marchioness of Quinworth" smile, but the smile belonging to Hale Flynn's wife, the mother of his children, and his friend.

Sometimes his only friend. She blew him a kiss from hands still clad in smart green gloves, for DeeDee always remembered what Hale had tried so often to forget: he, too, had buried a son.

❧

"Your sketch pads are stacked willy-nilly, you've arrived here two days before the rest of us with no explanation, and your lady's maid begged me for an extended holiday at her sister's—also without explanation."

Mama turned with military precision before the hearth in Joan's bedroom, for nobody could make skirts swish like Mama in a taking.

"Which holiday I gave her," Mama went on, "with pay, when in thirty years of service to the Flynn family, Bertha McClintock has never once mentioned a sister."

"Bertha has two sisters," Joan said, resisting the compulsion to tidy up her stack of sketch pads. "One named Joan, like me, the other named Deborah." Also a brother, though he was a disgraceful sot, according to Bertha.

Like Joan?

Mama picked up the wool plaid blanket folded across the foot of Joan's bed, shook it out and refolded it. The Marchioness of Quinworth was tall enough that she could fold most blankets without them touching the carpet.

Joan was an inch taller—the last time she'd allowed herself to be compared to her ladyship.

"Joan Flynn, if you think I won't ferret out what has gone amok, you're daft. Tiberius is keeping his own counsel, but if I ask him to send a few wires, I will soon have every detail of whatever disgrace you're about to bring down on this family."

When Mama was upset, her burr thickened, and she was nigh unintelligible now. That she'd press Tye into service rather than make Papa send her wires was part of the curious dance of consideration and selfishness that had always characterized Mama's dealings with his lordship.

"I grew bored in Edinburgh," Joan said, taking a seat on a window bench. "Everybody repairs to the country for the holidays, the Highlands are beautiful in winter, and I took a notion to travel on. Bertha fell ill and asked to turn back at such a small way station, I could not hire another lady's maid."

"And Miss Hartwell befriended you. I heard your bletherin' at supper, and not a soul contradicted you, but, Joan, I am your mother."

Mama tended to recall this when she was in want of other distractions.

"Must you make drama where none exists?" Joan asked, her tone as condescending as any the marquess himself might have employed. "Maids sicken, and they take winter journeys into dislike. Bertha is not young, and she does have family to the south."

No lies yet, though they were in the offing, like wolves shivering in the undergrowth, waiting to tear Joan's tissue of deceptions to shreds.

Mama settled onto the bench beside Joan in a cloud of lilac scent and green velvet fashion that went beautifully with her Celtic coloring.

"I am not interrogating you because I am bored, young lady, though after the past few years, I can understand you might judge me thus. As a parent, I have shortcomings, for which I am sorry." Her tone suggested she was more irritated than sorry, and yet, any admission of fault from Mama was a startling development. "Your trunks arrived two days ago, Joan. Most of your dresses are not yet pressed, some aren't even hung up."

Mistake. Every criminal supposedly made some minor mistake out of a suppressed desire to be thwarted in their wicked activity and brought to justice. Joan always tended to her own clothing when she traveled—something Bertha had never once objected to—but now Joan had allowed her mother to see the disarray in her bedroom.

"I'm letting my dresses air. Anything that travels by train needs to air." Joan rose but kept her steps measured rather than support the idea that she was fleeing from her own mother. "Take a sniff. Coal smoke is the very devil to get out of winter fabrics, and yet, I don't think Lady Balfour would like me flying my dresses from the battlements."

She held out the sleeve of her purple velvet dress, the one she'd worn on the train, the only one that might still carry a hint of coal smoke. Mama leaned in and took a whiff, as if in the manner of a wild creature, she might divine entire itineraries from a scent alone.

"This is such a pretty dress," Mama murmured, fingering the lacy cuff. "And shows to such advantage on you. If I needed a few small adjustments to my dinner dresses, could you make them without mentioning anything to your father?"

What on earth?

"Of course, Mama. I always have my sewing basket with me." Also her embroidery and her knitting. Those last had arrived with her trunks.

"I'm off to find your sisters," Mama said, rising. "Dora muttered something about wanting to learn to play hockey, for God's sake. I cannot rely on her father to curb such a notion either. He grows so restless when he cannot be regularly on horseback."

Such a comment might have been a criticism two years ago, but something had shifted in the way Joan's parents dealt with each other.

"Are you worried about Papa? He seems fine to me." As irascible as ever, without intending any real harm.

"He's humoring me," her ladyship said, hanging Joan's purple dress in the enormous wardrobe across from the fireplace. "We're trying, you know. Trying to learn how to get along when neither of us has a natural talent in that direction."

Right next to the purple dress, Mama hung a green brocade.

Joan considered what Mr. Hartwell had said, about conflict providing a certain excitement in a marriage and gaining a spouse's notice.

"You want to pay attention to each other," Joan

suggested, "but without being a bother. I can see how Papa might present a challenge in this regard."

Much less Mama, who let all and sundry know she was the brains behind the overflowing Quinworth family coffers, who'd left her husband for two years without a backward glance, and who thrived on gossip and social drama.

And Mama could not fathom why Papa spent so much time out on the land, in the company of sheep, horses, and fresh air.

Between the purple and green came an umbery brown that bordered on orange, the resulting palette sufficiently disquieting that Joan had to look away.

"I forget that my girls are no longer girls," her ladyship said. "You've hit it exactly: I want to attend to my husband, and not be a bother, and yet..." She trailed off, her gaze on the dresses in the wardrobe. She fingered the sleeve of the purple that looked so good on Joan.

"Whatever is wrong, Joan, I hope you know that your family will always love you. I have not been the most devoted mother, but I am loyal. Your father and siblings are too."

Mama kissed her cheek—Mama must kiss at least a dozen cheeks a day—and swished from the room, leaving Joan amid her dresses, sketch pads, knitting, and embroidery.

The time had come to put away her things, though, because no matter how many times Joan flipped through the pages of her sketch pads, no matter how long or hard she stared into the bottom of her empty trunk, the drawings she treasured most—the drawings she'd taken with her to have tea with Edward Valmonte and his mother—were no longer in her possession.

Like Mr. Hartwell's wife, looking in the mirror and seeing a form changing before her very eyes, Joan's inability to lay her hands on her sketches was proof, like nothing else had been, that Joan was, indeed, facing scandal.

When she'd hung her dresses up in their proper order, from bright to dark, and stacked her sketch-books in date order, and refolded the blanket at the foot of the bed in exact quarters, she went in search of Mr. Hartwell.

Nine

"AND HERE'S THE BANK DRAFT FOR THE INSURANCE premium," Dante said, adding the document to a stack on Hector's side of the desk. "Wouldn't want to forget that."

"God, no. The ghost of Mr. Shatner would haunt us for a certainty," Hector said, rising. "At least the sun's out. Shall I offer to take Margaret and the children into town with me?"

The sun was out, though it wouldn't be for long. Such was the reality of daylight and darkness in the depths of a Highland winter.

"If you take the children, the nursery maids will remember you in their prayers for years."

Dante rose too, because he'd spent the entire morning sitting behind the mahogany acreage of Balfour's estate desk, in hopes a certain nervous Englishwoman might come to further inspect a portrait.

Or a prospective spouse.

"They've even hung mistletoe in here," Hector said, an assessing gaze on the greenery overhead.

"At a gathering that's mostly family, there's little

harm in it," Dante replied, taking a place near the fire's warmth. "The MacGregor ladies are a comely lot."

"Fertile too," Hector murmured, taking a swig from his flask. A bachelor sharing a roof with a passel of babies, and not one but two women in anticipation of a blessed event, was entitled to his fortification.

And that tally did not include Lady Joan.

"The Quinworth daughters aren't hard to look on either," Dante observed, though Joan was clearly the best of the lot. Too bad she was burdened with Spathfoy for a brother.

"So why aren't they married?" Hector asked. "Their papa's a wealthy English marquess, and those women could have married into the best families in Europe—a German prince or an Italian count, at least. And yet, they're here, threatening to learn to play hockey with a lot of kilted heathen."

"German princes and Italian counts are thick on the ground. Kilted heathen with the luxury of time to play hockey have become worse than scarce."

Though why hadn't *any* of Quinworth's comely, well-dowered daughters married?

"I'm off to muster the troops," Hector said, putting his flask away. "Sand that bank draft, and I'll add it to the lot on my way out the door. If we're not back in three days, don't you dare marry that Englishwoman. She's trouble, mark me on this."

"All wives are trouble," Dante countered. "They'd say the same about husbands. Part of the charm of the institution."

Hector let him have the last word—continued employment being a dear privilege, apparently—and headed for the door. It opened before Hector reached it, and Lady Joan moved into the library.

Hector and Joan swung a few steps wide of each other, like predators observing the etiquette of the watering hole.

"My lady."

"Mr. MacMillan."

Nothing more, and yet, hackles had gone up on both sides, which was tiresome when Dante might marry the one and depended daily on the other.

The library door clicked shut, and Joan stopped four paces from the hearth.

"Good morning, my lady." They'd seen each other at meals and in the evening, when the house-party guests gathered in the largest parlor and tried entertain one another. More family would arrive as Christmas came closer, so Dante was biding his time and assessing his prospects.

"Mr. Hartwell."

Joan was quivering with some news, and in a rusty, sentimental corner of his heart, Dante experienced a pang of disappointment, for what could compel her to seek him out again in private, except proof that she was not carrying a child?

"You agreed to call me Dante."

"Dante, then."

She was a lady, and despite her ability to play marbles with the children or bluntly admit her recent folly to a stranger on a northbound train, she would hardly know how to discuss a woman's bodily functions.

And yet, he would not make it easy for her to dismiss him.

He waved a hand toward the painting over the hearth. "Have you come to assess the laird in all his dirt?"

"No. I have come to speak with you."

"Shall we sit?" An Englishman would send a footman for tea, and leave the library door open when he did. Those polite maneuvers would placate propriety and give the lady time to gather her wits, while bringing the temperature in the room down considerably.

Dante had not one drop of English blood in his veins.

Joan seated herself on the sofa, the warmest spot in the room. Dante took the place beside her, uninvited, and waited.

"You know I am in serious difficulties."

"I know you are in fear of scandal. You appear to enjoy good health, you have a comfortable roof over your head, and your pin money would keep most families in haggis, neeps, and tatties handily. What troubles you strikes me more as a challenge than a serious difficulty."

He'd baited her on purpose, because this pale, hands-clasped, red-haired martyr annoyed him on her behalf. Joan should be more like her mother, hurling thunderbolts of audacious charm, and leaving lilac-scented kisses on the cheeks of handsome men twenty years her junior.

Though Dante generally avoided the marchioness and her noisy chatter. Her own husband appeared to do likewise.

"I'm facing a challenge then," Joan said, hands clasped more tightly. "The challenge has become more pressing."

How could a woman be more pregnant? Twins

perhaps? She couldn't know that. He resisted the urge to pry her fingers apart and kiss her knuckles, as if asking for her to hand her troubles into his keeping.

"Tell me." Because a grown woman needed real comfort, not the nursery maid, kiss-it-better variety.

"He has my sketches."

Such torment inhabited those four words, that for Joan, they had to be of greater import than if the conniving bastard had got her with child.

"Explain yourself, my lady. You're not Michelangelo, that your every doodle and scrap of drawing paper can be attributed to you simply on the basis of your style."

Her chin came up, and her green eyes sparked with irritation. "I sign my drawings, of course. I'm proud of them, and they're quite good."

These drawings also had the ability to put the lady back on her mettle.

"Are they naughty drawings?" Though how could Joan execute naughty drawings when she was loath to study even her own unclad form in the mirror?

"They are not naughty. They're dresses, ladies' fashions, and they're brilliant. I wanted to impress him, to talk him into taking on my designs for his house of fashion. I wouldn't get public credit, of course, but everybody would know, sooner or later, and that would be enough."

So Edward Valmonte might be the weasel whom Dante needed to hunt down. Joan probably trusted his lordship from long acquaintance, trust being a necessary predicate to any seduction, and Valmonte had motive for stealing the drawings.

Valmonte's family enjoyed ownership of a

mercantile enterprise for two reasons. The viscountess was of French extraction, and financial practicality in the French was an eccentricity affectionately tolerated by their English neighbors.

The second reason Lord Valmonte could own a house of fashion was that it was considered an artistic undertaking, and his involvement in it that of tolerant patron and dilettante.

While Lady Joan, by virtue of her birth, would content herself with the backhanded credit for her talent given to her through polite—and not entirely kind—innuendo.

Dante ranged an arm along the back of the sofa.

"You're saying the scoundrel who took advantage of you has proof that you were private with him, if proof he wants."

Joan perched on the sofa lady-fashion—her back so straight it did not touch the sofa's upholstery.

"I recall now, sitting beside him before his mother's tea service, wondering if Lady Valmonte would join us—the invitation had come from her—but because I was too eager to show my work to somebody who might appreciate it, I did not wait for her."

"Such a great sin, wanting to share your enthusiasm with somebody who could reciprocate it."

His irony penetrated her fog of self-castigation, for she turned to regard him.

"Is your offer of marriage still open, Mr. Hartwell?" She might have been asking the coal man if he'd come around Tuesday next, the same as he had been for the past twenty years. And yet, her eyes were tormented with the sort of hopeless bewilderment

Dante experienced when the foreman had told him he'd grown too big—too strong?—to work the mines.

"Are you still willing to consummate the union and be a wife in every particular?"

Not that it mattered, for he wasn't about to cast Joan on the mercy of her dim-witted brother, her fluttery mother, or her grouchy father. He wasn't sure he trusted those sisters of hers either.

"Of course. I want children, Mr. Hartwell."

"I'm familiar with the condition, my lady. I mean no offense when I report to you that a husband likes to think of himself as more than simply his wife's captive stud."

The language was crude—and so honest—he wasn't sure she could comprehend his point.

Her chin dipped, her spine remained straight. "You said something the other day, in the nursery, that caught my attention."

His kisses apparently had not. Well, they'd have time to work on that.

"And?"

"You said that couples will sometimes row and spat to gain each other's notice. I think my parents have elevated this practice to a high, noisy, painful art. They've done better lately, but that's how they go on—good patches and rough patches."

Her words reminded him of a comforting truth: Joan Flynn was a bright woman, and nowhere near as self-absorbed as others of her station could be. She took an interest in her surroundings, and wasn't too proud to share her embroidery stitches with Margaret or play marbles with the children.

"I suppose many couples find themselves in a

similar pattern," Dante said, for he and Rowena had played their contentious games for years, though the arrival of children had reduced the volume of the marital noise considerably.

"I don't want us to be among those couples. I want us to be civil, Mr. Hartwell, more than civil, if possible. My family will worry, and I wouldn't want them to think—"

Oh, blast. She'd been doing so well with this honest entreaty routine.

"You don't want them to think that you've chosen beneath yourself out of an aging spinster's desperation, or as a result of a moral lapse. You want them to think that we're smitten with each other."

Honesty was a fine thing, also lowering as hell sometimes.

He took her hand and found it cold.

"Here is the great wisdom of taking me as your spouse, Joan Flynn. I will not judge you for having some pride. I have pride too. I will not judge you for finding yourself in a predicament you didn't see coming. I've landed in predicaments too. We're starting off with honesty between us, and that's no small gift. Assure that the honesty will be ours to keep, and our marriage will fare well enough."

He kissed her fingers then moved closer, slipping his arm around her shoulders.

She unbent slowly, curling down to rest her forehead at his throat. "We're not smitten."

At least she sounded forlorn.

"Smitten is for young fools putting a poetic label on their mating urges. What I want from you, Lady Joan, is a genuine interest in my children and my family.

You'll show Margs how to go on among the tabbies, you'll take Charlie in hand when she's to make her come out. You'll do your best with me and my rough manners and make a gentleman of wee Phillip."

"I can do that. You'll marry me?" She wanted so little in this bargain, while he was probably gaining entrée to any ballroom or house party the length and breadth of the realm.

"I will marry you, but there's one other understanding we need to reach."

She relaxed against him, nearly cuddled into him, her fears apparently relieved. "I can't help my family, but they mostly mean well."

"None of us can help our families, and I mean well when I raise this last topic: I expect fidelity between us. If we're to have a chance of making our marriage a cordial union, then we'll have none of that polite adultery your set finds so congenial."

The quality of her cuddling changed, became considering. "I am not a great proponent of polite adultery, or impolite adultery, if there is such a thing."

There were many ways to trample a wedding vow, though he couldn't expect her to know that.

"Your word, Lady Joan. Not a little slip, not a flirtation that gets out of hand, not a carriage ride that just happens to go nowhere slowly with the curtains pulled shut on the prettiest of summer days."

She patted his lapel. "They propositioned you, didn't they? The same hostesses who'd barely give you their gloved fingers in the receiving line groped you under the table and left notes in the pockets of your cape."

They'd done more than that, revealing themselves

to be a lot of bored, pathetic, aging schoolgirls whose morals would put mongrel dogs to shame.

"We will be loyal and faithful, Joan, or we'll not be married at all."

"We will be loyal and faithful." She kissed him on the mouth, a soft, sweet, unlooked-for gift that boded well for the vows they'd just exchanged. Dante had encircled her with both arms and begun mentally arranging for a special license, when a cold, imperious voice cut across the library from the doorway.

"What the *hell* do you think you're doing, taking liberties with my sister's person?"

❧

Tye hadn't raised his voice for two reasons. First, Balfour's house was rapidly filling with relations, neighbors, friends, and all manner of ears that would eagerly report the news of any Flynn family altercation.

For the Flynn family had been having altercations at house parties for as far back as Tye could recall.

Second, Joan was the one taking most of the liberties.

She was the sister closest to Tiberius in age, the most proper, and the most independent, which meant she was the most like him—and the one he fretted over the most as a result.

"You will not raise your voice at Lady Joan," Hartwell said, standing and assisting Joan to her feet. Then, with a bemused look, he added, "my lord."

Cheeky bastard—cool, cheeky bastard whose manners didn't desert him easily.

And yet, Tye would put the facts before Hartwell anyway, out of simple decency.

"Now see here, Hartwell, I've already explained that Joan has suffered a disappointment, and while no man likes to hear that he's being trifled with, the ladies can't be blamed for finding consolation—"

"Tiberius, please hush." Joan kept her hand in Mr. Hartwell's as she delivered her rebuke. "Mr. Hartwell is not a consolation."

"I'm not?" Hartwell's smile was indulgent, and...*tender*?

Tye did not exactly resent when his countess was right, but the accuracy of her surmises in certain areas did confound him.

"Mr. Hartwell had best not have been providing you consolation, Joan Flynn, or I'll provide him a demonstration of my pugilistic theories. You are the daughter of a marquess, while he...he is a stranger to your family."

The look Joan turned on Hartwell was unreadable. "Mr. Hartwell is not a stranger to me. He is, in fact, a friend. A good friend."

Hartwell nearly preened at this declaration.

"Friends don't compromise each other." Hester would laugh herself silly over that nonsense. She'd gone to great lengths to compromise Tiberius not so long ago.

Hartwell said nothing. He also allowed Joan to keep his hand in hers, of which the lady herself seemed unaware.

Joan's nose tilted up in a posture reminiscent of their mother. "If sitting beside each other compromises two people, then I delight to inform you that your countess has designs on Baron Fenimore."

Fenimore, great-uncle or third cousin or some

Highland relation to the MacGregor's, was older than Arthur's Seat. Hester had spent the evening beside him because he was more likely to nap than bother her with small talk.

"You and Hartwell were *cuddling*," Tye said, having acquired a happily married man's expert grasp of the topic. "You are not the cuddling sort, Joan Flynn."

Hartwell was trying not to smile. Too late, Tye realized what he'd said.

"And you are, Tiberius?" Joan countered, coming closer and towing a silent Hartwell with her. "*You*, who were the despair of our parents through at least ten social Seasons? Hester practically had to drag you to the altar by your...your *hair*, and nobody quite knows how she managed that."

Sisters and their illogic were the very devil. Tye advanced on Joan, hands on hips.

"I happen to *love* my countess, that's how she inspired me to marry her. You love your fabrics and clothing and all that folderol. You do not love *him*."

Hartwell brushed his fingers over Joan's knuckles. The caress was presuming as hell, but also seemed to steady Joan.

"I love to make pretty clothes, Tiberius, and I love to feel soft, pretty things in my hands. You love your horse. I don't see that this diminished your regard for Hester."

More nonsense, though Tye did adore Flying Rowan. Hester was fond of him too.

"You are trying to distract me, and it won't work. What the hell were you doing, practically sitting in Hartwell's lap, Joan? The next time you engage in such folly, it could be Mama or Quinworth who comes through that unlocked door. Do you want to be engaged to this man?"

Hartwell cocked his head, as if waiting for Joan's reply. That little relaxed gesture sent a trickle of foreboding down through Tye's middle.

"Joan, we don't know him, we don't know who his people are," Tye tried again. "He hasn't presented himself or his situation to me or to Quinworth to assure us that he can provide for you. Accost Hartwell under the mistletoe if you're in need of a diversion, but don't lurk behind closed doors with a man you don't intend to marry."

Tye knew better than to lecture any sister of his, but his concern was real. Hartwell had no pretensions to gentility. He was one of the rising buccaneers of industry, brash and bold about their wealth, and not at all respectful of the contribution the aristocracy made to the stability and sound functioning of the realm.

"Fine, then, Tiberius," Joan said, her smile naughty and proud at once. "I will only lurk behind closed doors with the man I *do* intend to marry."

She kissed Hartwell on the cheek without benefit of mistletoe, and made an exit from the library worthy of the marchioness herself. In Joan's absence, the only sound was the soft roar of the peat fire and the ticking of a longcase clock over in the corner.

Tye was torn between the need to sprint after her, and the urge to applaud.

"Before you start reeling with righteousness, two things," Hartwell said. "Maybe three."

"I should, first, kill you," Tye suggested, because Hartwell was owed at least a warning. "Second, I should bury your parts in a hog wallow; and third, I'll send Joan back to France."

Hartwell's smile was downright cheery. "You are welcome to try, *my lord*. You'll fail, on all three counts."

Yes, he probably would. Hester disapproved of violence, and this time of year, the hog wallows were frozen solid to a depth of several feet. Whatever Joan had sought in France, she'd come home, having decided she wouldn't find it amid the gaiety of Paris.

"I might fail," Tye said. "Because homicide would put rather a damper on Balfour's holiday gathering, and my manners have not deserted me to that extent, we'll never know. You *will* speak with my father."

Provided Tye had first evacuated Balfour's guests from within eavesdropping distance.

"Two things." Hartwell said again, quite calmly. "First, I can provide for Joan more than adequately. Not on the scale your family enjoys, but she'll never know cold or hunger or be left to fend for herself when she needs allies."

Hartwell's assertion bore an accusation an older brother could not miss.

"I have been as conscientious in my family duties as I know how to be, Hartwell, and though I love Joan dearly, *you* try telling her what to do."

"That was probably your first mistake, but I've no doubt your countess has disabused you of that tactic."

Hester loved it when Tye tried to order her about. She usually laughed herself silly, even before she started imitating him.

"Leave my countess out of this. I notice that while Joan was defending her actions with you, you did nothing to take up for her."

Except allow her to shamelessly cling to his hand.

"That's the second thing. Joan needed to be the one to tell you—you would not have believed me, and she doesn't need me to speak for her, in any case."

"You are a widower," Tye said, recalling some of the social intelligence Hester had passed along during one of their late night…chats.

"I lost my wife three years ago," Hartwell said. Nothing more, no manly gazing off into the fire, or sniffing into a handkerchief. Nothing sentimental about Hartwell's pronouncement at all, which suggested to Tye that the woman's death had, indeed, been a loss to her husband.

"Joan has been *off* somehow," Tye said, stalking past Hartwell to spear another chunk of peat onto the fire. "She arrived here early, dragging your entire party with her, no luggage, no lady's maid. Even my father—not the most devoted student of human nature—has noticed that Joan is unusually quiet."

"You are absolutely correct that Joan is coping with disappointment," Hartwell said. "Most women are by the time they're her age, but Joan has been honest with me. She believes we can have a respectful, cordial union, and I hope she's right."

Joan had not been honest with her very own devoted, loving brother. She was apparently determined to marry Hartwell, true enough, but she was not in love with the man.

Tye used a length of wrought iron to jab the fresh

peat to the back of the flames. "If you break her heart, I will kill you—socially, financially, emotionally. In every sense save for the criminal, I will end your life. My countess would expect no less of me, and it's the least I owe Joan."

"I believe you mean that."

Tye set the poker aside and replaced the screen over the hearth.

"Always nice to know prospective family has some basic English comprehension skills. When you meet with my father, they'll come in handy." With Mama, language skills were of no help whatsoever. "What was the third thing?"

"The third… Ah, yes. A drink, to celebrate the coming nuptials."

Balfour owned a distillery and served a whiskey that put angel choruses to the blush. Other breweries were blending their whiskies these days, mixing this barrel and vintage with that.

Tye preferred the old ways. And yet, he was enough of a new husband to understand the wisdom Hartwell had shown in this exchange with Joan. Joan had made her choice, and she'd stood by it, even to the point of having the last word with a brother who prided himself on his elocution and rhetoric.

And here Tye had thought her passion was limited to fabrics and stitchery.

"A drink would be appreciated. You'll want to pour from the decanter under the sideboard—plain, a bit dusty, and full of treasure."

Hartwell located the decanter and set out two glasses. Tye moved aside some bank draft or other and appropriated the comfortable chair behind Balfour's estate desk.

"Some people might think my sister is plain, and that she dresses so magnificently to compensate for her looks."

Hartwell brought him a drink, saluted, and downed a shot in a single swallow. "Those people would be idiots."

Tye took a savoring sip of indecently lovely whiskey. "My former admonition regarding your continued well-being stands, Hartwell: murder, in every sense but the criminal if you break my sister's heart. Other than that, welcome to the family."

Hartwell smiled and poured himself another drink. "Understood, *my lord*."

❧

Pandora was the smallest and youngest of the adult Flynns, which in Joan's opinion had also made her the most stubborn. That stubbornness was all too evident when she stood in the doorway to Joan's bedroom several evenings after Joan's engagement to Dante Hartwell had become fact.

"Good evening, Dora."

"Let us in, or we'll stand here in the corridor like a pair of drunken carolers until you do."

"We might even sing," Mary Ellen added evilly, for though they shared strawberry blond hair, Mary Ellen could sing like a nightingale, while Dora had from earliest youth been encouraged to merely move her lips when the hymns were sung in church.

"How seasonal of you," Joan said with irony

worthy of Tiberius in a foul mood. "It's late, I've had a very trying day—the entire week since leaving Edinburgh has been trying—and I have correspondence to tend to."

Correspondence to cry over, for Edward Valmonte's good wishes in light of Joan's engagement had been among the felicitations to arrive in the afternoon post. Joan tried to push the door closed—her sisters were not her friends and hadn't been for years—but Mary Ellen wedged her way past Dora and barged into the room.

Dora, of course, followed, but remained near the door. "We are here to tell you that you needn't marry this Mr. Hartwell for our sakes."

"Are you really? Thank you for those sentiments, and now I bid you good night."

Dora and Mary Ellen exchanged a look that included rolled eyes, exasperation, and the conspiratorial condescension of younger sisters who know they hold high cards.

About which Joan honestly cared not one single, bent farthing.

"You may bid us good night when you understand that we're in earnest," Mary Ellen said. "Mr. Hartwell is a handsome enough fellow, if you fancy the kilted sort, but if you think you must marry him so Dora and I aren't overshadowed by your continued... marital *availability*, then we can't allow you to make that sacrifice."

Though she was petite, Dora was in some ways most like their father. She said what she thought, regardless of the consequences, and while she

wasn't precisely nasty—sibling relations excepted—
she was blunt.

Mary Ellen, by contrast, had retreated into the role
of disinterested diplomat.

"Thank you," Joan said, though the sincerity of
their sentiment upset a balance that had emerged
between the sisters in adolescence.

An unhappy but stable, even rigid, balance.

"I'm not making a sacrifice," Joan went on. "One
tires of being leered at by the same bachelors and
having one's feet trod upon by the same tipsy baronets.
Mr. Hartwell needs a mother for his children, a hostess, and a chaperone for his sister as she makes the
acquaintance of Polite Society. Those are all worthy
projects, and I find his company congenial."

Oddly enough, this was all true.

Dora snorted and appropriated a seat on Joan's bed.
"You're hardly in his company at all. Tiberius has
appointed himself your guard dog, and Hester indulges
him. You're lucky to sit two seats away from your
intended at breakfast."

And yet, Dante had found quiet moments to
squeeze Joan's hand, to wink at her, to steal a peck
on the cheek even when mistletoe wasn't in evidence.

"What's really afoot, Joan?" Mary Ellen's question
was soft and held a hint of…worry. "Marriage is a
drastic, irrevocable step, and while Mama is trying to
put a good face on it, decent people don't marry far
below themselves by special license."

"You want to know if scandal is in the offing?"
They were entitled to worry, for scandal was knocking
on the very door.

"You are the most ill-natured creature," Dora said. "We're asking for information. Forewarned and all that. And stop pacing. You do it solely to make your skirts swish."

As Joan considered removing Dora bodily from the room, Mary Ellen came to roost in Joan's rocking chair.

"She's ill-natured only around you, Dora, and in all fairness, you're at your nastiest around Joan. And all over a silly dress? It's time for the two of you to move beyond that."

Dora lay back on Joan's bed, kicked off a pair of pink velvet mules, and crossed her ankles, as if getting comfortable for a nice long squabble.

"That dress was not silly," Joan said, recalling a green carriage dress with the loveliest peacock blue underskirt and a darker green gathered overskirt. That outfit was the first time she'd realized the potential of nacre buttons, and with a few plumes of peacock feather arranged both in a brooch and in the matching hat...

"Look at her," Dora said. "She's still in love with that dress, and all I wanted to do was borrow it."

Edward Valmonte was intent on blackmail, holy matrimony with all the intimacies attendant thereto was breathing down Joan's neck, scandal would likely come calling by Christmas, and Dora wanted to have this old argument?

Joan ceased her pacing before the hearth.

"Dora, I do not care that you typically spill coffee on every item of apparel you've worn for fifteen minutes. I do not care that I'd worked for weeks on that dress, for every moment was a labor of love. I do not care that you were in the act of borrowing it without my permission—which activity the law has unpleasant names for—when I came upon you trying to take up the hem. I do not even care that you ruined the dress for me when you went snipping away at it. I care very much that you would have looked ridiculous in that dress."

Dora sat up, her mouth open as if to fire off a retort.

"I told you," Mary Ellen interjected. "Joan isn't mean, she simply doesn't know how to express herself outside the sewing room."

Mary Ellen wasn't mean either, precisely, and yet, her comment—as insightful as it was—stung.

"That was a beautiful outfit!" Dora said, bouncing off the bed. "The perfect outfit for gaining Nathan Hampstead's notice—but, no. You would not allow me to wear it even the once, so all I had for the carriage parade was that infantile little cream business, and there he was, jabbering away to Matilda Carnes. He didn't even recognize me when I waved, and then they were engaged."

For the first time since childhood, Joan chanced a look at Mary Ellen in the midst of one of Dora's tirades. Not a conspiratorial look, but a look verifying that Dora was once again sounding sixteen years old, at the mercy of every adolescent insecurity, and passionately in love for the third time in as many weeks.

"Nathan Hampstead is notoriously shortsighted, Dora," Joan said gently. "He's also running to fat. Tiberius says the man plays too deep, as well. That cream business was your lucky dress."

For every girl needed a lucky dress. Joan had been designing hers for years.

"So you say now," Dora huffed, tossing herself onto Joan's fainting couch. "I was convinced at the time you wanted him for yourself."

This was news—also ridiculous. "You're daft. He's three inches shorter than I am. Do you know what he gazes at when we dance?"

Dora sat up and considered Joan from across the room. "I hate it when the fellows do that."

"We all do," Mary Ellen added. "Is this topic finally behind us?"

Peace on this subject would make a lovely wedding present. Joan knew better than to say as much.

"Dora, deep green does not become you. Your coloring is more genteel than my own or Mama's. She and I cannot wear the subtler colors, while you and Mary Ellen carry them off wonderfully. If you still want that dress, I'm happy to make it for you all over again, but we'll choose colors that flatter you."

"You wouldn't lend me the dress because I can't wear green?"

Not on your person. And yet, how odd to think that Dora—forthright, curvy Dora—could still feel stung by a long-ago sense of invisibility.

"Bad enough we all made our come outs in the shadow of a mama who commands every room she enters," Joan said, settling on the fainting couch beside Dora. "Much worse if we try to emulate her and fail."

"Joan was being protective of you," Mary Ellen translated. "My sisters are dunderheads."

Rather than acknowledge any dunderheadedness, Dora rose to pace.

"Is more protectiveness fueling this engagement, Joan? We know Eddie Valmonte was in your gun sights, and now he's to marry that Lady Bon-Bon. I thought you simply liked to talk dresses with him, but Mary El says Eddie's regard for you was becoming marked. I cannot see you talking about dresses with Mr. Hartwell."

"He wears the loveliest wool blends. Lamb's wool, angora, even cashmere."

Mary Ellen laughed, Dora joined in, and to her surprise—so did Joan.

"He won't be wearing any of those on your wedding night," Dora said, bouncing back up onto the bed. "Has Mama mortified you with that little lecture yet?"

"About five years ago," Joan replied, "but she was surprisingly encouraging about the entire undertaking." Which left one to wonder vague, uncomfortable things about one's own parents.

Though here was a difficulty—another difficulty: Would Mr. Hartwell expect to see his wife unclothed?

"First things first," Mary Ellen said. "What will you wear on your wedding day?"

"I can't make myself think about that," Joan admitted, because she had nobody else to whom she might have made such a confession. "I'll wear something, though I look ghastly in white. Fortunately, not everybody follows the Queen's example in this, even now."

"I have a lovely cream carriage dress we could alter

for you," Dora said. "Though I'm fairly certain it's in London. Possibly Edinburgh."

Which would not be a problem in this age of miracles. Dante had, in less than a week's time, procured the special license. To have a dress sent up from London would be no difficulty at all.

"Have you invited Edward?" Mary Ellen asked quietly.

Oh, God. Just when the day could not have become worse.

"Mama did the guest list, and I'm sure he's not—"

"You're sure he *is* on it," Dora interrupted. "Mama has never avoided a potential confrontation, and never held one in private that could be carried off in public. Blast and damnation. We ought to have said something to Papa."

"No matter," Joan said. "If Edward attends, he attends. We'll talk about dresses, which is all we ever really did."

That she could recall. His note hadn't mentioned blackmail, but it had confirmed that Joan's drawings were in his possession, and were likely to remain there. Edward was a viscount, after all. His coercion would be the smiling, sly variety.

"Which brings us back to our first order of business," Mary Ellen said. "You're getting married in a week's time, and everybody will come up from Edinburgh to look over this Mr. Hartwell. You'll need a dress."

Joan thought of her lucky dress, the one she'd designed and designed. The one she sketched in low moments, the one she saved for thinking about on bleak days and in black moods.

"There isn't time to make up something new," she said. "One of the qualities I treasure most about Mr. Hartwell is that he understands appearances for what they are—stage trappings rather than substance."

"Please don't inform Mama that appearances are of no consequence," Dora said. "She's confused on the matter. Mary Ellen's right, though. On your wedding day, you need a dress. For Mr. Hartwell's sake if not your own."

Dora, blast her, was not wrong.

"You need a dress," Dora reiterated, grinning, "and we're your sisters. You have to let us help you make it."

"Both of us," Mary Ellen said. "We'll forbid Dora to go near the coffeepot, and have Lady Balfour muster reinforcements if we need them. Hester would help, and Lady Balfour might as well. Between the ladies assembled here, we could sew you anything your heart desired."

How happy Mary Ellen was to contemplate this project.

And despite Joan's anxiety over the marriage, her fury at Edward, and her contempt for her own behavior—also her worry over the wedding night—how relieved Joan was to have her sisters' support.

Though for once, her heart's desire had nothing to do with sewing or fabric.

"I have some ideas, but they need refining."

"Come here, Mary El." Dora patted the bed. "I excel at refining."

"And so modest," Mary Ellen said, climbing onto the bed. Joan scooted to the foot of the bed, back supported by a bedpost, sketch pad open on her lap.

They spent an hour strategizing, until Dora threw the first pillow, and the second.

Before the room was coated in feathers—as had once happened when Joan was eleven—Joan had come up with a lovely, simple gown that could be made up in the time remaining. She sent her sisters on their way, tidied up the bed, and tried to calculate the fabric estimates, but made little progress.

Tears, it seemed, were also to be her newfound companions. Joan had just balled up Edward's infernal note, intent on pitching it into the fire, when a quiet knock sounded at her door.

Ten

"LET'S BE HONEST, MARGS," HECTOR SAID. "IF YOU don't want to spend time in my company, then I'll take one of the nursery maids along when the children and I fetch the post tomorrow."

His casual suggestion had Margaret bolting off the sofa as if a ghost had joined her in the library.

"Good evening, Hector." She'd been embroidering, peacocks or doves, something pretty and shimmery. By firelight, her birds seemed to flutter amid leafy green silk-thread boughs.

"Shall I light you to your bedroom, Margaret?" He'd had to lie in wait among the gentlemen in the parlor before tracking her here when the rest of the house was abed. For that much effort, a man deserved some reward.

"No, thank you. Would you rather I sent a nursery maid with the children to the village?"

He'd rather she left the children at home, rather she didn't sit them between the adults every damned time Hector took the sleigh to the posting inn, rather she didn't hover by the couch like a hare ready to bolt from cover when the hounds came too close.

"You should do as you please, Margaret. That was the point of my comment."

The point of his comment had been to provoke her into assuring him she loved spending time with him and wished he'd go into the village every day rather than every other.

When pigs danced the Highland fling.

She drew in a breath, which did agreeable things to her bodice. "The children benefit from—"

Hector took four steps closer, close enough to see the fatigue in Margaret's eyes. Firelight was usually flattering to women, softening signs of age, but the flickering shadows made Margaret look more like a shade than herself.

"You're up early with the weans each morning," he said, "then you put yourself at Lady Balfour's beck and call. At meals you barely say anything, and in the afternoons, you pretend you have correspondence to tend to if I don't get you out of this monument to dead pine boughs and holiday cheer. You're miserable, Margaret Hartwell, and I cannot abide that. If I'm making you more miserable, then you must say so."

Women comfortable with their needle had a competence of the hands that fascinated Hector, as if they played a musical instrument, except the result was pretty colors instead of notes in the air. Margaret opened her embroidery hoop and anchored her needle in a corner of the fabric. She folded the peacocks and doves away in neat, precise movements, so all the lovely birds were hidden from view, and a confusion of colored threads showed on the back of the fabric.

"The children need to get outside," she said. "Dante is busy wooing his investors and future in-laws, and I can barely keep straight the names of all the people we sit down to meals with."

Hector took the cloth bag into which she'd stuffed her stitching, and set it on the desk behind him. "The children will be fine. What do *you* need?"

The question baffled her, and that drove him...that drove him to distraction. Margaret Hartwell, whether she knew it or not, was what had held Dante's small family together in recent years. That she'd be uncertain in any regard was untenable.

"Dante is taking a wife," Margaret said in the same tones she might have reported fading eyesight or the loss of some other precious faculty. "Lady Joan is wonderful with the children, and she'll be a much better guide for Charlie than I could ever be. I like her, and she'll be good for Dante."

Insight struck, welcome and startling. "You want to hate Lady Joan. So do I."

"Not hate her...only resent her. This is very bad of me, for Joan is a good woman."

He'd come in here looking for a reckoning, and had found so much more—he'd found something he alone had in common with Margaret.

"You're worried about your brother," Hector said, taking Margaret by the hand and leading her to the desk. One didn't sit on desks in the households of earls, but one didn't stand on ceremony when wooing a lady, either. Hector hiked himself onto the desk, then patted the place on the blotter beside him.

For Margaret, the maneuver wasn't exactly

graceful—she was substantially shorter than Hector, but with his help, she managed.

"I *am* fretting about Dante," Margaret said, studying her slippered feet. "I'm worried about the children, and I'm worried about *me*. I should not burden you with my silly anxieties."

No honest, untitled Scot lived far from the fear of homelessness, but Margaret's fears went deeper, and Hector hadn't even suspected she harbored them.

Paper crackled under Hector's kilt as he shifted two inches closer, though he cared not if he sat upon the Christmas Eve menu or a draft of somebody's Last Will and Testament.

"You will always be welcome in your brother's household, Margaret, welcome and loved."

"So you say now, but soon Dante and Joan will start their own family, and dear old Aunt Margs will be towed along on family outings, invited to dinner parties at the last minute to make up the numbers. Who will speak to the women at the mills when they're too shy to bring their concerns to Dante? Who will remind Dante that his children go for days without seeing him? Who will keep an eye on Charlie's governesses and Phillip's tutors? Lady Joan is all that is kind, but—"

"The women in the mills can talk to me."

Though they typically did not. For the most part, Hector and the mill employees moved on opposite sides of the business's owner, and kept a wary, respectful distance from one another.

"They won't, though. Now that Dante has taken a wife, he will turn her loose on *me*. Joan will expect me to attend balls and teas, and wear fancy dresses, and Dante will be hopeful, when he recalls he has a sister, that Joan will succeed in making a lady of me. All for my sake, of course."

Part of Hector wanted to slap a hand over her mouth and roar at her that she need put up with none of that, that she was a woman of dignity and substance, and could control her own fate.

The other part of him had seen enough negotiations to know a more subtle course was called for.

"If you're confiding these worries to me, you must be very upset."

He was upset too, because sooner or later, one of the prancing ninnies frequenting the Edinburgh ballrooms would see what a treasure Margaret Hartwell was. She had the gift of managing without being seen doing it. Her visits to the mills were to take Dante his lunch, to put a bouquet on his desk, to count the number of Christmas baskets needed for the employees each year.

And yet, she knew the names of many of the women and girls employed at the mills, knew who was cousin to whom, and who was walking to church with the tobacconist's son. Hector had heard her passing along this information to her brother, making suggestions—suggestions only, of course—regarding promotions, and even which women would not work well together.

"I am upset," Margaret said, "and I fear I've taken out some of my ill temper on you."

Oh, he wanted to kiss her for that—he always wanted to kiss her, but particularly when she was being brave and honest, and *Margaret*.

Hector tucked his hands under his thighs and hunched forward. "You're right to be concerned for your brother, for your family. This marriage…"

Margaret hopped off the desk, which was probably prudent of her. "Dante is not in love, and while I'm sure Lady Joan deserves a man who loves her, Dante deserves a woman who loves him too. Rowena didn't, not at first. He was her unpaid mill foreman, and a way to have children."

Margaret had a temper, and Hector would love to see it unleashed someday—though not at him.

"They muddled along well enough, eventually." Though Dante had confided that he'd been relieved when the children arrived, because Rowena's expectations in the bedroom were no longer an issue in the marriage.

Rowena Shatner—Rowena Hartwell—had had inflexible notions about schedules, and about the universe running to the timetable she preferred.

"I didn't blame Rowena, of course," Margaret said softly. "If I could have a mill of my own and children, I'd marry a decent, hardworking man to get them."

"You're allowed to want those things, Margaret Hartwell." Though the part about the mill came as a surprise. "I wish I could give them to you."

She peered at him, as if somebody had misplaced the objectionable Hector, and some other fellow shared this late night tête-à-tête with her.

"You hide your sweetness almost as well as Dante does. I'm sorry I've been out of sorts."

"You've been nearly panicked." He couldn't give her a mill, and without benefit of matrimony, he wouldn't give her children.

But he *could* give her something to think about.

"When you go to bed tonight, consider what you want, Margaret Hartwell. You see your brother's marriage as cutting you off from the role you've loved, but it also frees you to pursue those fellows who can give you mills and children."

Which number did not include Hector. The pain of that should have been expected, and yet, it reverberated through him like the bells that would toll throughout the shire on Christmas morning.

For a long moment, Margaret studied the fire, saying nothing.

She was a pretty woman, though not in the striking, impressive manner of a Lady Joan. Margaret's beauty was soft, sweet, and subtle, but it would age wonderfully.

"Off to bed with you, now," Hector said, rising from the desk and joining her in the warmth nearer the hearth. "You'll go with me on tomorrow's jaunt into town?"

Because a doomed man was entitled to worship from whatever proximity he might torment himself with.

She nodded, and Hector ordered his feet to move. A fine old English tradition spared him the effort when Margaret left off studying the fire to peer up at him.

"Thank you, Hector, for listening to me. For not laughing, for not dismissing me." She kissed him, a somewhat awkward undertaking, because he was a foot taller than she, and slow to appreciate his good fortune. Margaret had to haul herself up his chest by bracing one hand on his shoulder and anchoring the other at his nape.

Once she arrived to her destination, however, she at

least permitted Hector time to be shocked and pleased, and—more important, to wrap his arms around her and kiss her back.

And then to kiss her back some more.

❧

"Mr. Hartwell." Lady Joan's posture and tone suggested she was surprised to find Dante standing at her bedroom door. The peculiar shine in her eyes suggested she was also unhappy, maybe on the same general account.

Well, so was he. In three days' time, they'd remove to Aberdeen, and the next day, they would marry. Tonight was possibly Dante's last chance to be private with his intended before they took their vows.

If they took them.

"May I come in? Should your brother find me lurking by your door, he'll do me bodily injury at least, or worse, lecture me to death."

"Tiberius believes in the proprieties," Joan said, stepping back.

"He does," Dante said as he slipped into her room, "unless he thinks he's unobserved with his countess beneath the mistletoe."

Then his lordship was a lusty English fiend—an encouraging revelation, that.

The door clicked closed behind him. "Does your call have a purpose, Mr. Hartwell?"

Mr. Hartwell. Something in Dante *wilted* at her crisp question. He took her hand—her fingers were cool—and tugged her over to the fainting couch.

"Yes, my visit has a purpose. We're a courting

couple. I have it on good authority that we're entitled to sneak behind a few hedges as the nuptials approach, though hedges are in short supply at this time of year."

And her infernal brother, her two sisters, or even her flighty mama seemed to lurk behind every one.

"We aren't a courting couple." She perched beside him, back straight, and ran a hand over the green velvet of her dressing gown.

"Then why is every single soul at this house party behaving as if we are? Why are we getting married in less than a week?"

The questions were meant to be rhetorical, to get Joan to *look* at him.

"That's a lovely dressing gown," she said. "Brown is a neglected color, but it becomes most men. Silk makes a much warmer lining than satin."

She'd *looked* at his dressing gown. The wilted feeling sank lower, to something worse than bewilderment, though he'd sensed tumult behind her growing quiet at meals. "How are you, Lady Joan?"

Her gaze went to the escritoire, where some crumpled attempt at correspondence sat on the blotter amid sketchbooks and letters neatly sealed with her papa's waxed crest.

"I am tired. My sisters came to call."

"Tell me." Because in her present mood, Dante would take any conversational gambit. He'd forgotten that marriage entailed this sort of work, and he'd never been very good at it—not with Rowena.

"Dora and Mary Ellen and I are not…not close. I'm the oldest, and because I'm tall, Mama seemed to think by the time I was fifteen, all my interests would be in common with hers."

Dante risked taking Joan's hand again. "She shares your interest in fashion."

Joan shook her head, some of the starch leaching out of her posture. "Mama likes to *wear* fashions, she has not the first clue how a dress is constructed, or which fabrics have what personality. Mama also overdresses—her wardrobe should be quieter, more elegant, but she likes noisy, fussy clothing."

Joan had probably grasped the difference between elegant and fussy by the time she was learning her letters.

"When your mother singled you out, your sisters resented it. Might we have this discussion under the covers?"

Now she looked at him, and not with the reckless glee of the prospective bride. "Under the covers, Mr. Hartwell?"

For the love of God. "Dante will do, seeing as we're private. You've banked the fire. Your feet have to be getting cold." So to speak. Her entire room was cooling down, for that matter, suggesting she'd banked the fire some time ago.

She studied her toes as if they'd arrived on the end of her feet all of a sudden. "I suppose sharing a bed with you should become a habit."

The notion appeared to confound her.

"A comfort," he said, "something to look forward to at the end of a long and sometimes trying day." Though he and Ro had never quite arrived to such a state.

When Dante expected dithering and equivocation

from Joan, she crossed the room and turned the covers down on the side of the bed closest to the fire. His respect for her rose, also his liking.

And his desire.

"Do you miss that? Climbing into bed with your wife?"

He came around to the opposite side of the bed, so they had the expanse of a big mattress between them, all cozied up with pillows, plaid coverlets, and tartan blankets.

"I'll explain it as best I can. Will you take your dressing gown off?" He shrugged out of his, which left him in a pair of black silk pajama bottoms.

"You don't wear a nightshirt?"

"I rarely wear anything to bed. One gets hot, and a nightshirt twists up, and then one wakes up and thrashes about." He sounded like Hector delivering a report, so he shut up.

Joan did not climb up into the bed, but rather, turned, sat, and swung her legs up together. Then she lifted the blankets and slid beneath them, all still wearing the green velvet dressing gown. She came to rest reclining on banked pillows rather than curled up under the covers.

"My sisters came to offer to help with my wedding dress. They surprised me."

Rather than hop up onto the mattress, Dante did as Joan had. Sit, lift, spin, tuck—which left them nearly a yard away from each other—rather like a married couple.

"An olive branch?" The headboard behind Dante's bare back was cool, and that was a fine thing.

"An olive branch I could understand. My family suffered a blow with my brother Gordie's death, and we've never really come right. Between my sisters and me, it's as if we all stopped maturing when Gordie died. I'm still seventeen, ready for my come out, Mama fussing at me incessantly. They're fifteen and fourteen, resenting me for something I cannot help."

"I had not thought you'd be lonely for the company of women." At the mill, the employees always seemed to be chattering and bantering with one another, casting sly looks and falling silent when Dante came into their midst, then bursting into more chatter—and laughter—the moment his back was turned.

"I'm not lonely, not exactly."

She was profoundly lonely. Dante hoped her husband could do something about that.

He rose from the bed and made a circuit of the room, blowing out the candles, one by one. "You asked about my first wife."

"I understand you loved her and you miss her."

The last candle brought him to Joan's side of the bed. He left that one burning. "Move over. If we're under the covers to keep warm, then a certain proximity will aid that goal."

Now, he sounded like Spathfoy. The earl's ability to acquit himself adequately under the mistletoe notwithstanding, Spathfoy was *English*.

"You want to *cuddle*?"

"Yes." For reasons he could not fathom himself.

She moved over, and he situated himself immediately beside her, then looped an arm around her shoulders and scooted down. Her dressing gown meant he was embracing mostly velvet, with a few inconvenient buttons and a tightly knotted sash.

"What are your expectations of this marriage, Joan?"

She shifted up, managing to elbow him in the process. "Are you having second thoughts? I hardly see how permitting you into my bed—"

"No second thoughts," he said, pressing a finger to her lips. "But I'd be lying if I said our nuptials never crossed my mind."

She subsided, her head on his shoulder. Her hair was still in a tightly braided coronet, and a hairpin jabbed into Dante's shoulder.

"Our nuptials are never far from my thoughts. I hope we shall suit, Mister—Dante."

He extracted the hairpin then found another. "It's hell when a husband and wife don't suit."

"I thought you loved your first wife."

"Love developed." More hairpins yielded to his questing fingers. "Rowena made it plain that she was marrying me to secure the mills and to secure children. She'd been an only child, and then lost her mother early. I eventually understood that this history made her unnaturally keen on having both her own way and a family of her own."

"She married you to provide her heirs. There's something of the old-fashioned aristocrat about that."

"Let me—" Joan turned her face into his shoulder, without his having to explain, and he searched out the last of her pins. "There. You don't typically sleep with all those pins in, do you?"

"No, but my evening routine is disrupted."

She settled back against him, her posture more

relaxed. Dante let his fingers tunnel through her hair again, as if searching for pins, but in truth he was simply enjoying the feel of her less tightly bound hair.

"That's lovely," she said on a sigh. "Tell me about your wife, for I'm an aristocrat, and I want children."

These parallels hadn't occurred to him—not consciously, but perhaps they'd driven him to seek her out late at night, when privacy was possible.

"How much do you understand about the conception of children?"

She yawned, delicately, of course. "That part is undignified, but quickly over. One need not belabor the specifics. My mother suggested it can become enjoyable, but Mama's given to exaggeration, and… she's loyal to my father, in her fashion."

Low expectations in a prospective wife were not a bad thing—were they? And yet, *undignified* and *quickly over*…well, they'd have time to work on that too, God willing. Decades of time.

"In the early years of our marriage, Rowena resented the hell out of me, and yet she expected marital intimacies with me. This created a befuddling awkwardness for me to which she was not sympathetic."

A beat of comprehending silence went by, which was fortunate. Dante could not have explained the peculiar challenge of his early married years any more articulately if he'd been, well, the Earl of Spathfoy.

"Oh, you poor man. And here I am, nearly a stranger, in want of the same intimacies so my child might have the fiction of legitimacy. What a muddle."

A tension in the pit of Dante's belly eased. However sheltered she'd been, Joan grasped the fundamental challenge of a man expected to regularly swive a woman who on some level resented the hell out of him.

"I want us to be friends, Joan. I want at least that, and friends are honest with each other. Will you bestow a friendly sort of kiss on your fiancé?"

❦

Edward's letter sat two yards away, a crumpled-up ball of malice and cheerful innuendo Joan had put from her mind for the duration of her sisters' visit.

Friends are honest with each other. Mr. Hartwell's words brought the letter and its ramifications slamming back to Joan's awareness with all the subtly of a hem ripping at high tea.

And yet...Joan's prospective husband was asking for something, something that had nothing to do with Edward's sly intimations. Snug in her fiancé's embrace, Joan felt a sense of security that she thought she'd left behind in Edinburgh, possibly forever.

"You want me to kiss you?" Joan was glad he'd asked, for chaste pecks on the cheek had only made her miss his kisses—his other kisses.

"We've kissed before," Mr. Hartwell said, drawing the covers around Joan's shoulders. "Kissing seems like a good place to start."

"To start—?" She thrashed up to her elbows, her dressing gown thwarting her for a moment. Mr. Hartwell lay on his back, his expression unreadable in the candlelight, but in his eyes... Hope? Expectation?

Vulnerability? Joan felt an abrupt and happy dislike for the late Mrs. Rowena Hartwell, though in all likelihood, the poor woman had been raised with the exaggerated propriety of the newly wealthy class.

And Rowena had had no brothers to give her even a passive understanding of the male of the species.

"Just a kiss," Mr. Hartwell said. "I've had one wedding night I'd as soon forget. With you, I'd like to try for a happier start to our marital life."

"Tell me about your wedding night—your first wedding night." Joan situated herself against him and wrapped her arm around his waist. The sensation of his bare skin against her forearm was odd, but... friendly, in a married sort of way.

"A gentleman doesn't kiss and tell, but suffice it to say, matters progressed with a great deal of awkwardness, tension, and silence. I was banished across the hall shortly thereafter. In the morning, I gave Rowena a pearl and gold bracelet, and she gave me a lot of dirty looks."

Clearly, he was telling Joan this because he wanted something better for them—as did she.

"We will improve on that memory." She kissed his cheek for emphasis, then decided to make her point more emphatically.

Her next kiss landed closer to his mouth, and Joan got a whiff of tooth powder. This close, she could also catch the scent of his shaving soap, and the smoothness of his cheek suggested he'd shaved as well as bathed before paying this call.

Her damned, dratted gown fought her, but Joan managed to arrange herself so she could kiss his mouth. The hand she'd draped across his middle slid up his chest— more smooth warmth—until her fingers encountered—

Abruptly she drew back. "I beg your pardon."

He took her hand in his, and used her index finger to trace his flat male nipple. "Think of me as a bolt of cloth, something expensive, that you can make into only one garment—a husband. Explore my every facet and quality as you decide on the design of that garment."

Beneath her finger, his flesh puckered.

"I like that, Joan. Kiss me again."

She liked the rasp that had crept under his burr. Liked the warmth of his skin, and the way his tongue flirted with her lips. By the time Joan recalled the need to breathe, she was lying half on top of her prospective spouse, her lips had developed new and exquisite sensitivities, and she'd come to loathe her dressing gown.

"Shall we anticipate our vows, Mr. Hartwell?"

He rose up like a sudden wave of half-naked male, inexorable and overpowering, rolling Joan to her back. "Do you know what it does to me, when you call me Mr. Hartwell and look at me like that?"

Whatever it did to him, he liked it. His eyes shone with approval and something more passionate, suggesting he liked *her*.

The next kiss was *not* friendly. It was hot and wonderful and noisy. Joan sighed and whimpered and bit him on the shoulder, then the ear, then the jaw. She squirmed in the confines of her velvet robe, and arched against her fiancé, and generally appalled herself with how easily she rose to the challenge he'd set her.

Every inch of his smooth, warm skin, every scent

and contour of his body—she wanted to own them all, with her hands, her mouth, her mind, and even— miraculous to discover—her heart.

"I understand what Mama was trying to tell me," she panted.

Fifteen stone of adult male was braced above her on his knees and forearms, his fingers brushing gently across Joan's brow.

"What did your mama tell you, lass? For surely no one has had to explain to you about kissing. You grasp that quite well."

Mama's exact words eluded Joan's recall. "She said it might take time, but if my husband's efforts in bed were well rewarded, mine would be too. Your wife—your first wife—she probably had no one to tell her what to expect. That could not have aided your wedding night."

He kissed her nose in a thoughtful manner. "Hadn't considered that, and Ro would never have admitted her ignorance. Not aloud. She thought me ugly, you see."

His tone held regret, as if he pitied the long-ago bride who'd shared such an awkward match with him.

"You are a handsome fellow, even my sisters admitted that much. I'm particularly fond of your eyebrows." Joan traced each one, thinking them akin to fox fur in their texture.

"It wasn't my eyebrows she objected to." Dante captured Joan's hand and drew it between their bodies. "May we please leave further mention of my late first wife for another time?"

"Of course." Preferably weeks in the future, at

least. Months or years might suit better. "Though if I had to object—goodness!"

He'd wrapped Joan's hand around his engorged member, skin to hot, smooth skin.

"You are in want of your drawers, Mr. Hartwell."

"I'm no' in want of me drawers, Lady Joan. Get acquainted, why don't you, as long as you've come to call?"

His burr had thickened along with this part of his body, the part Joan would learn even more intimately on their wedding night. As her fingers explored length, girth, texture, and response, she searched her memory.

She hadn't touched Edward thus, of that she was certain. The knowledge comforted significantly.

"Am I doing this right?" Because her prospective husband had gone quiet, all except for breathing that made his bare chest heave.

"Stroke me," he whispered. "Wrap your hand around me, and yes—God, yes. Like that, and don't stop. Please, don't stop."

The covers formed a cocoon of heat and darkness as Joan tactilely inventoried her prospective husband's most intimate attributes. He was smooth, rough, silky, hot, hard—a bouquet of textures like no fabric she could name. Dante's breath rasped past Joan's ear, his breathing became labored, and then, as if a sudden wind had picked him up, he heaved himself to his back and shoved the covers down.

He took himself in his own hand, and after a few rough strokes, groaned softly. By the light of the single candle, Joan watched his seed spurt onto his belly, gleaming like nacre on his fingers and ribs.

"Sweet, everlasting, holy…" He opened his eyes and regarded Joan with such wonder, she had to look away. "I hadn't planned that. Please believe me. I owe you every respect, of course, but I wanted to air some aspects of my—"

He lay amid Joan's covers, exposed down to his thighs, where the black silk was a shadow among Joan's scented linens. One hand was flung back against the pillow, while his male member lay in decadent repose amid the dark hair of his lower belly.

"My lady…" He cradled her jaw with his free hand and leaned up to bestow on Joan a kiss that combined heat, joy, and reverence in equal measures.

Mama knew a thing or two after all, for that kiss… that kiss *helped*. With Joan's worries, with her fears, with her sense that her life had run off its well-ordered, well-dressed rails. She kissed him back then wrestled her way off the bed.

She dipped a flannel in the wash water left close to the hearth for warmth, and brought it to Dante's side of the bed. He lay utterly passive, eyes closed, his breathing still deeper than normal.

"Shall I?" she asked, shifting so the candlelight fell across his torso.

"Madam, I could not stop you in my present state if I wanted to—and I do not want to."

The formerly thick, hard part of him was quiescent. "You're like a hedgehog all curled up and gone to sleep. I gather that scent is your seed?"

"Does it offend you?"

She started on his belly and sniffed. "Not offend. The scent is like a conservatory smell—earthy, and while not a fragrance, it's not a stink either. Does one—?" She gestured with the cloth.

He took it from her and rubbed himself briskly enough to wake up any hedgehog.

"Weren't we to cuddle at some point, wife-to-be?" He tossed the cloth in the direction of the hearth, where it landed on the hearthstones with a plop.

"So casual, Mr. Hartwell."

"Would you rather I got up and affected a bow? I might be able to manage it, or I might topple to my arse at your feet. I was sadly overdue for the pleasure you just bestowed on me."

He was teasing her, which was lovely and even lovable—though she didn't entirely understand his humor.

"Move over, sir. You are on my side of the bed."

He scooted a good two feet, into the middle of the bed, not clear to the other side. "That's intimate, knowing which side of the bed my lady sleeps on."

His lady. Not lady, as in Lady Joan, but lady as in the woman he esteemed above all others. Watching his hedgehog go to sleep was intimate too. Joan draped her dressing gown over the foot of the bed, and climbed in beside him. "You're telling me marriage is intimate."

"Ours will be, thank God."

His wrapped an arm around her and kissed her temple as he offered his prayer of thanksgiving, his tone suggesting the matter had given him concern.

Joan kissed his jaw, and yet, she was concerned too.

Her prospective husband sought to marry an intimate, honest friend, and she wished she could be that for him. She would try very hard to be that for him, because he intended to offer her nothing less of himself.

And yet, Edward's snide little note sat two yards away, making a mockery of Joan's marriage before the vows had even been spoken.

Eleven

"HALE FLYNN, I SENT YOU TO FETCH ME A BOOK. WHY are you back here empty-handed?"

Quinworth suspected DeeDee's exasperation was only partly feigned, for the prospect of losing a daughter to holy matrimony had overset her ladyship's nerves. Nothing would do but her husband of more than twenty-five years must read some Robert Burns to her, which his lordship was only too happy to do.

"My dear, Balfour House is a veritable gauntlet. I attempted the mission you set for me, only to find Mr. MacMillan stealing kisses from Miss Hartwell in the library. Having some familiarity with kissing, I can assure you these were not holiday greetings."

"You're the Marquess of Quinworth," DeeDee said, rustling about under the covers. "You clear your throat, look severe, and all in your path run for cover."

"The young lady was giving as good as she got, else I might have indeed cleared my throat and looked severe—though might I point out, that tactic never worked very well with you, madam."

Or with their children.

She preened as only Deirdre Flynn could preen before the man she loved. "Did you make only the one attempt, Hale? You were gone for more than a few moments."

His lordship took a seat on the bed at his wife's hip, close enough to catch a whiff of lilacs.

"I was trapped, trapped I tell you! I came up the stairs to report my failure to you, and what should I find but Spathfoy enjoying the privileges of a young husband with his countess. The household has gone mad."

Her ladyship's eyes began to dance. "Under the mistletoe?"

"I averted my eyes, my dear. One doesn't like to see one's firstborn son and heir so thoroughly taken prisoner by a woman half his size."

Her ladyship rustled around under the covers a bit more, the better to show off a peignoir that would make older men than Hale Flynn revisit naughty memories.

"This is a large house, Hale. You couldn't come up the maids' stairs? You had to stand there in your night robe, shivering with mortification while your son went down to defeat at the hands of his countess?"

How he loved it when she made fun of him. "I came up the footmen's stairs, and the sight that befell me…"

Had warmed his heart.

"Hale, if you want to live until morning, you'll stop being coy."

"Mr. Hartwell was coming out of Joan's room. I am dismayed to report that his hair was disheveled, and Joan hauled him back into her room for a parting kiss. A good, strong girl, is our Joan. She takes after her mother."

DeeDee stopped fussing her blasted nightclothes and laughed, the hearty, merry laugh Quinworth had fallen in love with decades ago.

"And I have missed all this excitement. Thank goodness for the foolishness of young people. Joan has had me worried these past few days."

She'd had her papa worried for longer than that, though matters appeared to be taking a sanguine turn.

"I'm again off in search of Mr. Burns, and mind you don't be snoring when I return, madam."

He kissed her cheek—a prudent husband didn't part from DeeDee Flynn without observing the civilities—and made his way back to the library, avoiding locations likely to be graced with mistletoe and kissing couples.

The library was still not, alas, devoid of occupants.

"You're Phillip, aren't you? Hartwell's boy? Isn't it late for you to be wandering the house?"

The lad remained where he was, sitting before the banked fire, a large book open across his knees. "Papa isn't in his room. I checked."

This was the serious little fellow who'd been spying from the balcony upon Quinworth's arrival at this Highland holiday bacchanal.

"Had a bad dream, did you? Heard some dragons under the bed?"

And where in this vast collection would Robert Burns be hiding?

"There are no such things as monsters, though Papa says Parliament comes close."

"The Commons certainly does. Don't suppose you've seen Robert Burns lying about somewhere?"

"Robert Burns was a poet and a great man," the child recited. "Burns begins with *B* and the *B*s are over there."

Burns was a linguistic genius, also a philandering disgrace, among other things, and yet DeeDee loved to hear her husband read his poetry. "Damned if you aren't right."

"Papa says you shouldn't swear, but Daisy swore at Fiona's rabbit when he got loose."

Fiona was Quinworth's granddaughter, Gordie's sole offspring, and the rabbit had been a gift to the girl from her uncle Tiberius—a bribe, more like. DeeDee had a soft spot for the damned rabbit, else it would be enjoying the hospitality of the stables.

The lad looked lonely perched on the hearthstones, his book too big for his lap, his spectacles making him resemble an orphaned owlet.

"You're not wearing slippers, boy. The womenfolk set great store by slippers."

"You're not wearing slippers either."

"I'm trying not to make a sound. Mind if I join you?" Because DeeDee might well fall asleep, given a few minutes to herself, and the woman needed her rest.

Young Phillip scooted over a few inches as Quinworth lowered himself to the hard stones. "Are you up past your bedtime, too, sir?"

"I am. Did you know your papa is marrying my daughter Joan?" Because people often forgot to tell their children the important things. Particularly people newly enthralled with each other's kisses.

"I like Lady Joan. She's no good at marbles, but

she smells pretty, and she doesn't cheat. Charlie likes her too."

"Charlene is your sister." Quinworth had done what research he could in the time allowed, not that Joan would have listened to reason regardless of any discovered shortcomings in Mr. Hartwell or his family.

The boy studied his book, though seated as he was, back to the fire, the words on the page would have been hard to decipher.

"Will you like having Lady Joan for a stepmama?" And weren't the lad's feet cold?

"It doesn't matter if I like her, though I do. Lady Joan explained that stepmamas understand about first mamas being important. I don't have to love Lady Joan, but I probably will."

"Even if she's no good at marbles?" The marquess had no familiarity with marbles as a pastime, but Master Hartwell apparently set store by the game, and he seemed a discerning young fellow.

"Papa is lonely," the boy said, turning a page of his storybook. "Lady Joan will be his friend, and he told Hector she can open doors. I thought footmen opened doors."

Interesting. Perhaps this was why Hartwell hadn't offered a single objection when Tiberius had arranged Joan's settlements so the funds remained indirectly under Joan's control.

"Ladies can help us make new friends," the marquess said. "They open doors to people we might not have otherwise met. It's a figure of speech."

"Papa needs money for the mills. He worries about it."

This, too, comported with what intelligence Quinworth had been able to gather. "Why doesn't your papa sell those fancy train cars, then?"

The child peered at a drawing of a fellow in armor brandishing a sword at a large, fire-breathing reptile.

"Because the train cars don't belong to him. Mama left one to me, and one to Charlie. They were a wedding present to her from her papa."

Good God. A wedding present made to only half of the couple? More research was in order, surely.

"The hour grows late, my boy. I think I'd best see you to your room. We're to fetch the Christmas tree tomorrow, you know. Nothing will do but we must emulate the Royal Consort's barbarian traditions. It's all quite jolly."

The child closed his book. "I don't want Papa to be lonely."

Despite his tender years, this small child knew loneliness well, as did the marquess.

"I will tell you a secret, young Phillip. Lady Joan has needed a friend for quite some time. I think your papa is just the fellow for her, and she's just the lady for him. It will be all right, you'll see."

Though Joan's loneliness had only recently come to her father's notice, and that largely because Hester muttered about it to Spathfoy.

With a less solemn child, the marquess might have tried for another wink, but Phillip lacked his younger sister's blithe—and loud—spirit. Quinworth rose and extended a hand down to the boy—Tiberius had been a great one for reading at all hours—and tucked the storybook under an arm, along with that old rascal, Mr. Burns.

"Let's to bed, shall we? Fetching the Christmas tree and cutting the Yule log are taxing adventures. You'll need your rest."

The child went along docilely, all the way to the nursery, where they made sure Fiona's rabbit was sleeping peacefully in his cage, then said their good nights. Quinworth turned his steps back to the bedroom he shared with his marchioness, but realized when he was most of the way there that he'd kept the boy's storybook along with Burns's poetry.

No matter. The marchioness was fast asleep when her husband returned to her side. Quinworth kissed her cheek, wished her sweet dreams, and blew out the candles.

He climbed in beside his wife and waited for sleep to claim him, as her ladyship rustled about on her side of the bed.

Hartwell was marrying *up*. Quinworth didn't particularly like that, but he respected it, and couldn't fault the man's taste in wives, provided Hartwell showed Joan every possible courtesy.

A father need lose no sleep in that regard, for Tiberius would kill Hartwell if Joan were less than pleased with her husband. Dora, Mary Ellen, and her ladyship would probably have a go as well.

Hartwell's motivation was plain enough, and not that unusual in these modern times, but why on earth would poised, lovely, well-dowered Joan accept Hartwell's suit—unless she was truly in love?

❧

"You will ride with me to the lake," Tiberius said, and from him, Joan supposed that was an invitation.

"We're in Scotland. It's a loch, not a lake. Though I must say, a kilt becomes you." Became him well, though Mr. Hartwell wore his with more casual swagger.

In the cavalcade of sleighs, Mr. Hartwell was farther up the line, with the Earl of Balfour, and Balfour's younger brother, Ian MacGregor. Some of the ladies had elected to stay back at the house and decorate the two trees that had arrived on yesterday's train, part of the batch the Prince Consort imported from Thuringia each year.

"Are you dressed warmly enough?" Tiberius asked. "There will be a wind, I'm sure of it, and some child or other will need to use the bushes, except there aren't any bushes in this blighted shire, and it's too cold to use them in any event."

He more or less threw Joan into the sleigh, then climbed aboard himself.

"Have you been draining your flask too often, Tiberius? It's a sunny day, at least, and the children need fresh air." While Joan needed to get the wedding ceremony—and wedding night—behind her.

He clucked to the horse, a hairy behemoth whose rhythmic trot set the sleigh bells jingling.

"No, I have not been tippling, though if you'd like a tot?" He shifted the reins and produced a leather-covered silver container.

"No, thank you." She'd beg a nip off her fiancé, later.

"If you detect a certain disquiet about the person of your brother, it's because I am worried for you. Hester says I am being ridiculous, though, and my countess is nearly always right."

"How could I possibly be a source of worry to you?" Joan asked. "You gained a promise from Papa that your sisters might marry where they pleased, within reason. I'm marrying where I please."

With the horse churning along, the wind was biting. Tiberius was seething about something as only Tiberius could, and Joan still hadn't come up with a strategy for dealing with Edward Valmonte.

For Christmas, might she please have some peace and contentment?

"Why this Hartwell fellow, Joan? He's notably ambitious, has no pretensions to gentility, and you barely know him."

Joan knew that Dante Hartwell had been lonely in his first marriage, though the man himself might not use that word. She knew he was decent and honest, and that he loved his family.

As did Tiberius, bless him.

"I am tired, Tiberius, of having my bosom leered at. I am sick to death of having the tabbies whisper about how it's a pity the only person in my family taller than me is my older brother—though I suspect in bare feet, Papa tops me by an inch or so. I'm weary of seeing crop after crop of simpering schoolgirls swan up the church aisles with their lords and honorables and *comtes*. Mama had even started muttering about German princes."

Until she'd said this to her brother, Joan hadn't realized how true the words were.

"But a mill owner, Joan? He watches you to see which fork you pick up first, as does his sister."

The path down to the loch curved, so Joan was

momentarily cast more snugly against her brother. Tye was solid, strong, and confident in his faculties to a point approaching arrogance, and Joan wanted—for the duration of one sweeping curve—to confide her situation to him in its entirety.

Edward Valmonte was born knowing which fork to use, and where to thrust his *fork* for best advantage.

"Mr. Hartwell might be watching me for the same reason you watch your countess, Tiberius, and the same reason Papa watches Mama."

Especially lately.

"Those two," Tye snorted. "I caught them lingering beneath the mistletoe yesterday morning and about had apoplexy at the sight. Mama is a force to be reckoned with."

Her son was only now realizing it? "Did you clear your throat and look appalled? Start lecturing them about decorum and children being underfoot?" Because Tiberius could deliver a prodigious scold any day of the week.

"I clapped his lordship on the shoulder as I fled the scene. It's Christmas, they've recently fallen back in love, and allowances must be made. Love is a form of madness in some people, and I don't think age or station has anything to say to it."

❧

"I want to disdain Hartwell because he's in trade," Tiberius admitted, accepting a nip from the Earl of Balfour's flask—for he'd drained his own before the hockey game had even started.

Asher MacGregor was cast in the same mold as

the rest of his family: tall, muscular, and green-eyed. His dark hair flirted with the chilly breeze as he and Tiberius watched the teams on the ice circle around the puck.

"You canna disdain a man who moves like that," Balfour said. "He's a demon with that stick."

On the ice, Hartwell leaped, spun, and came down with his stick already smacking the puck—hard—directly for the barrels marking the opposing team's goal. And in the next instant, he was off, ready to follow up, defend, or score as the opportunities arose.

"I can't fault his athleticism. I also can't feel my knees," Tiberius said. "And I wish I'd remained behind this morning to read stories to my son in the cozy privacy of the nursery. When there's a break, we're going back in."

For they captained opposing teams, of course. Behind them, near the bonfire, the children were enjoying hot chocolate and the doting attentions of the women, who had some gender-specific ability to ignore all the grace and power—and freezing knees—on display on the ice.

"I don't disdain Hartwell," Balfour said, capping his flask and mercifully allowing Tiberius's whining to go unremarked. "I respect the hell out of a fellow who can build up an empire on the strength of hard work, shrewdness, and daring. My own family took in paying guests, for God's sake, and that was hard enough, though the only thing they risked was the respect of their neighbors."

The puck shot forward, no less party than His Grace, the Marquess of Quinworth, defending for the southern team. A mad scramble ensued, and more than a little swearing—in Gaelic, English, and broad Scots—as players took off toward the northern goal.

"I want to disdain Hartwell," Tiberius said. In truth, he couldn't feel anything below about mid thigh. "I'm not succeeding very well at it. He treats Joan with utmost respect, though his manners aren't exactly polished."

"Ach, manners. Now those will keep a woman warm at night. I'm sure your countess would agree, though mine might argue the point. You're daft, Spathfoy, to carp about manners and disdain. Lady Joan is beautiful, well dowered, and knows exactly what an English marquess's daughter is worth to the bachelors prowling around the ballrooms. Christ, that had to hurt."

The puck had hopped up, as pucks will do, and clipped Balfour's younger brother Gilgallon on the arm.

"He's Scottish," Tiberius said. "He'll play more fiercely for the pain, or perhaps he's so cold he can't feel anything." For both teams were kilted in the interests of better mobility, or—Spathfoy suspected a sadistic streak in his in-laws—freezing several pairs of English ballocks into oblivion.

"Spathfoy, get in here!" Gilgallon called. "I need me wife to kiss it better."

Play suspended until Tye was in position on the ice, and then damned if it didn't feel glorious to skate all out for the sheer hell of it. In minutes, his lungs were heaving, and his focus fixed on whacking the bloody puck into the opposing team's goal.

The moment came, the sweet, surprising instant

when a clear shot opened up, with none to defend it. Spathfoy cocked his stick back and put every ounce of fraternal frustration, family concern, and sheer male exuberance into his swing.

The puck went aloft rather than skidding along the ice, and for a progression of heartbeats, Spathfoy purely admired the hurtling shape silhouetted against a blue, blue winter sky.

Somebody swore, and with the speed of thought, Spathfoy's internal admiration shifted to horror. A child had wandered onto the ice, outside the bounds of the makeshift field of play. She twirled, red braids flying out behind her, as if in her boots, she could practice the moves of the men on their skates.

Spathfoy's bodily reality became sympathy for every bullet ever aimed at a living creature: *Hit me, not the child.* For God's sake, not the child.

From nowhere, a kilted shape tackled the girl and went sliding across the ice with her, the ice cracking. The puck slammed into a meaty male shoulder, and the women came running down the bank en masse.

"She's all right," Hector MacMillan said, skating past Spathfoy. "He got to her in time, and she'll be all right."

The game broke up, as well it should when tragedy had been narrowly averted. Had the puck struck the child on the head…

"Tiberius!" His countess stood on the shore, swathed head to toe in the Flynn hunting plaid. The other skaters moved past him, back to the benches around the bonfire, back to the women and children.

Hester must have been watching, must have

understood that it was her husband's wild shot that had jeopardized the child. Perhaps she also grasped that Spathfoy could not make his feet move.

"Tiberius," she said again, striding onto the ice. "Charlie's quite unhurt, but my chin went numb an hour ago. Cease looking so virile and impervious to the elements, if you please, and stand at my back around the bonfire."

She reached him and wrapped her arms around him. His stick lay some yards away, though he didn't recall dropping it.

"I could have killed her," Spathfoy said, arms around his wife. Hester was quite petite, and with the added height of his skates, she felt like a child against him. "With one shot, I could have killed that girl or worse."

A shiver passed through him that had nothing to do with the cold.

"The child shouldn't have been on the ice, but the nannies aren't used to the cold, and Miss Hartwell was engrossed in cheering for the northern team. Are you all right?"

Spathfoy had no idea what his wife had just said, but he could see she was worried—could feel it in her continued embrace.

"I must apologize to the child, and to her father." He let Hester take his hand and walk beside him as she led him toward the bank of the loch. "I was worried about his manners. He has protective instincts that defy human limitations, and I was worried about his manners."

Hester gave him a look of wifely exasperation and let him clamber up the bank on his own.

❧

"You'll both join us for cards after supper," Spathfoy said, sounding very much like he was offering Dante the English aristocrat's version of a one-way trip down a dark alley.

"I'd be delighted to."

Spathfoy departed, no doubt to change out of his kilt now that the wedding entourage had reached the relative civilization of Aberdeen. The ceremony would be held at St. Andrews the following morning, provided both bride and groom showed up.

"I think he's trying to be friendly," Hector said, looking puzzled. "Hard to tell without his countess to translate."

Dante set aside the list of guests attending the wedding breakfast.

"I think it's tradition that the men hold a wake for a fellow's bachelorhood the night before the wedding. You may have this back, with my thanks."

He passed Hector the list of wedding guests, which had given him a headache, to say the least.

"You will not have a better opportunity for finding investors," Hector said, letting the list lie on the table between them. "Two dukes, a marquess, five earls, not including the two intent on getting you drunk tonight, a sprinkling of viscounts, and more barons and honorables than any one church should hold."

"They're all strangers to me, Hector." Dante hadn't much acquaintance with inebriation either, though its appeal was growing on him.

Hector stuffed the report into a satchel that went with them everywhere, even on this traveling circus of a wedding excursion. "Are you having second thoughts now?"

"The mills are producing capital steadily, the workers are happy, our products are respected, and our name is growing trustworthy. I don't *need* to refurbish and expand, I simply want to."

They were in the sitting room of the elegant hotel the MacGregors and Flynns had all but taken over upon arriving in Aberdeen. Balfour's countess had conferred with Joan, messengers had been dispatched, and all put in readiness—on less than a week's notice.

"The mills are producing capital," Hector said, snapping the satchel closed. "That's exactly why you can attract investors now. But your looms are aging, you need ventilation to keep up with the newest mills, a modernized loading dock would allow you to move a lot more raw wool in and finished product out, there's hardly enough light for the women to—"

Dante held up a hand rather than hear the very same arguments he himself had made to Rowena for five straight years—when they were speaking at all.

"My point is that business partners should have a sense of one another. A title does not make a man honorable."

Though lack of one certainly made his honor suspect in certain quarters.

Hector rose, and damned if Hector wasn't wearing proper trousers. "A title makes a man a gentleman with a pressing need to diversify his income, because nobody lives well off the land rents anymore. Polite Society took fifty years to realize diversification won't put dirt under their fingernails, and now they've caught onto the notion with a vengeance. Play cards,

Dante. Marry Lady Joan, ingratiate yourself with the
wedding guests, and turn wine into money at the
marriage feast."

Hector tromped off, satchel and biblical analogies in
hand, leaving Dante alone with another list—potential
investors known to socialize with Quinworth's
family—and check marks beside the names of those
who'd be attending the wedding breakfast.

The train ride into Aberdeen had been lovely. He
and Joan had had a compartment to themselves—
though visitors had been frequent—and he'd sat
beside her, listening to her chatter about her wedding dress, her niece Fiona's rabbit, her parents'
hot-and-cold marriage, and the menu for the wedding breakfast.

Joan had been nervous, and Dante had availed
himself of her hand. She'd blushed and chattered some
more, and then fallen silent, her head on his shoulder.

And in that silence, they'd been nervous together.

❧

"I must have said my vows properly," Joan said, smiling out the coach window at the crowd waving them
off, "because it appears we're married."

The coach lurched forward, the noise receded, and
Joan let her smile fade as well.

"I'm sitting beside you, and if we were not yet
married, I would be on the opposite bench—until we
were safe from prying eyes."

The sentiment was comforting, suggesting that
marriage had taken Mr. Hartwell by surprise too. He
grasped Joan's hand—maybe having small children

made a man prone to holding hands—and pulled the shade down.

"We still have the wedding breakfast to get through," Joan said, because that would be the true ordeal. Edward Valmonte, his mother, and his uncle had attended the service, his fiancée also in their party. A man who would bring a fiancée to a recent lover's wedding was a man who'd make good on threats of blackmail.

"I have it on excellent authority the menu for the wedding breakfast will be delightful, though I doubt I'll taste any of it."

"Don't let me get tipsy," Joan said, though she hadn't planned on that request. She hadn't planned on gripping Mr. Hart—*her husband's* hand so tightly, either.

"I wish you would," he said. "I wish you would trust that on your wedding day, your small misstep has been dealt with, you are safely married, and none can destroy the contentment and joy of the occasion. For Christmas, you should allow yourself to cease fretting and have some fun."

She shook her hand free of his and smoothed down the green velvet skirt of her wedding dress. The Christmas season had allowed her to choose a color far more flattering than virginal white would have been— also more honest.

"What token would you like for Christmas, Mr. Hartwell? I cannot imagine you've been anything other than a good, hardworking boy this year."

Her teasing fell flat and sounded condescending. Also nervous.

"I have been given a wife to cherish and hold dear, a mother for my children, a friend for my sister—who faces the daunting prospect of taking a place in Polite Society—and a lot of fellows to play cards with at family gatherings."

He apparently knew better than to mention love.

"Dora told me you'd been taken up by the press-gangs after supper. She said the smoke was so thick in the card parlor, you'll be airing your smoking jacket for weeks."

Joan's hand was taken captive again as her husband slouched down against the squabs and propped a boot against the opposite bench. This, too, was proof they were married, for a man would not have taken those liberties with a woman he was merely courting.

"Little sisters make the best spies," he said. "Just ask Charlie. I think Spathfoy was trying to make amends for nearly killing Charlie. Wait until that boy of his is in short coats. We'll see Spathfoy's hair turn white in the space of a year. You would have told me if the need for this wedding had grown less urgent, wouldn't you?"

Having a husband would be quite an adjustment—having *this* husband.

"I am not—I have not been—indisposed."

"That's unusual for you?"

The hotel approached, all decked out in holly and red-sashed wreaths, though blessedly devoid of mistle-toe. Joan wanted neither to remain in the coach with her smiling, relaxed husband, nor to go inside and face Edward and his innuendos.

Edward, who stood right beside his fiancée amid the throng lined up to welcome Joan and her new husband to the wedding breakfast.

"Might we finish this discussion later?" Joan asked

as Dante handed her down. "For the present, we have more good cheer to endure."

Twelve

"Too bad you couldn't have ended up with the likes of her."

Uncle Valerian's comment had been made with enough half-soused jocular bonhomie that several heads turned in Edward's direction. Thank heavens Mama and Dorcas were trying to draw the notice of some countess or other.

"I am content with my choice," Edward said, a diplomatic overstatement. Dorcas had a tendency to manage—witness her insistence that she join this outing in the North, and Christmas only two weeks away.

"I am content with your choice too," Uncle said, lowering his voice. "Get your hands on those settlements, my boy, and my contentment will bloom into glee."

Because that remark had also, no doubt, been overheard, Edward allowed his smile to become naughty. "It isn't the settlements I'm longing to get my hands on."

That was not quite a lie. Dorcas had permitted him only chaste pecks to her rosy cheeks—three so far.

Miserly little gestures that did not bode well for the succession Edward was intent on securing.

While Joan looked radiant, and when her new spouse had kissed her on the lips as they'd descended from their coach, the bride—*without* blushing—had kissed him back and cradled his cheek as if her every wish had come true in the church an hour past.

A fine show, but Edward gambled it was mostly show when he cornered the bride between well-wishers at the wedding breakfast.

"Where is your new husband?" Edward asked, sliding into the empty seat beside Joan. "He leaves his treasure unguarded on the very morning he acquires it?"

"Hello, Edward. My brother and father have taken my husband to introduce him to Their Graces. Perhaps it's your fiancée who should take more notice of your wanderings."

Her smile was positively diabolical, suggesting… Edward slapped aside the notion of Joan and Dorcas whispering in some corner.

"There's a duke here?"

"Moreland and his lady, a charming older couple who've formed a connection with the MacGregors. Her Grace enjoys the braw, bonnie lads in their kilts."

The wedding party had sported a small army of those.

Joan beamed in the general direction of a knot of people, one of whom was her plebeian—braw, bonnie, kilted—choice of a husband.

"You received my latest note, my lady?"

She took a nibble of cake off her husband's plate and chewed slowly, as if assessing the strength of the vanilla flavoring in the frosting. "Did you send me felicitations, Edward? I would have thought Lady Dorcas might have handled that formality for you."

Lady Dorcas, who was watching this exchange with undue interest from two tables over.

"I am happy for you, Joan. Sincerely happy, but you and I have matters to discuss if you are to have any chance at happiness as well. I have your drawings, and the lower orders are known to be possessive and old-fashioned regarding matters of chastity and marital fidelity."

Edward had made a life's work out of reading his mother's expressions, and he was becoming adept at reading Dorcas's as well. If Joan were truly unconcerned about her evening in Edward's private parlor, if she were daring him to start scandal, she would have laughed, patted his hand, or asked him to renew her acquaintance with Dorcas.

Instead, the lady's gaze went to her husband, who was smiling at something a tall, lean, older gentleman had said.

"You were naughty, Lady Joan, *very* naughty, and while you might feel compelled to confess that naughtiness to your new husband—wedding nights can be so awkward, can't they?—you won't want your lapse bruited about among Polite Society. You will meet me the day after tomorrow at the tea shop just off Wapping near the green. Three of the clock, sharp."

"How do you know I'm not off on a wedding journey?"

Not a go-to-hell, not a slap to the face. He wished she'd do both, and he wished ladies' fashions were a lot more profitable than they had been in recent years.

He also wished Dorcas's casual perusal wasn't turning perilously close to inconvenient curiosity.

"Nobody travels with the Yule season approaching, and your Scotsman will make a great fuss over the New Year, as they all do. Your family will want to make sure he doesn't gobble you up whole, too, so for the next few weeks, you and I can see a bit more of each other."

Because she was the bride, and it was her wedding day, Edward leaned over and would have kissed the lady on the cheek, except a large hand clamped down on his shoulder.

"Ach, get yer own lady to take liberties with," said a jovial male voice. "I can assure you this lady is spoken for and will remain so for the rest of my natural days."

Edward rose to greet the groom, the first time he'd come face-to-face with the man—or face to chin, for Joan had married a veritable brute.

"Edward, Viscount Valmonte, at your service. Old friends like to offer good wishes on such a felicitous day."

How it galled to play the pretty, but from the calculation in Hartwell's eyes, Edward could not be certain—not absolutely, positively certain—that the groom's jocular warning hadn't been in deadly earnest.

Which was good. If Joan had a jealous husband, she'd be all that much more likely to meet Edward's demands.

Edward bowed to the lady. "Happy Christmas, Lady Joan."

He sauntered back to the company of his fiancée, whose cheek he did kiss, right there in public, where Dorcas couldn't do a damned thing to stop him.

❦

Dante's objective was simple: he wanted no dirty looks from the new Mrs. Hartwell come morning. How to achieve that goal as yet eluded him.

"You've married a lazy man, Mrs. Hartwell." He confessed that sin while taking Joan's cloak from her shoulders. They'd seen the last of the guests off, smiling and waving in the chilly afternoon air as clouds had hastened the early darkness common in December.

"You're not lazy," Joan said, more tiredly than loyally. "If Hector had his way, you'd do nothing but work. How did I get mud on this hem?"

"I am lazy. Hector equipped me with a list of the wedding guests, and in the time I might have memorized the names of every wool supplier in the realm, all I could keep straight is that Moreland is the one with the pretty duchess."

Of all the titles who'd come to see Lady Joan Flynn's hasty wedding, the duke and his lady had seemed to genuinely wish the couple well.

"Her Grace took an interest in Balfour's situation."

Much of Society had taken an *interest* in Lady Joan Flynn's downfall, though they'd at least been polite about it. One well-dressed, smiling lord or lady after another had found a moment to accost Joan, while Dante had been dragged from guest to guest by Balfour's family. He'd not known whether to return to her side and force her to present her lowborn spouse to her friends, or leave her in peace to make what excuses she could.

"The maids can tend to your hem in the morning," Dante said. "I've left instructions we're not to be disturbed."

The day had been a progression of revelations, such as any wedding day between relative strangers might be. Joan had been a beautiful bride, for example. Not pretty, not well dressed, not even blushing, but beautiful.

"But my hooks—"

Beautiful, though not eager. Dante twirled a finger. "I'm competent to unhook a dress, if you'll permit it?"

"Of course." She presented her back and swept her hair from her nape, the gesture brisk and... unseductive.

"Are you nervous, Joan?" He started at the top, grateful that the myriad hooks meant this wedding night could get off to an unhurried start.

"I'm still Lady Joan, not that it matters."

He suspected it mattered a great deal. "I'm nervous, my lady. The vows cannot be consummated without your participation."

The nape of her neck turned an interesting shade of pink. "One gathered as much."

He rested his cheek against the bump at the top of her spine, wishing she'd turn around and gather her husband into her arms. "Promise me, no dirty looks in the morning."

She didn't laugh—perceptive of her. "I'll want the lights out."

Dante went back to unhooking her dress, because he'd progressed less than halfway down her long, graceful back. "We can manage in the dark."

Though her request made him uneasy. Whose face would she rather see on her wedding night? Prancing lordlings by the dozen had bowed over her hand, and Valmonte had been on the verge of stealing a kiss.

"We can even manage so you need not see my face at all," he said, though the offer made him angry.

More hooks came undone, while Dante realized he'd made an offer he could not support. If Joan wanted him to toss up her skirts and rut on her from behind, like some ram after the ewes in spring, he could not accommodate her.

"I like your face very well," she said. "But I'm not…"

She wasn't in love with him, which notion shouldn't bother a man who'd used his wedding breakfast to make the acquaintance of dukes, earls, and viscounts. "You're not what? Not ready? Putting off the intimacies won't make them any easier. Not for me."

"I'm not pretty."

Of all the daft—

Six more hooks to go, and Dante dispatched them in silence. Rowena's looks had been average—pretty enough—but she'd been so confident of her father's affections, of her entitlement to deference as a function of her father's wealth, that pretty hadn't come into it.

Not ever.

"No, you're not pretty." He pushed the sleeves of the dress off her shoulders, slowly, slowly, revealing pale skin and elegant curves. "You're beautiful. Pretty is for schoolgirls, shopgirls, and debutantes. Pretty is for bouquets and hillsides. You have dignity, poise, charm, wit, and courage. God save me from a wife whose sole attribute is mere prettiness."

He'd puzzled her. In the cheval mirror, he could see auburn brows knit and mental gears turn—while he tried to undress her.

"You're handsome, though," she retorted—accused.

"All the ladies were inspecting you today, admiring your kilt—*and your knees.*"

Her comment laid a trap of some sort, one neither a homely husband nor a handsome one could crawl out of with her regard for him intact.

He started on the bows of her corset cover. "I'm relieved to have their inspection over with, if you want the truth. Relieved the ceremony is behind us. This is a fetching dress."

"I hadn't time to add much lace," she said, reminding him that clothing and fabric served in conversation with Joan much as the weather might for others. "Mama thought my dress plain."

"She said it was daringly elegant. I heard her." At least three times. While the marchioness had no doubt been sincere and well-meaning, each repetition had left Joan more nervous and uncertain. "The color is lovely on you."

Dante had just unknotted the lacings of her stays— she apparently didn't believe in lacing herself to oblivion—when Joan turned to face him.

"You truly like this color? As greens go, it's on the pale side."

She was pale, and the strain of the day put shadows beneath her eyes. Perhaps she fussed her clothing because that was something a woman could control, even a wealthy, titled woman.

"Demure, not pale," he said, thanking whatever merciful deity had inspired his vocabulary. "But, Joan?"

"Mr. Hartwell?"

"You need not be demure with your husband. You can be honest. If the notion of coupling with me horrifies you, then say so. It's been only ten days since you boarded my train, and there's still some time when uncertainty—"

The god of inspired vocabulary had dispensed a solitary favor and then fled the scene. Dante fell silent rather than do greater damage.

Lady Joan stood before him, her bodice gaping away from her underlinen, her hem sporting a few dashes of mud. Between uncertainty and fatigue, Dante endured a stirring of sentiment—longing, protectiveness, affection—despite their circumstances.

Despite everything.

"I want to have a wedding night with my wife, but more significantly, I want her to enjoy that wedding night. If that means we wait, then I will wait."

If heaven were merciful, maybe he'd wait only until morning.

Joan was not inclined to offer him ready assurances. Hope sank, but didn't go completely under, because the lady was still standing before him in dishabille, looking both puzzled and determined.

"I am not pretty, but you are handsome. We'll muddle through, Mr. Hartwell, and without anybody handing out dirty looks in the morning."

He'd amused her. Thank heavens, he'd amused her.

"Help me with this infernal neckcloth thing," he said, lifting his chin. "Hector knotted it up as if he wanted to strangle me."

Because Dante did not use a valet, and knew nothing of what was fashionable, while Hector had studied up on the matter of cravats and neckcloths and ties prior to the wedding.

"It's a jabot," she said, "old-fashioned and French, owing to the formality of the occasion. You might need it if we're ever to present you at court."

"Now you'll give a poor Scottish lad nightmares on his wedding night."

She draped the lacy French thing over his shoulder, as if it were a pet. "What next?" she asked, stroking the lace. "Is this where we climb under the covers and become man and wife?"

He wanted more than that for her and for himself too, but had no clue in which direction *more* might lie. "You didn't enjoy your wedding day, did you?"

Another stroke of pale fingers over lace. "Today wasn't awful. My family loves me, and that was…was a gift. Even my sisters."

He unpinned a spray of lily of the valley from her hair. "You seemed happy enough at the church."

"I had you beside me at the church."

He passed her the little bouquet, a bit wilted but still fragrant. "I'll be beside you in that bed, too, and in life. The two go together, and you'll be beside me."

Dante looked forward to that, in fact, but didn't push his luck by telling her as much. Instead, he turned her by the shoulders and nudged her in the direction of the bedroom.

"I'll call for you in a few minutes," she said, apparently grasping his scheme. "When I'm under the covers."

"I will not cross that threshold until you summon me."

But they would emerge from their bedroom as man and wife—if he didn't bungle this wedding night too.

How had Joan not realized what a good-looking fellow she'd married? In his wedding day finery, Dante Hartwell had been the handsomest man of the entire gathering—tall, muscular, broad-shouldered, and imbued with a sort of bodily confidence even Tiberius didn't manage in a kilt.

Far handsomer than Edward Valmonte, who'd looked effete in his gray morning attire and white gloves.

Clothes did not make the man, Joan decided, hanging her wedding finery in the wardrobe, though they might do a great deal for a lady. Her dress needed more lace, another flounce at the hem, another dash of piping or embroidery, but she hadn't had time to create that additional camouflage.

Now, her only camouflage would be darkness.

She peeled out of the rest of her clothes, tended to her ablutions, and donned the sheer nightgown she'd chosen from her trousseau. In darkness, the embroidery on the hems and seams would go unappreciated by her husband, but Joan would feel it against her skin.

In the next room, Mr. Hartwell stirred, possibly banking the fire or pouring himself a drink.

For warmth, Joan also put on the silk-and-velvet night robe that went with the nightgown, then brushed her teeth and took down her hair.

A bride was to leave her hair unbound.

A bride was also supposed to be chaste and at least infatuated with her groom, if not in love with him.

Joan braided her hair, climbed onto the bed, and called to her husband. "Mr. Hartwell, you may join me."

He sauntered into the bedroom interminable

moments later, waistcoat undone, the first few buttons of his shirt open, cuffs turned back. "You don't dither about before bed. That's a fine quality in a wife."

Dithering would not have solved anything, would not have made the specter of Edward Valmonte and his presumption any easier to banish.

"Do you need help getting undressed?" Though clearly he had the process under way without her help.

He peered in the general direction of the bed. Joan had turned the lamps down, but the fire in the hearth still cast some light. "Stay where you're warm, lass, and I'll be along shortly."

Joan's feet were cold, and the rest of her wasn't exactly cozy, either. The notion that Dante Hartwell would join his body to hers—and this time spend his seed inside her body—was neither repugnant nor enticing, but merely…odd.

Water splashed, then a toothbrush tapped against a basin. The mattress dipped long moments later.

"Are you nervous, lass?"

She'd dodged that same question previously. "Yes. You?"

"A wee bit. I've admitted as much."

He settled about two feet away, which wouldn't do much to warm Joan's feet.

"You've done this before," she pointed out.

"Not for quite a while." He kindly did not remind Joan that she'd apparently done it before too, which was the very reason they were sharing a wedding night.

That lowering piece of self-castigation illuminated an insight for Joan: Edward Valmonte had stolen her good name, and he still threatened her future. Joan might placate Edward with more designs or with money, but under no circumstances could she allow Edward to taint the intimate aspects of her marriage.

But how to go on?

Sir, would you please impale me on your hedgehog? "Have you decided what to give your children for Christmas?"

"Those two are easy. Charlene is happy with anything—storybooks, hair ribbons, dolls. Phillip is a mechanical sort—he can spend an hour with a spinning top—and he likes his books too."

Joan's parents wouldn't have had such ready answers about their children. "What would you like?" She'd asked him this before, and his answer had been a lot of flattery and indirection.

"Margs will knit me a scarf. Hector will find me a good bottle of whiskey. The women at the mills send a basket of jams and such."

He had employees, not only family. Did Edward Valmonte's seamstresses and cutters send him a basket of jams for the holidays? Joan scooted a foot or so closer to her husband's side of the bed.

"Do you find presents for the children yourself, or leave it to Margaret?"

Or would he pass that responsibility on to Joan? She hoped he would, and might even ask him to. Good heavens, what was *she* to give him for Christmas?

He shifted, such that when Joan stretched out her chilly foot, she encountered his calf. His bare, warm, hairy calf, because her husband slept without the benefit—or hindrance—of clothing.

"I find my own gifts for the children—a papa's

prerogative to put some sort of imprimatur on the holidays. Margaret and Hector deal with the employees' Christmas baskets."

He shifted up onto his side, facing Joan. "What shall I get you for Christmas, Mrs. Hartwell?"

"You've given me your very name. That's gift enough." Also his trust, his respect, his kisses…so many treasures, and all of them as undeserved as they were precious.

He rolled to his back again, suggesting she'd provided the wrong answer.

"I don't want your gratitude, Joan. Loyalty, fidelity, and a good-faith effort to make something of this marriage will be a fine bargain on both of our parts. The marriage is as much opportunity for me as it is convenient for you."

Joan did not want *a fine bargain*, but she did want the warmth her husband's body gave off. She yielded to the craving and snuggled right up to his side. His arms came around her, as if they'd spent many nights visiting their way to shared sleep.

"I kept my nightgown on."

"I know, lass. I'll forgive you that modesty if you kiss me."

She kissed him, and the contour of his lips told her he was smiling. "You should kiss me too, sir. My feet are cold."

"You need your husband to warm them up?"

She needed her husband in so many ways. When Dante kissed her, when he held her and spoke of loyalty and fidelity, then nasty notes and misplaced sketches seemed far away and insignificant.

"Shall I take off my nightgown?" She didn't want to, but Dante was naked, and the intimacies she'd tried hard not to dwell on were commencing.

"You feel safer with it on," he said, shifting to blanket her with his body. "I'll try not to tear it."

Gracious. "I can stitch it back together if you do."

He nuzzled her ear, sending a shivery feeling down Joan's spine. "Kiss me some more, Mrs. Hartwell."

He'd been calling her that since they'd shut out the rest of the world nearly an hour ago, but his voice had taken on a rasp, and her new name had become an endearment.

Also a dare.

She threaded one hand in his hair and used the other to cradle his jaw, the better to know exactly *where* to resume kissing him.

"You shaved again." He'd also used his tooth powder, bless him. This detail reassured Joan, as a memory of Edward's wine-soured breath tried to intrude.

Dante rubbed his cheek against Joan's in answer. The movement rubbed his chest against Joan's too.

"I love silk," Joan said, kissing his smooth jaw. "I think I'll love it even more by morning." Because silk turned every touch—even a touch of chest to breasts—into a caress. Did all married women know that?

Did married *men* know that?

He resumed kissing her, and his tongue came calling, politely at first, then more boldly, until Joan caught on and paid a few calls of her own.

"Your nightgown, woman—"

He tried to lift her hem, but it was trapped under her hips. Joan raised her hips and encountered…*her husband.*

"Careful," he whispered, right near her ear. "Your kisses have inspired me."

He was hard, ready, and naked, while Joan... worked her hem up, not quite to her waist. "I like kissing you too."

In fact, she liked *him*. Liked that he could tell her he wanted no dirty looks between them in the morning—a modest, honest ambition she could share and fulfill. She wasn't so keen on his hand covering her breast through the silk of her nightgown, for Edward had touched her thus—groped at her—and it had been purely unpleasant.

"Don't go shy on me," he whispered, scraping a fingernail over Joan's nipple. "Tell me if you like that."

"Do it again." The sensation was...unnerving. Agitating but pleasurable, not the rough squeezing she'd been subjected to by the viscount. "I'm not sure. It's different." Inspiration struck, and Joan reached between their bodies. "Maybe it feels like when I do this?"

She brushed her thumb over the smooth head of his cock. He retaliated with a similar caress to her nipple. For a few minutes, under the covers, in the warmth and darkness, they experimented with a call and response of caresses, until Joan was panting beneath her husband, and battling an urge to...*squirm*.

"If you keep that up, Mrs. Hartwell, I'll spend, and we'll have to start all over."

Was he complaining? "Is that bad?"

He laughed—or possibly groaned. "Spread your legs, love, and leave off teasing a newly married man."

This made sense, that instead of his legs braced

outside of hers, he should be between her legs, and yet, the position was unbearably *marital*.

"We're about to consummate our vows, aren't we?"

"Aye, as long as you're willing."

Something blunt and warm nudged at Joan's privy parts. The sensation was novel, and neither pleasurable nor painful.

"Hold still a wee bit while I get my bear—there." A forward maneuver, and that blunt warmth began insinuating itself into Joan's body. "You're wet, God be thanked."

"Am I supposed to be?" She thought perhaps she was, because having established her wetness, her husband seemed to gather a sense of purpose.

"I love that you're wet," he said, kissing her cheek. "And you're luscious and hot and wonderful too." More kisses, to her jaw, her ear. Gentle, beguiling kisses to go with a careful joining of their bodies.

His compliments were curious, and accompanied by the peculiar sensation of a male body entangled with Joan's in the coital act. She wanted to ask him if she should *do* something—kiss him back perhaps? But they'd already kissed for some time—and interrupting her husband as he sought to consummate their union didn't seem quite the done thing.

Hold still, he'd said.

The bed bounced rhythmically, distractingly. Dante's breathing became labored, Joan's nightgown bunched up between their bodies, and the temptation to squirm nigh overwhelmed her self-restraint.

"A bit more," her husband rasped. "Almost… Ah, blessed, holy…*God*."

She held still as he thrashed and thrust, until like a locomotive, he decelerated, moving more and more slowly until he came to rest against her.

That was it then. They were married, and though Joan felt a sense of disappointment that was somehow physical, and her feet were still not warm, she was also left with a puzzle.

If she'd undertaken this behavior with Edward Valmonte, she could not recall it, not in any detail of sight, sound, scent, or sensation. Kisses, yes, some rough handling of her breasts, and then Edward's weight—insubstantial compared to Mr. Hartwell's—but nothing more intimate than that.

Another reason to thank God.

Joan kissed her husband's temple and brushed a hand through his hair, grateful beyond measure that, despite her disappointment and cold feet, her only memories of this intimacy would be with her very own Mr. Hartwell.

Thirteen

WORSE THAN DIRTY LOOKS FROM A NEW WIFE WERE NO looks at all, and the sinking conviction that dirty looks were deserved. A man on his second wedding night should have at least pleasured his bride.

Fortunately, Joan did not seem aware of her husband's poor showing, while Dante could focus on little else.

"Do you favor coffee, tea, or chocolate?" Dante asked, though sitting across from him at the small breakfast table, Joan was entirely capable of pouring her own drink, and looking elegant while she did. He simply wanted to know her preferences.

"Chocolate, I think, to celebrate our first morning as man and wife." Her smile was a crumb, tossed his direction as she turned the pages of the Aberdeen newspaper. Hector didn't read the paper with that much focus. Dante himself—

She studied the page as if it were holy writ, or as if she indeed sensed that her one and only wedding night had been less than she deserved.

"They used your word: *demure*. They say my dress

was a demure, elegant concoction in a shade between celadon and jade, with tastefully understated lace adornment suited to the solemn joy of the occasion."

His lovemaking hadn't put a smile like that on her face—yet. He vowed that one day soon—one night very soon—it would.

"Your chocolate, madam. I gather you're pleased with the account of the wedding?"

"I'm pleased with the account of the dress my sisters and I made for the wedding."

Dante wasn't pleased, though the dress, the wedding, and the bride had been lovely. His sole consolation lay in the realization that the wedding night had attained the goal of confusing the paternity of any child Joan might bear nine months hence.

He nonetheless battled a compulsion to take Joan by the hand and drag her back to bed, so he might acquit himself well enough to put *that* smile on her face in the next twenty minutes. The wedding night had been a success from a pragmatic perspective, and only from a pragmatic perspective, but as a lover, he'd finished the race well behind a dress.

At least he'd finished. With Rowena...

He snipped that thought off like a loose thread that could unravel an entire seam, even as he admitted that such memories had contributed to his lack of deliberation with Joan the previous night.

"What will you do now, with your demure, elegant, tastefully understated...dress?"

She stirred her chocolate, much as a general might have stirred chocolate while looking over his battle maps.

"I will add more lace, perhaps a lavender lace fichu, a stripe of purple embroidery about the hem, bodice, and cuffs." The chocolate was set aside, while eggs and toast grew cold on Joan's plate.

"You'll fuss it up," Dante said, taking a bite of his eggs. "Is that your mother's influence?"

And could he order Hector to develop some reports on ladies' fashions? Because apparently, the topic would figure prominently in marital conversations. Perhaps he should have spoken to his wife of silk and nacre in bed?

"My mother?"

Dante put a bite of egg on a corner of toast and passed it to his wife, whose figure, he had occasion to know, had little need for her corsets.

"You said your mama likes to dress loudly, too much flounce and whatnot. You looked lovely yesterday, and I know every person with eyes in that church envied me my bride."

Joan clearly wanted to argue—not to the point of dirty looks—but she instead took the toast.

"Thank you. I *felt* pretty, though my wedding dress isn't my lucky dress."

The first time he'd shared breakfast with Rowena, she'd given him a list of rules she had wanted enforced in the mills, half of which had been damned silly. The list had been a test—would Dante prove himself a fool by enforcing the rules they both knew were silly, or would he prove himself a fool by battling his wife over silly rules?

They had been so young, so unsure of themselves, and so unable to trust each other's support. He felt a stab of compassion for his immature, furious first wife—and for her husband.

Dante knew better now—or hoped he did. "What is a lucky dress? Should I be searching for a lucky kilt?"

Though he suspected he'd been wearing his lucky kilt yesterday, wedding night disappointments notwithstanding.

"It's *that* dress," Joan said, sitting back, eggs, toast, chocolate, quite possibly *husband*, and even her unimpressive wedding night forgotten. "That dress you put on, and you feel like the smartest, most lovely, beneficent woman in the world. You feel like your best self, and like you want to share that best self with all of creation. A lucky dress is comfortable, too, though, and it need not even be all that showy. It's your lucky dress."

"Can a woman have a lucky dressing gown? The one you're wearing is fetching."

And held together with nothing but a sash, or pair of sashes, inside and out.

"I love that you tease me," Joan said, tucking into her eggs with a hint of a smile. "Friends tease each other."

"Spouses do too." Had she recognized the sexual innuendo? Her smile held a fortifying hint of mischief. "Would you please pass the butter, and what do you mean, the dress makes you feel beneficent?"

He asked, because a marquess's daughter might have a different view of spending money than a mill owner's wife. Joan's pin money was spelled out in the settlements, and wasn't much more than Dante set aside regularly for Margs.

"Beneficent to me is sweet, openhearted, in love

with the world," Joan said, passing him the butter. "Generous of spirit."

Like a woman should feel after her husband had shown her a proper wedding night.

"You'll not be making one of these lucky dresses for Margs, then. She can nigh bankrupt me with the Christmas baskets she gives out to the workers each year."

Dante had yet to have his annual argument with Dear Margs on this topic, though it was imperative that expenses be kept to a minimum this year more than ever.

"You do Christmas baskets." Joan's look was the farthest thing from dirty—she *approved* of the Christmas baskets, God help him. "Do you hand them out yourself on Boxing Day?"

"I hand them out with Margs, because she insists that Hard-Hearted Hartwell be seen committing at least one act of wanton generosity. When we send the workers home on Christmas Eve, we send them home with the baskets."

Joan set aside the next bite of eggs and toast her doting husband had so generously provided her.

"You expect people to work on *Christmas Eve*?"

Dante spread butter on his scone—something a doting wife might have done for him.

"They expect to be paid; I expect them to work. It's a quaint system, but has a certain pleasing symmetry. Will you finish those eggs?"

She considered her remaining eggs, she considered her chocolate, and then she considered her husband, and still she didn't give him a dirty look.

She gave him a *pitying* look.

"The holidays are an occasion to celebrate, Dante. People need times to celebrate, to gather with family and express their thanks for the good things in life. Especially when winter closes in, so cold and dark, we need Christmas to cheer us."

He was a papa. He didn't need anybody to explain Christmas to him. Christmas was about storybooks and spinning tops for the children, mistletoe for the maids and footmen.

A free ham for the workers, rum punch, that sort of thing.

"We need coin to pay our rents," he said. "While we're sitting on our backsides, singing carols and swilling wassail, those rents go unpaid." On that point, he'd never taken issue with Rowena. "Besides, Christmas is more English than Scottish. We Scots focus on the future, on the New Year, and the opportunities it brings."

"So you give your workers New Year's Day off?"

Now *his* eggs had gone cold, but he finished them anyway. A new husband needed to keep up his strength, for marriage encompassed many nights when a wife might need her spouse's warmth.

"We relax our vigilance about tardiness on Boxing Day and New Year's, and we close ninety minutes early on Christmas Eve. Any day my people work and the other mills are silent is a day when I'm making profit and the others aren't. That profit is what keeps the mills safe, and puts the Christmas hams in those baskets."

He was happy to explain business to his wife. Joan

was a smart, sensible woman, and fifty years discussing ladies' fashions would be a trial to any husband.

"But if the other mills are silent on Christmas Eve and New Year's, then you wouldn't be falling behind them by giving your workers a holiday."

"Suppose not. Might you pass me the paper?"

"Maybe we English need Christmas more than you Scots do, but Christmas is still important to the Scots."

Christmas pudding was important to them, witness all that nonsense in Balfour's kitchen over the damned pudding. Dante didn't reach for the paper though, because he had a sense his new wife was about to deliver her version of a dirty look.

Over his business practices—an oddly cheering thought. They had years to learn each other's preferences at the breakfast table *and* in bed, after all.

"I'm willing to concede that Christmas has its uses," he said, "else I would not be attending Balfour's holiday house party. Then too, the Yuletide festivities brought you to me, for which I must esteem them greatly."

He assayed a smile and got nowhere with it. Perhaps Lady Joan could accept only compliments to her clothing.

"Dante, please give the workers Christmas Eve and Boxing Day off. Families need to be together at Christmas, and the ladies will work all the more happily in anticipation of your generosity."

Not a dirty look, not a pitying look, but *a hopeful look*.

"They'll miss two days' pay, Joan. Some of them will miss it terribly."

"I have pin money. Surely we can cover two days' pay out of my pin money?"

She made this offer without hesitation, suggesting either it was important to her, or she had no idea what two days' wages amounted to for three mills' worth of hardworking women and girls.

He named a figure, because he knew to the last groat what it took to keep labor on the floors of his—their—mills.

"If I let you cover the wages, who will make up your spring dresses, my lady?"

She waved a hand, no lace at the cuff of her dressing gown. "I make up my dresses—I enjoy it, and I get ideas when I'm doing the cutting and stitching. I have enough fabric to keep me busy for years. Give the ladies time away from their labors, Dante. I'm asking this of you, and making my funds available to see it done."

Her casual offer provoked all manner of thoughts and feelings.

Dante was arguing with his new wife, and nobody was shouting, slamming doors, or silently fuming.

Then too, Joan did make up her own dresses. When he'd inquired of her sister Dora about Joan's whereabouts several days ago, Dora had delivered a lecture on what it took to put together a lady's dress, from sketch to finished garment. According to Lady Dora, those tasks had absorbed his fiancée's every waking hour.

Beneath those realizations lurked another: Joan wasn't wrong. When morale was good, the mills were more productive. Even Hector grudgingly admitted that much, though Margs had to bludgeon him into it.

"I can't let you squander your pin money."

"I've been squandering my pin money for years on dresses. It's my pin money to squander, isn't it?"

"It absolutely is." Just as Margs's pin money was hers, and Dante did not allow himself to wonder what she did with it.

"Well, then. I believe we have a bargain." She smiled, a faint, smug, mysterious smile that was more maddening than a world of dirty looks, for he didn't want a *bargain* with his wife.

He wanted a marriage, and he wanted that smile from her not for his concessions at the mill owner's negotiating table, but for his ability to please her as her husband.

And as her lover.

❦

The first day of Joan's married life was both pleasant and harrowing.

Breakfast was nerve-racking, but civil enough. For luncheon, a private dining room was reserved for such members of Joan's family as hadn't returned to Balfour House for the balance of the holidays.

Tiberius kept shooting her concerned looks across the table, while trying not to get caught at it. The Countess of Balfour offered to take charge of the wedding presents, and Joan's sisters promised to organize the thank-you notes.

After lunch, Hector hovered about looking like a small boy in need of the facilities, until Dante disappeared with him to some location where men might spend an afternoon talking business in private.

And then Tiberius, looking intent on an awkward discussion, sat himself down beside Joan.

"You seem to have weathered your wedding night without serious injury."

Awkward indeed.

"Unlike your countess, Tiberius, I chose a husband already broken to the bridle. Mr. Hartwell has been the soul of consideration." Though Mr. Hartwell needed to learn a thing or two about celebrating holidays.

"If his consideration ever lapses, you will come to me, Joan Flynn. I'm still your brother, and this entire wedding came about far too suddenly. If he anticipated the vows with you, I could understand…?"

Tiberius had more in common with their papa, the marquess, than he knew, for the purpose of this interrogation was to convey love and support, after a fashion.

"We did nothing of the sort, Tiberius. I'm Joan Hartwell now, and I promise you, should Mr. Hartwell's felicity toward me lapse, I will be on your doorstep bag and baggage."

The relief in his eyes suggested this falsehood was what he'd needed to hear, though Joan would never turn her back on the husband who'd stepped forward to avert a scandal of her own making.

Her conscience piped up, sounding very like her brother: meeting with Edward Valmonte was a betrayal of her vows, for Dante Hartwell interpreted those vows to include loyalty and fidelity, both. Lying was not in any way a show of loyalty.

"If Hartwell's felicity lapses," Tiberius replied, "I will ruin him."

"Spathfoy," said a pleasant male voice from behind Joan's chair, "shall I have the same chat with your countess? Offer her asylum if the pillaging Hun she married ever abuses her affection? Assure her that her husband and the father of her children will be subjected to social and financial disaster upon my whim?"

Tiberius rose, and a moment of silent male combat ensued—all tough glances and jutting chins that was really quite dear.

"No need, Hartwell. The lady's own brother offered me the same assurances."

Across the table from Joan, Matthew Daniels—brother to the Countess of Spathfoy—winked at Joan.

All in good fun, then.

The second night of Joan's wedded life was less easily deciphered. Her husband had been dragged off to play cards with the gentlemen, while Joan endured tea with the ladies. Because Dora chose to linger in Aberdeen—shopping, of course—talk did not touch on Joan's wedding night.

Overtly.

The sly glances and knowing smiles when Joan excused herself said enough.

Her husband had told her not to wait up for him, so she braved their chilly bed all on her own, and didn't wake until a large, warm, male body curled around her from behind.

"Missed you," Dante whispered, kissing her ear. Then a pause, while his breath, redolent of tooth powder, fanned over her cheek. "Go back to sleep, love. Your menfolk have fair worn me out."

Joan drifted in slumber, torn between a desire to renew intimacies with her husband—they were married, and she had a sense that what had taken place on her wedding night was merely a prelude to how matters might eventually go on—and a need to hide herself away from him.

Hide herself, and the deceptions she'd perpetrate on him.

❧

The subtlety required of a new husband was exhausting. Also daunting.

Spathfoy had taken himself back up to Balfour House, amid some glowering and handshaking, while Joan's mama had kissed Dante's cheek and given him speculative looks he was at a loss to fathom.

The marquess, oddly enough, had been the one to pat Dante's shoulder and quietly admonish him to: "Give it time, lad. Our dealings with the ladies benefit from patience. God knows, we try theirs."

Margs and Hector had boarded the train, the children shouting and waving with them, and then Joan had declared a desire to go shopping.

The previous night, Dante had damned near cut his throat shaving in the dark, then climbed into bed next to his new wife, determined to improve on his initial showing in the marriage bed.

He'd tried an experimental kiss, missed Joan's cheek and bussed her ear. She hadn't so much as twitched. Hadn't rolled over to ask him about his evening, hadn't touched his face to appreciate his machinations with soap and razor.

And yet, he'd awoken that morning to find a silk-clad wife plastered to his side.

Daunting.

"Shall I accompany you on these shopping raids, my lady?" Dante asked his wife when the train had disappeared from sight. "Seeing and being seen out and about is doubtless part of why we've been allowed a few days here in Aberdeen without your family's company."

Without their meddling.

"They left us here so they might resume their bucolic holidays," she said, taking his arm. "And we were seen by quite a few people at the church when we took our vows."

Her tone was a bit off, insofar as a husband of two days could tell such a thing. "Was it hard to say good-bye to your family?"

The train station was a busy place, right on one of Aberdeen's main thoroughfares. People came and went all around them, mostly happy, some harried. The scent of the place was "winter travel." Wet wool, cold air, and mud, overlaid with the meaty fragrance of fresh bridies sold by the street vendors.

"Hard to say good-bye?" She twitched at her hems as Dante escorted her back to the street. "Yes. They worry. I wasn't sure they would, but they do."

About her. "Are *you* worried?" He could not be more specific—about their marriage, about the scandal it might have caused versus the scandal it should have averted.

About his abilities as her sole source of intimate pleasure for the next few decades.

"Not as worried as I was. Let's get you back to the hotel so Dora and I can start on our shopping."

He accompanied her along the busy streets, glad to have a woman on his arm who didn't mince about, forced to a doddering pace by excessive corsetry or boots more stylish than practical.

And yet, Joan was quiet, and that quiet suggested that even *less worried*, she still had concerns she kept to herself.

"I'd be happy to go with you this afternoon," he said as they marched along. "Fabric shops aren't exactly enemy territory, particularly if they sell wool."

"I couldn't ask it of you. I can linger over bolts of cloth the way some men become absorbed with choosing a horse to purchase. When the fabric is purchased, one must consider thread, binding, linings, that sort of thing. I wouldn't want to bore you so early in our marriage."

She walked more quickly, though the day was as close to sunny and pleasant as December in Aberdeen could be.

"I'm glad to see the last of your family for a few days," Dante said, and that slowed his wife's pace. "They're decent, but I had some notion that endless games of cards might result in more than hours of cigar smoke, casual insults, and petty bets."

Surprisingly modest bets, in fact.

"I thought men enjoyed cards. I thought you hatched up grand schemes over hands of whist, decided who was to stand for which seat in the Commons, that sort of thing."

He drew her back from the curb lest a passing dray

splash mud onto her hems. "So did I. Hector assured me I'd pick up some hints about who's amenable to investing in the mills. I've since realized Hector himself has never sat through an evening of cards with such as your family. He does not know how business is done among the wealthy and titled any more than I do."

They didn't conduct business over cards, or while playing hockey, or during drinks before or after dinner. Perhaps Dante ought not to have admitted as much to his new wife, but if he wanted her trust—and he did—then he had to offer his own.

In vain, apparently.

All Joan had to say when they gained the hotel lobby was, "Dora and I will be back by tea. I'll expect you to save your company exclusively for me when I return."

She kissed his cheek, while Lady Dora pretended to study a couple across the room admonishing a porter to be so very, *very* careful with their luggage.

"Enjoy your shopping."

Dora grabbed Joan's arm. "We always do."

And away they went, leaving Dante feeling…restless. No, not exactly restless…

Orphaned.

His sister and his children were on their way back to the cheerful company at Balfour House, his wife was reveling in the blandishments of Aberdeen's fabric shops, his man of business had for once agreed to leave him in peace.

What was he supposed to do with himself when abandoned for an afternoon the day after his nuptials?

An office in Aberdeen might be possible with additional investments in the mills, so Dante took himself out walking the city during the limited hours of daylight. He had no idea how far he'd wandered, but he must have traveled in a circle, because when he left off trying to compose a letter to Hector, he found himself about three blocks from the hotel.

A bookshop sat across the street, and next to that, one of the tea shops starting to spring up in the larger British cities. He considered stopping in for a cup—tea with Joan was still two hours distant—when both Joan and Dora emerged from the bookshop. They spoke briefly, and then Dora ducked back into the book- store, like a pirate returning to her smuggled treasure.

Dante had lifted his hand to wave at his wife when she marched into the tea shop alone—no sister, no maid—and took a seat in the window, across a small table from none other than Edward Valmonte.

Who had been waiting for her.

❧

"I'm not sure marriage agrees with you, my dear."

Edward lounged back, looking honestly con- cerned, for which Joan purely hated him. Women perfected the drawing-room art of appearing kind while they politely assassinated another lady's marital chances or her entire reputation. False compassion on a man was...

Joan wanted to hit Edward with a closed, bare fist, not a polite slap with her open palm.

Or dress him in pink lace—soiled, ill-fitting pink lace, like a...a bawd.

"Marriage to Mr. Hartwell agrees with me entirely. Give me back my sketches, Edward, and I'll rejoin Dora at the bookshop next door. Nobody need know you're a thief as well as a seducer."

He hadn't brought the sketches, though. Joan could see that much, and the last thing she'd do—the very, very last thing—was heed another invitation from Edward to join him somewhere private.

"Not a thief, certainly, though some might consider that other accusation flattery. Would you like some tea?"

For the sake of appearances, she should order something. "Darjeeling, please."

He placed their order and waited until the tray had been brought to the table, the service laid before them.

And now, she would have to serve him. He knew it too, as evidenced by the smirk lurking in his gray eyes.

Joan sat back without even taking off her gloves. "My sketches?"

"*If* you left any sketches with me, I have misplaced them—temporarily, I'm sure. Won't you pour?"

"I'm not in the mood for tea, though if you aren't more forthcoming, my lord, I might accidentally spill that pot some place your unborn children would regret."

The smirk vanished, replaced by an appraising gleam that—God help her—bore as much approval as speculation.

"I'm designing Maison du Mode's ladies' fashions for this spring in these weeks before Christmas," Edward said, pouring for Joan and then himself. "My ideas are the best ones my mother has seen, from me or even from those poseurs in Paris, and Mama has a very discerning eye. I noticed something, though, Mrs. Hartwell."

The scent of the tea was soothing, and yet, Joan would not partake of even a sip in Edward's presence. Neither would she correct his form of address—she was still *Lady* Joan—when her wedded status was a source of significant comfort.

"I'm all attention, Edward. You noticed something. How fascinating. Perhaps you'll notice that you are in anticipation of holy matrimony, and I doubt your fiancée would be pleased to know how you comported yourself with me while newly engaged to her."

Edward shot his cuffs, which were not exactly pristine. "I noticed signatures on the back of each page of a certain sketchbook. Legible signatures, one of them accompanied by the date of our little encounter."

The tension Joan had been carrying inside for two weeks congealed into despair.

"Signatures proving the sketches are mine, the designs are mine—assuming forgery isn't among your many criminal gifts. You've stolen my good name, Edward, stolen my ideas, and forced decisions on me I should not have had to make. Give me back my sketches."

He stirred his tea, as if answers might float up from the tea leaves.

"I wish I could, but alas, I'm in a quandary. As long as I have that sketchbook, I have evidence that you were quite, quite private with me not two weeks prior to your wedding, for the sketches are also dated. If I surrender those sketches to you—assuming I can find them—then you have proof the lovely spring dresses on my mother, my fiancée, and half the aspiring cits in the realm were your fashions, and not mine."

The only thing worse than being coerced was being coerced by somebody who lacked a shred of sense.

"My designs are not fashionable, Edward. Hoops are growing wider, skirts more elaborate. My designs are not *à la mode* and you know it." They were designs that made a tall, slender woman appear graceful, rather than like the handle of a bell too wide to pass through any door.

"Another quandary, dear Joan, for though skirts *are* growing wider—which means they're costing a great deal more to make—the Queen herself finds that style nothing less than a fire hazard, and will not wear it. Mama reminded me of this when she was cooing over those sketches."

Edward hated Joan for this, clearly, because every design of his own that Joan could recall was for more of those ridiculously wide hoops, contraptions in which a woman could sit only with the greatest of care, and could barely manage to dance at the balls where she wore such finery.

And the Queen was not tall. She was quite, quite short.

"Fine, then," Joan said, rising. "You may have those designs with my blessing. Not a soul will notice that those dresses closely resemble what my sisters, my mother, and I will wear, right down to the flounces and buttons, and we'll wear our dresses much sooner than anybody can purchase the ones you stole from me."

Edward caught her wrist, and while Joan knew she could tromp on his instep and twist away from him—*thank you, Tiberius, for being a protective brother*—she could not cause a scene two days after her own wedding.

"Please do resume your seat, my lady."

She cast a meaningful glance at the steam curling from the spout of the teapot, and Edward dropped her wrist. She did not sit down.

"Make your threats, Edward, for clearly, you have more of them up your sleeve."

Edward rose, as a gentleman must. "Not threats, not to a woman whom I esteem greatly. I will express my regrets that, should you in any way intimate those designs are yours, I will make it plain to the gentlemen in my clubs that a certain lady and I worked on those drawings together, at a time when neither one of us was wearing a stitch. Lovers do that sort of thing, you know."

They took their clothes off, completely off, as Mr. Hartwell took his clothes off before joining Joan in bed.

Standing toe to toe with Edward, so close Joan could smell his gardenia eau de cologne, Joan missed her husband. Dante did not deal in intrigue and innuendo; he did not sneak about and steal; he did not wear lady's perfume...

He did not deserve a wife who slunk around, meeting weasels in tea shops when she ought to be shopping for Christmas gifts.

"Keep the sketches, Edward. Your crime will go unpunished, and if you seek to sully my reputation,

I am married now, to a man with delightfully old-fashioned notions about those who mean his wife ill."

"Then his notions about marital fidelity will be similarly old-fashioned."

The door banged, making a bell tinkle with incongruous cheer, while Joan's insides turned colder than the air outside.

"I must be going, Edward, or Dora will be here, asking questions about why you've lingered in Aberdeen without your fiancée."

"I'll expect more sketches by the end of the month," Edward said quietly, the way a chaperone might inform a debutante of a tea stain on the very bodice of the young lady's presentation gown. "That gives you weeks to come up with summer ideas, and they don't have to be finished—just enough that I can—"

Joan cut him off with a wave of a purple glove. "Show your mother, and continue the farce that your creative genius has finally borne worthy fruit. I can't force myself to create beautiful dresses, Edward. The ideas come or not, without my willing it so."

Had he any understanding of creativity, he'd grasp that much, but such were Edward's limitations that he expected beautiful fashions to march onto the page on a schedule.

She nearly felt sorry for him, dwelling in such darkness while his family expected him to be the artistic engine for their house of fashion.

"I'll want you to do Dorcas's wedding dress," Edward said. "Start on that first, and it had better be good."

What Edward lacked in understanding, he made up for in audacity. "But a wedding dress—"

"Your own was lovely," he said tightly, trying to take the honest compliment from the words, "and you had little time to create it. I want a wedding dress, Joan, for starters, and then I'll want some summer dresses, too."

"*Lady* Joan."

"The title won't help you when the rumors fly—nor will they assist Mr. Hartwell to find the funds he's been trying to drum up between waltzes and weddings."

Edward leaned closer, as if he'd steal a parting kiss to Joan's cheek, but that she could not bear. She nudged at his half-empty teacup, and—alas—warm tea spilled down his trouser leg, and the cup bounced off his boot.

"My apologies," she said as she turned to leave. "And you forgot to wish me happy Christmas. My regards to your fiancée and to your dear mama."

Fourteen

WHAT DID IT SAY ABOUT A MAN THAT HIS FIRST WIFE regarded marriage to him as an occasion for dirty looks, and his second had an assignation with a handsome young lord within two days of her wedding?

Though as assignations went, a meeting in a tea shop was not particularly clandestine—a cheering detail.

"More buttered peas?" Joan asked.

"Please." For Dante had worked up an appetite marching around the darkening city, arguing himself out of an old-fashioned duel of honor. What decided him against such dramatics was the fact that Valmonte, having a title, could credibly claim honor prevented him from meeting a man of much lower station.

Then too, Valmonte might kill him, and where would that leave Margs, Phillip, and Charlie?

Where would that leave Joan?

"You seem preoccupied," Joan said, spooning buttered peas onto his plate. "Are you anxious to get back to your reports?"

He was anxious to shake some answers out of his wife, and yet, by the candles adorning their table, she looked shaken already. Tired, preoccupied, not nearly in the pink.

"I undertook Balfour's house party to widen my circle of acquaintances among the titled and monied, and that plan has been…delayed." Though not thwarted, certainly. He was married to a marquess's daughter now, may God have mercy upon them both.

Joan put her fork down, peas spilling off of it. "I'm sorry. I never considered how marrying me might interrupt your plans. Is it urgent that you have these introductions?"

What was she asking?

"Important, but not urgent, and the holidays were a convenient way to see the goal accomplished. You haven't eaten much, my lady."

She organized her peas, tidied them into a corner of her plate the way a man arranged the cards in his hand in anticipation of a round of betting.

"May I ask you a question, Husband?"

No, he would not consider an annulment if there was no baby. Of that, he was certain—though one marriage to a reluctant bride had been one too many.

Christ.

"Ask."

"Did you marry me for my dowry? If you did, that's entirely understandable. I should bring something to the union, after all, besides scandal and bad judgment, but if money is—"

She was herding peas at a great rate. Dante took her hand, relieved it of her fork, and laced their fingers.

"Do you want an annulment if there is no child?"

She gripped his hand more snugly. "Certainly not. I want to understand our situation."

Oh, the delicacy of the aristocracy.

"Come," he said, drawing her to her feet. "Unless you're in want of tea or sweets?"

She made a face Dante had often seen on Charlie, an expression that restored a man's faith in his future—some.

"No tea, thank you. I'm learning to enjoy coffee and chocolate."

He walked with her to their bedroom, leaving the dishes in the sitting room for the silent, unobtrusive hotel staff to deal with.

"Shall I unlace you?"

"Please."

The prosaic exchange of a man and his wife at the end of their day, though Dante had every confidence Joan would again use a lady's maid when they rejoined the Balfour house party.

While he had no intention of hiring a valet.

"Did you and Dora make many purchases this afternoon?" Dante asked as he started on Joan's hooks. The ladies had come home empty-handed, though the shops would deliver parcels anywhere, for a sum.

"Dora is book mad, the way some people are horse mad, or cannot stop themselves from gambling. She is on a mission to find books for every member of our holiday gathering. What did you do with yourself this afternoon?"

They might have had this discussion over dinner, except Joan had interrogated him about the mills—how many employees, what ages, what hours did they work?

"I walked the city, looking for a place to set up offices near the docks. How many hooks can one dress have?"

"My back is longer than most women's," Joan said, as if admitting a fault.

"Your back is beautiful." A correction more than a compliment, so he tried again. "You are beautiful." Physically beautiful, but also beautiful in a way that confounded him, and should have been impossible, given what he'd seen at that tea shop.

No reply as her sleeves loosened from her shoulders and Dante resisted the temptation to kiss her nape.

Because he was an idiot, quite possibly an idiot married to an unfaithful wife. Though again, a meeting in a tea shop was not the stuff of adultery per se.

"You asked about our situation," Dante said, tugging Joan's sleeves down her arms and untying the bows on her chemise and corset cover. "What exactly would you like to know?"

She stepped away, heading for the privacy screen.

"Where shall we live, for one thing?" Her undone clothing rustled softly as she moved, not the same crisp swish and sway of a lady in public; rather, the sartorial whisper of a woman with whom a man was intimate.

"I have houses in Edinburgh and outside Glasgow, and rooms in Newcastle." The rooms were his. The town house was Charlie's, the country house, Phillip's. He started on a circuit of the room, turning down lamps. "Each dwelling is comfortable enough."

"Where are your mills?"

"Outside Glasgow, not far from the Clyde." Not far from the house, either.

"Do you weave cotton or linen?"

He was tall enough to see over the privacy screen, so he knew Joan was poised with her hands braced on the washstand, head down, as if a great weariness beset her. He turned to the wardrobe and began disrobing rather than intrude further on her privacy—or be caught staring, for Joan was tall too.

"We handle some linen and some cotton, but mostly wool. We're dependent on the Americans for the cotton, and that bunch hasn't sorted themselves out yet. Linen is less risky over the long term, but wool we have in abundance right here. Leave me some wash water, if you please."

"Of course."

Until they were in bed—Joan in her silk night-gown, of course—it went like that, a question from Joan, an answer from her husband, and no questions at all in the opposite direction.

"You asked about our situation," Dante said, blowing out the last candle and climbing onto the bed. "May I assume you want to know how we're fixed?"

"Yes."

How to explain it?

"In one sense, we're wealthy. The mills are profitable and worth a great deal. We keep our equipment and premises in excellent repair, and we turn out a good product. None of it—not the land, the looms, the facilities, the houses—is mortgaged."

"And in another sense?"

Well, damn. Joan lay on her back, reclining amid the pillows, hands folded over her middle. Dante had seen tombs decorated with saints in such a pose.

"My side of the bed is a bit chilly," he said, which was an utter untruth *in one sense.* "Would you mind paying a call on your husband?"

Was that a smile threatening her saintly impassivity? By the limited light of the banked fire, Dante could not be sure, and yet, Joan shifted and rolled and boosted herself across the bed and tucked herself against him.

"Hello, Husband. Can't have you taking a chill."

He wrapped his arms around her, arranged her braid so it wasn't trapped between them, and endured the slide of silk over his thighs as Joan got comfortable.

"In another sense," he went on, as if a woman's nearly naked body were not pressed to his, "we are cash poor, the same as any old duke trying to live off his land rents. I made the decision years ago to pay off the debt on the mills rather than amass personal assets, and that means any major difficulty—a roof collapsing, a strike, a fire—and we don't have the capital to rebuild."

This had been a perpetual argument between him and Rowena.

"Have you insurance?"

Insightful question, and Dante's best counterargument. "Of course, but there's no insuring against a strike."

Joan scooted around again, her arm draped over Dante's belly as if she'd keep him from pitching away in a high wind.

"Nobody can prevent strikes, though your Christmas baskets are a form of insurance, however small. I doubt my brother has explained as much of the family finances to his countess."

He nuzzled her crown, because her hair was tickling his cheek. "You've mentioned that your mother takes an interest in commerce."

"She used to. Now, I'm not so sure what occupies Mama's time. Ordering my father about, mostly. I'm not a spendthrift, Mr. Hartwell. I will manage within my pin money handily. We will have household budgets, and I'll manage within those too."

To reply to those brisk assurances with a declaration of love would not do, but Dante was that grateful for Joan's insight.

"I worry about money," he admitted softly. "I'm the son of peasants, many people depend on me, and I worry about money. You have married down, Lady Joan."

Though he was learning that other concerns could eclipse money on his list of anxieties.

"I married well," she said, kissing his jaw. "Of this you may be certain, sir: I will not add to your burdens and worries."

He cuddled her closer rather than tell her she already had.

⁓

Tell him.

Tell your husband Edward Valmonte is threatening you, your marriage, possibly even your husband's business prospects.

Dante's cheek was not as smooth as it had been the past two nights, and Joan liked that. She did *not* like the sense that in addition to possibly carrying a child, she had brought the potential for her husband's ruin into the marriage.

"You cannot help but add to my burdens," Dante said. "Now I must wrack my brain to come up with a Christmas gift for you. Please assure me I needn't buy a token for Spathfoy too."

"Tiberius would be mortified to accept any gift from you. He holds himself accountable for Charlie's mishap on the ice."

She felt him sorting through Charlie's various mishaps, for the child had several a day.

"Your brother is an idiot, though he grows on one. Shall I make love with you, Mrs. Hartwell?"

The question was quiet and casual, punctuated with a kiss to Joan's temple. She liked that too, even as Edward's attempt to kiss her cheek earlier in the day lingered on the edge of her awareness.

"I would like…you shall make love with me," she said. "I want us to begin as we intend to go on, as a real couple, enjoying real intimacies."

"You enjoyed them, then? Our wedding night intimacies?"

She had…and she hadn't. She sensed that her answer mattered, though, and not every husband would be considerate—or courageous—enough to ask.

"I was nervous." She was nervous still, for many reasons.

"I was as well. I think we established that. What would set you at ease?"

This question too was quiet and casual, and yet, it bore worlds of significance, about the man Joan had married, about what that man deserved from his new wife.

"I'm nearly on the shelf," Joan said, tracing the

curve of her husband's ribs. "I *was* nearly on the shelf. I was the older sister, the lady of my father's house for several years in Mama's absence, the sibling Tiberius could rely on to help keep family matters organized."

"You are a formidable lady."

A formidable lady, defeated by a fool and his schemes.

"Your assessment is generous, and yet, you're right: I've grown used to thinking of myself as competent, and in this wife business…"

Dante shifted, wrapped his arms around her, and heaved up, so Joan was—just like that—straddling her husband.

"Listen to me, my lady. The genius of the institution of marriage is that husband and wife enter the race from the same starting line at the same time. We're fumbling around in this marriage together, hoping good luck, good faith, and time will mature our union into a partnership. I'm hoping that, at least."

Another question, delicately put. "I am too, desperately."

He cradled her cheek against a warm, callused palm. "I believe you, so we must have frequent negotiations, about how to go on, about how not to go on. You will have notions about Charlie and Phillip that haven't occurred to me, and I might have a few ideas about this baby you'll find worthy of your consideration."

He was asking Joan for permission to hope that their marriage could become a partnership in every way—and deftly reminding her that children, *a baby even*, depended on Joan's ability to have these negotiations with her new husband.

"For Christmas, you want a real wife," Joan said, which she desperately hoped she might be for him.

"A wife, a lover, a mother for my children. Yes, I've been a good boy, Joan Hartwell, and my hopes for this Christmas are high."

While Joan hoped to placate Edward with a few drawings—for now. She curled against her husband, felled by the realization that after summer fashions, Edward would clamor for autumn dresses, and so on.

She had *not* been a good girl, but she was damned if she'd allow Edward's venery to blight her entire marriage.

"Tell me about the lover part," she said. "I had the sense that our wedding night, as pleasant as it was, was not the great passion the poets allude to, and that the fault for this may lie with me."

Or with her husband's consideration of her?

"Pleasant." Dante groaned the word. "Pleasant is a place to start, but we can aim much, much higher."

Joan expected a discourse from her husband on what he sought from his wife under intimate circumstances. Mama had suggested that ordering one's spouse about in bed was one of a marriage's great pleasures, and Joan was willing to be ordered.

Such was her sense of indebtedness to her husband.

Mr. Hartwell's notions did not exactly comport with Mama's views.

"Make free with my person," he said, placing Joan's hands on his chest. "And allow me to make free with yours in any manner that brings you pleasure."

Merciful saints. "Your chest feels like..." Not like any fabric Joan had touched previously. He had a dusting of springy hair, but then came warm skin, resilient muscle, and unyielding bone. Under her palm, his heart beat in a slow, steady rhythm.

"While you feel like heaven," he said, gliding his hand over the silk of Joan's nightgown. "Do you like it when I touch your breasts?"

"Touch them, and I'll give you a report."

Her retort provoked a smile, and all manner of touches. Gentle, firm, teasing, cherishing, all through the gossamer barrier of silk. And then his mouth—hot, damp, and disconcerting—drawing on her and causing sensations that...

"How shall I make free with your person, Husband?"

She wanted to kiss him, but he had only the one mouth, and that one mouth was wonderfully busy.

"Touch me," he whispered as he switched breasts and arched up beneath Joan.

Oh.

Oh.

"Am I to move, then?"

"Move, wiggle, tease, stroke, pet, *fuck*..."

Once, when Tiberius's horse had stepped on his foot, Joan had heard her brother mutter that same word. Repeatedly. Even the horse had looked abashed.

"Say that again," she whispered, tugging her nightgown up past her hips so hot skin brushed hot skin. "Say it."

"It's vulgar," he replied, using a particular hard, smooth part of him to stroke over Joan's sex. "I should not use such language before a lady."

"I'm your lover," Joan said, lowering herself enough to trap that same part of him between their bodies. "Make free with your naughty talk."

"Then fuck me," he said softly, as much dare as invitation. "Take me in your hand, Joan, and put me inside you."

And here came a revelation: Joan desired her husband.

She wanted to be a good wife to him, because she owed him that and she'd taken vows, but she also desired, even *needed*, these marital intimacies with him.

She wrapped her fingers around his shaft and positioned him. "Like this?"

And oh, this was *better*.

For as he glided into her body, shallowly, slowly, by maddeningly patient increments, Joan's husband also dallied with her breasts.

"Move, Joan. Don't make me do all the work."

"Move how?" For all she felt was that undifferentiated urge to squirm, though now she also wanted to scream.

He went still.

"That doesn't help," Joan said, trapping his hands against her breasts, lest the misguided man cease all his efforts at once. "I prefer it when you move."

She preferred it *frantically* that he should resume moving. *Frantically and immediately.*

He curled up and kissed her, hard, a reminder that kissing could be part of this too, which was true enough, but rather beside the—

"You move here," he said, his hands guiding Joan on either hip. "Pleasure yourself, use me to gratify your passion."

She wanted his caresses to her breasts, but with his bare hands on her bare hips, he showed her an intimate, interesting rhythm, that took all of her concentration.

"Like this?"

"Exactly like that."

His hands fell away. Without ceasing her undulation, Joan put his palms over her breasts again. "Please."

Bless him, he obliged, until sensations began to pile up on each other, resonate, and overlap. Heat and wanting swamped Joan from within, as well as a sense of freedom twined around a longing of the body and the heart both.

"Joan, slow down." Dante's hands were back on her hips, trying to still her movements, but she could not allow it. If anything, she wanted more—

"Please, love. I'll spend if you can't—"

She kissed him to stop his prattling, because something bright and novel was welling up from inside her, or from *him*, inside her. His grip on her tightened, and he hilted himself hard against her, while all Joan wanted to do was to keep thrashing, until, until—

She could not think until *what*, because her husband had gone still again, breathing hard, his arms wrapping Joan in a fierce embrace.

"Good God, woman." A hoarse, wondering endearment. "Good God Almighty."

Her body vibrated with longing, she was breathing hard, and her husband had subsided utterly.

"Are you all right?" Because their previous attempts at marital intimacies had not been as athletic. "Dante? Is anything amiss?"

"I am not all right. I am *married*."

"You sound pleased." While Joan was bewildered, for surely this flustered, anxious, dissatisfied feeling was not marital bliss?

"I am slain on the altar of your passions. Again, dammit. Joan, I'm sorry."

Naughty talk had served her much better than her husband's silly poetry, for Joan's passions left her with an inconvenient urge to weep.

"I made free with your person, Husband."

"My early Christmas present, and yet, I sense your own efforts were not similarly rewarded." He pushed her braid over her shoulder, a gentle touch that invited Joan to cuddle against him. "Talk to me, Joan. I left you hanging, didn't I? I left you hanging again."

He was already threatening to slip from her body, and the sensation underscored a sense of emotional emptiness. "I don't know what you mean."

And they would soon make a mess of her nightgown.

"Here." He snatched a handkerchief from the night table. "To catch my seed."

More vulgar talk, though not half so inspiring as his earlier pronouncements.

"I don't know as I'm fit for this aspect of being a wife." She made use of his linen, and found some consolation curling onto his chest.

"You are fit for this," he said, patting her silk-clad bum in a manner that had to be husbandly. "You most assuredly are. The fault lies with me. My self-restraint is out of practice, but I'll make amends. I promise I'll make frequent, sincere amends. You deserve to find your pleasure, but I hadn't expected such passion in a new wife. My delight renders me…incompetent. I'm sorry, and I'll find my balance soon."

His apologies were heartfelt and comforting, though

Joan still wasn't exactly certain what he apologized for. Dante Hartwell was many things—honest, pragmatic, honorable, passionate, and hardworking—but incompetent was not among them.

He continued to stroke her backside, which soothed the riot inside Joan, and yet, she fell asleep wondering: If she were honest with her new husband, if she confided her situation to him, and explained to him exactly how great a liability he'd taken on when he'd married her, would he have any interest in making those frequent, sincere amends?

Would he have any interest in remaining married?

❧

"You allowed your sister to marry a man whose finances you hadn't thoroughly investigated?"

Asher MacGregor, Earl of Balfour, could not resist an opportunity to needle the oh-so-competent Tiberius Flynn, Earl of Spathfoy. Petty behavior, true, but Spathfoy was an English lord much in need of needling, and a host's holiday generosity compelled Balfour to tend to the oversight.

"I hadn't time to investigate Hartwell's finances," Spathfoy said, tying a crooked pink bow on a sprig of greenery. "And though you Scots might do it differently, in England, a girl's papa is the one looking over her suitors."

"I've found something at which you do not excel," Balfour remarked, snatching the mistletoe from Spathfoy and untying the bow. "Who dresses you, Spathfoy? Your bows positively droop."

"My countess dresses me, and undresses me, and

she has no complaints about anything drooping. Your bow isn't much better than mine."

"Mine is jaunty, yours droops. Where shall we hang this?"

"I don't see why we're the ones assigned this task," Spathfoy groused, picking up another sheaf of mistletoe and choosing a red ribbon. "The footmen would be happy to take it on, and the maids would cheerfully direct them."

Balfour rose to poke up the fire in the library's enormous hearth. "In the first place, the ladies assigned this task to us so we wouldn't be underfoot in the kitchens. No less personage than the Duchess of Moreland has passed down her family recipe for some German sort of holiday cake, and nothing will do but Hannah must teach it to the ladies of the assemblage."

"So when are we to raid the kitchen?" This bow was no better than the last, though Spathfoy appeared to admire his own handiwork.

"The stuff has to bake, Spathfoy."

"No, it does not. Have you never eaten cake batter, Balfour? Never dipped a larcenous finger in the sweet, creamy— You're not tying your share, old man. Stop wandering about and get back over here."

Balfour heeded the scold because it was deserved. "More droopery. He can steal cake batter like a schoolboy, but a simple bow eludes him. What shall we do about Hartwell and your sister?"

The only bows left were white, which meant they were reaching the end of this inane exercise.

"I've threatened him with worse than ruin if he

trifles with Joan's affections. I think this is my best one yet."

"For God's—" Balfour left off wrestling a sheaf of mistletoe and a ribbon that wouldn't stay snug about the stems. "A charming effort. There's hope for you, Spathfoy, and while I approve of some judicious threatening when it comes to one's sisters' suitors, I invited Hartwell here in part to explore some business opportunities with him."

A large, blunt, half-English finger came down on the half hitch of Asher's bow. "It works better this way, though if you try to entrap my finger and take liberties with my person, my threats will all be reserved for you, Balfour."

"Don't flatter yourself. I'm getting your countess eyeglasses for Christmas. You'd best enjoy her misguided attentions while you have them, Lord Droopy Bows."

"Hartwell strikes me as a good man," Spathfoy said when Balfour's bow—by far the best of a bad lot—was complete. "Prudent, hardworking, shrewd, devoted to his children. His sister approves of him."

And those last two attributes—devotion to children and a sister's regard—would carry weight with Spathfoy, as well they should.

"He has some odd notions," Balfour said. Scottish notions, he suspected. "Rather than build up cash reserves, he's paid down debt."

"Mortgages are available when cash is in short supply." Spathfoy gathered up his pile of bound mistletoe, which—let it be noted—was about half the size of Balfour's.

"Mortgages are available when a business is on solid footing. When trouble strikes, nobody lends a bloody groat, regardless of how much sound management, potential profit, or equity remains to secure the loan. I say we hang some mistletoe in each bedroom."

"I hardly need mistletoe to undertake kissing in my own bedroom, Balfour. And if you do, then my profound condolences to your count—"

Balfour tossed a bouquet of mistletoe and ribbon at Spathfoy's chest. "You have no holiday spirit. Dickens wrote a story in which your sort figured prominently."

Spathfoy rose and deposited Balfour's missile in a plain wooden crate piled high with beribboned greenery. "You're saying Hartwell could use some investors."

"For an Englishman, you're a quick study. Hartwell is now family to you, your sister's welfare bound up with his. Before I involve myself, my brothers, or my brother-in-law in his business, I thought I'd give you the opportunity."

Spathfoy rooted through the mistletoe, selecting a fat bundle bound with red ribbon. "You were being polite, then, allowing me to bat first?"

"What are you doing with that?"

Rather than answer, Spathfoy leaped onto Balfour's estate desk in a single athletic bound, nearly landing on a stack of bank drafts and correspondence. "Your countess will thank me." He tied the mistletoe to a lamp hanging over the desk—tied it off center—then hopped down, nimble as a cat.

"For an English galoot, you move quietly. And yes, I think you and your father ought to have first go at investing in Hartwell's mills. He oversees them himself, lives within walking distance of them for much of the year, and employs mostly women."

Spathfoy stood back, hands on hips, surveying his feeble attempt at decoration. "I thought it was the hemp mills that restricted themselves to women."

"And the hemp mills have had a notable lack of unrest among their workers. Hartwell says women are more reliable, they drink less, they're content with modest wages, and they do better fine work. Why in the bloody hell did you hang that over my desk? I'll be interrupted the livelong day until the berries are all gone."

And Spathfoy would sneak down here in the dead of night to hang fresh mistletoe, until Balfour had been kissed to within an inch of his life.

"I'm being generous," Spathfoy said, picking up the box. "You're Scottish, so generosity is a foreign concept to you. This way, you need only sit upon your lordly, kilted arse, looking conscientious and businesslike, and you'll gather up kisses. Let's be off, shall we? We have at least three dozen bundles yet to hang, and this is a large house."

"You'll talk to Hartwell about his mills?" Because generosity was *not* a foreign concept to the Scots, and Balfour had once been a man with few supporters and many mouths to feed.

"Come along, Balfour. The ladies are depending on us."

"I hate it when you're coy, Spathfoy. It hardly becomes an Englishman of your self-importance."

"You're just jealous." Spathfoy moved toward the door, the pied piper of mistletoe. "I have consequence and dignity, and better than all that, I have strategy."

"You have a big, nattering English mouth. You'll talk to Hartwell?"

"I've invited MacMillan to join us for cards tonight, and my countess has taken Miss Hartwell under her wing. You and I are off to hang some mistletoe in the nursery."

Where Hartwell's children were corrupting the youth of the Scottish Highlands, and likely aggravating a fat rabbit as well. Balfour followed his lordship into the chilly corridor, hustling to keep pace.

"*Our niece* is in that nursery, Spathfoy. Fiona and her damned rabbit will tie us to the bookshelves and make us read fairy tales until spring, and Hartwell's get will assist her."

"If I'm inclined to invest in Hartwell's mills, that doesn't preclude you from doing likewise, you know."

"You'd invest jointly with me?" The question had to be asked, though Spathfoy was fairly leaping up the stairs with his box of mistletoe.

"I never said that, though I cannot speak for my father's judgment in these matters—or my mother's. They're headstrong, those two. They consider you family, and try as I might, I cannot dissuade them from the notion. Mama's Scottish antecedents might have something to do with her confusion."

Or with Spathfoy's pride.

They reached the floor upon which the nursery was located, as was made obvious by the boisterous rendition of "Silent Night" ringing down the hallway.

"The children are in excellent voice," Spathfoy remarked, heading for the nursery suite.

"And the maids are likely half-swizzled."

Three-quarters, from the sounds of their caroling. "Why are we starting up here, Spathfoy? The footmen come up only to trim wicks, tend the grates, and deal with that damned rabbit. That mistletoe will go to waste."

"Frederick is a good fellow, Balfour—for a rabbit— and if you're not a good earl, for Christmas I'll find Frederick a lady rabbit to keep him company. I might anyway. A lonely rabbit is an offense against the natural order, according to my countess."

For God's sake. The Lord of Misrule was making an early start on the season. "Have you been at the eggnog, Spathfoy? You're taking this holiday spirit thing a wee bit too far."

Spathfoy paused outside the nursery suite door, while the children shifted into a version of "Greensleeves," which had lyrics children ought not to be singing.

"You don't want to spend the morning hanging three-dozen sprigs of damned mistletoe any more than I do."

"Language, Spathfoy. We're preparing to storm the nursery, after all."

"And likely to endure the kisses of the nursery maids." Spathfoy did not exactly need to steel himself to make that sacrifice, judging from his piratical expression.

"And we'll kiss the little girls, and that damned rabbit, too, but *why?*"

"So that when we turn to our next objective—*the kitchens*—we will have our reinforcements with us."

"Because," Balfour said, helping himself to two sprigs of mistletoe, "if we have the children with us, nobody will be scolded for snitching batter or biscuits."

"Or for stealing kisses."

Fifteen

To Hector's surprise, cards among the wealthy and titled wasn't much different from cards among the unwealthy and untitled. Men drank, they complained about the cards in their hands, they muttered about the other fellows having good luck, and bragged on their own skill.

Earls, however, lamented not knowing what to give their countesses for a Christmas token. They offered terse condolences to one another upon the misery of having a child in the nursery who was—sorry to hear it, laddie—teething.

Or colicky.

Balfour's brothers had been at the table, along with Hector, Balfour, and Spathfoy. Connor MacGregor favored singing the old Highland ballads and lays to a teething child, and had gone so far as to share a few verses of a wee tune he'd devised for the very purpose.

Gilgallon thought a child best soothed by slow rocking in a papa's arms, while Ian MacGregor had found that reciting the 23rd Psalm had a calming effect—on the papa, if not the child.

Mary Frances's husband, Matthew Daniels, had said little, but had done considerable justice to the decanters.

Daft, the lot of them, though Connor had a beautiful bass-baritone singing voice.

Hector had excused himself as the hour approached midnight, having the sense that play would be for something other than farthing points in his absence.

He made his way to the library, not only in search of a certain bonnie lassie awake past her bedtime, or not exclusively in search of her, but also because something had teased at the back of his mind, niggled, like a shutter banging somewhere distant in a big house on a windy day.

The library was occupied, else there would have been no candles lit on the towering Christmas tree. The entire room smelled like a German forest—brisk, piney, and cozy at the same time.

"You'll ruin your eyes, Margaret Hartwell." But what a lovely picture she made, curled in one corner of the sofa, her feet tucked under her, a book open on her lap.

"I'm not reading." She uncurled and stretched, which made her bodice seams strain. "I was thinking. You've been excused from the card table?"

She was less fussy around him since they'd shared a kiss. Hector's purpose for visiting the library had been to root around on the vast desk, because he had a sense some document or other wanted sending to Aberdeen, or some memo hadn't been forwarded to its proper destination.

"I excused myself. I've never endured such a herd of nannies fretting over their charges. What were you not reading?"

She held out the book, which necessitated that Hector approach the sofa. "Miss Austen. She has a bracing wit."

"I tried reading some of that stuff," he confessed, setting the book aside and taking the place beside Margs. "At first I thought she didn't like men very much, and then I thought she didn't like *anybody* very much—though she did enjoy wielding a skilled pen."

"If you like English prose." They shared a look, one that agreed that English prose was a lesser class of discourse than Scottish prose. "I wonder if I'll end up like Miss Austen."

Whatever tugged at Hector from the depths of the desk would keep. "You'll pen sniffy novels and content yourself without husband or children?"

The notion gave him a pang. Margs was a natural with children, and they adored her. She had the gentle knack of inspiring compliance without giving orders.

"I'll be the family spinster, visiting this or that relative over the holidays, confiding my petty woes and wants in a tidy journal that nobody will read until some niece or other finds it two decades after my death, and thinks what a funny old thing Aunt Margs was."

The fire gave off a nice peaty warmth, and the candles on the tree added to a sense that the entire world had left Hector these few moments of privacy with a quiet, pretty woman who was in need of…reassurance.

"Your brother has married well, my dear. Lady Joan will see you matched with some wealthy fellow, one who can look after you properly."

"I suspect Dante married in part for me and the children."

304304304304

304304

"He might have," Hector said, rising lest he take Margaret in his arms and offer something other than reassurance. "He also married her because she could open doors for him that all the waltzing and card playing in Scotland could not."

To give himself something to do, Hector took up the brass candlesnuffer from the mantel and carefully put out the candles on the tree, one by one.

"Do you think so? I'd rather they married because of a sudden, overwhelming attraction."

Half the candles were out, which was a fine way to occupy a man when his thoughts were turning to mistletoe and futile dreams, but the room grew darker with each candle snuffed.

Rather like Hector's dreams.

"You're a romantic, Margaret Hartwell, if you believe in sudden mutual passions. Don't worry, your secret is safe with me."

As was she. One indulgence, one kiss, could be forgiven as a lapse inspired by wassail and mistletoe, but for Hector to again take advantage of the late hour and the solitude would be ungentlemanly.

"My secrets are safe with you, of course. My person is probably safe with you as well, as is, of course, my antique and useless virtue."

The homey fragrance of beeswax and candle smoke joined the peat and pine of the library as Hector snuffed the last candle. "You sound unhappy to be assured of honorable treatment."

She sounded peeved, in fact.

"Was Balfour courting your loyalty, Hector? Was he making subtle overtures to entice you away from Dante?"

He set the candlesnuffer down on the mantel, but didn't pay enough attention, for it went clattering to the hearthstones. "Was Balfour *what*?"

"Was he exploring whether you might come to work with him? Might tell him Dante's secrets, so he could purchase Dante's mills the next time the women are of a mind to strike?"

He set the snuffer on the desk—a reminder to explore the desk later, because something still nagged at him.

"What are you going on about, Margaret? The card game was merely friendly, or as friendly as a card game can be when Daniels and Spathfoy must be so English, and the MacGregors so Scottish."

Though they *had* asked him a number of questions about the mills, and about Dante's role in running them. Casual questions.

About Hector's role.

He sat abruptly.

He wanted to run a mill, true. Wanted the day-to-day decisions, the balancing of profit with practicality and decency. Wanted to know that some far-off child was trudging to services warmly wrapped in wool that Hector had had a hand in making available to the child's family at a reasonable price.

And he wanted…

"I'm loyal to my employer, Margaret Hartwell. Doubt whatever else you like, but not that."

Though if he had his own mill, he'd certainly not waste his limited time discussing business with Margaret.

"Damn you men."

Hector had time to think, "*Margaret never curses,*"

before a surprisingly strong shove sent him over onto his back, and a not particularly happy female straddled his middle.

"I shall be an old maid, and you'll be writing up Dante's reports, and all the while, Hector MacMillan…"

He loathed to see Margaret upset, though the feel of her—skirts bunched, her knees snug against his hips—was fearsomely agreeable. "Margaret, what are you about?"

She leaned down, the better to glower at him. "If one of those earls or their wealthy relations offers you a job managing their affairs, you take it. I've watched Dante for years, pretending that humble origins haven't cost him, that his regard for Rowena was genuine and not manufactured in the interests of his ambitions."

Insight struck, warm and sweet. "You daft wee woman, you fancy me."

Not as two people orbiting the same mill owner might have a friendly regard for each other, but as a woman who waited up late in a lonely library might fancy a man who made excuses to visit that library.

"Aye. I fancy you. I fancy your kisses too."

"Those, you may have." As for the rest of it… Hector urged Margaret down into his embrace. He was familiar to her at a time when much was changing in her world; he was safe and could be trusted not to pursue a woman above his touch. Dante might have the balls to seize Lady Joan's hand when it became available; Hector couldn't view marriage from as mercenary a perspective.

"You're humoring me, you dratted man."

He kissed her cheek, then her eyebrow. "Aye." He should lock the door.

He kissed her nose instead.

She sighed, a soft exhalation of frustrations, insecurities, and who knew what else.

"I don't take well to teasing," she groused. "I want your kisses, Mr. MacMillan."

He wanted all of her, for the rest of his days, but Dante would not allow that, and forcing Margaret to choose between her brother and a prospective husband of exceedingly modest means was beyond him.

"Kiss me, then, wee Margs. Cease yer bletherin'."

They kissed and talked until the small hours, falling asleep entwined on the sofa. Hector eventually roused and carried a drowsy Margaret to her bed, kissed her forehead, and left her to dreams more pleasant than his own could be.

For he'd recalled what had bothered him so, what had nagged at his conscience.

He'd seen Dante write out the bank draft to renew the insurance policy on the mills, but Hector could not recall passing a missive containing the document to the postmaster in Ballater. In the morning he'd assure himself the bank draft had been sent, come mistletoe, wassail, or even a spinster with a taste for his kisses.

❧

Joan had married a working man, and the difference between her husband and the other men she'd had occasion to study at close range fascinated her.

The marquess, like generations of landed gentlemen

before him, typically rose and rode out early, at least several mornings a week if the weather were fair. He might grab his fowling piece and tramp his woods when game was in season, or take a fishing pole and spend an hour or two on a handy riverbank. Riding to hounds between harvest and planting was his dearest delight—after his marchioness, of course—regardless of the weather.

Quinworth had correspondence to tend to, and a secretary to assist with it, but business was an afterthought on his schedule.

Tiberius lived life less at leisure, in that he spent more time with his commercial interests—and with his countess—but he, too, ordered his day as much for pleasure as productivity.

Dante Hartwell *worked*.

In the week he and Joan had spent in Aberdeen, Joan had awoken every morning to find her husband in a dressing gown, sitting with a single lighted lamp, a cup of coffee by his elbow as he read some pamphlet, report, letter, or newspaper. He went to bed the same way—reading—until, with all the lights out, he'd take Joan in his arms and make slow, sweet love to her.

If they took a carriage, he read in the carriage. If Joan went out of an afternoon to pay a call or browse the shops, she'd come back by teatime to find him scribbling away at figures or dashing off a note to Hector or one of the mill suppliers or managers.

His fascination with matters of business intrigued her, even as she acknowledged that for the first time in her life, she was becoming acquainted with jealousy.

"What shall you do, Wife, on this our last day of

freedom before we must return to the loving arms of our families?"

"I haven't found you a Christmas present yet," Joan said, and perhaps it was English of her, but a present to her husband on their first shared Christmas was important.

"Make me something with these clever hands of yours," he said, reaching across the breakfast table to clasp Joan's hand. "Something to remind me of my wife."

"I don't know much about men's fashions." Joan visually measured his shoulders. For embroidered handkerchiefs would not do. For all she knew, Charlie and Margs were giving him embroidered handkerchiefs. "Waistcoats have always fascinated me."

Dante set his paper aside and topped up Joan's coffee. "Why is that?"

Her brother or her father would have gone back to their newspapers had she made her observation at the Flynn family breakfast table. Her sisters would have rolled their eyes while her mother gave her a pitying look.

"You can tell a man by his waistcoats. The waist-coat is one aspect of his clothing that allows for some color and some individual style, and what a fellow does with it gives insight into his character."

He added a half teaspoon of sugar, a dollop of cream, and a dash of cinnamon to Joan's coffee, then set it by her plate.

"Your brother is a sober and elegant man, then, with a hidden streak of daring."

"Yes." Exactly, precisely.

"And Hector is desirous of more notice than I give him."

Joan took a considering sip of perfect coffee. "Many men wear plaid waistcoats, especially here in the North."

But in this conversation—about waistcoats, her family, and her husband's man of business—Joan grasped a sense of exchanged marital confidences, and that appealed to her more than the coffee she was learning to savor.

"Hector is restless," Dante said. "I'm not sure what to do for him. If I give him any more responsibilities, he'll have no time for sleep. He churns out reports and memos and calculations almost faster than I can read them, but when it comes to the mills…"

Joan took a turn reaching across the table and squeezing her spouse's hand. "When it comes to the mills?"

"Nobody had to show me how to take apart or put together a loom. I can't say I was born understanding how one works, but with a few tools, I soon figured it out."

"Sewing is the same for me. I see a dress, and know how it's put together, and often, how it might have been done better—a different fabric, a different piecing scheme, or different lining."

Again, her family might have scoffed at that offering, but Joan was coming to understand that her family did a lot of scoffing at one another.

While Dante Hartwell listened.

"For me, the broken piece of equipment is a chance to leave the perishing paperwork on the desk for a change and do something of practical value. Coal mining was like that too."

All Joan knew about coal mining was that it was dirty, dangerous, brutally hard work. "In what sense?"

"A man who digs a ton of coal knows that people will be kept warm by that coal, locomotives will roll across the land burning coal, industry will turn coal into all manner of products. Coal matters."

Viewed through her husband's eyes, yes, it rather did. "And Hector lacks your ability to repair a loom? Aren't there others with that skill?"

He withdrew his hand, maybe the better to concentrate on Joan's question. "Margs has the same ability. It's the damnedest thing. An entire crew was struggling to get a new dye vat through the loading dock doors, and it looked like we were going to have to tear down the factory and rebuild it around the damned vat. Margs came by with my lunch, or some such rot, and she quietly suggested we turn the thing on its head, angle it so, and buy an inch of purchase by taking the doors off their hinges."

"And you listened to her."

"I either listened to her or had wider doors installed on the one mill I can honestly say I own. She glowed for a week over it."

Margaret's brother still glowed with the memory of his sister's cleverness. Had Tiberius ever been that proud of his sisters?

"You should talk to Hector," Joan said, taking another sip of coffee. "Ask him in what direction his ambitions lie. My father once said an ideal toady is lazy, smart, and proud. Such a man will delegate work efficiently and take enough pride in the results to ensure they're competently rendered, and yet, he'll lack the ambition to leave his employer, much less establish a competing enterprise."

Papa's diatribe had gained Joan's notice, because it suggested he was not the simple hounds-and-horses man Mama and Tiberius sometimes made him out to be. Judging by her husband's expression, Papa's thinking had gained Dante's notice too.

"Hector is not a toady."

"I don't think your Mr. MacMillan is lazy, either."

On that thoughtful observation, Joan picked up her small stack of correspondence, despite a lack of enthusiasm for its contents. The good wishes of Society acquaintances on the occasion of her wedding—and so on and so forth, *dearest Lady Joan*—were not half so interesting to Joan as her marriage.

She was falling in love with her husband. Yes, he worked incessantly, but he also *listened* to her. He was patient with her in bed, and tender, and he wrote notes to his children and his sister among his other correspondence, and—

Something Dante had said floated to the surface of Joan's musings.

"I thought you owned three mills." She was sure he'd said as much, repeatedly.

"I own the one," he said without glancing up from whatever he read. "The other two are held in trust, one each for Charlie and Phillip. The rail cars are part of the same trusts, and there's stock too."

Unease slithered down Joan's spine. Ownership was not a detail. She was sure she would have taken note if her husband had explained this to her earlier.

"And the houses?"

"Charlie owns the town house, Phillip the country house. I'm trustee over the lot of it for some time yet, and I'll end up with minority shares fairly soon." He'd nearly muttered this, so intent was he on some column of figures.

Joan lifted her coffee cup to her lips, but the contents had grown tepid.

Her husband owned one mill. A single mill. He had not even a house to call his own.

They had not even a house to call their own.

Abruptly, the buttery scones and crisp bacon Joan had enjoyed with her coffee threatened to make a reappearance. She was upset with herself, for not ascertaining her husband's relative poverty before she'd married him, and she was upset for Dante.

This arrangement was Rowena's doing, Joan was sure of that. The woman had been so resentful of the need to marry to secure control of the mills that she'd organized her affairs to keep Dante from ever having title to them.

Idly Joan leafed through her correspondence, not even seeing the letters she held, but needing to do something with her hands.

"You're quiet," Dante said, peering over the rims of his gold spectacles. "Planning another assault on the shops?"

The last epistle in the stack bore a familiar elegant script, and Joan's queasiness was joined by a dull throb behind her eyes. "I suppose I ought to, lest I return to the Highlands without anything to give my husband for Christmas."

"We're not poor," Dante said, a touch defensively.

He apparently understood her the way he understood one of those complicated looms in the mills he did not own.

"We're not wealthy either," Joan said, regretting the words as soon as she'd uttered them. Regretting was an acquired skill, and she would soon excel at it.

Dante took off his glasses, folded them slowly, and tucked them into a pocket of the waistcoat he wore beneath his dressing gown—a muted version of the Brodie hunting plaid.

"I will provide for you, Lady Joan. You will never go hungry. You'll never be without a comfortable roof over your head. You'll never want for safety and a place to come home to."

He didn't mention that her children would all be legitimate, and for that, her nascent love acquired an element of admiration.

"I don't need more than that, and if your incessant work is undertaken in the misguided belief that I do, please know that you're mistaken. I simply did not understand that these…assets belonged to the children. I understand that now."

Whatever he'd expected her to say—that Rowena woman really had much to answer for—his raised eyebrows suggested it wasn't that.

"We're set up well enough," he said. "I'll organize the figures, and we'll go over them together. The children hold title, but I've allowed no mortgages on their assets, and all the profits from the mills and the estate are mine to do with as I see fit." He leaned over the table and kissed her cheek. "*Don't worry.* If we're prudent and a bit lucky, things will be fine."

That he would be honest, that he'd offer her a tutorial on their finances, reassured her no small amount.

And yet, Joan did worry. She was a new wife preparing to have yet another assignation with a scoundrel who could ruin not only her good name, but her husband's apparently precarious finances as well.

❧

Some men did not have the knack of being married, and Dante feared he might be one of them.

Joan was patient and affectionate with him in bed—even passionate—but he sensed she'd yet to find her pleasure in his arms. A man never knew for sure, particularly with a woman he'd made love to only a half-dozen times, but a husband had instincts, and Dante's were coming to dread the end of each day.

Again.

And now this little tête-à-tête over breakfast had upset Joan to the point that she was putting a hand to her belly and probably fearing starvation.

"Why don't I come with you this morning, Wife? We'll bill and coo before the shop owners, do the newlywed bit, and earn some bargains in the name of the recently married."

He should not have mocked their wedded state, for Joan rose, her hand on her stomach.

"That's very generous of you, but you ought to put our last day of peace and quiet to use here. Tomorrow it's back to the children and the holiday nonsense and being cheerful guests at a busy house party."

She hurried off to the privacy screen, leaving Dante with cold coffee, scones that turned to the consistency of hockey pucks when cool, and kippers—which a new husband could ingest only if the tooth powder were particularly effective.

His gaze fell on the correspondence Joan had been reading. She'd left the table in such a rush that the last letter remained open beside her plate.

The sound of water pouring into a porcelain basin came from behind the privacy screen, and then Joan set about brushing her teeth.

Dante picked up the letter, though spying made him ten kinds of a cad. He endured the beating from his conscience because whatever was in the letter might have contributed to his wife's upset.

Though learning of their relative poverty certainly hadn't cheered her.

> *My Dearest Lady Joan,*
>
> *Time for another cup of tea in the company of a woman I esteem greatly. Shall we say, two of the clock, same location? Likely to be less custom at that hour—a consideration I'm sure you'll appreciate. Until next we meet, I remain,*
>
> > *Entirely Yours,*
> > *Valmonte*

Dante set the note down exactly where he'd found it, feeling the need to wash his hands.

And get drunk.

And break something precious, delicate, and pretty into a thousand pieces.

Stronger than all those urges, though—and they were strong indeed—was a need to understand.

Valmonte had brought a female with him to the wedding, a possessive sort of young, well-fed female, who'd clung to his lordship's skinny arm and barely left his side for the duration of the wedding breakfast.

A fiancée sort of female, and Joan had told Dante in one of their earliest conversations that she'd misstepped with an engaged man. Misstepped *once*, and she'd considered it an overwhelming folly, made possible only by strong drink and misplaced trust in the blighter's gentlemanly honor.

To hell with that.

"If you'll take a maid with you," he called out to his wife, "I can bury myself in calculations and be ready for Hector's interrogations when we return to Balfour House tomorrow."

Joan tapped her toothbrush on the side of the basin. One, two, three times—he already knew this habit of hers, along with a dozen others. She emerged in her dressing gown, her unbound hair cascading over one shoulder.

"You are very dedicated," she said, taking a seat at the vanity and separating her hair into three skeins. "I admire this about you."

"Don't admire me." And how was it, that even as Joan prepared for an assignation, Dante loved the sight of her nimble fingers bringing order to all the fiery chaos of her hair? "I like business. I like the challenge and uncertainty of it. I expect even if we do eventually grow wealthy, I'll not hire lackeys and managers. Some men need to drive their own curricles rather than ride around warm and dry inside a coach."

"Some women need to make their own clothing, even though they could well afford to have others see to it." She wrapped a ribbon around the end of her braid, tied a bow, and arranged her hair in a coronet on her head. Joan wasn't in any way attempting to be seductive with her toilette; her hairstyle was prim, and yet, the sight of her stirred husbandly urges.

"Would you come back to bed with me if I asked it of you?"

"Yes." She went on sliding pins into her hair, no hesitation, no blush, nothing to indicate she found the request an imposition. "I like your ambition, Dante. I understand it, even. I can't imagine letting somebody else tend to my wardrobe. My clothing is part of who I am in a way that might not be entirely healthy. I expect commerce is like that for you."

"I thrive on it." But in a sense, he'd thrived on the sheer grueling drudgery of the mines too. "Come to bed with me, Joan."

They'd never made love by the light of day, and a winter morning didn't exactly provide a flood of sunshine, but it did require another increment of trust on the part of his wife.

She withdrew a few pins from her hair while Dante wheeled the breakfast trolley to the corridor then locked the door to the sitting room.

"You're not getting undressed?" Joan asked when he returned. She certainly hadn't shed any clothing. No matter how intimate they were, Joan remained in her nightgown, a proper, decent English wife.

"You might like me with my clothes on for a change."

She sat on the edge of the bed. "Or I might not."

Did a woman intent on meeting her lover agree so easily to intimacies with her new husband? Did she all but ask for her husband to come naked to the bed? And why meet in a damned tea shop if Valmonte was Joan's lover?

Dante took a place standing before her, their knees nearly touching. "Undress me, then." A taunt more than an offer, and Joan picked up on the ambiguity of it.

"If you like."

She unbelted his dressing gown, pushed it off his shoulders, and laid it across the foot of the bed. "You have nice clothing. I noticed that about you when we met on the train."

"Not when we met in the ballrooms?"

Next she unbuttoned his waistcoat, an unpretentious affair in a dark plaid associated with his mother's clan.

"Everybody puts on finery for a social evening. Is the silk lining for warmth?"

She ran her fingers over the pale green fabric, as if she could learn things by touch that the fabric wouldn't confide to anybody else.

"I like the feel of it."

He liked the feel of her fingers undoing his cuffs, too, but he did not like the sense that he was trying to prove something by taking her to bed. Old feelings, of despair mingled with arousal, rose up from his first marriage.

She peeled him out of his shirt, which meant only his plain black kilt remained, and Joan made short work of that.

He stood naked before her, half-aroused, wishing he'd never started this encounter. Men in love were fools, but they were supposed to be happy fools when anticipating the consummation of their passions.

"You don't mind that I see you naked," she said, wrapping cool fingers around his shaft.

Rowena would never have been so bold—poor lass. "I'll cover up if the sight offends you."

"I like looking at you," Joan said, scooting back on the bed. "You are what the local ladies would call a braw, bonnie lad."

Her Scottish accent was flawless, and her legs... Her long, pale legs, flashing at him from beneath her hems, drew his focus from questions of motivation and fidelity to the matter at hand.

"Someday, Joan Hartwell, I'd like to see you as God made you," he said, following her onto the bed. "Someday, I would love for you to flaunt your wares for me."

But only for him.

He prowled on all fours across the bed, until she was beneath him on her back.

"I'm skinny," she said, scooting her dressing gown and nightgown up to her hips with about as much seductiveness as if she were piling up the dirty laundry. "I haven't much bosom. A woman who creates dresses becomes aware of these things."

Was that why she agreed to meet with Valmonte? Because the attentions of a wealthy, titled young man made her feel less insecure?

"You're daft," he said, kissing her temple. "Does a woman's bosom run her husband's household, so he comes home to peace and tranquillity every night? Does her bosom protect her children from all harm, and teach them their letters? Does her bosom scold a man who thinks to take on winter without his scarf and gloves? Can her bosom squeeze his hand softly at that exact moment when he feels most alone in the world?"

She kissed him, probably to shut him up, and she was smiling. "Help me get my dressing gown off."

A concession, perhaps. Dante obliged, and in the pale light, Joan wearing only a silk nightgown was luscious.

"You would tell me if I were imposing?" Dante asked as he arranged himself once more over his wife. Would she tell him if she loved another?

Would she tell him if his lovemaking were a disappointment?

"Making love with my husband could never be an imposition."

How certain she sounded.

"Then do me a favor," he said, nuzzling at her shoulder. "If you take a notion to wrap your legs around me, indulge yourself." She had discovered this maneuver the previous night, and the leverage it had given her had rendered Dante's efforts to hold back, to wait for her, hopeless.

Again. In any other circumstance, he would account himself a man blessed with abundant self-restraint. In Joan's arms, he had yet to demonstrate that quality to his own satisfaction, let alone hers.

He made love to her, plied her with as much tenderness and patience as passion and marital devotion could inspire, until he faced the choice of spending or losing his erection. He pushed himself through a weak, halfhearted finish, and again thought of many such encounters with his first wife.

"Did I do something wrong?" Joan asked when Dante's breathing had returned to normal. Her question held train cars full of uncertainty, while her touch on Dante's hair was the embodiment of tenderness.

He waited to hear how his genteel lady wife would comment on his most recent poor showing, but she said nothing more. He slipped from her body and rose from the bed, sad, disgusted with himself, and not a little afraid for his new marriage.

"Why do you ask?"

She propped herself up on her elbows, her nightgown leaving everything below mid thigh in plain view. "I did something wrong. You don't deny it."

He moved behind the privacy screen, wet a cloth, wrung it out, and brought it to her, then returned to the only corner of the room where she couldn't see him, and tended to his own ablutions.

"I'm preoccupied," he said. "I've started looking at how much I should borrow to make some repairs to the mills." He wasn't even tempted to peek as a silence suggested Joan was making use of the cloth he'd given her.

"You were thinking of figures while we…while you—"

Mrs. Hartwell, who had an assignation to keep in less than four hours, was growing upset.

"What were you thinking of?" Dante asked, tossing a wet rag with undue force at the washbasin, glad his wife could not see that fit of pique. "Were you cutting out a new dress, selecting a book for your sister?"

"Dante?"

He came out of hiding to find his wife kneeling on the bed, her braid untidy, her expression guarded.

"I'm sorry." He sat on the bed beside her, feeling as if he'd just completed a double shift digging at the bottom of a hot, airless shaft. "A man likes to acquit himself well when attempting to satisfy his wife's passions."

Needed to, in fact, with increasing desperation.

She had the hem of her nightgown between her fingers, rubbing it back and forth, the way Charlie stroked the satin edging of a blanket for comfort. Joan's expression said she did not in any fashion comprehend his point.

Which, unaccountably, reassured him. What sort of wanton wife doesn't understand when her husband apologizes for failing to satisfy her?

"You satisfy my passions," she said, sounding hopelessly uncertain. "If I had a larger bosom, or more shapely hips, I might satisfy yours better."

He tackled her, had her flat on her back beneath him, her legs loosely encircling his hips.

"We have been married barely a week. One day, my dear, you shall strut about our bedroom in the altogether, and you will enjoy it. You will enjoy driving me daft with those long, strong legs of yours, with your elegant shoulders, and your lovely bosom. You will not even notice how such a display torments and delights your husband. That's how comfortable I hope you'll be in your own skin."

"You haven't seen my bosom."

"Nor your delightful bum, nor a bit of red hair not quite the same shade as what's on your head. *Not yet.*"

That gave her something to puzzle over, as if Dante had begun speaking in a foreign language, and Joan was able to catch just enough to make a faulty translation. He helped her off the bed, kissed her soundly on the mouth, and smacked her gently on her backside.

Joan remained quiet as they both dressed, and as Dante laced her up in anticipation of her shopping expedition. He bit back another offer to accompany her, bit back a thousand questions, and stifled an incongruous reprise of the erection that had become so unreliable not twenty minutes earlier.

"I'll be glad to get back to the Highlands." Joan sat before her vanity in a fetching ensemble of brown wool with red piping. She positioned a silly, elegant confection with pheasant feathers on her head, then tilted it to the right, studying the effect in the mirror.

"Your family will be relieved to see you've endured the first week of marriage without mishap." Though Dante and his wife had just had a mishap, and were perhaps headed for something worse than a mishap.

"My sisters will interrogate me." The angle of the hat went from attractive to perfect. Smart, elegant, and fun without sacrificing an ounce of sophistication.

"About—ah, about the wedding night. What will you tell them?"

Joan rose, a magnificent testament to exquisite style. She appropriated a matching parasol from the wardrobe and graced her husband with a sweet smile. "I shall tell them being married to you suits me wonderfully, in every regard."

She tidied up the correspondence on the table, tucking most of it away in a valise of some sort. Valmonte's damned note, she casually balled up and pitched into the fire.

Dante escorted her to the lobby, where one of the hotel maids waited to accompany her ladyship to the shops. When he'd kissed his wife farewell, he returned to their rooms alone and lay down on the bed, the better to wallow in his wife's scent.

Of course Joan had destroyed Valmonte's note. The remaining question was whether Valmonte would destroy Dante's marriage.

⁓

"How appropriate. You've invited me to dine with a mongrel." Joan took her seat in the brightly lit tea shop without allowing Edward to assist her.

The aspersion was unfair. Joan liked Fergus, for all the dog had bad taste in owners. The terrier perched in the crook of Edward's elbow, looking jaunty and dapper in a canine waistcoat in a red, black, and yellow tartan pattern.

"Insult me all you please," Edward said pleasantly, "but I could hardly abandon Fergus to fend for himself. Mama would leave him to freeze in the mews if she had her way."

Edward kissed the top of the dog's head and earned a lick to his cheek in response.

"Have you brought me some sketches in your reticule, perhaps? Christmas draws near, and I wanted to present Lady Dorcas with a few ideas."

Joan drew off her gloves, and when she wanted to

slap them across the cheek Fergus had just kissed, she instead took the lace of her cuff between her fingers.

"I have been in the constant company of my new husband, Edward. I have some ideas, but if I'd spent hours with my sketchbook this week, Mr. Hartwell would have remarked it. He would also notice that I was sketching dresses not for myself, but for a woman of a different conformation entirely."

Edward set the dog on the floor, where it obediently sank to its haunches. The affection between owner and dog was not feigned, and what did it say about Edward's family, that he had to protect his pet from his own mother?

"What shall I give my fiancée for her Christmas token, then?" he asked, his tone belligerent. "I am relying on you, Lady Joan, and you will not like the consequences of my disappointment."

The lace of Joan's cuff had the soft, uneven texture her fingertips craved, and yet to stroke the lace would betray the nerves unsettling Joan's stomach. Children twitched at their hems and petted their dolls to settle nervous stomachs.

And fiddling with a cuff was a good way to weaken its stitching.

Joan sat back, hands in her lap. "Lady Dorcas is fond of sweets. Give her a recipe book. Give her French chocolates. Give her something that shows you have paid attention to her wants and whims, not a dress to advertise the ideas you've purloined from me."

"She likes chocolate," Edward said, tugging gently on the dog's ears. "I like chocolate too, probably the only thing we have in common, but I need that dress, Joan."

He sounded honestly regretful to be bullying her.

"Hire a Frenchman. They're full of ideas."

"I tried that. In the first place, Frenchmen cost a prodigious sum of money. In the second, they gossip. All I need is for tattle to circulate that Uncle tipples and Mama—"

He fell silent, his expression shifting from a house bedecked for the holidays to a house denuded of all wreaths, window candles, cloved oranges, and mistletoe.

The change was intimidating. Joan picked up her gloves rather than give in to the compulsion to fiddle at her lace.

"Edward, you are a *gentleman*. You are threatening my reputation, my happiness, my marriage, my everything over a few fancy dresses, and I haven't done anything to deserve such treatment from you."

She made the appeal as much for him as for herself, because Edward Valmonte wasn't given to meanness. He was a charming flirt, frivolous, and also—Joan had bet her future on this—harmless.

"I'm glad you understand what's in the balance here, Joan. And don't forget the harm to your sisters' reputations if it becomes known you took up with Mr. Hartwell to avoid the scandal of your behavior with me. Then too, from what I hear, dear Mr. Hartwell is looking for funds—perhaps he knows fancy dresses cost a fortune, and they are what his new wife needs to be happy."

Was that what Society thought of her, that she required *dresses* to be happy?

And what did it matter what Society thought— what did Dante think?

Joan withdrew a pencil and small sketch pad from her reticule. "Place your order—yours and Fergus's. I won't be having anything."

"Stay with Lady Joan," Edward instructed his pet, and the dog shifted to sit at Joan's feet when Edward rose.

Joan's lucky dress would not work on a woman of Lady Dorcas's dimension, but the dress Joan had been considering for Dora's Christmas gift might. Full sleeves and generous skirts, but along softer lines than most women were wearing lately. Pastels, of course, a fairy-tale blue with not pink, but—

What? What would flatter Dorcas's coloring and provide an eye-catching contrast without being a trite red or black?

Edward returned to the table and kept his bullying, threatening mouth closed.

"The bodice is always the biggest challenge," Joan muttered. "Get that, and the neckline, skirts, and hems fall into place."

"If you say so."

"The foundation color isn't much of a challenge. Dorcas will look lovely in blue, but the contrasting and complementing shades…"

She wasn't about to ask *his* opinion.

The sketch took about fifteen minutes to complete, and when it was finished, Joan wasn't satisfied. Edward, however, was wreathed in smiles.

"There, you see? You think you must wait for inspiration, but you're wrong. *Mater artium necessitas* and all that. I'll expect more invention from you when you return to Edinburgh."

Necessity was the mother of desperation, in Joan's opinion, and desperation was conducive to stupidity rather than invention. She'd been desperate to hear somebody rhapsodizing over her designs.

And now somebody was.

"The hems need work, but nothing too fancy," she cautioned. "Peach and a soft, understated light brown for contrast. Think of a roe deer on a sunny winter's day."

Edward stroked Fergus's head absently, and Joan shifted her skirts aside, lest his hand touch her clothing.

"Brown, blue, and peach? That's different."

"Different is what gets a woman noticed, provided it isn't too different. Dorcas has a lovely bosom, an excellent complexion, and a pretty laugh. She can afford to take small risks with her wardrobe."

Why couldn't Edward, the man who was to marry Dorcas, *see* this?

"When can you have a finished design to me?"

Giving him the sketch had been a mistake, for now, like an ill-trained dog, his bad behavior and unreasonable expectations had been rewarded.

"You finish it. Ask her what she thinks of your creation, modify the details and palette to suit her preferences. You can do that much."

He was so absorbed with the sketch, he didn't even react to the insult. God help Lady Dorcas.

"You know, Edward, I might tell your wife I've designed her wedding dress at your insistence." Joan liked that idea exceedingly. "Tell her you weren't talented enough, that you made an offer you couldn't live up to. I might even tell your mother you've threatened me with ruin if I don't yield to your schemes."

He folded the sketch in exact thirds and tucked it away, and with it went a piece of Joan's happiness, a piece of her integrity.

"You're welcome to take tea with Mama any time you please. Provided she hasn't overindulged in the Madeira, she will likely applaud my enterprise, for it's all that stands between her and economies she's incapable of exercising. And as for Dorcas..."

He picked up his dog, setting the beast on his lap, pouring cream from the small pewter pitcher into a saucer, and letting the dog lick from the plate.

"Dorcas," he went on, "would never have allowed herself to be private with a bachelor, much less take spirits with him in quantity. She'd find my willingness to maintain silence on your behalf for a few silly dresses generous. Her own silence I cannot guarantee."

As the dog lapped at the cream, Joan came to a daunting realization. Edward Valmonte was frivolous by nature, but circumstances had made him desperate, and like any beast backed into a corner, he'd become capable of viciousness.

Joan was his last, best hope of solving whatever problems he considered so dire, and he would go to any lengths to see his scheme come to fruition.

The dog kept licking, though not a drop of cream remained.

Edward set the empty saucer out of reach of Fergus's tongue.

"There's a good fellow." He rose with the dog in his arms. "A half-dozen more sketches will do for now, and you should know, Dorcas and I will attend Lady Quinworth's New Year's ball. I could hardly turn down an invitation from the family of one of my oldest and dearest friends, could I?"

He leaned in to kiss Joan's cheek, but she pulled back.

"You haven't paid your bill yet, Edward. I'll wish you good day."

Not happy Christmas. Joan would never wish him or Lady Dorcas that again.

She tugged on her gloves and left without a backward glance.

❧

Joan hurried out into the gloom of a midwinter afternoon, though Aberdeen was so far north, the daylight was all but gone. She paused on the corner and pulled her scarf up around her chin.

The tea shop glowed merrily as a few snowflakes danced on a chilly breeze, shoppers bustled all about, and down the street, a charity choir mangled Handel's "Hallelujah Chorus."

While behind the cheerfully decorated window of the tea shop, Edward lounged with his tea, his little dog, and Joan's sketch. For Christmas she'd given Edward exactly what he wanted and did not deserve, while she'd given her husband lies and looming scandal.

Dante was at that very moment likely back at the hotel, glasses perched on his nose while he wrestled with some column of figures. He toiled not for his own gain, but because he managed his children's legacy, and felt responsible for the people he employed.

While Edward fed cream to his terrier from a porcelain dish.

Fergus had apparently had enough indulgence, for Edward rose, donned his greatcoat, and left the shop. He set Fergus down when they reached the stoop, and Fergus lifted a short back leg right at the top of the steps.

As if to give the dog privacy, Edward glanced about at the passersby, his gaze lighting on Joan less than four yards away.

"You waited for me," he said, coming down the steps. "You needn't. Shouldn't you have a maid or some footmen with you?"

His concern was ludicrous—Joan's maid was in the bookshop—and his dog was done turning the snow yellow.

Edward scooped up his dog, and right there in the busy street, kissed Joan's cheek. "You forgot to wish me happy Christmas, Joan."

The air was thick with coal smoke overlaid with wet dog, but what nearly gagged Joan was the additional scent of Edward's cologne—though she'd once found it pleasing.

"You'll bring me those sketches," Edward said. "I've been a good boy, and a little Christmas token between intimate friends isn't too much to ask."

Against her cheek, the cold leather of his gloves made a tactile contrast to his soft words and presuming kiss.

"I am not your friend, intimate or otherwise. And you may call me Mrs. Hartwell." Of that, she was dead certain.

In the soft light from the tea shop windows, something flickered in Edward's eyes. Regret, or remorse? "You will bring me those sketches."

Behind the window, people were laughing and talking, gobbling up sweets, and making holiday plans. All that good cheer, all that noise and merriment, had only made it easier for Edward to trespass on honor and long acquaintance.

With a sense of inevitability, Joan took in a breath and prepared to negotiate with Edward a time and place where she might pass over the sketches without drawing the notice of her family.

Or her husband.

But something happened. She took in a steadying breath of cold Scottish air, and felt...

The bodice of her dress.

She, who was too skinny for fashion, felt the bodice of her dress confining her breasts and her breathing. While Edward stood there, one supercilious eyebrow arched in anticipation, Joan felt for the first time a sense of being confined by her fashionable attire.

Because Dante laced her up snugly, because he fed her sweets, *and because she was apparently to have a child*.

"I will not provide any more sketches, Edward, not without compensation, not without an acknowledgment of my work. *Now* you, Lady Dorcas, and your little dog may have a happy Christmas."

She might have slapped him, so stunned was his reaction—so satisfying.

"I assume you understand what 'no' means, Edward, but let me explain something further. I am *married*, and my husband will be the father of my children. I cannot have a parasite like you threatening my family's future, and if that means you tell all the world that I spread my legs for you, then be prepared for them to hear also that you lured me into your trust, plied me with drink at least, and otherwise behaved like a man who holds his intended in no esteem whatsoever."

"You can't do that," he said, taking a step closer. "I'll tell everybody you begged me for attention, and I felt sorry for you. A woman of your modest endowments and excessive height doesn't get many offers."

Fergus whined, as if Edward clutched him too tightly.

"You make odd noises," Joan said evenly. "Your breath stinks, and you say stupid things when engaged in your petty attempts at seduction." And the best part? "Your wardrobe lacks style and imagination. Why Fergus puts up with you, I do not know."

She flounced away—flouncing was supposed to be great fun, wasn't it?

"Where are you going?" Edward called as Joan strode off toward the bookshop. "This isn't finished! I have those sketches, and I will not keep silent!"

"I'm going shopping for a Christmas present for my husband," Joan called back, though a lady never raised her voice. "And for all I care, you can run back to your mama and tell her whatever lies you please."

❦

When traveling alone, Dante bought himself a second-class ticket and looked for a compartment full of the weary, downtrodden, or cup shot. Though the stink of such company might be trying, they tended to be quiet enough to let him do some reading.

The return to Balfour was undertaken in a

first-class compartment, which Dante and his wife had to themselves.

More's the pity.

"You're quiet," he observed. He wanted to ask her what she'd sketched for Valmonte in that same tea shop, but he already knew: Joan sketched dresses. Occasionally, she'd sketch a dress worn by her mother or her sisters, but the occupant of the dress was often an afterthought, chosen to better exhibit the garment itself.

Joan put down the book she'd been reading, some old novel. "I've been thinking. Have you ever been to Paris?"

Why, yes, of course. Every crofter's son who came of age toiling in the mines went larking off to Paris at the first opportunity.

"I don't speak French." He read it well enough, because he needed to understand contracts written in French.

"That's no matter, they all speak English."

No, they did not. Many of the French understood English, but just as Dante was loath to exhibit his poor pronunciation before the French, they hoarded up their English abilities for their own purposes—and for their own entertainment.

"You've been, I take it?"

"Many times. I would love to show you Paris." Her enthusiasm for the journey did not show in her gaze, which was fixed on a bound edition of one of Dickens's dolorous epics.

"We'll go someday, then." Someday when the mills were adequately financed, Margaret's situation was settled, Hector wasn't vibrating with a restlessness that boded ill, and Joan wasn't having assignations with skinny viscounts.

"Might we go soon?"

Her simple question held controlled desperation, the ladylike version of panic, and abruptly, Dante could not abide the deception that had joined them in their private compartment.

He put an arm around his wife, closed his eyes, and spoke as gently as he could. "Why did you meet Valmonte in Aberdeen, Joan? He's engaged, you're married. To me."

The shock of his question rendered her smaller against his side.

"Edward is an old friend. We shared a cup of tea."

Joan had not shared anything with Valmonte, except her time and her sketch. Perhaps she'd been anxious that news of her meeting might get back to her husband, but then, why meet in a public tea shop and sit in the very window?

Dante honestly did not want to accuse his wife of infidelity, not even in his thoughts.

"I don't care for him," Dante said. "He doesn't mind his tongue in the gentlemen's retiring room, and he lets his mother run roughshod over him. The family business seems to fall entirely to the uncle, while Valmonte minces about town, having tea with other people's wives."

She picked up her book. "I can hardly avoid his company. He and Lady Dorcas will be at Mama's New Year's ball. They'll show up at all the best entertainments, and you and I will be invited to his wedding."

She came to a pair of pages that hadn't been cut. "Were you spying on me, Dante?"

They were to exchange prevarications, which was usually the way of it when a marriage faltered.

"I'm interested in opening offices in Aberdeen. Any time a port city acquires rail access, trade there booms, and Edinburgh has become quite expensive. I was acquainting myself with the commercial real estate available in Aberdeen, and happened to see you."

He fished out his penknife, appropriated her book, and slit the pages cleanly free of each other.

She accepted the book back, but didn't open it. "So you'll be spending time in Aberdeen, while the children and I remain where?"

He'd been thinking of establishing Hector in Aberdeen, though Joan didn't seem upset to relocate her husband there.

"The Glasgow property is home to the children and Margaret. I prefer it for its proximity to the mills."

For what fine lady didn't aspire to live within walking distance of a trio of wool mills?

Joan stared at her book for the next thirty miles of their journey, while Dante kept his arm around her and pondered what he might have said, should have said, and didn't say.

"Maybe this spring," Joan said as the train lost momentum on the approach to some way station, "I'll pop over to Paris and do some shopping."

The hell she would.

"Long journeys at this point are probably not well-advised. Do you know yet if you're expecting a child?"

A child would bind them together, and as the train hurtled toward the cold, dark mountains, Dante accepted that he wanted to be bound to Joan. Not only legally, but morally, emotionally, intellectually, financially, all the ways a true couple became entangled.

"I'm not certain. My digestion has been tentative, but that's to be expected amid so much upheaval."

Upheaval, indeed.

"In the interests of giving you some peace amid this upheaval, we might consider separate quarters upon our return to Balfour House."

The train bumped over some junction in the tracks, jostling everybody aboard, the way that question to Joan jostled all of Dante's dreams for a shared future off their marital rails.

He could not lie down night after night beside a woman who was dishonest with him.

"Separate quarters might be for the best," Joan said. "I appreciate your gentlemanly consideration."

She cuddled closer, her book apparently forgotten, while Dante stroked her arm and nearly choked on his consideration.

❦

Tell him, tell him, tell him.

That Dante would suggest separate sleeping quarters not ten days into the marriage was a sign of consideration, and yet, like pretty clothes that only drew attention to a woman's plainness, to Joan, the effect wasn't considerate at all.

"Thank God," Dante muttered as the train slowed

on the approach to Ballater. He tucked his lap desk into a satchel apparently made for it and reached for Joan's book. "I can carry that if you don't want to put it in your reticule."

A mundane bit of thoughtfulness. Their marriage would be full of thoughtfulness and devoid of trust.

"I'll carry it." They decamped for the platform when the train pulled into the Ballater station. Dante fussed with the lone porter over their baggage, and soon, they were in the frigid darkness, awaiting the arrival of a sleigh to take them back to Balfour house.

"Come along," Dante said, tossing the porter a coin to mind their trunks. "We can get something to eat over at the inn."

"An inn?" Joan had never taken a meal at a country inn, and the prospect sounded dubious from a gusta-tory standpoint. "Are you hungry?"

"And cold," Dante said, his breath puffing white in the night air.

Down the street, laughter burst from a two-story granite structure festooned with lanterns and wreaths.

"Very well." How difficult could it be, to sit beside her husband while he downed an ale and a meat pie? Joan dutifully tucked her gloved hand over his arm and pre-pared to march off, when a ripping sound stopped her.

"I'm caught," she said, freeing herself from Dante's escort and stifling a curse. "My hem is caught, and I can't—"

She couldn't turn to inspect the damage because she was *caught*. Her favorite aubergine dress, the one with the lavender lace and flounces about the hem, the one she considered her prettiest for everyday and travel, was doomed to catch, snag, and be injured by circumstances. One curse wouldn't be enough; one language worth of curses wouldn't be enough to express her sheer frustration.

"Hold still," Dante said, kneeling. "I'll have you free."

"That's not the point." He was bareheaded, kneeling at her hems, and Joan was desperate to make him understand. "I've torn the hem, ruined the lace. Now the lace will drag in the snow, and I'll step on it, and it will tear further, and the entire petticoat is at risk, and I *love* this dress. I sewed every stitch of it, tatted every inch of the lace. I chose the fabric and made the patterns, I love—"

He rose holding a scrap of lavender lace, and used it to dab at Joan's cheek. The sensation of hot tears on her cold cheek, of the rough-soft lace against her skin, put the moment into higher relief than a simple torn hem merited.

"It's only a dress, Joan. You can make another."

Dante spoke gently, he touched her gently, and he might just as gently give up on their marriage.

He hadn't believed her lies about that tête-à-tête in the tea shop. The next time Edward commandeered Joan's presence or her sketches or her time, Dante wouldn't be fooled by those lies either.

Joan wrapped her hand around his, around the frivolous bit of little lace he'd used to dry her tears. The lace was worth nothing, while her husband meant so much to her.

"I don't want to sleep apart," she said, tugging him closer by virtue of their joined hands. "I don't want anything to come between us."

He rested his forehead against hers, so their breath joined, and a startling patch of warmth touched Joan's brow, like a kind thought might touch her mind. The laughter came again, and somebody took up a song about the wise men, long journeys, and hope.

"I followed you, Joan, the second time you met with him. The first time was by chance, but then I saw Valmonte's note, his *summons*, and followed you. I should not have dissembled, but he's of your ilk, a handsome young lord, a gentleman by birth. Nonetheless, I suspected his motives. I did not trust—"

She kissed him, quickly, because the cold was threatening to make her teeth chatter. "I did not deserve your trust. Edward certainly did not deserve mine, and he's about to make such trouble."

"Valmonte was the one who used you ill?"

Down the snowy street, the revelers at the inn had fallen silent, while a lyrical duet lifted into the night, like the single star sending a beacon of hope long ago.

To withhold details from Dante now would be to protect Edward, and a cheering, simple thought made Joan's decision effortless.

Her marriage mattered to her more than anything. More than pretty clothes, pretty society, pride, familial associations, titles, appearances, *anything*. She would become Mrs. Dante Hartwell in truth, and the rest of the world—and their little dogs—could all have a Happy Christmas without her.

"Edward is the scoundrel, and I suspect he duped me with an invitation to tea, purportedly from his mother. I'll tell you all of it, but let's find some ale and a meat pie." She kissed him again, more lingeringly.

"Aye," Dante said. "We shall. Before our lips freeze together."

⁂

Scandal was not *necessarily* bad for business.

Dante rubbed his eyes, and for the thousandth time, resisted climbing into bed beside his sleeping wife. After the Christmas Eve tree lighting, he'd remained awake, rearranging figures and wrestling emotions.

Joan was embroiled in a situation that could bring ruin not only to her, but also to Dante's businesses, and to Joan's family. For Quinworth's brood, the scandal would be temporary, particularly if they distanced themselves from Joan's folly, though Joan's guilt over the inconvenience to her family would be eternal.

A drink to settle the nerves was in order, or to take the edge off the worries keeping Dante awake.

He could not foil Valmonte's scheme.

He could not protect Joan from the ridicule and judgment of her peers.

He most certainly could not attract investors from among Joan's family, which meant going hat in hand to the banks or continuing on the present course, reaping profit, but with a sense of disaster looming when a roof gave, a loom broke, or a strike threatened.

Fire, thank God, could be insured against.

He rose, kissed his wife's forehead, and took himself into the darkened corridor, a frigid place even in Balfour's commodious dwelling. Despite the challenges facing him, Dante enjoyed fierce satisfaction that Joan had entrusted him with her problems, surrendering a burden she should never have been made to carry.

"What are you doing out of bed?" The question came from Spathfoy's father, who managed to look dignified even at this late hour.

"Fetching a nightcap. Join me?" The Marquess of Quinworth was Dante's father-in-law, and yet, they'd hardly exchanged two words since the wedding.

"If I tarry with you over a drink, my marchioness will fall asleep in my absence, for which I will be scolded in the morning."

This scold didn't bother his lordship much, based on the affection in his tone.

"A wee dram, then," Dante said. "We can toast the health of our ladies."

"And the Queen, of course," Quinworth said, a small English nudge to his son-in-law's cultural ribs.

"Two wee drams, then, for—"

In the darkness at the end of the corridor, a pale, shadowy blur disappeared around the corner, a blur about the size of a cat, but closer to the ground.

"What was that?" Quinworth asked. "Has Frederick got loose again?"

Dante hurried down the corridor, the older man keeping pace. "Frederick?"

"My granddaughter Fiona's damned rabbit. He's a complacent enough chap, though lately, Fiona says he's looking peaked and wan."

They were nearly running, but quietly, in deference to the sleeping household. "That rabbit weighs a good stone at least," Dante said, for he'd made Frederick's acquaintance on many trips to the nursery. "He's no more peaked and wan than Spathfoy's gelding."

"Or Spathfoy himself," Quinworth said as they rounded the next corner.

Just in time to see a bunny tail disappearing toward the stairs.

"That's not Fiona's bunny," Dante said, anxiety tearing at him. "That's the rabbit I bought Joan for Christmas. If it gets outside in this weather—"

"It will hop out to the stables and dine on oats and hay until spring," Quinworth said, sounding more stern than optimistic.

"It can't hop to the stables through more than two feet of snow," Dante countered.

They next spotted the beast at the top of the main stairs, which it descended with enough speed to suggest the rabbit knew it had pursuers and wasn't in any mood to be caught.

"We should fetch the hounds," Quinworth said. "This time of year they get mopey, and a bit of a run—"

"They'll tear my Joan's Christmas present to pieces, all over Lady Balfour's carpets."

That brought the older fellow up short at the bottom of the steps. "Well, it was a good thought. Perhaps one couple, on a leash—"

"That way!"

They thundered off, past the formal parlors, in pursuit of one downy little tail that moved not at a panicked speed, but at the speed of a damned rabbit out to have a lark at the expense of its supposed betters.

Spathfoy emerged from the library, drink in hand. "What is this commotion?"

"Damned rabbit is loose," Quinworth said. "I say

we get the hounds, but Hartwell isn't in the mood for indoor blood sport."

"We're starting a fresh hand," Spathfoy said, swirling his drink. "You can get another rabbit sent out from Aberdeen, for God's sake. Come join us, and get out of this freezing corridor."

"Capital notion." The marquess appropriated his son's drink and downed it in one swallow. "What's the game?"

"That rabbit," Dante said in low, furious tones, "is my sole gift to my lady wife, for she loves soft, comforting textures. I'll not sit about choking on your cigar smoke while yonder rabbit roams at large, vulnerable to dogs, cats, weather, or zealous cooks. Get off your lordly arses and help me find Lady Joan's gift."

Father and son exchanged glances that blossomed into identical smiles. Spathfoy snatched back the glass and bellowed into the library.

"You lot! Hartwell says to get off your lordly arses and help him find his wife's rabbit!"

The next two hours saw Dante, Quinworth, Spathfoy, Balfour, his three brothers, his brother-in-law, and the night porter tearing around the house, amply fortified by many a wee dram, until the hunt converged outside the nursery.

"The little bugger went this way," Connor MacGregor muttered. "Damned near skinned m' knees on the stairs, chasing him here."

He took out a flask and tipped it up, and up some more.

"I nearly had the blighter in the library," Spathfoy said, taking out his own flask. "That is one quick rabbit."

"That's a sober rabbit," Balfour said. "The odds are stacked against us."

"It's a missing rabbit," Gilgallon said, adding a few Gaelic curses at rabbits, their progeny, their tails, and their rabbity ideas about Christmas.

"Rabbit haggis sounds good about now," Matthew Daniels added. "And I loathe haggis."

They were panting, more than half-tipsy, and had spent their Christmas Eve in pursuit of Dante's Christmas present rather than whiling away the evening at cards.

Would they have been as generous with their time had they known Dante was all that stood between Lady Joan and endless scandal?

The nursery door opened, revealing Charlie in nightgown and ratty braids.

"You're all up past your bedtime," she said. "May I stay up too?"

A pale, furry blur shot between her slippered feet, directly into the warmth of the nursery.

"There's the little bas—blessed bunny!" Spathfoy roared.

A general melee followed, with seven grown men and one little girl trying to crowd through the doorway at once. The child, like the rabbit, was sober and fresh from her slumbers, with the result that at least three of her uncles suffered an elbow to some inconvenient location.

"We've got you now," Dante said to the little gray beast, who sat serene and fluffy before the box in which Frederick resided. "Quinworth, get the door."

Such were the bonds forged in the hunt field that the marquess obeyed Dante's command smartly.

"He'll not get out now," Balfour said. "Little wretch owes me two hours sleep beside my countess, and at least four bottles of the finest—for God's sake!"

Frederick's head popped up over the edge of his box, an enclosure with sides about two and a half feet high.

"That's a tall bunny," Gilgallon said, foreboding in his tone, "and likely a fast bunny too."

"Frederick is a quite good size," Charlie observed. "And oh, look, they're making friends!"

Dante hadn't given the second rabbit a name repeatable in polite, sober company, but the Infernal Beast also went up on its back legs to touch wiggly, pink noses with Frederick. A conversation of some sort transpired between the rabbits, consisting of sniffing, interspersed with moments of unblinking, leporine consideration, followed by more sniffing.

"They could start fighting any moment," Quinworth muttered. "Buck rabbits aren't to be trifled with— prodigious teeth and claws, you know."

"Frederick is a gentleman," Charlie said, as if instructing a slow student in a familiar catechism. "Who's his new friend?"

"Frederick is a fat, indolent parasite and a disgrace to the male gender," Spathfoy muttered. "But even a rabbit bestirs himself when his territory is threatened."

A moment passed, while grown men recovered their wind, two rabbits exchanged bunny-greetings, and a small child hoped none of the adults would notice the hour.

"Charlie, you should be back in bed," Dante said softly, because Phillip and Fiona slept nearby.

"Oh, good luck with that," Spathfoy grumbled. "I was about to invite the child to join us for cards. It's the bunny's turn to deal."

Charlie beamed at the earl. "You were?"

"He was not," Dante retorted, trying to figure the best angle to attack the rabbit so it wouldn't disappear under a wardrobe or into some gap in the wainscoting. "Spathfoy was teasing."

Phillip emerged from the dormitory. "Teasing about what? You're all up past your bedtimes, and Father Christmas won't visit us."

Charlie's hands went to her hips. "He will too. Lady Joan promised!"

Fiona appeared on Phillip's heels, making the playroom just the sort of crowded, dimly lit space in which a pair of rabbits might run riot until dawn.

"Is there a lid to Frederick's box?" Dante asked. And where were the nursery maids at such an hour?

"We don't use it," Fiona said. "Frederick likes to come out and play, though lately he's been—"

"Peaked and wan," her uncles said in unison with her grandfather.

"Rabbit haggis," Gilgallon whispered.

"Get the lid to the box," Dante instructed his daughter. "If we can chase Lady Joan's pet in with Frederick, we can separate them before they take up arms against each other."

"Frederick is a gentleman," Charlie said again as she rummaged behind a toy box for a square of wood. "He won't take up arms against a guest under his roof."

Dante was directly behind the loose rabbit, who was absorbed touching noses with Frederick. "Nobody move."

The nursery became the still, quiet place it ought to have been at such an hour. Soundlessly, Dante crouched behind the rabbit, reaching slowly, slowly toward the errant gift. He'd just touched soft, soft fur, when the dratted creature shot straight up—

And into Frederick's box.

Frederick's head disappeared.

"They're going to be friends!" Fiona said, clapping her hands as Dante slapped the lid onto the box.

"Got you." He held the lid down, expecting a furious thumping and squealing to ensue, but all in the box was quiet.

The menfolk exchanged uneasy glances, while Quinworth, in a grandpapa's blend of command and cajolery, spoke to the infantry. "Off to bed with you now, children. Father Christmas is doubtless on his way even as we speak."

"Silly English tradition," Connor commented.

"Which you will observe when your children are toddling, if you don't already," Spathfoy countered.

The children turned for their beds, just as the box thumped loudly, repeatedly.

"Let Frederick out," Fiona cried. "They're having fisticuffs, and Frederick is too sweet and dear and kind and—"

Dante angled himself between the child and the rabbit box, and cracked the lid.

He dropped the lid abruptly, while the thumping went on in a merry rhythm.

"They're fine," he managed.

"But I can hear them fighting!" Charlie said, tugging on Spathfoy's restraining hand. "It isn't good to fight with your friends, especially when you're the only bunnies in the entire Highlands."

"They're…" Dante looked to the other men for reinforcements, and found only suppressed, incredulous mirth and darting gazes. "They're doing the bunny get-acquainted dance. Sort of a bunny version of the Highland fling. I don't think Frederick will be peaked and wan after this. Listen, nobody's yelling in there."

The thumping paused, then resumed.

Both little girls looked dubious. Phillip turned and headed for his bed. "I'll not be the reason Father Christmas passes this house by. The dancing bunnies can go hang."

The child had management written all over him, and the little girls fell in behind him. Quinworth closed the dormitory door just as seven grown men tried to quietly fend off hysterical laughter.

And failed—utterly.

Sixteen

"We need a nightcap," Spathfoy announced, because Hartwell's pursuit of the rabbit had been more than a new husband's dedication to a good impression on Christmas morning.

"My cellars will be empty by Hogmanay," Balfour groused. "Never saw such a lot of Englishmen for drinking whiskey as you, Daniels, and Quinworth."

"Marriage to a Scotswoman will do that," Quinworth replied, all equanimity.

Spathfoy draped an arm over Hartwell's shoulders, lest Hartwell, like his rabbit, go darting off into the shadows. "You married an Englishwoman. She seems happy enough with her bargain."

But Joan was also worried. Spathfoy's fraternal intuition told him as much, backed up by his countess's observations.

When Hartwell ought to have offered some remark about a Scotsman's ability to keep a woman happy, he tromped along in silence and made no move to cast off Spathfoy's arm.

"Early days in a marriage can be a challenge,"

Connor MacGregor offered, with the peculiar delicacy he demonstrated about twice a year. "Though Lady Joan watches her new husband the way Quinworth's hounds might watch those rabbits."

"More affectionately," Gilgallon suggested. "Maybe the way the rabbits were watching each other."

This engendered more merriment, and yet Hartwell didn't join in, even when they gained the warmth of the library, where the Christmas tree lent its pleasant scent and holiday cheer to the entire room.

"You're quiet, Hartwell," Quinworth said as Balfour poured drinks. "Has chasing the rabbit worn you out, or does my daughter have something to answer for?"

Hartwell accepted his drink, though the gesture had an odd, dazed quality.

The fire crackled cozily in the hearth, shadows danced across the carpets and walls. Father Christmas was no doubt making his way up the drive that very moment.

"Spathfoy mentioned that even a rabbit will defend his territory," Hartwell said softly. The other six men comprehended his tone, for they left off suggesting names for Lady Frederick's progeny.

"I am far from a rabbit, but I'm not a wealthy, titled, elegant gentleman either, and my territory is under attack."

"Bad form on somebody's part," Quinworth said, tossing back a nip. "Not the season to behave uncivilly. Come tell Father Christmas what's afoot, and maybe with the aid of his elves, we can put some coal in an appropriate stocking."

Spathfoy had never been more proud of his father, which probably said more about the quality of Balfour's nightcaps than Spathfoy's filial sentiments.

"Tell us," Spathfoy said. "Joan is my sister, and a woman of eminent discernment. If she chose you to do the bunny dance with, then we're rather stuck with you too."

"Your refined speech will provoke the man to call you out," Balfour commented, ambling off to the sofa. "I'm your host, though, Hartwell. You're Scottish, so you know your every comfort and care is mine to fuss over. Tell us what's troubling you."

"And I'm purely bored," Connor added, taking a seat beside Balfour. "Entertain me with your worries, and I'll be less concerned about my wife's interesting condition."

Everybody silently drank to that sentiment. Hartwell took a seat behind the desk, and he looked good there, if tired and worried.

"Lady Joan did not marry me out of any sudden upwelling of tender sentiment. She has been preyed upon and taken advantage of by a scoundrel of the first water, and I've considered everything from calling him out to killing him to lay my wife's fears to rest."

"Killing always sounds good," Daniels noted. "But the justice of the peace will take a dim view of it, particularly if Joan's detractor is wealthy and titled."

Hartwell's tale didn't take long in the telling. Joan had been foolish, but understandably so, given her passion for her dresses and Valmonte's charm and flattery. Hartwell had been everything noble, particularly given that Joan's titled and wealthy relations had not made any overtures of a financial nature to her new spouse.

"Bad tidings, this," the marquess said when Hartwell fell silent. "Joan and her mama both become fierce when pursuing what matters to them. And you're right, holding Valmonte accountable will be hard, for he is titled. The wealthy part, however, is open to debate."

Every pair of eyes went to the older man.

"In what sense?" Hartwell asked.

"Men gossip, and they drink, and I'm an old fellow with nothing better to do on the occasional afternoon than lounge about my clubs, reading the papers, and lamenting the youth of today."

Spathfoy had yet to see his father lounge or engage in anything so tame as a lament. "You have the floor, sir. What have you heard about Valmonte?"

Because this was what Hartwell needed. Not a title, not even that much wealth. He needed information and the courage that came from knowing he did not stand alone.

And Spathfoy needed to apologize to his sister—for failing to protect her, for treating something she was passionate about as a mere feminine fancy, and for doubting her choice of spouse.

❧

A letter of resignation was a difficult document to draft. Hector's attempts kept turning into memoranda—of all Dante should do upon Hector's departure, of how Dante ought to choose Hector's replacement, of how badly Hector hoped Margaret would find happiness.

Which was a lot of balderdash. Hector hoped Margaret would wait for him to make a proper fortune, like a sea captain's wife waited, sometimes years, for her husband to return from his journeys.

"It's no damned good," Hector informed an enormous black-and-white cat that had arrived with the Daniels household and taken to lurking in Hector's room. "It's like you and that damned rabbit. You share an owner in wee Fiona, but you and the rabbit can never be more than friends."

The cat squinched up its eyes, looking sagacious and regal, as cats will.

A commotion in the corridor momentarily disturbed the cat's display of indifference, provoking the beast to pop down from Hector's desk and sniff at the door.

"That has been going on all night," Hector said. "Some sort of scavenger hunt or midnight caroling without the tunes. Putting out the children's presents, I suspect."

Though the children would be getting a blessed lot of presents, based on the commotion Hector had heard.

"Makes it hard for a fellow to think."

The thought of Margaret pursued by the titles and nabobs Lady Joan could introduce her to weighed on Hector with a sort of morbid fascination. Those fellows wouldn't know what to make of quiet, sensible Margaret. They would dance with her, decide she had no conversation, and completely overlook—

He took up his pen again and kept his epistle short this time. The sooner he found a position with some opportunity to it, the sooner he could rescue Margaret from the imbeciles twirling about the ballrooms.

He had some money, he had brains, he had ambition, and Margaret wasn't greedy. Maybe even by next Christmas...

By next Christmas, Margaret could be married to somebody else and have a baby on the way. She wouldn't know Hector was leaving his post in search of betterment unless he told her.

Hector sanded his letter, let the cat out, and when he should have climbed into his own bed, he instead stole off in the direction of Margaret's room.

❧

Joan's mattress finally, finally dipped and jostled with the weight of her husband finding his slumbers. He lay on his back, two feet and one world away from Joan, much as he had the previous two nights.

"Has Father Christmas taken to turning his reindeer loose in the house?" she asked.

"Aye. And his elves."

Joan had not been a wife long, but something in Dante's voice sounded different to her. Beneath the covers, she scooted closer. "Dante? Is something troubling you?"

Something more than a wife about to bring scandal and ruin down on all and sundry, and over some silly dresses.

"You told me Valmonte lured you to his house with an invitation to tea from his mother, who supposedly wanted to talk over a new dress with you."

"And like a fool, I snatched up my sketch pad and parasol—"

He shifted onto his side, so he faced her, though the banked fire revealed little of his expression.

"Like a woman who trusts those she's known for years, you obliged. And then Valmonte met you, and you started sketching. I've seen you sketching, Joan Hartwell. You become cast away with it, as if sirens have you in thrall."

"Not lately I haven't." Lately, she hadn't sketched anything except her husband's features, his hands, even the way his kilt draped over his knees.

"Valmonte plied you with drink and took advantage, and he thinks to continue abusing your trust and your good name. Is there anything you haven't told me?"

They weren't quite nose to nose, weren't touching, and that was fortunate, because abruptly, Joan had difficulty speaking around the lump in her throat.

Yes, there was something she hadn't told him, though the words would seem self-serving now.

"What are you planning, Dante? You aren't thinking of calling him out or dumping him on a ship bound for the Orient, are you?"

"I'd like to, but your family had other suggestions."

Though she wore nothing except her silk nightgown, Joan abruptly felt as if she'd donned a heavily boned corset and laced it much too tightly.

"I won't leave you, Dante. Not for them. Not for appearances. Unless *you* send me away, unless you ask it of me, I won't endure one of those genteel, nasty Society separations. I never meant to shame you, never meant to shame myself."

Never meant to do anything except hear somebody murmur a few appreciative comments about pretty designs that Joan took more pleasure in creating than she had in anything else.

Strong arms hauled Joan across the remaining distance, until she was plastered against her husband, wrapped in his embrace and crying as if her heart would never mend.

"Wheesht, love, none of that. Hush now, hush."

"But I've made a terrible muddle out of what might have been so sweet—"

"You're sweet," Dante said, kissing her. "And dear, and you must not worry. Nobody's leaving anybody. Nobody's creating any scandal. We'll reach an agreement with Valmonte."

But Joan was in the grip of a tantrum of the heart, and while part of her knew she ought to rein herself in, another part of her would not be dignified—*or alone*—any longer.

"You cannot trust Valmonte, Dante. He's desperate, an animal backed by pride into a dirty corner of arrogance. He's all fight and no honor. I love you, and I will not allow somebody I love to face such—"

This kiss was as tender as the last, but more fierce. "Say that again."

"I cannot allow a varlet like Ed—"

"Not that, the other. Say it."

What had she—?

The constriction around Joan's emotions loosened, more swiftly and thoroughly than if someone had taken a knife to her laces.

"I love you, dearly. Completely. I love my husband.

I am profligately proud to be Mrs. Dante Hartwell, and I love my husband. I always will."

More fierce, delighted kisses followed as Dante wrestled himself over her. He wore not a stitch, and every warm, solid inch of him was lovely in Joan's arms.

"We'll buy Valmonte's silence," Dante whispered. "Tie it up in a bow and never let anybody pry it open. You're right that he's desperate, Joan, and a desperate man will take even a poor bargain if it's presented as his only option."

Joan wrapped her legs around her husband's flanks and locked her ankles at the small of his back.

"Do not say his name ever again in our bed. I hate him and the entire vain, silly, venal company he keeps. I love you. I love you. I love you."

Something rent as Dante levered up on his arms—silk from the sound of it.

And Joan felt freer still.

"My nightgown," she said, trying to wiggle free of the silk with fifteen stone of husband atop her. "Get rid of it, please."

He lifted away another two inches to bunch fabric up in his fist. "You're directing me to toss aside your nightgown? We've ripped it, Joan, torn it properly down the middle, and you—"

She snatched it from him and pitched it who knew where. "Stop blathering about a lot of silly fabric. Make love with me."

This hurling of verbal thunderbolts was great fun when undertaken naked under the covers with her husband. Dante rolled them though, putting Joan on top.

"You make love with me as well, Wife, and that's a bargain we'll both enjoy keeping."

Abruptly, Joan's nakedness was not under the covers, but rather, perched atop her spouse, illuminated by firelight—and a blush.

She curled down against him, nose to his chest. "This is quite intimate, this absence of clothing."

"Shall I fetch you another nightgown?"

He would, too. He'd climb of out the bed, march naked across the room, and look away while Joan's modesty came between her and the man she loved.

"I cannot bear to turn loose of you for even that long," she said, which was nothing more than the honest truth. "Though this is not dignified."

"Don't suppose it is dignified, but I love you too, Joan, and this trust you show me is more precious than dignity. Kiss me."

She showed him her trust, kissing him with all the ferocious possessiveness in her, then with protectiveness, and ultimately with a pure, roaring passion for him and the intimacies a husband and wife were entitled to give each other.

She showed him a few other things too—how much she enjoyed kissing him, how dearly she delighted in running her hands over every inch of him, how ferociously tender her embrace could be.

Dante likely would have joined his body to hers slowly and carefully, but Joan was having none of that. She'd discovered a pleasure greater than silk or velvet against her skin, better than crisp linen or delicate lace.

Her husband, as God made him, as close as he could get, skin to skin, breath to breath, passion to passion.

When he was intent on nudging and teasing, Joan gloved him in a single, exquisite roll of her hips—and then gave in to the compulsion to keep moving.

"You have hair on your chest," Joan said inanely, but the sensation of his bare chest rubbing against her breasts was novel, raw, and delightful.

"While you—" He guided her up so he could get his hands on her breasts, and the feel of his callused fingers and palms on her flesh was better than lace.

"Don't you stop," she whispered, bracing her hands on either side of his head, the better to meet him thrust for thrust.

Sensations robbed her of speech, sensations of pleasure and yearning and intimacy.

But also of anxiety, that she would again find herself some minutes hence, lying beside a sated husband, feeling all manner of tenderness, but also distance, and disappointment that she was not his equal in passion.

"I love you," Dante said, low, harsh words accompanied by his arm lashed tightly across her back. "I love you, and nothing and no one will change that, *ever*."

His declaration set her free, hurled her beyond worries and wishes into a pleasure so pure, the Christmas star itself could not have shone more brightly. Dante was with her in that pleasure, closer than thought or touch or any experience Joan might have foreseen when she'd taken her wedding vows.

When she'd endured with him in that light as long as she could, other pleasures awaited her.

The pleasure of lying spent upon her husband, both of them panting and naked, both of them needing the other's continued touch.

The pleasure of letting go—of pride, appearances, loneliness—everything, to trust that a shared future of any description would be the greatest gift imaginable.

The pleasure of a silence devoid of secrets and devoid even...

Even of shame.

"My love, are you crying?" Dante's hands on her back could not have been more tender, which only provoked Joan to worse lachrymosity.

"Of course, I'm crying. I've torn my favorite nightgown."

"Now will you let me fetch you another?"

The naughty wretch was laughing at her, and well he might. They faced ruin, very likely parenthood, and who knew what else. Their families had front-row seats for the entire farce, and Dante was naked and laughing in her arms.

"If I do allow you to fetch me another nightgown, and I'm not saying I can bear to let you go for that long, may we tear that one as well?"

And then Joan was naked and laughing in her husband's arms too.

◦❦◦

Christmas Day had been a circus, with Hector twitching at every slammed door, Margs looking preoccupied, the children shrieking and galloping, while inside Dante, a stillness had taken root, a solid quiet that had to do with knowing his wife would not leave him or forsake him.

Even if he bungled today's encounter with Valmonte. The plan was simple: List for Valmonte every gambling debt known to the collective MacGregor and Flynn males. List the business debts Quinworth, his lady, Balfour, and Spathfoy had been able to unearth. List the gambling debts Valmonte's mother had amassed, probably without informing her son of her peccadilloes.

And offer to make it all go away for a signed confession of rape. Quinworth would hold the document, and he'd be in a position to slander Valmonte without revealing particulars if the need arose.

Joan shifted her rabbit to one side and kissed Dante's cheek.

"Don't trust Edward. He's a weasel without honor, meaning no disrespect to weasels." She cuddled Babette closer—Lady Frederick—though the cold at the Ballater station didn't seem to bother the wee beastie.

"You like that rabbit."

"I like that you bought me something soft and warm to cuddle while I wait for you to return from Edinburgh. Very thoughtful of you."

And the rabbit would spare Joan's cuffs and hems from the twiddling and stroking she inflicted on them when nervous, for Lady Frederick thrived on affection.

"I won't kill Valmonte," Dante said as the conductor blew a single, long whistle blast.

"Also very thoughtful of you. I wish you'd let Tiberius accompany you."

Dear Tiberius had sat next to Joan at breakfast, and Dante had overheard the words "profoundly sorry," "remiss," and "apologize."

Truly, Christmas was a season for miracles.

It would take a miracle to make Valmonte see reason, but for Joan, Dante would try.

She accompanied him onto the train and kissed him good-bye so thoroughly the rabbit began to protest against Dante's chest.

"Don't kill him," Joan said as the "All aboard!" was called. "Lady Dorcas has plans for him, and I have plans for you."

The trip down to Edinburgh took hours, and in those hours, Dante occupied himself as he typically did on board a train—ciphering, estimating, projecting, and rearranging assets and liabilities, until almost every contingency could be accounted for.

Almost.

≈⁂≈

"You're doing what?" Margs shouted.

"Lower your voice, Margs," Hector pleaded. "It's for the best that I leave."

He'd not found a way to share his plans with her last night, though he'd shared his kisses and a great deal more. Then Christmas Day had been too hectic, and now, on Boxing Day, Hector had tracked Margaret to the library.

She paced away from him and from the wilted greenery above him, her blue velvet skirts swishing. "You would abandon Dante *now*, when he's taken a new wife, his household is in chaos, and these titled relations haven't a spare coin to invest?"

"They have spare coins. I did a report—"

Fury made Margaret Hartwell beautiful. Her normally placid eyes turned stormy, her pretty features

animated with passion. Hector wasn't about to report
on *those* conclusions.

"Bother your reports! Dante needs you, the children will miss you, and I—"

Hector's future hung on her next words, for never
in his wildest imaginings had he envisioned that
Margaret might object to his departure.

"And you?"

"I understand ambition," she said, her back to
him as she fussed with a small table tree adorned
with red ribbons. "I have some myself, in case you
hadn't noticed. I'm not like Rowena, though. Simply
because I have ideas for how to better manage mills
staffed almost entirely with females, that doesn't mean
the world owes me a mill."

"I'd love—I'd like to hear your ideas, all of them."

She turned, a small red bow in her fingers.

"Well, you won't, because you've some fool notion
that another employer will offer you greater opportunity
for advancement than Dante will. My brother thinks the
world of you, relies on you, and has taken great pains to
bring you into every facet of the mill's operations, when
another employer would have never—"

The bow in her fingers came unraveled, or unraveled the rest of the way. Margaret flounced over to the
desk and began opening drawers, one after another.
She set the little ribbon aside and piled the usual
accoutrements of correspondence on the desk—paper,
penknife, ink, sand, documents, more documents.

"What are you looking for?"

"Needle and thread. This bow isn't stitched like the
others, and that's why it has come unraveled."

Hector moved closer to the desk, intent on knotting the dratted bow around a tree branch tightly enough to put the discussion back onto relevant topics. "I'll see to it, but you can't be rummaging about in—What's that?"

"A bank draft," Margaret said, apparently satisfied that needle and thread were not among the desk's contents. She would have returned the documents to their original locations, but Hector swiped the bank draft, ribbons forgotten.

"This is made out to the company that insures the mills."

"And quite a sum it is," Margaret replied, tucking away everything she'd just found inside the desk. "I'm surprised Dante left it sitting about."

"What's today?" Hector's voice sounded far away to his own ears, and pinched with dread.

"Boxing Day, December 26. It ought to be called Sore Head Day, given how quiet the menfolk are. For the children we could change the name to Naps and Bellyaches Day, but for me, Out of Patience Day might serve."

As Margs nattered on, Hector stared at the bank draft, his entire future staring back at him, bleakly.

"We'll send it by special messenger," he muttered, "but it will be late by several days. As long as no losses occur during the lapse, the policy will likely be reinstated. I'm sure this happens all the time, the post being unreliable, holiday schedules upsetting everything."

But this lapse, this failure to see funds where they needed to be, exactly when they needed to be there, was indicative of an unreliability nobody would tolerate in a business manager.

And Dante had reminded him to get the damned thing sent off.

"You needn't tell Dante," Margs said gently. "It's one bank draft, Hector. You've seen a hundred of them safely on their way, and this one will be no different."

Margaret was generous and kind, the two qualities Hector valued in her most. He was about to tell her as much when Balfour came striding into the library, followed by some rough-looking fellow Hector did not recognize.

"There you are. Miss Hartwell, good morning. MacMillan, this fellow has a telegram for your employer. Says it's a business matter. In Hartwell's absence, I thought to direct him to you rather than Lady Joan."

"Telegram for you, sir," the fellow said. He was a harried sort of man, tall, gaunt, weary. "I was told to see it delivered personal, and wait for a reply."

"Open it," Margaret said. "Dante would want you to open it, Hector. If it's urgent, he won't be able to tend to it until he's concluded his business in Edinburgh."

Hector took the telegram, knowing in his bones the news had to be bad.

And it could not have been worse.

He read the words, read them again, then passed the slip of paper to Balfour, who offered a short, dirty oath in Gaelic.

"There's been a fire at one of the mills, Miss Hartwell, on Christmas Eve. The loss of the structure is complete. MacMillan, you'll want to remove to Edinburgh immediately. If you hurry, you can intercept Lady Joan on her way back from the station."

Margaret leaned heavily against Hector, who put his arms around her, as much to comfort himself as her, while the insurance payment lay on the desk directly under the wilted mistletoe.

Seventeen

EDINBURGH OBSERVED THE TRADITION OF BOXING Day, when gifts were delivered to servants and tenants, and the better families received callers by the hour.

Dante took advantage of tradition and joined the polite throng in the Valmonte formal drawing room, declining a liveried footman's offer of champagne, wassail, or rum punch.

"Mr. Hartwell," Valmonte said, sauntering forward. His lordship was pink about the ears, suggesting his choice had been the rum punch, probably for most of the afternoon. "A pleasure and a surprise. Is your new wife with you?"

In spirit, she certainly was.

"I've been entrusted on her behalf to discuss some sketches with you, Valmonte."

"Proper address would be 'my lord,' but in a display of holiday cheer, I shan't quibble. Did you bring the sketches with you?"

Dante patted his battered traveling satchel when he wanted to backhand his bloody lordship into next year. "I have documents with me right here."

"Some privacy is in order," Valmonte replied—quick study that he was. "My personal office will do."

Dante followed Valmonte past servants rushing in all directions, past a small parlor where an argument was in progress between Valmonte's mother and uncle, into what looked more like a sitting room with an escritoire than any office Dante had seen.

"May I offer you a drink?" Valmonte asked.

He lifted a glass stopper from a cut crystal decanter, his every gesture imbued with languid grace.

Dante closed the door. "My mother's people were Brodies. Do you know what their clan motto is?"

Valmonte poured a drink, apparently for himself, which was all to the good, for he'd need it.

"Alas, clan mottoes are not something I've studied at any length. I assume that's the Brodie plaid you're wearing?"

"My wife gave me this kilt for my Christmas present. She sewed every stitch herself, and it fits beautifully, though she took not a single measurement." She'd tucked him into it that morning and pronounced it his lucky kilt.

Valmonte swirled his drink, his smile sly. "Very talented, our Joan."

That knowing, coy smile and the equally offensive use of the plural possessive almost undid Dante's self-restraint, but Joan had forbade him to do murder. As Valmonte lounged against a sideboard, the cost of which would have fed a Highland village for a year, Dante was grateful for Joan's prohibition.

"The Clan Brodie motto is simple: 'Unite.' My wife's brother reminded me of that, and you're right about *my* Joan. She's exceedingly clever, brilliant even, and she's also brave and honorable."

Two qualities Valmonte lacked. He must have sensed some point was being made, for he left off grinning at his drink.

Brandy, from the scent of it, not even a good Scottish whiskey.

"She sews well," Valmonte said. "An accomplishment most women of her rank wouldn't be caught dead admitting, but I consider Joan a dear friend and conclude she can't help herself. Some people must gamble. Joan must stitch. You've brought me some sketches, Hartwell?"

No, Dante had not. He'd brought paperwork. A more astute businessman would have noted the difference.

"Joan is brave, honorable, and loyal to those she loves," Dante said, limiting himself to the most relevant of her virtues. "She hates you."

And well she should. This parasite had had the gall to attend Joan's wedding, to *threaten* her at her own wedding breakfast after taking shameful advantage of her, violating her trust, and exploiting her vulnerabilities.

"The creative souls are often at the mercy of their passions," Valmonte said with a shrug. "You might remind Joan I said as much."

He took a delicate sip of his drink, while down the corridor, the argument escalated, and Lady Valmonte ranted about her station having certain expectations a glorified clerk would know nothing about.

"You'll forgive my mother," Valmonte said, his

lordly congeniality acquiring a forced quality. "The holidays are a strain on her."

Dante appropriated the seat behind Valmonte's elegant little escritoire. "Did your dear mama approach the holidays worrying about whether her ruin at the hands of a gentleman she trusted would become common knowledge?"

Valmonte did not set his drink down. He *positioned* it, carefully, on a black lacquered tray encircled by a green dragon.

"Dear me," he drawled. "Has Joan embellished a tale of liberties stolen and virtue compromised? It wasn't like that. A fellow of your humble origins can't be expected to understand that your betters must be allowed their small lapses. We don't take them seriously, and if Joan brought some experience to your union, well, then—"

"Shut up."

The very novelty of being interrupted likely stopped the idiot's yawping.

"You lured Joan to your home with an invitation to tea, supposedly from your mother. You further indicated that a discussion of dress designs would be the topic of choice, and thus Joan hurried here, sketchbook at the ready, eager for an enjoyable social call. You plied her with strong drink at least, took liberties no gentleman would have taken, and then threatened to expose Joan to ruin for having become your victim. I suggest you sit down."

Dante pointed to the chair opposite the escritoire. In Valmonte's first display of prudence, he took the indicated seat.

"Did you have to beat this confession from your

new wife, Hartwell? Joan's fairly bright. I cannot imagine she'd confide such a tale in you willingly. She should be—"

Dante's hand shot across the desk and grabbed Valmonte by his fussy, old-fashioned cravat. "If you say my wife should be ashamed, they might be the last words you utter, you miserable pollution of the human race."

More than Valmonte's ears turned red. His entire face would have gone nicely with a cheery Royal Stewart plaid.

Dante thrust him back into his chair. "You and I will transact a wee bit of business."

Valmonte fussed the lace at his throat, which, alas, no longer lay in such tidy, pristine folds. "I can have four footmen here in a minute flat, Hartwell. Joan behaved foolish—"

Dante flexed his fist, and Valmonte fell silent.

"I will geld you before you reach that bellpull, *your lordship*. A belated Christmas gift to my wife. And just as you made sure there were no witnesses to your violation of Joan's trust, your accident with the fireplace poker will also go unwitnessed."

Valmonte's expression became considering— respectfully considering. "You should be angry with Joan. I assumed she'd kept her—our—indiscretion to herself, and you married her none the wiser."

"You will cease making assumptions about my marriage, my wife, or what I knew when. This is a confession of rape." Dante laid the document before an abruptly pale viscount, and set the engraved silver pen and ink stand by his skinny wrist.

"Why should I sign this?" His voice quavered, which was some gratification.

"Your mother's debts exceed anything she can repay from her pin money. Your house of fashion is a house of debt. Your personal finances aren't in terrible disarray *yet*, but if Lady Dorcas calls off the wedding, then you won't have her settlements to keep your aristocratic ship of mismanagement afloat for another ten years."

Valmonte was so assured of his place in life that his arrogance amounted to a sort of innocence. He was also taken by surprise and not entirely sober.

Dante felt no pity for him whatsoever.

"My friends and Joan's family expect you to sign that confession, in exchange for a sum certain that will cover the Valmonte personal debts. That's not a bad plan, but I've devised an alternative."

Though he hadn't discussed the specifics with anybody, including his wife. Still, Joan had to know a confession of rape could easily redound to the discredit of the victim, regardless of its uses against the perpetrator.

"Joan told her *family*?"

"Spathfoy and Quinworth hate you too, and Balfour called you a disgrace to your patrimony. His sister was more eloquent than that, but the one you'll have to worry about is Lady Quinworth—assuming you don't have an accident with the poker and the andirons before you leave this room. Oh, and Connor, Ian, and Gilgallon MacGregor bear watching too."

A few beats of quiet went by, underscored by the happy murmur of holiday socializing from the front of the house.

"Give me the damned pen."

"Na' sae fast, laddie. What my family wants is important, but what Joan wants matters more. You own a house of fashion, such as it is. I'm prepared to buy it from you."

Valmonte blinked, looking not like a proud viscount but like a slightly drunk man going prematurely bald, who knew his overindulgences would cost him more than a clear head.

"Listen, Hartwell. Maison du Mode, having aspirations in artistic directions, is the only means my family has to make money without offending the genteel strata of Society we occupy. I don't expect one of your humble origins to comprehend the strictures a man in my position endures."

Valmonte could make longer sentences when under the influence than Dante could when dead sober.

"A man of my *humble origins* understands that times have changed, Valmonte. You can't keep your mama in furs and diamonds on the land rents alone, particularly not Scottish land rents. Sell me the business, and you can invest the proceeds to generate interest income."

Valmonte picked up the pen, a little silver business that might have served equally well as a dagger, were the man clever enough to wield it. "Mama will kill me if I sell that place."

While buying Valmonte's business would mean a fat mortgage on the only mill Dante owned outright.

"Your mama will kill you? And when you cower before your mother's tantrums, does Lady Dorcas find an example for how her marriage will go on?" Rather than ask that question, Dante might as well have swung the cast-iron poker at Valmonte's balls, and because that was a cheering realization, he didn't stop there.

"Bad enough that you watch your family's fortunes drain away one ball gown, carriage, or gambling debt at a time, but what will your children have, Valmonte?"

"My sons will be gentlemen, my daughters, ladies."

Oh, for God's sake.

Any aspiration Dante had ever held to the status of gentleman drifted up the flue like so much ash. Gentlemen could be scoundrels, sneak thieves, seducers, and cowards.

How much better to be Lady Joan's plain, simple, devoted husband.

"Sell me the business," Dante said. "Joan might keep the name the same, though I won't encourage that. Remove to Paris where everything is cheaper, rent out your properties to men of my *humble origins*, and invest what capital you have."

Hector could have written entire memos for the idiot about that plan, the only one that held a prayer of rescuing Valmonte from penury before his children were grown.

"That advice is my holiday gift to you, Valmonte, but my patience is at an end. This is a contract of sale, and the amount is the same. You either admit you're a rapist, or you give up a business you're not running very well to begin with. Choose."

"I'm not allowed to read them?"

"How much time did you give Joan to gather her wits before you stole her sketches and her good name?" Moreover, Valmonte likely could not comprehend a business document if he were given all day to decipher it, and Dante wanted to breathe the fresh Scottish air sooner rather than later.

Valmonte peered at the contract of sale, which Dante had kept as simple as such an agreement could be. The confession, by contrast, was problematic, because Valmonte could later credibly claim he'd been forced to sign it under duress.

In which case, his lordship became the victim, not Joan.

Valmonte dipped the pen and pulled the contract for sale closer.

"Sign legibly," Dante warned, "and all three copies. Send your uncle around to Balfour's town house to vouch for your signature."

For Dante had already signed the documents, and had stepped off the train long enough to pass a bottle of good whiskey to old MacDeever, and to have the man and his porter witness Dante's signatures.

"What's the third copy for?"

Valmonte didn't sign the documents so much as he sketched an affectation of a signature, but did this man know nothing of business?

"I'll store the third copy in my bank vault, where moth, rust, or fire cannot destroy it, nor thieves break in and steal it."

Nor thieving viscounts pretend the contract had never existed.

Valmonte sat back when he'd decorated the third copy with his penmanship. "Now what?"

"Now I own a dress shop with airs above its station. You'll have a bank draft within the week." And

Dante's mill—Love Mill—would carry a substantial mortgage too.

His first, but well worth the debt.

"It's a house of fashion," Valmonte sniffed. "Worthy of any of its rivals in Paris or London."

"I'd like the key to my house of fashion," Dante said. "Now. And lest you think to clean out the cash box or make off with the inventory, the doors to the place are under surveillance by fellows I trust who are, *alas*, of humble origins. If you or any member of your family come on the premises, you will be politely escorted at all times."

Valmonte replaced the pen in its stand, his expression perplexed. "I can't think like you do. You're not a gentleman, and I'd never steal—"

"Exactly. I am not a gentleman, so you'd best quit talking while you're still alive and able to sire children." Dante rose, before Valmonte's attempted thieving from Joan resulted in multiple accidents all around. "Either of us can repudiate that contract in the next three business days, but by Friday, that deal is final."

Valmonte rose as well, by virtue of bracing both hands on the desk and pushing to his feet like an old man or a young sot. "It says that?"

"Second page, paragraph seventeen. Prevents an argument of duress, and limits excuses about fraud in the inducement."

Which was so much Mandarin to the *gentleman* blinking at Dante. "We're done then?"

"I'm finished with you, unless I or my family hears the first hint of discredit to Lady Joan's name." Dante would have to rely on his betters to patrol those borders, because he belonged to not a single club that his lordship would dine in even as a guest.

Valmonte fingered the fringe of the brocade bell-pull, but didn't summon anybody. "I wouldn't have signed that other, about the rape."

Dante tarried, because Valmonte wasn't rattling his toy swords—or pokers—at this juncture. "Why not?"

"Because I didn't. One imbibes, you know, then imbibes a bit more, and certain functions diminish. Even if I'd entertained such notions—and I'm not admitting that I did, not for very long—Joan could talk about those damned sketches for hours, and it grew late, and well…I *didn't*."

"You're sure?"

"Have you ever tried to take liberties with a properly dressed woman? A moat, drawbridge, and portcullis could not defend her virtue more effectively than all those petticoats and bustles and knickers… Particularly in winter. To say nothing of her damned corsetry. Unless she's enthusiastic about the business too, importuning a properly dressed woman is a futile undertaking."

And Joan had not in any way been enthusiastic about the undertaking. That Valmonte knew as much was bad enough, but Dante let him live anyway.

It was, after all, Christmas.

"Go to Paris," Dante said. "And my regards to your mama and fiancée."

He collected two copies of the contract and showed himself out, eager to present to Joan the happy developments of the day.

❦

"Ye mun stop pacing," Margaret said. "Dante will get here when he gets here."

Hector took a seat then popped right back to his feet, while Joan exchanged a look of mutual exasperation with Dante's sister.

"Hector, he won't blame you," Joan said. "The holidays throw everything into an uproar, and mills are prone to fires."

Dante would blame himself. He'd construct some male fancy of surpassing logic that made him as responsible for the day's dismal events as if he were laird of a medieval Highland demesne and answerable only to God.

While Joan, too, felt that the tragedy at the mill was her fault. If she hadn't distracted Dante from the business upon which he thrived, if she hadn't added scandal and holy matrimony to his already taxing schedule, if she'd let him focus on finding the investors he'd sought—

"That's him," Margaret said as the front door to Balfour's elegant town house swung solidly shut outside the family parlor. "Let me tell him, Hector. You'll muck it up."

"I'll tell him," Hector shot back. "I'm his man of business, and I'm responsib—"

Joan rose and went to the door. "Out, both of you. I will convey to my husband this news, and you will stop carping at each other. Things could be much, much worse. Dante is sensible, and he will agree with me on that."

Joan had debated wearing black, though. In this

holiday season, she'd considered wearing the most somber attire a woman could don.

"Greetings, all." Dante positively swaggered into the family parlor, a cozy, comfortable space Balfour had turned over to Joan's use. "My lovely wife, you've joined me a day early, but happy Christmas."

He kissed her, his kilt swinging about his knees.

"Happy Christmas, dear Husband. Hector and Margaret, you will please excuse us?"

"Yes," Dante said, drawing Joan closer to the fire. "I have glad tidings to share with my wife. Be off with you two. Find some mistletoe, a wee dram, and a cozy parlor of your own."

Hector took Margaret by the elbow and drew her from the room. The door had barely closed before Dante's arms were around Joan and his mouth on hers.

"I was so naughty, Wife. You'll have to spank me for it, I'm sure. I did not follow Spathfoy's instructions. I did not behave with anything approaching prudence. We're in debt. Wonderfully in debt. For the first time in years, I've taken on substantial debt."

He kissed her again, as if this debt was the best gift the holidays might have produced.

Joan kissed him back, because for one moment, she wanted to imprint on her memory this impression of Dante Hartwell suffused with joy. Whatever had transpired with Valmonte, Dante had acquitted himself well, and he was magnificent in victory.

"Dante, I have some news."

He linked his hands behind Joan's neck, his arms a heavy weight on her shoulders. "Are ye well? You look pale. Valmonte shared with me some news, too. I think you'll want to hear it."

"Dante, you should hear my news first." She drew him close and hugged him fiercely. "The mill you call Love has burned to the ground. The structure is a complete loss."

The shock of it went through him the way cutting off the gas doused a bright lamp to nothing more than a lingering whiff of smoke. One instant he was alive with joie de vivre and full of his accomplishments, the next he was relying on Joan simply to keep him upright.

"A fire?"

"Christmas Eve. We're not sure how it started. Hector will leave for Glasgow tomorrow, if you ask it of him." As would Joan; she hoped he knew that.

Dante lifted his forehead from Joan's shoulder, his gaze terrible. "And our people? What about our people? I employ a hundred women and girls at each mill, and—how many lost, Joan?"

"Not a one. You closed the mills for Christmas Eve. Your people were home stuffing themselves with ham, neeps, and tatties."

He sank onto a sofa as if he'd taken a bullet from an unseen assassin. "Not a one?"

"Not a watchman, not a mouser, as far as we know." Joan took the place beside him and let him absorb that miracle, which, as endlessly wondrous as it was, might be the last good news for some time.

"They'll not go hungry," Dante said fiercely. "We can add a second shift to the two mills remaining, or a third shift for those who are willing, and the insurance settlement will let us rebuild come spring. Rebuilding will employ more than a few of the men-folk, and we can finally modernize the facility." He looped an arm around Joan and drew her close, kissing her temple. "We'll manage. We've had setbacks before, but we'll manage."

And now, she had to tell him the rest.

"There won't be any insurance money, Dante. Hector found the payment for the policy in Balfour's library after it had come due. Today was the first day he could send it, and it's in the post, but the policy will have lapsed."

Hector and Margaret had explained to Joan how insurance worked, Margaret in particular using terms and examples Joan could comprehend.

"The bloody insurance has lapsed?"

"Hector said that's what happens when a payment isn't made on time."

Dante stared into the fire, his expression intent rather than thunderous. "Hector would know, though I'll want to check for myself. Each mill has its own policy, and Love is the newest acquisition. Its policy might read differently. This complicates things."

This complicates things.

The only asset Dante owned outright and a significant source of his income went up in smoke, and to him, it was a *complication*.

"I love you," Joan said. "I know that doesn't help, it won't rebuild any mills, but you know my settlements are available if you need them. Tiberius won't fight me on that, in fact, he might—"

Dante kissed her. "Hush a moment, dear heart. I'm thinking."

The moment became five minutes, then ten, with Dante staring into the fire, while Joan's eyes grew heavy. She dozed off against his side, relieved he'd taken the news so well, but hurting for him, that his endless hard work had earned him only...

More hard work and a wife who'd needed something as simple as insurance explained to her.

Eighteen

"FIONA SAYS FREDERICK'S NOT PEAKED AND WAN WHEN Babette is with him." Phillip stroked a small hand over Frederick's furry back.

The rabbit did, indeed, look more cheerful as he reclined against the wainscoting of the nursery's playroom. His eyes were bright, his nose in constant motion, and though Babette was at present paying a call on Joan's lap, Frederick had a contented air.

A *smug*, contented air.

"Frederick will be a papa," Dante said. "This settles a fellow down."

Dante's thoughts would not settle down. He'd spent yesterday in Glasgow, sorting out the aftermath of a fire and watching Hector work himself to exhaustion, while Margs acted as his lieutenant, and Dante...

Tried to make himself useful.

No insurance would be forthcoming. Hector had made certain of that.

"Why is Frederick to be a papa? Because he married Babette?"

Dante picked the rabbit up and settled in beside his son on the hearth rug. "Yes, more or less. Rabbits do these things a bit differently, but Babette will be the mother of his babies."

Frederick was soft to the touch and shamelessly willing to be stroked and petted. No wonder Joan enjoyed the company of her rabbit.

"Lady Joan is going to have a baby," Phillip said, running a single finger down Frederick's back. "I heard her talking about it when the ladies were knitting."

No, she was not. She wasn't to have a baby or a dress shop or much in the way of luxury. Dante had until the following day to repudiate the contract with Valmonte, and while the chore needed to be dealt with, he didn't look forward to it one bit.

"I don't think there will be a baby showing up any time soon, lad. Not for us, though Frederick will be a papa by spring."

If a dance competition were held the length and breadth of Scotland, Frederick and Babette would have won top honors in the Bunny Fling.

Phillip left off petting the rabbit. "Lady Joan will have a baby by autumn. She said she might name a boy Christopher, because she got exactly what she wanted for Christmas."

Oh, Joan. Dante had lost a mill—mills could be replaced—but Joan had been nearly certain she'd at least have a child to love. While Dante was relieved Valmonte would have no continuing connection to Joan, he also knew she'd already grown attached to the notion of motherhood.

"Maybe by next Christmas," Dante said. "Though

that will take some fast work. We should put Himself back in his box."

Phillip gave his father an impatient look. "It doesn't take a year for a baby to grow."

"What would you know about it?" Dante teased. "Are you considering holy matrimony? Perhaps the scullery maid who sneaks you biscuits will be waiting for you under the mistletoe?"

Phillip produced one of his rare, sweet smiles. "I'll never get married. Girls are silly and bossy, and they never like to get dirty. May I hold Frederick? Lady Joan said if she has a girl, then you should choose the name."

Dante passed the rabbit to Phillip, who sat cross-legged before the fire. "Do you recall every bit of gossip you overhear?"

"I heard them this morning. I can remember what I heard this morning."

"This morning?"

"They were giggling. Girls giggle too."

A sensation rippled down Dante's spine, a sparkling sense of possibility, of hope. "You're sure you heard the ladies this morning?"

"Lady Quinworth, Lady Balfour, Lady Joan, Fiona's mama. They were quite silly. Lady Quinworth said she refuses to have a granddaughter named Babette. I like the name Babette, and Frederick does too. His favorite girl name in the world is Babette."

Dante rose, his thoughts hopping about like so many loose rabbits. "Put Frederick back in his box, my boy. I can't think you'd fancy a sister named Babette."

"Babette Bunny Hartwell. It's better than Charlene."

"It's awful. Don't you dare mention it to Lady Joan."

"I'm to call her Mama. She said we could if we wanted to."

Dante kissed the top of the boy's head, because Phillip was smiling again—twice in one brief conversation. "Then so you shall, and I shall be the papa."

The rabbit wiggled his nose, one papa to another, and Dante left the nursery at something close to a sprint.

≈≫

"Leave off raiding Balfour's decanters long enough to answer some questions."

At Dante's command, Spathfoy paused mid pour at the library's sideboard.

"You're a member of this family for little more than four weeks, and already you're giving orders. Your atrocious manners suggest Joan has been remiss in her uxorial duties, Hartwell, and I'm sure my mother—"

"Cease yer bletherin', Spathfoy," Balfour said, passing the glass to Dante. "How is the situation in Glasgow?"

"Smoky," Dante said. "Subdued chaos at the remaining mills as we sort out how to fill all the orders, keep everybody employed, and stop Hector from clothing himself in a hair shirt. They're managing, though. That's not what I wanted to ask you about."

"A toast," Spathfoy said. "To the New Year."

Balfour lifted his glass. "Not very original, Spathfoy. But Hartwell can likely use any excuse to take a tot. If you won't allow us to invest outright, we'll lend you whatever you need."

Dante paused, his glass halfway to his lips. "I wasn't about to ask for a loan."

"Of course you weren't," Spathfoy said, shooting a glower at Balfour. "But we heard about the insurance. Miss Hartwell mentioned it to Lady Quinworth, who told my father, and—"

"What did you want to know, Hartwell?" Balfour interjected.

Dante took a fortifying sip of a smooth, fruity whiskey. "How soon do the ladies know they're carrying?"

The quality of the very air in the library changed.

"Long before they tell us," Spathfoy said. He took up a slouch against the mantel, above which, the Highland laird still strutted about on a life-size canvas. He'd been a papa, that laird. Dante could tell from the twinkle in his eye.

"I think they know at the very moment of conception," Spathfoy added.

"They suspect, anyway," Balfour said. "My countess, who would fill every room with bouquets, abruptly took the scent of most flowers into strong dislike. I didn't put the signs together until the child was born, but that was the first clue—and not two weeks after conception, as nearly as I can calculate."

"That soon?"

"My mother claims to have conceived me on her wedding night, and said she was queasy within a week," Spathfoy volunteered with a smugness that suggested the timing was his doing.

"Mary Frances's situation with Fiona was apparently different," Balfour said, reaching above the estate desk to yank down a wilted sprig of mistletoe and toss it into the fire.

"Your footmen won't thank you," Spathfoy observed as the greenery blackened and curled to ashes.

"Next Christmas we'll all descend on your household, Spathfoy," Balfour muttered. "We'll see who has the happiest footmen."

"About the ladies," Dante interjected. "They can tell within two weeks?"

"I should think so," Spathfoy said.

"As loath as I am to agree with yon Lord of Mistletoe about anything," Balfour said, finding more mistletoe over the sideboard and another sprig affixed above the library's globe, "my sense is most women can tell fairly quickly if they've conceived. I came to that conclusion when I practiced medicine, and my experience as Lady Balfour's husband confirms it. Now I have a question for you."

Balfour had been trained as a physician. Dante had forgotten that.

"They can tell," Dante murmured. Rowena hadn't been forthcoming about such matters, and Dante hadn't dared interrogate her.

"Hartwell, finish your drink. One senses you need the fortification," Spathfoy said, pushing off the mantel and steering Dante to the couch.

Balfour came around with the decanter.

"As for my question, and please pay attention, Hartwell: If you weren't inviting us to invest in your mills, and you won't accept a loan now, then why were you willing to disrupt your entire holiday to accept my invitation to Balfour House?"

Perhaps they would name a daughter Babette after all.

"I don't think he heard you," Spathfoy said. "The Scots can have very poor hearing."

"I heard him. I did want investors, or thought I did." But he'd found so much more.

"Then why don't you want them now?" Balfour asked, taking an armchair by the fire. "Shipping is a chancy business. We're seeing only the first hints of what steam can do, pirates continue to plague us, nations go to war, navies get unpredictable when attempting to justify themselves in times of peace—"

Spathfoy resumed his place at the mantel. "And the New Year will be here before you make your point."

"My point is that diversification is sound business. I would like to invest in your mills, Hartwell."

"As would I," Spathfoy added. "I'm half-Scottish, and nobody works harder than a Scot in pursuit of coin. Investments in Scotland strike me as a sensible use of my wealth, and my parents agree."

"You both need to know something," Dante said. "I never got a signed confession from Valmonte, nor would I ask for one now. Of all his transgressions, the one covered in that document was apparently not among them."

Some throat clearing went on, some sipping of whiskey.

"Well, then," Spathfoy said, raising his glass. "If you didn't get a signed confession, what did you get?"

"A bloody dress shop."

Spathfoy fell prey to a sputtering cough before mirth overcame him, Balfour's guffaw soon degenerated into hooting laughter, and Dante kept to himself that the name Babette Hartwell was growing on him by the minute.

~∽⌀~

"My lady?"

Before her eyes opened, Joan had the thought, "He's back," and yet a curious midafternoon lassitude kept her sprawled beneath the sheets.

"Mrs. Hartwell?"

"Mmf."

The bed dipped, the scent of Dante—pine and spice, husband and delight—wafted across the sheets. "I have married a slugabed. Fine quality in a wife."

He snuggled up next to her, a hairy muscular leg tucked against her backside, his chest to her back.

"Mrs. Hartwell, you've neglected your wardrobe."

For him, she would make the hard slog up from a delicious nap. "How are the mills?"

"I remark on a complete lack of attire, and you ask about the mills. The mills are abuzz. We had a miracle, according to the women. The first time old Hard-Hearted Hartwell gives them Christmas Eve off, and the fire has no victims. I've never seen such a lot of smug, busy women. I'm Happy Christmas Hartwell now, according to them."

His hand, callused and warm, paid a call on Joan's breast.

"I missed you," Joan said, wiggling closer to him. "I am already accustomed to sleeping with my husband. You'll not be traveling without me again soon, sir, not even for two nights."

"You're sleeping through teatime. Balfour said you might be prone to napping."

The hand so charmingly full of Joan's breast made no lascivious overtures, but remained, a pleasurable addition to the pleasurable sensations of clean sheets and friendly husband.

"What would his lordship know about my naps?"

"He's a physician. Are you well, Joan?"

"I am quite well." Also naked. Why on earth hadn't she indulged in such decadence before her marriage? "I believe I sleep better without clothing."

"You sleep better when you're carrying my child."

The sweet, sleepy sense of well-being in which Joan had been wallowing expanded, to encompass an aching tenderness toward her husband. She shifted, the better to cuddle against his chest.

"I am carrying," she said. "The other ladies have confirmed the signs, though it's very early days."

"Earlier than you know, my love."

A note of smugness in his tone had Joan burrowing closer. "What does the loss of the mill do to our situation, Dante? A child is an expense, but I can make do on little, I assure you. My pin money is excessive, and—"

"The loss of the mill, the oldest and least productive of the three, will be the concern of my investors, and of Margs and Hector MacMillan."

"Hector blames himself, Dante, but anybody can forget the post."

"I blame myself. I expected Hector to be at my beck and call, to have no holidays with his own kin, to step and fetch and do the work of three men, as if a mind that astute should be content with endless clerking and haring about."

Joan kissed the center of his chest and laid her cheek over his heart.

"You told him that, didn't you? Of course you did, and probably with Margs right there to hear every word." Hard-Hearted Hartwell, indeed.

"We were standing on the weaving floor at Hope, with more than a shift of employees looking on. I didn't admit to him I was responsible, I roared it. Productivity suffered for all the shouting and betting going on."

"I'm so proud of you." Maybe a wife shouldn't say those words, but the way Dante kissed her ear suggested he'd needed to hear them.

"Better late than never," Dante went on. "The ladies cheered like sailors, Margs loudest of all. Hector has more than a few admirers." He patted her bare bum, a scrumptious blend of possession, affection, and naughtiness in a single glancing caress. "I don't hate the mills, but I'm glad to know they'll be in good hands with Hector."

She kissed his chin. "And Margs?"

"And Margs. I suspect we'll soon see a merger of interested parties there. Are you falling back asleep?"

"I like sleeping naked. Perhaps it's fortunate I never knew this, though in other regards, I can't say naïveté served me well. You never told me how you left things with…"

She didn't want to say his name. Not in bed, not when enjoying the freedom of an unclad state for one of the first times in her adult memory.

"About that."

Dante's hand ceased its slow, soothing pattern on her hip, though beneath her ear, Joan still felt and heard the steady tattoo of his heart.

"Should I get dressed, Husband? I'd rather remain with you here."

"If you go down to tea in the altogether, I won't answer for the consequences."

"Wear your lucky kilt. We'll find some consequences you might like." Impending motherhood was making her daft, also happy, and yet, a serpent remained in her marital garden. "What were you about to say?"

"I met with a certain party as planned and can assure you he'll never cause you another moment's trouble. He's removing to Paris, in fact, and taking his harpies with him."

Contentment shifted again, to encompass profound, enormous relief, and gratitude bigger than a Highland summer sky.

"Thank you, Dante. Thank you, thank you. I could not have a better Christmas gift from you, though I love Babette dearly, of course."

"Not as dearly as wee Freddy does, but I've another gift for you. For us."

"So many gifts. I am your wife, I have Charlie and Phillip and Margs to love—Hector, too—and this baby—"

"Is our baby, Joan Hartwell. I know you don't want certain names brought up in our bed, but you need to know that when a man overimbibes, his ability to perpetrate certain kinds of mischief deserts him. Your sketches were the objective of his venery, not your virginity. *You gave that to me.*"

A shiver passed over Joan, a delighted, elated disbelief, anchored at the same time by a bodily knowing. "To you?"

"You were a maid when you came to my bed. You're to be a mother now, and I'll be a papa again. We're a fine team, Mrs. Hartwell."

"I'm to be—"

That Dante would have loved any child born to them was a measure of his heart, but that their firstborn would be his in every sense moved Joan beyond happiness to a transcendent, intimate joy.

"We're to be," he corrected her. "We'll also be late for tea, though I've one more small parcel to lay at your feet."

"No more," Joan said, wiping her cheek against his shoulder. "No more, Husband. My heart cannot hold any more glad tidings."

He dabbed at her cheeks with a corner of the sheet. "Women are emotional when they're on the nest. It's nothing to fret over."

She smacked him, which had about as much effect as if she'd smitten him with a swath of lace. "I'm so much more than on the nest. I'm Mrs. Dante Hartwell, and I love you, and I never thought beyond—Oh, you are awful."

So she kissed him for an awfully long time, all the while sensing patience in him and great good cheer to go along with a rising arousal. When she let him up for air, she was straddling him, her braid coming undone, the covers in a tangle around them.

"You are trying to distract me," Dante said, tracing

a finger along the side of her jaw. "Flaunting your rosy wares, accosting me with your charms. And to think you once valued your modesty so exceedingly."

He was teasing her, and the matter he alluded to was more complicated than modesty, having to do with trust, self-confidence, pride, and love.

"So say your piece, and then I have plans for you, Mr. Hartwell. We're not finished celebrating our holidays."

"No, we are not. I bought you that silly dress shop. I had a bit put aside, and we'll have some investors in that venture too, at least until we can buy them out. But nobody would hear of me taking a mortgage, and Spathfoy said it would be seen as a hobby for you, an eccentric indulgence, like a collection of teapots, or—please stop crying, Joan. I wanted to make you happy. All I wanted was for you to be happy."

She mashed her nose against his neck, hard, because tears and joy both had reached proportions too great for one lady to manage.

"I wanted to make *you* happy," Joan said. "I wanted to be a good wife to you, to be worthy of your respect and affection. I wanted you to be p-proud of me."

He let her cry, let her kiss the daylights out of him, and cry some more. When she could compose herself, to the extent a woman naked in bed with the most wonderful husband in the world could compose herself, Dante held her, his cheek pillowed against her hair.

"You're pleased, then, to have a dress shop of your own? We'll be firmly in trade, whether you're simply sketching the dresses or handling the ledger books. I won't have you on your feet greeting customers all day."

"Of course not. We'll hire snooty Frenchwomen for that, and this will be the best fun, Dante. Ladies pay dearly for their fripperies, too. Trade can be lucrative."

He laughed at this profundity. "We'll have a portion of the profits from the mills, and I have a few other ideas, if you don't object to ventures involving family. We won't starve, unless you deny me leave from this bed."

"We've missed tea, haven't we?"

And this would cause talk and knowing smiles, and Joan could not be less concerned. She stretched atop her husband, luxuriously, having her first experience of that condition known as "not a care in the world."

"I can fetch you some clothes," Dante said, hugging her soundly. "What shall you wear to your first dinner as a purveyor of fine ladies' fashions?"

She would wear a smile, certainly, and it could well be a permanent addition to her wardrobe. "Choose anything, provided I can remove it easily."

Dante rose from the bed, not a stitch on him, and crossed to the wardrobe. "These aren't likely to fit you much longer."

And what did that matter? Instead of patterns and fabrics and lace, Joan's awareness was drawn to the line of her husband's shoulders, the sculpted tapering of his ribs, the—

Oh, dear. They were going to miss dinner as well.

Though they did decide one thing before Joan again fell asleep in her husband's embrace some while later. If the child was a girl, she would be named Joy Babette Hartwell.

If you enjoy romance
set in the Scottish Highlands,
then be sure to read on
for a taste of

The Laird

Book 3
in Grace Burrowes's
Captive Hearts series

"Elspeth, I believe a Viking has come calling."

At Brenna's puzzled observation, her maid set aside
the embroidery hoop serving as a pretext for enjoying
the Scottish summer sun, rose off the stone bench, and
joined Brenna at the parapets.

"If Vikings are to ruin your afternoon tea, better if
they arrive one at a time," Elspeth said, peering down
at the castle's main gate. "Though that's a big one,
even for a Viking."

From her vantage point high on Castle Brodie's
walls, all Brenna could tell about the rider was that he
was big, broad-shouldered, and blond. "Our visitor is
alone, likely far from home, hungry and tired. If we're
to offer him hospitality, I'd best inform the kitchen."

"He looks familiar," Elspeth said as the rider swung
off his beast.

Brenna had the same sense of nagging familiarity.
She knew that loose-limbed stride, knew that exact
manner of stroking a horse's neck, knew—

Foreboding prickled up Brenna's arms, an instant before recognition landed in a cold heap in her belly.

"Michael has come home." Nine years of waiting and worrying while the Corsican had wreaked havoc on the Continent, of not knowing what to wish for.

Her damned husband hadn't even had the courtesy to warn her of his return.

Elspeth peered over the stone crenellations, her expression dubious. "If that's the laird, you'd best go welcome him, though I don't see much in the way of baggage. Perhaps, if you're lucky, he'll soon be off larking about on some new battlefield."

"For shame, Elspeth Fraser."

Brenna wound down through the castle and took herself out into the courtyard, both rage and gratitude speeding her along.

She'd had endless Highland winters to rehearse the speech Michael deserved, years to practice the dignified reserve she'd exhibit before him should he ever recall he had a home. Alas for her, the cobbles were wet from a recent scrubbing, so her dignified reserve more or less skidded to a halt before her husband.

Strong hands steadied her as she gazed up, and up some more, into green eyes both familiar and unknown.

"You've come home." Not at all what she'd meant to say.

"That I have. If you would be so good, madam, as to allow the lady of the—*Brenna*?"

His hands fell away, and Brenna stepped back, wrapping her tartan shawl around her more closely.

"Welcome to Castle Brodie, Michael." Because

somebody ought to say the words, she added, "Welcome home."

"You used to be chubby." He leveled this accusation as if put out that somebody had made off with that chubby girl.

"You used to be skinny." Now he was all-over muscle. He'd gone away a tall, gangly fellow, and come back not simply a man, but a warrior. "Perhaps you're hungry?"

She did not know what to do with a husband, much less *this* husband, who bore so little resemblance to the young man she'd married, but Brenna knew well what to do with a hungry man.

"I am…" His gaze traveled the courtyard the way a skilled gunner might swivel his sights on a moving target, making a circuit of the granite walls rising some thirty feet on three sides of the bailey. His expression suggested he was making sure the castle, at least, had remained where he'd left it. "I am famished."

"Come along then." Brenna turned and started for the entrance to the main hall, but Michael remained in the middle of the courtyard, still peering about. Potted geraniums were in riot, pink roses climbed trellises under the first-floor windows, and window boxes held all manner of blooms.

"You've planted flowers."

Brenna returned to her husband's side, trying to see the courtyard from his perspective. "One must occupy oneself somehow while waiting for a husband to come home—or be killed."

He needed to know that for nine years, despite anger, bewilderment, and even the occasional period of striving for indifference toward him and his fate, Brenna had gone to bed every night praying that death did not end his travels.

"One must, indeed, occupy oneself." He offered her his arm, which underscored how long they'd been separated and how far he'd wandered.

The men of the castle and its tenancies knew to keep their hands to themselves where Brenna MacLogan Brodie was concerned. They did not hold her chair for her, did not assist her in and out of coaches, or on and off of her horse.

And yet, Michael stood there, a muscular arm winged at her, while the scent of slippery cobbles, blooming roses, and a whiff of vetiver filled the air.

"Brenna Maureen, every arrow slit and window of that castle is occupied by a servant or relation watching our reunion. I would like to walk into my home arm in arm with my wife. Will you permit me that courtesy?"

He'd been among the English, the *military* English, which might explain this fussing over appearances, but he hadn't lost his Scottish common sense.

Michael had *asked* her to accommodate him. Brenna wrapped one hand around his thick forearm and allowed him to escort her to the castle.

⁂

He could bed his wife. The relief Michael Brodie felt at that sentiment eclipsed the relief of hearing again the languages of his childhood, Gaelic and Scots, both increasingly common as he'd traveled farther north.

To know he could feel desire for his wedded wife

surpassed his relief at seeing the castle in good repair, and even eclipsed his relief that the woman didn't indulge in strong hysterics at the sight of him.

For the wife he'd left behind had been more child than woman, the antithesis of this red-haired Celtic goddess wrapped in the clan's hunting tartan and so much wounded dignity.

They reached the steps leading up to the great wooden door at the castle entrance. "I wrote to you."

Brenna did not turn her head. "Perhaps your letters went astray."

Such gracious indifference. He was capable of bedding his wife—any young man with red blood in his veins would desire the woman at Michael's side—but clearly, ability did not guarantee he'd have the opportunity.

"I meant, I wrote from Edinburgh to let you know I was coming home."

"Edinburgh is lovely in summer."

All of Scotland was lovely in summer, and to a man who'd scorched his back raw under the Andalusian sun, lovely in deepest winter too. "I was in France, Brenna. The King's post did not frequent Toulouse."

Outside the door, she paused and studied the scrolled iron plate around the ancient lock.

"We heard you'd deserted, then we heard you'd died. Some of the fellows from your regiment paid calls here, and intimated army gossip is not to be trusted. Then some officer came trotting up the lane a month after the victory, expecting to pay a call on you."

Standing outside that impenetrable, ancient door,

Michael accepted that his decision to serve King and Country had left wounded at home as well as on the Continent.

"I *begged* you to take me with you." She wrenched the door open, but stepped back, that Michael might precede her into the castle.

She had pleaded and cried for half their wedding night, sounding not so much like a distressed bride as an inconsolable child, and because he'd been only five years her senior, he'd stolen away in the morning while she'd slept, tears still streaking her pale cheeks.

He searched for honest words that would not wound her further.

"I prayed for your well-being every night. The idea that you were here, safe and sound, comforted me."

She plucked a thorny pink rose from a trellis beside the door and passed the bloom to him.

"Who or what was supposed to comfort me, Michael Brodie? When I was told you'd gone over to the enemy? When I was told you were dead? When I imagined you captured by the French, or worse?"

They stood on the castle steps, their every word available to any in the great hall or lurking at nearby windows. Rather than fret over the possibility that his wife had been unfaithful to him—her questions were offered in rhetorical tones—Michael stepped closer.

"Your husband has come home, and it will be his pleasure to make your comfort his greatest concern."

She looked baffled—or peevish. He could not read his own wife accurately enough to distinguish between the two.

"Have you baggage, Husband?"

Yes, he did. He gestured for her to go ahead of him into the hall. "Last I heard, the coach was following, but I haven't much in the way of worldly goods."

"I'll have your things put in the blue bedroom."

When she would have gone swishing off into the bowels of the castle, Michael grabbed her wrist and kept her at his side. She remained facing half-away from him, an ambiguous pose, not resisting, and not exactly drinking in the sight of her long-lost husband, either.

"What's different?" He studied the great hall he'd stopped seeing in any detail by his third birthday. "Something is different. This place used to be…dark. Like a great ice cave."

She twisted her hand free of his.

"Nothing much is different. I had the men enlarge the windows, whitewash the walls, polish the floors. The room wanted light, we had a bit of coin at the time, and the fellows needed something to do."

She'd taken a medieval hall and domesticated it without ruining its essential nature, made it comfortable. Or comforting? Bouquets of pink roses graced four of the deep windowsills, and every chair and sofa sported a Brodie plaid folded over the back. Not the darker, more complicated hunting plaid Brenna wore, but the cheerful red, black, and yellow used every day.

"I like it very much, Brenna. The hall is welcoming." Even if the lady was not.

She studied the great beams twenty feet overhead—or perhaps entreated the heavens for aid—while Michael caught a hint of a smile at his compliment.

That he'd made his wife smile must be considered progress, however miniscule.

Then her smile died. "Angus, good day."

Michael followed her line of sight to a sturdy kilted fellow standing in the doorway of the shadowed corridor that led to the kitchens. Even in the obscure light, Michael recognized an uncle who had been part older brother and part father, the sight of whom now was every part dear.

"Never say the village gossip was for once true! Our Michael has come home at last." Angus hustled across the great hall, his kilt flapping against his knees.

A hug complete with resounding thumps on the back followed, and in his uncle's greeting, Michael found the enthusiasm he'd hoped for from his wife.

"Surely the occasion calls for a wee dram," Angus said. His hair was now completely white, though he was less than twenty years Michael's senior. He wasn't as tall as Michael, but his build was muscular, and he looked in great good health.

"The man needs to eat before you're getting him drunk," Brenna interjected. She stood a few feet off, directly under crossed claymores that gleamed with the same shine as the rest of the hall.

"We can take a tray in the library, woman," Angus replied. "When a man hasn't seen his nephew for nigh ten years, the moment calls for whisky and none of your fussy little crumpets, aye?"

Brenna twitched the tail of her plaid over her shoulder, a gesture about as casual as a French dragoon swinging into the saddle.

"I will feed my husband a proper meal at a proper

table, Angus Brodie, and your wee dram will wait its turn."

Angus widened his stance, fists going to his hips, suggesting not all battlefields were found on the Continent.

"Uncle, Brenna has the right of it. I haven't eaten since this morning. One glass of good spirits, and I'd be disgracing my heritage. Food first, and then we'll find some sipping whisky."

Brenna moved off to stick her finger in a white crockery bowl of roses, while Angus treated Michael to a look of good-humored disgruntlement.

"She runs a fine kitchen, does our Brenna. Do it justice, and find me in the office when you've eaten your fill. I'm that glad you're back, lad."

He strode off, the tassels on his sporran bouncing against his thick thighs, while Brenna shook droplets of water off the end of her finger.

"Does my uncle often cross swords with you?"

She wiped her finger on her plaid. "He does not, not now. He leaves the castle to me. I'm sure your arrival is the only thing that tempted him past the door. What are you hungry for?"

He was hungry for her smiles. A soldier home from war had a right to be hungry for his wife's smiles.

About the Author

New York Times and *USA Today* bestselling author Grace Burrowes hit the bestseller lists with her debut, *The Heir*, followed by *The Soldier*, *Lady Maggie's Secret Scandal*, and *Lady Eve's Indiscretion*. Her Regency and Victorian romances have received extensive praise, including several starred reviews from *Publishers Weekly* and *Booklist*. *The Heir* was a *Publishers Weekly* Best Book of 2010, *Lady Sophie's Christmas Wish* won Best Historical Romance of the Year in 2011 from RT Reviewers' Choice Awards. *Lady Louisa's Christmas Knight* was a *Library Journal* Best Book of 2012, *The Bridegroom Wore Plaid*, the first in her trilogy of Scotland-set Victorian romances, was a *Publishers Weekly* Best Book of 2012, while the second tale, *Once Upon a Tartan*, was an RT Reviewers' Choice award winner for 2013. *Darius*, the first in her groundbreaking Regency series The Lonely Lords, was named one of the iBooks Store's Best Romances of 2013.

Grace is a practicing family law attorney and lives in rural Maryland. She loves to hear from her readers and can be reached through her website at graceburrowes.com.